OVERTHROW

PREVIOUS BOOKS BY DAVID POYER

Tales of the Modern Navy

Deep War

Hunter Killer

Tipping Point

The Cruiser

The Towers

The Crisis

The Weapon

Korea Strait

The Threat

The Command

Black Storm

China Sea

Tomahawk

The Passage

The Circle

The Gulf

The Med

Tiller Galloway

Down to a Sunless Sea

Louisiana Blue

Bahamas Blue

Hatteras Blue

The Civil War at Sea

That Anvil of Our Souls   A Country of Our Own

Fire on the Waters

Hemlock County

Thunder on the Mountain

As the Wolf Loves Winter

Winter in the Heart

The Dead of Winter

Other Books

Heroes of Annapolis

On War and Politics
(with Arnold Punaro)

The Whiteness of the
Whale

Happier Than This
Day and Time

Ghosting

The Only Thing to Fear

Stepfather Bank

The Return of
Philo T. McGiffin

Star Seed

The Shiloh Project

White Continent

OVERTHROW

THE WAR WITH CHINA AND NORTH KOREA—FALL OF AN EMPIRE

DAVID POYER

ST. MARTIN'S PRESS
New York

First published in the United States by St. Martin's Press, an imprint of St. Martin's Publishing Group

www.stmartins.com

The Library of Congress Cataloging-in-Publication Data is available upon request.

ISBN 978-1-250-22056-1 (hardcover)
ISBN 978-1-250-22057-8 (ebook)

First Edition: December 2019

10 9 8 7 6 5 4 3 2 1

What matters Death, if Freedom be not dead?

No flags are fair, if Freedom's flag be furled.

Who fights for Freedom, goes with joyful tread

To meet the fires of Hell against him hurled.

—Joyce Kilmer, "The Peacemaker"

I'll tell you what war is about, you've got to kill people,
and when you've killed enough they stop fighting.

—Curtis LeMay

I

WHAT MATTERS DEATH

1

Brunei Bay, Brunei

THE heat was sweltering. But then again, they were nearly on the equator.

Daniel V. Lenson leaned on the rail on Vulture's Row, high on the island of USS *Franklin D. Roosevelt*. His windblown hair, once sandy, was starting to gray. Crow's-feet from years at sea seamed a tanned face. He wore khakis with black flight deck boots. A garrison cap with one star was tucked under his belt. He slumped as if bone weary, but with head unbowed. Two staffers stood behind him. One was a blond master chief with eyes as bright blue as the bay below. The other, a husky marine with a slung carbine.

"Admiral, about time to head over," Sergeant Gault said.

Dan nodded. "In a minute," he muttered.

The marine was almost a family retainer by now. His elder brother had died covering the retreat of the Signal Mirror mission Dan had led in Iraq. They'd run into each other in Pearl, and now Ronson Gault was an aide. The other man, Master Chief Donnie Wenck, had been with Dan on several Tactical Analysis Group missions, investigating emergent naval threats, and served with him since the start of the current war.

Lenson rubbed his chin, contemplating the second mightiest mass of military power yet assembled in this conflict. Tugs scurried about near the bay entrance. A jeep carrier maneuvered for the channel in. Tenders lay alongside hastily emplaced floating piers, and the clatter of generators and power tools filled the inner basin. New Burke-class destroyers and reactivated Spruances pulled out of mothballs lay at anchor, riding to a stiffening northeasterly wind. Beside another tender, slim black needles were rafted out. Hunters, autonomous submersibles that screened task groups on the move, and searched out mines and enemy submarines nearer an enemy coast.

The assault fleet was being assembled at two points: Cam Ranh Bay and this remote, undeveloped harbor on the northern coast of Indonesia. Olongapo would have been closer, but the Philippines were still avoiding commitment. The sultan of Brunei had been more welcoming.

An enormous assemblage . . . but to its commander, a disquieting massing of irreplaceable assets. Concentration invited attack. The Chinese had to know they were here. Their satellites had been shot down, but high-altitude drones were hard to detect. Indonesia had cracked down on its Chinese minority, but a spy could be buried in their command structure. Or eavesdropping on Allied comms.

Dan had ordered combat air patrols three hundred miles out, and drone jammers posted on the hills. Army antiair lasers, and a harbor security team alert for undersea intrusions. THAAD missile batteries were posted on the Spratleys, which had been retaken in the opening months of the war.

Still, he worried. He took a deep breath, fighting a dread he couldn't share with anyone around him . . . only with his wife, and she was back in Washington. He coughed into a fist, trying to clear a smoke-damaged trachea. "Donnie, what'd this morning's test tell us?" he rasped.

The master chief slicked back an unruly cowlick. "Missile came in from due south. A Coyote mated to a booster, off an Aussie Poseidon out of Edinburgh. To test our vulnerability to suborbital attack."

Dan frowned. A suborbital could leave Asia headed north, circle the planet, and hit the task force from behind. "How'd we do?"

"Army radar picked it up first. Satellite cuing a tenth of a second later. Took it with an Alliance from *La David Martin*. Backup, the Patriot battery on the mountain. All constructive—we didn't actually fire. Dr. Soongapurn's still evaluating, but it looked to me like we were on the money."

Dan nodded, only mildly reassured. A single warhead from the enemy's secretly built arsenal of superheavy thermonuclears could destroy everything around him, which was most of the striking power of the Ninth Fleet.

The war had started three years before. Distracted by a trivia-obsessed press and paralyzed by politics, America had estranged its allies and handed the strategic advantage to its enemies. Judging the time right for bold moves, President and Chairman for Life Zhang Zurong had knocked out communications and reconnaissance satellites, then invaded Taiwan and Okinawa. When a U.S. carrier battle group sailed, he'd destroyed it, killing ten thousand servicemen and women.

The analysts had predicted any twenty-first-century great war would be over in weeks. No economy could sustain cyberwarfare, blockade, and the lavish expenditures of lives, ordnance, ships, planes, missiles, and money a major conflict would devour. And nuclear weapons, they said, would constrain escalation and limit the battlespace.

Not one of those predictions had come true.

Instead the conflict had spread like wildfire in a drought-stricken forest. North Korea attacked the South. Iran and Pakistan fell in behind China. Zhang invaded India and Vietnam, and a massively powerful artificial intelligence called Jade Emperor demolished American financial, industrial, and power networks in the Cloudburst. American carriers, too vulnerable to risk, had been held back from battle. Submarines, destroyers, and cruisers had borne the brunt of war. They'd paid a heavy price in blood, damage, and lost ships.

For the first year, the Opposed Powers had won every battle.

Until Operation Recoil. Requipped and retrained, the Navy and Air Force's first strike against the Chinese homeland had derailed Zhang's second offensive. But Dan's flagship, USS *Savo Island*, had been left adrift and on fire. He'd been shot down in a helicopter as he shifted his flag, and barely escaped with his life.

Since then, the sea lanes had been secured. Marines and the Army had landed on Taiwan, igniting a battle that was still raging. Japan had rejoined the Allies and was retaking the Ryukyus.

Here in the South China Sea, Dan had been part of a raid on the enemy's south coast. Operation Uppercut had softened up Hainan and Hong Kong, but a tactical nuclear attack on the sub pens went badly. Mines and air strikes took a heavy toll. The Allied raiders returned with heavy damage and serious losses.

But now a starving, disease-racked China was growing desperate. A thermonuclear strike on Hawaii had nearly destroyed Honolulu. With dozens of other American cities held hostage by heavy Chinese ICBMs, a frightened president hadn't dared retaliate.

Step by step, the God of War was advancing on both home countries. Each year, Mars exacted more sacrifices. Each year he demanded greater risks, more lives, more treasure.

And no one yet could see how this war might be ended.

"Sir, 'bout time we headed over." The master chief huffed, exchanging glances with the sergeant.

"Uh, one more second, okay?" Dan wasn't eager for the confrontation ahead. "You can call the car, and tell Captain Skinner."

He fingered the stars on his collars. His enemies in Congress had made it clear they were his only for the duration. But his actions in the Taiwan Strait, clearing the enemy's subs from the central Pacific, and most recently off Hainan, had earned him a reprieve. The Chief of Naval Operations, the Commander, Indo-Pacific Command, and the Commander, Ninth Fleet, had given him Task Force 91—the ships in this bay and others, forward deployed in the South China Sea.

It looked impressive, but after Allied losses in the last operations, most of what remained had been committed to the ongoing battle on Taiwan. Dan had gotten what could be spared. New construction, many with unblooded crews. Retreaded ships. Reserve air squadrons. His expeditionary strike groups were built around *Hornet*, *Bataan*, and a jeep carrier, *Liscome Bay*, plus a combined Vietnamese/Indonesian/Australian landing force centered on *Makassar*, *Surabya*, and *Adelaide* and protected by Australian frigates and submarines. The ground forces were primarily from Indonesia. He would have heavy carriers in support, but they would be held far back, protected by an antiballistic missile cruiser.

Operation Rupture would land on, occupy, and hold Hainan Island as a base for further operations. The first Allied seizure of Chinese territory. But they would face desperate resistance from an utterly determined enemy.

He couldn't shake what the Deputy Pacom had told him in Cam Ranh Bay. This invasion was the last gasp. Political support was gone. Strikes and riots were shaking the United States. The Allies were out of money, ships, troops, and resolve.

But Intel said China was suffering too. Zhang was fighting rebellions in Tibet, Xinjiang, and Hong Kong. His armies were suffering heavy casualties in Taiwan on the Vietnamese front, and in the Ryukyus. The enemy being thus engaged all around his periphery, the Joint Chiefs expected Dan to bring to battle whatever reserves remained. Once those were destroyed, the way could be clear for a landing on the mainland, in Hong Kong or the other restive provinces of south China.

He gripped the splinter shield, throat suddenly constricted. If he could pull it off, it might end the war. But if he failed, thousands of troops and sailors would die. And the war would grind on, and trillions more in treasure be wasted, in vain . . .

Turning abruptly away, he stepped into the flag bridge. Where a stoutish captain was studying a diagram on a nav screen, with younger officers and chiefs around her.

As most senior officers preferred to, he stuck with staff he'd served with and could depend on. Like Wenck and Gault. Amarpeet Singhe, a sharp-edged but competent strike specialist. Colonel Sy Osterhaut, Army, who'd planned the first Hainan strike with him in the basement of Camp H. M. Smith. Kitty Pickles, the captain, who'd helped ferret out replacements for scores of gas turbine engines defectively machined in a cunning cyberattack.

One lieutenant, though, was new. Sloan Tomlin was a WTI, a Warfare Tactical Instructor. He'd earned his antisubmarine/antisurface warfare patch out of San Diego, then done a readiness production tour out of PACOM, focusing on Chinese tactics. And Tomlin was well connected; his grandfather was high up at a well-known defense contractor.

Dan glanced over their shoulders. "Steaming formation?"

Pickles shook her head. "The sortie plan, Admiral."

"Want to give a gander, sir?" Tomlin asked.

Dan wasn't sure about the kid yet. The WTI had tactical acumen, and Tomlin knew the new tactical AI system, Sea Eagle 2.0. But he seemed to regard his admiral as a not terribly bright elder statesman. Or maybe even a doddering figurehead. "When I get back. Polish it up until I can't find anything wrong."

"Aye aye, Admiral.—Yessir, Admiral." In unison, they tapped off semi-ironical salutes. He grinned back and stepped into the elevator, headed down.

THE cavernous hangar echoed with the rattle of air wrenches, shouts, staccato beeping as autonomous forklifts puttered past. Dan wended through mountains of palleted supplies. At the far end F-35s and helicopters were being worked on.

On the quarterdeck, faces turned his way. The keen of a bos'n's pipe pierced the din. *"Task Force 91, departing,"* the ship's 1MC stated as bells rang out.

A tall spare figure, "Torch" Skinner, *Roosevelt*'s skipper, offered a salute and a handshake. Dan told him where he was going, then headed down the slanted steel openwork of the brow. His car was waiting at the bottom, the driver in Indonesian army greens. Gault and Wenck got in the back.

Next stop, Mobile Logistic Force South.

THE admin building was Lego'd together out of gray and tan modules connected by graveled walkways. On a slope overlooking the airstrip and harbor, it was surrounded by chain link and concertina. A sandbagged guard post was backed by a security force barracks and an Arrow/Oerlikon air defense battery. A sign read *Allied Com-*

mand, South China Sea/Forward Operating Base Brunei Bay/Naval Facility Indonesia. A solar array glittered up the hill.

His chief of staff and deputy task force commander was waiting. Short, balding, Captain Fred Enzweiler was as colorless as they came, but since Dan's squadron command, he'd kept Dan's desk visible under the deluge of administrivia. Three foreign officers accompanied him. The most senior was Major General Triady Isnanta. Swarthy, with prominent cheekbones, Isnanta headed the Korps Marinir, the Indonesian version of the Marines. He would command Rupture's landing force. Dan shook hands with him, then with Admiral Ramidin Madjid, Indonesian Navy. They'd served together years before in an anti-pirate task force. The third man, Admiral Vijay Gupta, commanded Indian Navy operations in the South China Sea.

In what had to be a calculated snub, they were kept waiting in the lobby for twenty minutes. Admitted at last to a conference room, Dan found it empty, with no sign of the standard cookies and fruit juices. Its single huge window overlooked the harbor. "Is the admiral coming?" he asked the chief who'd shown them in. She simply smiled nervously.

At long last the door opened, admitting a small man in brilliant, obviously new summer whites. Lee Custer was polished like a piece of antique silver. His carefully cut hair was platinum. He wore a heavy gold watch that had probably cost Dan's annual salary. He could have been sent straight from Central Casting to play the take-charge admiral. Beside him Dan felt rumpled, potbellied, and underdressed in shipboard khakis. Custer didn't have a bad combat record either. But his handshake was reluctant, and he avoided Dan's gaze as he muttered, "Good to see you."

"Yes, sir. Good to see you too." Not that either man meant it.

Custer had been in line for command of Task Force 91 after the incumbent suffered a heart attack. But Bren Verstegen, Ninth Fleet, had made clear the assignment was impossible. "There's no way we can have someone with that last name in charge of an operation this risky," he'd said.

Dan guessed it was really someone higher up the chain who'd made that call. This administration seemed uninterested in strategic direction, but they paid microscopic attention to the optics. The upshot was that Custer, a vice admiral, was directing the logistics element supporting the invasion fleet, while outranking Dan, whose two stars were only temporary. A topsy-turvy situation that might strike civilians as trivial, but that in terms of personal relationships could get ugly.

And any ugliness could impact the support his ships received—food, fuel, repairs, logistics—the classic "beans, bullets, and black oil" of World War II logistic-speak.

So he made an effort to smile, and offered Custer the seat at the head of the table. The other man pulled a chair up, whisked it with a monogrammed handkerchief, and lowered himself cautiously. He opened with, "Let's get some ice water in here." Then, to Dan, "There's a significant weather event impending. Close to typhoon force winds predicted."

Dan nodded. "I've put the word out as SOPA to make all preparations for a storm."

SOPA was Senior Officer Present Afloat, which made Dan responsible for the physical safety of all the ships below them.

"Including getting under way?" Custer asked.

"Weather guessers tell me that shouldn't be necessary. And I'd rather not, considering."

"All right, your decision. As the . . . senior." Custer nodded to a staffer. "Commander, let's get started."

The briefing descended into mind-numbing detail as mid-grade officers reported on preparations to support the fleet. Combat hospital units, setting up east of the harbor. Fresh food supplies, backed up by bulk rations. Tugs, to retrieve damaged ships. The Indonesian general asked about rice. Custer reassured him food stocks would be adequate.

Unless, Dan thought, shipping ran out. A torpedo, a missile attack . . . if they lost too many of their hastily converted transports, the "rice" could indeed run short. As could ammunition, batteries, spare parts, fuel . . . He shook the worry off and lifted his head. "I'd like to discuss the progress of battle damage repair. Are we still backlogged from Uppercut?"

Custer nodded to another briefer. Slides and graphs appeared. Timelines. Milestones. Dan took notes, as did Enzweiler beside him. The general picture was encouraging, to his surprise. The support forces were working around the clock, to judge by the lights that burned ashore and on the tenders all night long. The atrophied industrial base back home, and a thirteen-thousand-mile logistic tail, had been shored up by Japanese additive manufacturing shops. You couldn't 3-D print an Aegis radar switching module, or a ten-ton bronze screw for a destroyer, but you could crank out a rocket body, a duct fairing for an F-35, or a radome for a Phalanx.

Enzweiler said mildly, "So you predict we'll be at ninety percent of ships returned to ready status by S-day." Their sailing day, seven days ahead of D-day on Hainan.

"We can promise ninety percent availability. Maybe even ninety-five."

"Okay, great." Dan checked his notes. "We'll leapfrog the mobile base up at D plus ten?"

"Correct. Cover the initial movement with *Monocacy* and *Rafael Peralta*. Deploy Army ABM on Day 1, then follow that with the mobile logistics once the shield's up."

"Hospital facilities?"

Custer waved it aside. "*Mercy* and two converted cruise ships. Plus the MASH back here in Brunei."

"A combat support hospital," a staffer piped up, but fell silent after a directed-energy glare from the vice admiral. The lieutenant looked at the floor, then got up and left.

Dan was studying his notes again when something flashed at the corner of his vision. For an instant he thought it was a floater, or something in his eye. Then he caught the horrified stares as heads jerked around toward the huge window.

His breath caught in his throat. He squinted into sudden light.

A pillar of fire was ascending out in the harbor.

The floor shook. Ice rattled in glass pitchers.

"*Down,*" he yelled. Grabbing Enzweiler and the Indonesian general, he pulled them to the deck with him.

As they hit the carpet the window burst inward in a hurricane of scything shards that snapped like bullets as they slammed into wood, plastic, metal, flesh. The sound and vibration arrived then too, a volcanic *CRAAAAACK*. It went on and on, accompanied by a horrific rumbling, as if some subterranean empire was collapsing in smoke and brimstone and fire. The building quivered on its foundations. The walls jerked. The room rocked, knocking the large-screen displays off the walls to crash and shatter. Then the vibrations trickled away, to silence again.

Dan lay full length, waiting for the next shock. Screams and moans from around him penetrated the siren aftersong of the detonation. But after a minute he cautiously got to his knees. Then to his feet, crouching, ready to dive again. He peered out the glass-less gape of the blown-in window.

Fire and smoke blanketed the roadstead.

A ring of ships lurched outward as if blown by a heavy wind. A shock-driven wave was recoiling from the shore, lifting interference peaks that poked skyward in quirky rocking pyramids of white water. Transports and destroyers rocked ponderously on their anchor lines, topsides smoking or aflame. A frigate lay canted hard, blown onto the shoal water that ringed the deeper central basin of the bay. Small craft wallowed, also on fire. As he watched, one tipped its bow skyward and slid beneath the waves. The slim black needle of a hunter drone waterbugged randomly here and there, its computer brain scrambled by the close-in shock.

Custer climbed to his feet, face blanched. He passed a hand over it, smearing his cheeks with blood and spotting his whites. "No warning," he muttered, to no one in particular. "No warning. We should have clobbered them before, the first time they went to nukes."

Dan consulted his phone, and was surprised to find it working. He had eight messages. More popped as he scrolled. "It might not be a missile," he muttered.

"Then what?" asked the Indian admiral, Gupta.

Wenck and Enzweiler had their phones out too. "No cuing from any source," the master chief said. "Nothing since the test this morning."

Dan scrubbed his face, careful to keep his hands away from his eyes in case he'd picked up any shards from the deck. Which sagged under them now with a weary groan. "We'd better get outside," he muttered, than called aloud, "Evacuate the building."

"No. No! There'll be radiation," Custer countermanded. "Shelter in place. We need masks. NBC protection."

"I don't think that was a nuke," Dan told him. "We'd have had a whopping EMP pulse. It would've killed our phones."

Custer went scarlet. "Not a nuke? Fuck you, Lenson! That was no conventional explosion."

Dan didn't contradict him. But he was getting the bad feeling that hadn't been an enemy strike at all. He shaded his eyes and peered out again, to where the smoke had lifted into a turbulent black and ocher mushroom that was still raining pieces of orange fire down all around the roadstead.

At where the ammunition ship USNS *Mount Hood*, pulled out of mothballs and reactivated for this operation, had been anchored. With six thousand tons of bombs, shells, and missiles, plus hundreds of tons of fuel. Furnishing a full third of the munitions reserved for the imminent invasion.

At least, it had until about two minutes ago.

Fred Enzweiler inspected his phone. "OOD on *FDR* reports: Large explosion, vicinity *Mount Hood*. Fire. Debris. No evidence of ship now visible."

"Holy fuck," Wenck breathed. They stood staring out, until a renewed groaning underfoot motivated a stampede for the door. Which was jammed. General Isnanta grabbed a chair, hammered the remaining glass out of the window with it, and vaulted out for an eight-foot drop to the grass. Two junior staffers followed. The others milled about until someone grabbed the conference table. Seized by many hands, it was instantly converted to a battering ram.

They burst into the hallway to find more destruction and several moaning men and women. All seemed to be still alive, though. Dan peered back into the conference room. Everyone still there was at least sitting up. Maybe they hadn't actually lost anyone. At least, here at headquarters.

But out in the basin would be a different story. He'd seen large conventional explosions before. He'd seen nukes too. Far too close up for comfort, in USS *Horn*, off the coast of Israel. If this hadn't been a nuke, it had to rank close to the scale of one.

But then, this wouldn't be the first time in history an ammo ship had gone up.

And usually no one survived to explain why.

Sergeant Gault came running from the car, carbine at the ready, as Dan was snapping orders to Enzweiler. "We can't rule anything out," he told the deputy. "A drone sub, midget, some form of undersea penetrator—even UDT swimmers. Check with harbor security. If this was an attack, I want to trap them inside the harbor."

Enzweiler turned away, stammering into his phone. Dan stood shaking, only now accepting at gut level what had happened. Regardless of the cause . . . a long-range autonomous torpedo, careless munitions handling, or even some too-hastily-assembled missile . . . they'd just lost any chance of making S-day on time. The lurching, burning ships, the wrecked piers with blown-apart stacks of supplies, made that all too clear. Not to mention losing a shit-ton of ammunition. It had been in short supply all through the war, and *Hood* had stocked hundreds of millions of dollars' worth of advanced weaponry.

Custer, behind him, was dabbing at the blood on his cheek with the monogrammed handkerchief. "Fucking politicals," he muttered.

Dan blinked. "Excuse me?"

"I had us on schedule. You've wrecked the invasion. Mooring an ammo ship in the basin! Asinine!"

Dan frowned. "In the . . . ? But it had to be here. Inside the anti-submarine defenses."

"Why not off to the east, at least? In that side loch? Not in the middle of the fucking anchorage!"

"That class draws thirty-eight feet loaded. No way she was going in the side loch." Then he frowned. Why was he defending himself? If Custer'd had a problem with where one of his ships was anchored, why hadn't he brought it up before? *He* was the logistics honcho.

"Oh, *you'll* be okay," Custer sneered, blowing his nose and examining the result. "You won't pay. Just like you didn't for running away when that German tanker got hit. When you offered the Chinese

Hornet on a plate. Then stepped on Tim Simko, and took his job. That's why we'll lose this war. Cowards in the White House. Fuck-ups running the Fleet."

What the hell, over? Had the guy taken a shot to the head? "Uh, I don't think we're on the same page on any of that, Lee."

"Yeah? I know the score. *Admiral*." His tone set quote marks around Dan's rank. "How DC favors politically connected golden boys like you."

Golden Boy? Dan thought. More like Shitlist Sam. He caught astonished looks from around them. This was no place for an all-star face-off. "Look, we don't have time for this. Let's all get to work, mass-casualty mode, see if we can get these fires put out." He told Enzweiler, "Have the staff watch officer get boats out there. Every ship with a ready boat, throw a corpsman in it. Bring the wounded ashore." To Custer he snapped, "What about that combat hospital unit? Are they ready to take casualties? Let's jump on this. I'll just have to get back to you, on the rest of your sad little shit fit." He turned to Gault. "We're headed back to *FDR*. I'll run the rescue effort from there."

Custer's fists were clenched, face still fiery. Blood trickled from one nostril. Maybe he was more badly injured than he looked. "You were SOPA," he gritted out. "I'll make sure you're held responsible!"

"That's good, Admiral. Do your worst." Dan turned away, slipped on a blood-slick patch of grass, but recovered and jogged on down the hill. Cursing not Custer, but himself. Was there any way he could have prevented this? He didn't think so. But the bottom line was, a lot of people were dead. A ship, lost. Others, badly damaged. Custer would try to pin the blame on him. Not that he cared. In the grand scheme of things, blame would be a light load to bear.

Far worse was that the long-awaited invasion had just been set back. For weeks, if not months.

And the enemy hadn't even done it.

Somehow, they'd just totally fucked themselves.

2

USS *Savo Island,* Hawaii Oparea

TWO hundred miles off Oahu, the predawn ocean heaved with sullen swells.

From some massive storm, far over the horizon. Out of sight, but drawing nearer.

High above the sea, Captain Cheryl Staurulakis, USN, lowered her binoculars and sighed. Slight-framed, she wore heavy black boots and starched and ironed blue flameproof shipboard coveralls with silver eagles pinned to the lapels. She wore data-driven BattleGlasses and a helmet stenciled CO. A faded, much laundered olive and black shemagh was draped under it as a flash hood.

Her cropped blond hair was faded too. Her cheeks were pinched and pale, blue eyes deeply hooded. Flash gloves were tucked into her belt. A gas mask hung at her hip. Around her on the cruiser's enclosed bridge stood four crew members, each so busy with his or her respective screen that Cheryl was the only one looking out the slanted windows.

She sighed again, scratching an irritated red patch under her wedding band, then jerked her nails away. She crossed to a grizzled older man. "Chief Van Gogh. We clear?"

"Surface radar shows range clear to the north, Skipper, two eight zero to zero eight zero. Some sea return. Occasional rain squalls."

She raised the binoculars again and took a final sweep along the horizon, squinting into the glare off the undulating sea. Fluffy clouds floated miles off, bellies highlighted with the first pinking glow of dawn. Gray tentacles of rain trailed from the nearest. Frowning, she pressed a button on the side of her Glasses. A scatter of contacts appeared, picked up by satellite, radar, sonar, remote sensors, and woven into a seamless net of data by the ship's computers. She toggled screen to screen. The main body lay behind her, the carrier and supply ships nestled at its heart. Farther out, unmanned UAVs and submersible Hunters prowled, extending the early warning perimeter frigates and destroyers had furnished in earlier wars.

She closed her eyes, remembering.

She'd been on the bridge like this when her previous ship had been hit. Two missiles had slammed in high, wrecking the helo hangar, a radar-controlled 20mm, the after stack and intakes, and half the ship's antennas, including both after phased arrays. Another had exploded at the main deck level. The last had punched in low, leaving a four-foot hole at the waterline, major blast damage, and raging fires deep in the old cruiser's belly.

They'd barely made it back, threading enemy-occupied islands and creeping across hundreds of miles of hostile sea to finally reach a friendly port.

And burying too many good men and women at sea.

They'd joined the man whose ring she still wore. Eddie "Chip" Staurulakis's fighter had never returned to the carrier after the raid on the bases and airfields around Ningbo. A victim of enemy fire, the Navy said. At first, she'd wanted to find out who'd sent him into the heaviest antiair defenses in history, and make them pay. She'd sent inquiries, screamed at his squadron commander. But as the months passed, her rage had cooled. So many others had died too. It was just . . . the war.

But so far, she hadn't identified anyone who'd actually witnessed him go down.

Which could mean, couldn't it, that he was still alive . . . somewhere.

She shuddered. Her eyes snapped open. She clicked a button on her throat mike. "Combat, CO."

"Combat aye." The Combat Information Center, four decks down.

"Ready to go to war, XO?"

"Go, ma'am."

"See that squall to the north?"

"Ten minutes before we're in it. No worries."

She sighed again and clipped the binoculars back into their holder. She'd loved the old *Savo*. Though it bore the same name, this new ship felt colder. Less responsive. Far more capable, of course. But for some reason she, its captain, didn't feel she'd yet connected with it. That deep emotional link was missing.

Those who'd never been to sea insisted a ship really couldn't be alive, or have a personality.

Maybe you had to experience it to know.

Or perhaps this latest minting of steel and electronics, fire and electricity was simply too new, too young, to be truly an individual yet . . .

Her musings were interrupted by the beep and hiss of an encrypted voice transmission. *"All stations this net, this is Pyramid. Stand by . . . OTC passes . . . Comex, Comex,"* a speaker droned overhead.

Pyramid was the exercise coordinator, back on the carrier. Lifting her head, Cheryl called, "Commence exercise. Bos'n, sound general quarters. Shift conn to CIC. All hands, clear the bridge."

An electronic bonging began. *"General quarters. General quarters,"* the 1MC announced. She wheeled, pulling on gloves, and headed for a heavy stainless steel door that opened onto a small elevator.

Eighteen seconds later, flashes far over the horizon reflected off the low clouds. But by then the wheel on the helm console moved without human hands, humming a lullaby to itself. The high pilothouse of USS *Savo Island* was abandoned.

ROLLING slowly, the massive cruiser purred through the sea. No human figure moved topside. Her smooth, steep-slabbed sides were featureless, save for the glitter of crystallized salt on gray paint, the snap of a single flag far aloft.

USS *Savo Island* was the third ship named to commemorate

a battle fought north of Guadalcanal in 1942. The first had been a Casablanca-class escort carrier. Commissioned in 1944, CVE-78 had received a Presidential Unit Citation for action in the Western Carolines, Philippines, and Okinawa.

The second *Savo*, a Ticonderoga-class cruiser, had transferred to the Pacific Fleet just before the current war. Cheryl had been her operations officer, then exec, and finally skipper. After receiving battle stars for actions in the Taiwan Strait, the Battle of the Central Pacific, and the East China Sea, that second *Savo* had been scuttled after a nuclear attack on Hawaii—her topsides wrecked by the shock wave, her bottom blown out by demolition charges.

Some of the crew manning this third namesake had been aboard her as well.

The primary mission of the first cruiser of the new Savo Island class was antimissile defense. Its Alliance interceptors were AI-enabled to discriminate between the decoys and live warheads of heavy ICBMs. It carried railguns and beam weapons to defend the task forces it would accompany to war. Armored, compartmented, and sealed from the outside air, it was designed to survive. A dynamic access network provided high-bandwidth data exchange among air-, surface-, subsurface-, and ground-based tactical data systems. Instead of shafts and reduction gears, it was propelled by podded Tesla truck motors using power converted from an AC bus, driven by gas turbines looted from commercial airliners.

Following the commissioning ceremony in San Diego, they'd had gotten under way for shakedown exercises with air and submarine services in the Southern California oparea. After a shipyard availability, they'd headed to Hawaii for ballistic missile defense qualification and certification.

Today was the last and fiercest day of their final fleet exercise. The crew was looking forward to a few days of liberty afterward, following too many weeks of hard, exhausting training. So was she, having missed far too much sleep trying to get a new build to sea in wartime.

From there, if they passed this final exam, *Savo* would be assigned to one of the strike groups being formed for the counteroffensive.

To a "secret operation in western pacific," as her classified orders read. It would take them into high-threat areas close to enemy coasts. More than that, she did not know. There was scuttlebutt, but she didn't join in. Loose lips still sank ships.

After three years of war, blockade, and cyberattacks, China was wounded. But as the cliché went, wounded animals were the most dangerous.

Down on the broad flat foredeck, doors suddenly jerked, then folded back. A white turret enclosing something resembling a large reflecting telescope purred up into view. The turret housed a complex assemblage of beam tubes, casings, mirrors, lenses, and radiators. Cables sprouted from the barrel.

Once fully extended, the turret paused. Twitched.

Then suddenly slewed and elevated, pointing off to starboard. Stabilizing, the cylindrical protuberance nodded slowly up and down as the ship rolled. Attentive. Waiting. Looking expectantly toward the far horizon.

THE first CICs, Combat Information Centers, had been curtained radar shacks behind destroyer bridges during World War II. Now *Savo*'s was buried deep, an armored, hermetically sealed, shock-cradled, radiation-shielded citadel for the remaining human crew. A second citadel aft housed the damage control, engineering, and electrical teams, along with a backup control station.

Four decks down, Cheryl paused to check a freshly painted warning at the base of a door. Then undogged it, slipped through, and slid into the central seat at a command table.

The air was cold here. The overhead dead black, the lighting muted. Officers and chiefs sat to her left and right, and console operators within speaking distance. Seven large-screen displays surrounded them, with a video wall of three directly ahead, one to each side, and two behind. When linked to topside cameras, they gave a 360-degree view around the ship, in both visible and infrared. At the moment, though, the forward screens were oriented toward the threat. Voices murmured. Air-conditioning hissed. Cooling fans hummed.

She nodded to the tall young man seated to her right and settled a helmet on her shoulders. Matt Mills had been the operations officer on the old *Savo*. Now he was her exec, second in command.

"Standing by for automatic, Captain," he muttered.

"Alice, this is the CO," Cheryl voice-identified herself to the combat system. Formerly ALIS, the missile defense subprogram of the older Aegis combat system, the enhanced tactical AI was now AALIS. Advanced ALIS, and all but another crew member now. It could fight the ship on its own, make tactical decisions, select and deploy sensors and weapons faster than human thought. One more generation, Cheryl often thought, and human beings would be warriors no more.

Only prey . . .

"Good morning, Skipper." A neutral tone, the pitch and intonation neither male nor female.

"Hello, Alice. Threat axis three five five. Scan and report."

The images on the left and central screens tilted backward, deepening into a 3-D display, and populated with symbols. Surface contacts. Aircraft. Missiles. Subsurface contacts. Only a few were from the ship's own radar. Most were from the JTIDS network. Encrypted, jam-resistant, and nodeless, it aggregated data from MOUSE nanosatellites, drones orbiting high above the sea, and autonomous gliders cruising beneath the thermoclines. Yet another layer of extra-ionospheric imagery came from the Missile Defense Agency sea-based X-band radar, riding in a heavily guarded patch of sea north of Hawaii.

Beside her Mills bent to a touchpad. He hooked and tapped. The symbols began flashing. He touched his boom mike. "Alice, TAO: Fire control key inserted. Prepare for auto control."

"Alice aye. Data collection complete. Ready for auto control. Request batteries released."

Cheryl reexamined the screens inside her helmet, then clicked on an exterior camera. Deep into the war, the eastern Pacific was devoid of commercial shipping, and no one in his right mind ventured out in a pleasure craft. But she checked anyway before leaning forward. "Alice, CO: Initiate auto control mode. Batteries tight."

A keyboard clicked, and the screens transformed. One displayed live video from the mast-mounted camera. Another, moving steadily over the waves far below as dawn glittered over their crests, was a live feed from a drone five thousand feet up and fifty miles north. Its view was momentarily obscured by cloud, then cleared.

Five streaks of fire were traveling so close above the waves that the shock waves from their passage ripped the crests apart into mist. As if the sea itself was unzipping, revealing white lacy underthings. They traveled not in straight lines, but in a complex interweaving pavane, as if handing off the lead one to another. But second by second they were closing on *Savo*, and the higher-value units behind her.

Voices in her earbuds, a drill-worn litany from checklists and photocopied ponies taped to consoles. *"Lock on, tracks 2031 through 2036."*

"Warning bell forward deck. Visual confirm, forward deck clear. Nulka active decoys to auto ready."

"ECM reports: Consistent with YJ-25."

Developed from the YJ-18 during the war, the Chinese YJ-25 "Salvage" was a submarine-launched antiship missile. It carried a two-hundred-kilo warhead, but the real threat lay in its speed. A final ramjet stage sprinted in at over Mach 5, making it impossible to take down with the weapons most Allied ships carried: medium-range Standard missiles, the short-range Stingers mounted as last-ditch defense two years before, even the 20mm Gatlings that were the last resort.

She wasn't looking at real YJ-25s, of course. These were targets, look-alikes for test purposes. But if they couldn't be stopped, neither could the real thing.

The symbols drew nearer, still accelerating. The video juddered, trying to continue tracking them, but it jerked back and forth crazily. Then suddenly they were gone, blotted out by the gray murk of a squall.

Cheryl shifted in her chair and zoomed the forward camera in on the tubular assemblage on the foredeck. It still gave that queer impression of mechanical intentness, tracking slightly up and down as the deck rose and fell, like a cat intent on the random hoppings of a bird.

"Tracking," the laser console operator called from behind them.

"Request batteries released," AALIS said again.

She nodded. "Released."

The screen froze. The lights dimmed, flickered. The fans in the consoles around her dropped an octave.

"Pulsing," AALIS said in Cheryl's earbuds.

A faint beam appeared in front of the assemblage's muzzle. It wasn't colored, or solid. It was only really visible when a burst of spray came over the bow and flashed suddenly into steam. It wasn't continuous. It stuttered, the massive capacitor banks below the forward deck charging and discharging ten times a second. Brief pulses didn't overload the thick sea-level atmosphere and break it down into plasma, which would spread and diffuse the beam. But so long as the laser was focused properly, if the pulses could dwell on the same spot for a quarter second they would burn through an inch of tungsten steel.

"Dwelling," the console operator called. "Dwelling . . . stand by—"

A flash lit the gray cloud in the overhead imagery. *"Splash Track 2035,"* AALIS said. On the left-hand screen the scarlet symbol winked out.

But a buzzer sounded. The soft voice of the operator came on the circuit. *"Beam tube overheat, forward mount."*

"Beam overheat forward. Standing by to shift to aft projector," AALIS murmured.

Cheryl bit her lip as plumes blasted from the white barrel. Liquid nitrogen, piped into the cooling jacket at four hundred pounds per square inch. They'd had problems before with that mount. Given a few seconds to chill, usually the LAWS came back on the line, but the technicians from Naval Surface Warfare Center had warned that if they were supercooled too often, the fragile laser elements would crack. She shifted to the aft camera. Noting, as she did so, that the squall clouds had closed in. Were nearly, in fact, on the ship.

The broad, flat afterdeck began with ranks of flush-mounted

hatches just aft of the deckhouse. They sealed vertical launching tubes for Standard and the new Alliance missiles, for improved cruise weapons, and close-in Sparrows in six-round packs. Aft of that was a second laser mount. And aft of that again, another gray turret.

"Shifting to after laser . . . correction . . . possible beam degrade due to rain. Assigning tracks 2031 and 2033 to railgun," AALIS said in her ear.

That aftermost turret came alive and swung to face north. Unlike the thick-barreled white pods of the LAWS, railguns more nearly resembled conventional cannon. But their long tapered barrels were square, not round. Instead of explosive shells propelled by hot gas, they "fired" electrically driven hardened steel projectiles at two miles a second. AALIS's gun control subroutines tracked the projectiles and separated them into submunitions four hundred yards from the target, increasing the hit probability sixteenfold.

Mills said into his throat mike, "Designate to railgun. Auto engage."

"Batteries released when in range," Cheryl confirmed.

She'd barely finished speaking when the first slug cracked out in a dancing blaze of sparks and a shaft of white fire. The blaze was actually burning steel, half from the projectile, the rest stripped off the conducting rails by voltage and velocity. The barrels recoiled, aimed again, fired once more. The slugs were inexpensive, the electricity about a dollar a shot, but the barrels were only good for about four hundred rounds before the conducting core eroded and velocity fell off a cliff. The railgun fired three times with twenty seconds between rounds, *bam . . . bam . . . bam*, then swung briskly back centerline and lowered its barrel, as if satisfied with a job well done.

AALIS spoke in her ear. *"Track 2031 splashed. Track 2033 splashed. Ceasing fire, railgun. Ceasing fire, LAWS. Nulka returned to standby. Archer localized. Designate Archer Alfa. Range one hundred and ten miles. Tracking outbound. ID as hostile."*

Cheryl hesitated, frowning. "Archer" was shorthand for the launching platform for hostile missiles. But the incoming threats hadn't been launched from a hostile ship.

Which meant . . . what? "Uh, Alice, CO. Identify archer."

"Archer Alfa squawks IFF emulating US Navy P-8 IFF."

The P-8 Poseidon was a patrol and antisubmarine aircraft, modified, in this instance, to support live fire training. Cheryl lifted her eyebrows, smiled at Mills, and shook her head. "Uh, Alice, recheck. That's a valid IFF."

"Negative. Target is squawking false IFF."

She exchanged another glance with Mills. *Uh-oh*, he mouthed. *She's at it again.*

In previous exercises AALIS had seemed a bit *too* suspicious, a mite *too* spring-loaded to misidentify friendly aircraft as threats. Cheryl had logged the issue in her after-action report, but maybe the patch the software developers had sent wasn't fixing the problem. She was opening her mouth again when the AI said, *"Warning bell forward. Taking Archer Alfa with enhanced range Standard."*

She hit her throat mike. "Negative. Negative! Hold fire—"

But a magazine hatch drove open in the video from the foredeck. A burst of flame dazzled the camera, followed by a whiteout of cottony smoke.

A raised voice from behind a blue curtain. "Sonar reports, high-speed screws. TWS reports, torpedo in the water! Single torpedo. No ping. Wake homer or passive acoustic. Bearing zero eight zero."

Cheryl clicked her mike again. "Alice: resuming semiauto control mode! Acknowledge."

"Acknowledge return to semiauto mode."

Mills, beside her, was barking "Come left, steer two six zero" into his mike. "Activate Rimshot. Shit bubble decoys. Stand by on CAT."

Rimshot, installed in blisters along the hull, replaced old-style passive degaussing with an active magnetic-signature management system that could finesse the apparent location of a large ferrous body, such as a ship's hull, to trigger magnetic exploders into premature detonation. The bubble decoys generated false sonar returns.

And the Countermeasure, Antitorpedo, was their last line of defense: a small-diameter, very fast torpedo designed to home in on incoming weapons. Unfortunately, *Savo* only carried a pod of four, since the Submarine Force claimed priority on them. But the incoming practice weapons had inert warheads. They might damage the screwpods or the sonar blisters, if they struck home, but they wouldn't sink the ship.

But that wasn't her main concern just now. The hundred-and-forty-pound warhead of an armed Extended Range Active Standard, just now igniting its sustainer engine on the northern horizon, could easily bring down a P-8. "Warn them," she snapped to Mills. "Get on the coordination net and pass verbal warning. RIM-174 active Standard on their tail." To AALIS, "Designate the SM you just fired as Vampire."

"Interrogative, Captain. This is own ship weapon."

Cheryl bared her teeth. Why was the fucking machine *arguing* with her? "This is the CO. Alice: I say again; designate Vampire and take for target. *Confirm!"*

"Designated as Vampire Five," AALIS said, but unwontedly slowly. What was that nuance in its tone, Cheryl wondered. Doubt? Resentment at being contradicted? No, absurd. That had to be her own fears surfacing. Her own lack of trust in the AI. Which was, after all, only responding according to programming.

"CIC, Sonar. Screw noise. Torpedo close."

She had to stop the errant missile before it was out of range. But she couldn't engage with a second Standard. They were programmed to avoid each other during multi-salvo firings. Likewise, she wasn't sure the railgun projectile, fast as it was, could overtake the rapidly departing missile, and she really had no time to make the calculation.

And she couldn't help wondering, in some detached corner of her mind . . . was this how Eddie had died? Enemy fire, the Navy said. But a lot of ordnance had been flying around. She'd wondered then if it had been blue on blue. Which might be why no one would admit to actually seeing him go down.

She shook that off. If she didn't fix this, there'd be more widows, and widowers. The patrol plane was still calmly headed outbound, with apparently no inkling of what was on its way. Unfortunately, only one possible action remained to her. "Alice: Engage Vampire Five with LAWS as soon as track is established. Engage torpedoes with CAT if decoys fail."

The computer said, *"Interrogative, Captain. Warning! Doctrine violation. You are directing me to engage own ordnance, already*

assigned to hostile air. Also, after LAWS mount is currently as-
signed to tracks 2031, 2032, 2036."

"Fuck me," she muttered. "What the hell's this bitch trying to do? You give her a direct order, and she *argues* with you."

Beside her Mills was typing furiously. "We're not raising them, voice," he muttered. Meaning, she supposed, the Poseidon. It was still outbound, oblivious to the doom closing in from its blind zone dead astern. And behind the exec, the antisubmarine officer seemed to be vying for her attention too.

Unfortunately she didn't have time for either. Cheryl sucked in a deep breath and tried to keep her tone level, her pronunciation clear. Too-marked inflections tended to confuse the voice recognition soft-ware. "Alice: I confirm that order. Ignore doctrine violation. Designate own-ship Standard as Vampire Five. Drop previous targets. Engage with LAWS!"

"Engaging track 2038 with LAWS—"

A glance at the screen told her 2038 was the bomber. She shouted, "Negative, *negative!* Engage outgoing *own-ship Standard* with LAWS!"

Beside her Mills murmured, "You're confusing her, Skipper. Go to manual mode?"

Cheryl twisted, to meet the gaze of the laser console operator. The petty officer had the outgoing missile centered on her screen, the Playstation-like controller cradled on her lap. The range was clear. The squall had moved on. Cheryl nodded to the operator. "Aft LAWS to manual mode," she told her boom mike. A second later, AALIS rogered.

"Tracking," the console operator said, slumped in her chair, intent on her screen. Her thumbs tightened on her controller. "Pulsing."

In the aft camera, the barrel-like mount steadied. The lights flick-ered again. Once again the cooling fans whirred downward as the laser sucked energy first from its own capacitor banks, then from the ship's generators.

A second passed. Then another. Plumes of white vapor burst from the laser. The beam, stuttering ten times a second, seethed the hu-mid air in front of the muzzle. No one spoke.

Why wasn't it working? Cheryl half rose from her seat, intending to supervise over the console operator's shoulder, but Mills brought up the video from her sight in the CO's helmet.

The outgoing missile was a black cruciform, its exhaust a bright dot centered between the fins. It was so dazzling that the usually intense dot of the outgoing beam, focused to burn through metal and detonate anything flammable, was invisible. The crosshairs of the dual reticle showed it as properly centered. The beam readout showed it as properly focused.

But nothing was happening.

She tensed, realizing suddenly and with a sinking heart what was wrong. Centered in the superheated plume of the sustainer exhaust, the beam *couldn't* focus. Diffused by the engine's shock wave, the burning dot of the laser, nearly as hot as the surface of the sun, might heat the gas plume behind the engine, but it wouldn't stop the missile. If anything, the added energy might boost its velocity.

But before she could react the operator's voice came over the circuit. *"Shifting to manual aiming,"* she said in the same detached tone. The laser-spot slid out of the engine-glow and refocused, to the side, between the rim of the engine nozzle and the port fin.

It held there, dwelling unwavering as the tail-root turned red, then white-hot.

With a burst of flame, the fin disintegrated. Fire burst from one side of the missile. Then it lurched, rotated, and exploded in a soundless, detonative violence. A moment later all that remained was flaming debris, gyrating and tumbling as it soared downward toward the sea far below.

"Splash Vampire Five," the operator said.

"Splash Vampire Five," AALIS confirmed.

Cheryl was taking off the helmet, exhaling at last, when a red LED ignited on the console. "Aft LAWS overheat fail," the operator muttered. At the same moment the old-style 21MC box in front of her clicked on. *"CIC, After Steering. Just heard a heavy impact back here."*

She twisted to face the ASW officer, at his own console. "Didn't we get the CAT off?"

"Never left the tubes, Skipper. Somehow the firing code got disabled. Was trying to tell you, but you waved me off."

"CIC, Main." Lieutenant Jiminiz's voice. Another hand from the old *Savo*, Jiminiz was fleeted up to chief engineering officer now. *"Dispatching damage control team to check out impact aft of frame 260."*

She hit the lever. "Very well, CHENG. Report damage. Any hull penetrations."

"DC aye."

The overhead speaker beeped. *"All stations this net, this is Pyramid. OTC passes: Finex. Finex. All stations report."*

"Shit," Mills muttered, beside her. "That was so fucked up, Skipper. We didn't look good at all, on that one."

"Unfortunately . . . I've got to agree." She leaned back in her chair, rubbing her face and thinking *Fuck Fuck Fuck* real hard so she wouldn't say it out loud in front of the crew. Or worse yet, snap at them. Relieved that at least they hadn't shot down their own range services.

But sobered, disappointed, and angry. The most modern ship in the fleet. AI-enabled. With the newest weapons. But the software patches weren't working, her tactical agent was trigger-happy, her lasers overheated, and the antitorpedo countermeasures were duds. How could she take a ship to war in this condition?

She shuddered, fighting off memories of bodies in the passageway outside sick bay, of the screaming of the wounded, of the burned . . . She wasn't going to go through that. Not *ever* again.

"A word, XO." She jerked her head toward the access door.

In the passageway, she gave him instructions. "We'll have to cancel liberty, Matt. I'm sorry, but there it is. We just aren't ready. We have too much to do. Before going in harm's way."

He sucked in air between those gorgeous white teeth. "I agree, but . . . crew's not going to be happy."

"We're going to *war*, XO. You remember how close we cut it last time. This ship's built tougher, I think. But the enemy's learning too. If we want to come back this time, we need all systems operational. Everyone at the pitch of training. Nothing left to chance."

"No argument, Skipper. Just pointing out . . . well, never mind." He shook his head, looking away, obviously wondering how he was going to sugarcoat this one for the crew. "Maybe . . . pass it via the Goat Locker?"

She grimaced. "It's gotta come from us. We could let the department heads make exceptions, if there are really good reasons, and we don't need that specific person to correct the casualties." She sighed, giving in to the inevitable. "I'll get on the 1MC, give them the word myself."

A few minutes later, as men and women left their citadels and *Savo Island* turned for port, the PA system crackled. They looked up, pausing in their work as their commander spoke.

"This is the Captain.

"Thanks, everyone, for your hard work getting ready for these exercises over the past weeks. There, and in the shipyard, you've given a thousand percent.

"Unfortunately, today's exercises uncovered significant shortcomings in several areas of material, training, and software. We have to correct them before we go to war. We must *correct them, before we go to war.*

"Thus, I'm sorry to say, I'm canceling liberty in Pearl. I know it's disappointing, but I have no choice. Once we make port, if everyone turns to with a will, I might be able to cut loose for one night's Cinderella liberty. But that's all I can promise. The Fleet needs us on the line when the big push comes. Which I understand is nearly on us."

She let up the button, wondering if there was anything else she should say. What would her old mentor, Daniel V. Lenson, have ended the bad news with? She hovered, licking her lips. Frowning.

"Once again, thanks for your hard work. I'm sorry I have to call for more. I'd just rather we paid in sweat now, than in blood later.

"This is your captain speaking.

"That is all."

3

The Pentagon

THE lithe woman striding toward the river entrance wore a tailored gray suit and low gray suede heels. Night after night of exchanging sleep for toil had pressed creases into her forehead and left shadows under her eyes concealer didn't hide.

At the granite steps she touched her left ear, and pulled a lock of hair over it. Then halted, pressing a hand to her forehead.

A momentary dizziness. The old sense of having been here before.

No, not exactly déjà vu, Blair Titus thought, trying not to wince as she resumed climbing the broad staircase.

Because, truly, she *had* been here many times. As defense aide to Senator Bankey Talmadge. As the staff director to the Senate Armed Forces Committee. As undersecretary of defense, her current position, with offices on the third floor in the E Ring. And for the twice-weekly meetings of the Joint Chiefs' Pacific War Working Group.

Uniformed guards inspected her ID, took temporary possession of her phone and briefcase, and pointed her through the security gate. It promptly warbled a warning.

"Titanium, in my leg and hip," she explained.

The male sergeant nodded, looking only a little apologetic. "Still have to check you out, ma'am."

A thin female soldier wanded her in a side room as the others looked through her briefcase and scrolled through her phone. "Can you hurry?" Blair said at last. "I'm due in the Tank."

"Sorry," the trooper said, but didn't speed up her inspection any. She seemed particularly interested in the Manolo Blahnik kitten heels, and in Blair's white silk blouse and thin gold torque. Blair pressed her lips together, holding back a sigh.

Finally the guards seemed satisfied she hadn't suddenly become a major threat to national security, instead of part of its defense. Blair took back her Coach briefcase and marched on up the ramp, heels clicking. Summer sun falling through thick safety glass windows made the polished floor tiles glow.

She remembered all too well why the windows were shatterproof. Unfortunately, on that day years before in New York, she herself hadn't been.

At the next security station two staffers joined her. The older one carried a briefcase, the younger a tablet under one arm. When she veered into a corridor they wheeled with her, precisely, in step.

THE Blairs had been shakers in national politics since Francis Preston Blair had moved to Washington to start a pro–Andy Jackson newspaper. After being defeated in a bid for Congress two years before, Blair Titus had reluctantly accepted an offer from the opposition to help bridge the expertise gap as the country plunged into war. Now she was the undersecretary for strategy, plans, and forces at Defense. And deeply suspect to the peace wing of her own party.

But the country needed her, as much as if she were in uniform. Like her husband, Dan.

The second set of guards waved them through. "Go ahead, ma'am." She smiled tightly, and went on in.

CONVENING today was what Dr. Edward Szerenci, the national security advisor, called the HTWG—the Hostilities Termination Working Group. Szerenci loved coining acronyms. Its task, as the name implied, would be to find a way to end three years of desperate conflict. She'd worked all this week researching history, pulling together alternatives, and going over the options with her staff and experts from academia.

She wasn't ready. But then, no one had been ready for this war, either.

The meeting room, opening off the already highly secure Intel Center, looked like any bland windowless conference space, though newer and better furnished than anything at the White House. But it was even more heavily shielded than the West Wing. A scanning console would detect any transmitting devices. She helped herself to coffee at an urn, taking it black, but stirred in sugar as she surveyed the room.

The operations deputies were ranked along the wall, as usual. And, as usual, looking even tenser and more sleep-deprived than their principals. They were there to listen, since they'd have to execute whatever was agreed on. She noted bulky, slow-moving Helmut Glee, the Army chief of staff. Gray, birdlike Absalom Lipsey, Joint Chiefs Operations. Rotund, pain-racked Dr. Nadine Oberfoell, from the Office of Cyber Security, in a wheelchair now—that was new. No sign of Nick Niles, Dan's former CO, now chief of naval operations. Oddly, there seemed to be no one from Indo-Pacific Command, the main warfighting CINC, either. But there were reps from State and CIA. Good.

"Blair, you look wonderful. As always," said a professorial-looking fellow in a blue tweed jacket.

"Hello, Kevin." Dr. Glancey was a historian from Stanford.

A cleared throat from behind her. "Kev. Blair." Gray-suited, silver-haired, the national security advisor patted her shoulder.

"Ed," she murmured.

Szerenci sighed, looked at the pastries, then back at her. "I like the gray. In the hair? Adds to the gravitas. Not that you didn't have plenty before."

"Thanks," she said reluctantly, brushing that rogue lock down over her misshapen ear again. She and Szerenci had clashed more than once. But he kept her on the list for policy meetings. Maybe as devil's advocate?

Maybe.

"How's Admiral Dan doing? Any recent word?"

"I don't hear from him that often, Ed. I'll probably learn more about what he's doing here today, than what he can tell me."

Szerenci looked past her, and not for the first time. "There's Rick. Guess we're ready to start."

Husky, fiftyish General Ricardo Petrarca Vincenzo was the chairman of the Joint Chiefs. In terms of protocol he and Szerenci were roughly equal, but here at the Pentagon, Vincenzo would chair the meeting while the security advisor sat to his right. Blair found her own place halfway down, between Glancey and the CIA rep, Tony Provanzano.

Vincenzo poured himself a glass of water, and opened. "Welcome, everyone. The purpose of this meeting is to staff out options for the second Allied Heads of State conference in Jakarta. We're going to scramble up the agenda today. First, overall picture. Then, enemy situation. I need everyone to keep your presentations brief. Eight minutes. No more. Then we'll review the strategic balance. Finally, we have to staff out a way to end this thing. And it would be good if we could present it as a consensus.

"Obviously, this is compartmented. There'll be an official minute, but no personal notes can leave this room." He waited a beat, then nodded to the first briefer.

A screen lit at the end of the room. The first image was the JCS logo. Four swords behind a shield, surrounded by a laurel wreath.

She knew the background, but forced herself to listen for any new developments. Vietnamese forces, backed by US airpower, had halted the Chinese south of Hanoi. A CIA-controlled Islamist rebel group had destroyed Jade Emperor, the main Chinese AI, ending cyberattacks on the US. The American artificial intelligence, Battle Eagle, was recovering the initiative. After being stymied for weeks in ferocious battles, the Marines and Army were finally making progress in Taiwan. A combined US/Indonesian force was readying for the invasion of Hainan, although a recent accident in Brunei would push back the date. Finally, and most critical for the future, Allied war production was rising.

"So far, so good," Vincenzo remarked. "And a long way from where we started. Especially in equipment and munitions. How about the enemy situation? Tony?"

The CIA rep beside Blair clicked through several slides. Again, she knew most of what he presented. A major outbreak of a lethal influenza was decimating both the Chinese and Vietnamese armies. Beijing was reinforcing, but the new troops were poorly trained, hungry, sick, and ill-equipped.

Provanzano said, "But we can't underestimate the depth of sacrifice the Chinese may be willing to make. The leadership's determined to hold out. Worst case, they can fall back on their nuclear retaliatory force. Which so far has kept us from escalating."

"We've been working to right that balance," Szerenci put in.

The chairman nodded. "Hold it there, Tony. Right, that situation's evolving. I'd like to hear from STRATFOR next. Then MDA."

The general from Strategic Forces—nuclear weapons, both sea-, land-, and aircraft-delivered—took them though a sobering recap of Allied efforts to recoup a shortfall that had, Blair reluctantly admitted, probably been part of the reason for the war. Working in secret for a decade, and using nuclear material the North Koreans had traded for food and oil, the Chinese had built a large class of very heavy intercontinental missiles. In throw weight, accuracy, and number of independently maneuverable warheads, they were superior to anything in the American arsenal. Seventy MIRVed ICBMs had been targeted against major cities in the continental United States. Up to seven hundred warheads, though probably some were decoys.

More than enough to kill a nation, according to the analyses.

A bulleted slide flashed up. The general said, "Two points in Premier Zhang's ultimatum bear repeating. First, US forces and nuclear weapons bases will be dealt with 'by any means necessary.' He's proven that by taking out the *FDR* battle group and Pearl Harbor. Second, and most threatening: 'Any aggression against Chinese soil will be answered by a similar level of destruction visited on the American homeland.'"

"It's always slippery judging intent," said Provanzano, beside Blair. "But it's a credible threat. That's the consensus of the intelligence community."

"Which is why the administration never committed to retaliate," Szerenci said. "I know it looked like cowardice, and it's not how I would have proceeded personally. But it's defensible. Withholding a response, trying to keep the war conventional as long as possible. Until we could regain parity, then superiority.

"If we'd only built the force I kept recommending for years . . . well, water over the dam." Szerenci took off his glasses, massaged closed eyes, then looked to Vincenzo. "Shouldn't we clear the room now, General?"

The chairman glanced at the staffers lining the walls. "Thank you, gentlemen. Ladies. Principals only from here, if you don't mind."

WHEN the room was cleared, Szerenci pointed to Strategic Forces again. "General, sorry for the interruption, but you understand why. Tell everyone what you've done to retrieve the balance for us."

The screen cut to a massive missile shouldering its way out of a silo. In the video, flame and smoke burst up all around it. It rose into the sky, trailing flame and a gigantic pillar of white smoke.

"The biggest ICBM ever built. The Earth Penetrator Heavy," the general said. "We started with a SpaceX heavy booster. Each missile packs a dispenser bus with four hardened earth-penetrating reentry bodies. Each reentry body carries an uprated W91 device with a total output of twenty megatons. The biggest warheads ever put on a missile.

"But the real difference is, terminal velocity. Boosted by a modified Trident engine on the way down, the EP Heavy payload will hit the ground at twice the speed and with far more energy than any previous reentry body. The hardened penetrator can punch through two hundred meters of granite. Since the warhead energy couples to the target via seismic shock, the harder the rock and concrete they encounter, the more destructive the shock wave they generate.

"These things will blast mountains apart."

Dr. Oberfoell stirred, straightening in her wheelchair. "I sent around a document about Battle Eagle's recent compromise of the enemy's command system. We may be able to cut their strategic re- sponse time by as much as eighty percent."

The general smiled at her, which Blair found ghastly. Considering what they were actually saying.

Szerenci looked pleased too. "First we slow down their reaction times. Then hit them with a punch heavy enough to destroy their mobile launchers before they can leave their tunnels." Somehow he'd taken the lead from the chairman. He pointed down the table. "But what if they manage a partial launch? Say we destroy eighty percent of their capability. Twenty percent of seventy is fourteen. Double that to be safe. MDA, can you stop twenty-eight missiles headed for American cities?"

Blair sucked air, dizzy again. Not from déjà vu this time, but from disbelief. Rational human beings were discussing this? She started to speak, but the missile defense rep was passing around graphics showing intercept probabilities. She stared down at hers.

"Bottom line, to answer your question directly, sir, we estimate twenty percent of the remainder will get through."

"That takes us down to two to three, right?"

"Two to three on US cities. Yes sir. With several warheads each, though. Since they're MIRVed."

Into a dead silence Szerenci said calmly, "Acceptable?"

No one looked at anyone else for a few seconds. Across the table from Blair, Dr. Oberfoell reached for the water carafe. Filled a glass, and sipped from it.

"Acceptable," Szerenci concluded, this time with a falling inflec- tion.

Vincenzo leaned back in his seat. "Let's hope it doesn't come down to that. But it would be great to regain dominance. The question I'd have is, does Zhang know the Heavy exists? If we're talking deter- rence, secrets don't deter. Demonstrated capabilities do."

"We developed it in secret," the STRATFOR general said. "Other- wise we risked a preemptive strike."

"Of course. Sure. But when do we tell *them* what we can do?"

"We reveal it at Jakarta," Szerenci put in. "At the Heads of State conference. The way Truman told Stalin at Potsdam." He looked around. "Sense of the meeting?"

Nodding. Murmured agreement. Blair felt numb, but finally forced herself to nod too. Maybe the fear factor would work. Maybe. Certainly handing the nuclear advantage to China hadn't.

If they could end the war at the price of three American cities . . .

"Let's take a break," Vincenzo said, and got up. This time, none of them met the others' eyes. And several lined up, gazes downcast, at the door to the little attached restroom.

SPEAKING slowly and heavily, Vincenzo reviewed strategy next. "The two-pronged plan we implemented last year is working. Uppercut and Causeway succeeded. At immense cost, but the troops came through. Taiwan will be ours shortly, if all goes as planned.

"We brought forward our buildup this year. Stockpiled. Built a supply train. Secured replacement weapons and aircraft from Israel, Britain, and the EU, and reconstituted our own industrial base. The enemy's penned in, and weakening.

"Currently, a combined Vietnamese-Indonesian ground force, supported by the US, Vietnamese, Indian, and Australian navy and air force, is preparing to land in Hainan. Occupying that island will position the Allies to develop operations into Hong Kong. Up to now, I've resisted any suggestion we land on the mainland. But if the Indonesians prove as tough as they look, I might say yes. Drive a wedge into south China, and maybe the regime will fall."

"Korea," Szserenci prompted.

"That was my next sentence, Ed. That plan's been looked at by the refugee government and approved by the interim head of state. Toppling one of the Opposed Powers will weaken morale of the others. Leading, again, to possible coups."

The chairman steepled his fingers. He too looked sleepless and tormented. But also grimly determined. "We've come back from where we were. And we have a path forward, in the near term. But this war could still go either way, if home front resolve weakens and production drops, or there's a major defeat on the battlefronts. Or if some unforeseen unknown clobbers us on the back of the head.

"That brings us to war termination. Which Dr. Szerenci and the SecDef are going to get asked about in Jakarta. I asked Dr. Glancey to give us the historical perspective first. Professor?"

Beside her Glancey stood. He cleared his throat, looking around. "As I've told many of you before, we're in unexplored territory here."

The professor locked each of their gazes in turn, as if at a graduate seminar. "Modern conflicts don't terminate when both adversaries are balanced. Unless both are exhausted. Their economies wrecked. And usually, not even then. After lives have been sacrificed, atrocities alleged, populations propagandized and mobilized for total war.

"What's worked before? Overwhelming force has to be demonstrated by one side. But that's not all; a corresponding requirement is for the other side to accept the impossibility of victory. Operation Barbarossa demonstrated overwhelming force. But Stalin refused to accept defeat. So termination did not result.

"In World War I, termination occurred through a combination of military exhaustion, famine, propaganda, and psychological collapse. In World War II, pure military defeat and loss of territory, in the case of Germany, and blockade and bombing, including nuclear weapons, in the case of Japan. In the Cold War, economic collapse and a yearning for freedom."

He sighed and looked away from them all. "Unfortunately, there will be no more one-sided nuclear wars. We've gamed this over and over, at the War College and at Stanford. In ninety percent of the runs, there proved to be no way to terminate hostilities short of a nuclear exchange."

Blair leaned forward, so he could see her. "What happened the other ten percent of the time?"

He looked down at her. "A coup. Followed by total collapse."

"A military coup. In China?"

Glancey looked away again. "Not always, Blair."

She waited a moment, but apparently no one else was going to ask. "You mean . . . here?"

"Let's not go there," Vincenzo cut in. "We may not agree with the administration. But we still operate under civilian control."

"The overthrow didn't come from the top," Glancey said. "We don't see it, in this room. We have enough to eat, drivers, personal protection. But people are angry out there. They're afraid. It only happened once in our simulations. But that one occurrence came from below. Something more like . . . a revolution."

Murmurs of protest, shaking of heads. Vincenzo frowned. "So how *do* we end this, Professor? You keep telling us what we can't do, how impossible termination is. But every war has to end. How the *fuck* are we going to tie up this one?"

Glancey spread his hands. "I could give you some song and dance, General. Or insist no one knows. But, really, I just told you how it ends. Ninety percent of the time, with central nuclear war."

More silence. Blair shifted in her chair, only now acknowledging the ache in her injured hip. She caught Oberfoell's eye across the table, and cleared her throat. "Nadine, can you help out at all? You said Battle Eagle could slow their responses. Can it possibly disable their heavy missiles completely, now Jade Emperor's out of action?"

"We're working on that," the cyber director said. "Believe me. As I said, we can degrade their command. But we haven't found a way in to the missiles themselves. Before it was destroyed, Jade advised them to isolate everything. But, as I said, we haven't given up."

"Cybersabotage is worth pursuing," Szerenci said. "But if nuclear war is the foreordained end, we need to strike first. With EP Heavy, followed by a massive counterforce laydown from all three legs of the triad. All out. Nothing held back."

Blair reached for the carafe, and sipped water with a suddenly dry mouth. "That's a dark vision, Ed."

"It's not one I wanted, Blair. Contrary to what you seem to think."

"Maybe now's the time to make a peace offer, Ed. Ricardo. At Jakarta? Let's at least . . . perhaps an armistice proposal. A cease-fire. There are elements that might respond." She almost said *I talked to them in Zurich*, but didn't. Only Szerenci knew that, and it would be all too easy to get branded as a traitor if that meeting became known.

But Szerenci shook his head. "No, Blair. I understand. Believe me. But it's too late to talk peace.

"The Allies made that mistake in 1918. Letting the enemy survive, but humiliated, so he could come back twice as strong.

"It's time to bring China to its knees, forever. Leave it a scorched wasteland. Like Sherman said, leave them only their eyes to weep with. Kill so many people they'll never dare threaten us again."

Into the shocked silence that followed he said calmly, "Does that sound 'dark,' Blair? We've known since the test at Alamogordo this moment would come someday. That's how this war will end. The only way it *can* end."

He reached for the carafe, and the chill tinkle of ice was the only sound in the room. "We can wish all we like," he added, "But the only thing we can do now is make sure that when it's over, more of us are left, than of them."

4

Taiwan

SERGEANT Hector Ramos is riding a motorized ammo cart north after three days off the line at Battalion Aid. He's twenty. An E-5, even though he's been in the Corps for only two years. He's not tall, but he's muscular. His black hair's buzz cut under the helmet. His right temple is shaved and microstitched under a sprayed-on bandage. He wears an eagle, globe, and anchor tattoo, a red plastic rosary around his neck, and fresh, spanking-clean battle dress. The backs of his hands as he grips his carbine are slashed with dark scars from the kill room of the chicken plant he worked at before ICE gave him a choice: enlist, or be deported.

The burns on them, though, are from battle. He's a two-island Marine now. The first was Itbayat, northernmost of the Philippines. There he earned a Purple Heart, the Combat Action Ribbon, and the Asiatic-Pacific Campaign Medal.

Right now he's riding a robotic weapons carrier down a winding road onto the plains of northern Taiwan. A lanky white woman in battle Cameleons and a smart helmet is clinging to the handgrips in the passenger seat. Intermittent blasts flicker and rumble on the horizon ahead.

The front. Where he'd fought for weeks, before being sent back with the walking wounded.

He'd caught a bullet in the helmet and blacked out. When he came to again he couldn't remember his name. The platoon commander interviewed him brusquely, snapped photos of the helmet and his bleeding scalp, and told Iron Dream, the sexy-voiced intersquad AI the troops called Wet Dream, that Staff Sergeant Hector Alfonso Ramos was going to the rear for evaluation. And also, to put him in for his second Heart.

Hector had protested, and been told that he'd just gotten an order.

The next thing he remembered was a field shower, then a metal framework clamped to his head. A needling pain as a spiderlike machine click-click-stitched his torn scalp. A bandage. A shot. Then a hot meal.

Followed by an instantaneous toppling, under a tent pocked by the endless rain, into a sleep like death itself.

THE battle had ground on longer than anyone had expected, fueled by a sense on both sides that this might be the climactic campaign of the war.

Operation Causeway, the invasion of Taiwan, began with battle drones and submarines cutting off enemy reinforcements and resupply. Then the Marines landed. The first wave seized an airfield and port on the east coast. Once that toehold was covered by missile support, air defense in place, armor landed, and logistics coming in, they'd driven inland. Linking up with resistance forces, they'd punched west into the central mountains. The Army landed in the south, but was stalled by AI-controlled autonomous armor.

Since then, the Army had pinned the bulk of the enemy as the Marine Third and the Nationalist 905th went toe to toe with the Chinese First Amphibious Mechanized and the 45th Airborne Mechanized. After the first days hardly anything digital had functioned. Both sides were jamming and emping from the Ka-band down. The clouds of drones vanished, dropped like dead buzzards by the rain, the mountains, and raptor UAVs that soon expired in their turn.

The Marines cowered in the mud under furious barrages. Charlie had better artillery than the Allies and more ammo stockpiled than Intel had predicted. The result was head-to-head butting, a deadly, grueling ground game. The platoon had taken heavy casualties, dead, wounded, blown apart by creeping mines, brains scrambled by microwaves, blinded by ocular interruptors, both Marines and their robotic counterparts.

Ramos had fought side by side with one of those robots, immortalized now in Division tradition as the Last CHAD. C323 had thrown himself on a grenade, then, with wires hanging from a demolished chest, manned a machine gun post until it was overrun.

Now all the Combat Humanoid Autonomous Devices were gone, "dead" or broken. The human marines had taken heavy losses too. But they'd finally punched through the mountains, and were hitting the enemy's last reserves. At least, Intel said these were the last.

Operation Causeway was reaching a desperate climax. From where he stood, even Hector could see that.

BUT now he's heading back to the front, and trying to find the platoon. Scanning the sides of the road as he and Patterson jostle and bump along. Rivulets of blood, diluted by rain, slide this way and that under the cans of ammo in the cargo bed. "Why does it just fucking rain and rain," she mutters through gritted teeth. "Have we seen the sky since we fuckin' landed?"

Ramos doesn't answer. He's concentrating on the road. Looking for ambush sites, IEDs, and the creeping mines that sense movement and home on body heat.

Lance Corporal Patterson, beside him in the jolting cart, was a girls soccer coach in Pennsylvania before the war. He's seen her broken-field sprint through barrages in two sets of jelly armor, carrying ammo and freeze-dried plasma. Today her dirty face is streaked with rain. "So how'd he get it?" she asks him.

Hector can't remember what they were talking about. He shakes his head carefully, so as not to dislodge anything. "I don't know, Wombat."

"You don't seem to know fucking shit-all these days, Sergeant."

"Not first 'a tell me that. I thought—"

He's interrupted by a skinny marine at the side of the road flagging them down. The guy looks shaken. No rank insignia, but no one wears them in combat. "Pull over. Halt," Hector tells the cart. He casts a wary glance past the loner, but sees only paddies. "What's the deal, jarhead?"

"Harlen, PFC. First 'a the Third. You got comms back to Higher?"

"Not right now. Why?"

The marine shoots an apprehensive glance over his shoulder. "Might wanta call this in. Or at least, go see."

Hector frowns. "See what?"

"Right down this road. Half a klick?"

He glances at Patterson. She shrugs. "Climb aboard," he tells the PFC.

He unslings his weapon and checks the seating on the magazine as the cart jolts and whines, threading a blasted village of smashed homes. The rutted road, once asphalt-paved, has been chewed into mud again by treads. It's littered with the usual trash of war. The unmistakable possum-stink of rotting meat, garbage, shit, and smoke makes the air the cart shoves him through somehow thicker, almost liquid. A smell he barely notices anymore.

"There it is," yells the PFC, pointing.

"Slow down," Hector tells the cart.

"Oh, fuck me," Patterson breathes.

A river's engraved a shallow groove across the land, framed by perhaps four hundred meters of swampy soil on either bank. Cupped by long arcs of barbed wire, topped by rusting concertina, on the shores lie hundreds of bodies. No. Thousands. Motionless, except for the stir and flutter of quarreling crows and gulls. But atop slim steel towers, barrels still sweep the fence line.

"Halt," Hector snaps to the cart. "Those are facial-rec MGs on those pylons." He searches the sky, but doesn't see anything up there. The dronehawks have done their job.

"We gotta call this in," the joe says again.

"I'm getting video." Patterson holds up her battle phone.

"I'll call it in, dickhead," Hector says, "but you need to rejoin your unit."

"I lost them. Got separated." The guy looks desperate. "Can I come with you?"

"Only if you wanna fight," Hector tells him. "'Cause that's where we're headed."

He nods, and Hector tells the cart, "Reverse, retrace to main road, return to loading point." Motors whining, tires spinning in the mud, it obeys.

IT's still raining when they get back to the platoon. The Marines are marching forward. Marching. On foot. Along a muddy, shell-blasted, waterlogged sunken road between bare paddies whose dikes have been blown apart by shells and trampled by retreating Chinese armor. Rifles and Gussies slung, a long, swaying, trudging line of men and women.

Like the Romans, Hector thinks. He didn't learn much in school, but remembers a picture of the legions on a road. Little Lieutenant Ffoulk hikes with them, dirty as the rest, her oversized butt swaying as she marches. Blown over a cliff in the mountains, she refused evacuation. When she spots Hector she squints and signals him up. Her gaze sharpens on his uniform. "Sergeant. What, they're not issuing Cameleons anymore?"

He doesn't salute. That would mark out leaders for drones, for snipers. "Lieutenant. No, just these left."

"Who's this mutt?"

"Lost his unit. Wants to fall in with us till he can rejoin."

"Fine by me, take him. You back in battery, Ramos?—Hey, Patterson. Lance Corporal, you stick with me.—Ramos, I say again, you with us, Sergeant?"

"Affirmative, Lieutenant. Where's my squad, ma'am?"

"I gave Karamete your squad. We lost Glasscock. I'm gonna need a new platoon sergeant."

"How about . . . how about Clay?"

She squints again. "The Top got his legs blown off back in Chishang, remember? Sure you're okay, Marine?"

"Yeah. Yeah, I forgot." He shifts his boots in the mud. "Uh, Dolan's senior to me."

"Blinded by an ocular yesterday. You're getting the platoon, Staff Sergeant. Like it or not."

"Uh-huh. Aye aye, ma'am. Uh, we brought ammo in the cart."

"So I see." She nods to the vehicle. "Cart: Drive up the column. Stop every hundred yards so the troops can pick up ammo. When you're empty, return to your charging point." The AI beeps acknowledgment and moves out.

She brings Hector up to date as thcy trudge on. "Armor punched through up around Heping. The Japanese allies are hitting the beach at Yilan, up to the northeast. Higher think this thing might be breaking loose.

"Here's the plan. Pei's trying to withdraw to the capital. If he can dig in there, make it a three-block war, we'll pay in blood. Division vants us to drive northwest and cut him off. We get behind them, this thing's over." She readjusts her pack, wheezing. "So about two klicks, we're gonna mount up and see how far we exploit the breakthrough. You and Wombat stick with me. Got a special mission if we get there. Oorah?"

"Oorah," Hector says. But really, he cares not at all. Suddenly his head aches, and once again, he can't remember exactly who he is.

TO his astonishment, the tanks really are waiting. Smoke rises ahead, between the green steep mountains, and the hollow high roar of jets and the crump of bombs reverberates down the valley. The rain pelts down steadily as the company climbs aboard, second platoon in the lead. No trucks, no thin-skins. Just the tanks, gray and scarred with whatever the slants have been throwing at them.

They push northward through heavy rain and desultory shelling all that afternoon. The pace isn't exactly breakneck. The road twists and switchbacks like a fleeing rattler. The tanks growl and lurch and skid around shell and bomb craters. The marines cling like lice to the rusty rebar hastily welded on as handholds, Red Army–style. They wait while combat engineers repair a bridge. Then push on through deserted hamlets, terraced paddies, above a river that foams and swirls brown as melted chocolate as it rushes south.

They dismount in front of an enemy roadblock at some nameless crossroads. Hector sets his squads, trying to figure how the old Top would have done it. They lay down fire, but before they can advance the resistance melts, pelting away into the paddies, or just dropping their weapons and standing along the road, hands up and mouths open.

Most of these guys aren't even in uniform, just dirty civvy clothes with red armbands. Locals? Volunteers? Hector wishes the Marines had some friendlies with them, to figure out who's what.

Ffoulk gestures angrily for the newly surrendered troops to pick up their rifles again. She calls up an app on her tablet, and speaks into it.

"Zài dàolù shàng reng wuqì," a speaker on the tank bellows. They hesitate, staring at the pudgy black woman perched on the Abrams. She gestures again, peremptorily, with her carbine. The turret begins to rotate toward them. They scramble to pick their weapons up and throw them into the mud.

The tank revvs again, its steel track plates crunching over rifles and machine guns, reducing them to scrap. Disarmed, their recent enemies squat along the road, hands up. Some grin and wave as the tanks speed by, though they quickly recoil, ducking, as the tracks blast mud into their faces.

The Marines run into another block five kilometers on, at a pinch in the valley. This takes calling in close air to growl off several hundred rounds of 20mm into pockets of resistance. Followed by a salvo of tank shells, this allows them to ram through again.

The valley opens. The road descends, becomes four lanes of concrete. The armor leaps ahead, their riders gripping tight as baby possums on a mother's belly. Shaken off, they'd be smashed into paste by the vehicles behind.

Ahead, skyscrapers grow.

AS dusk creeps closer they grind into the outskirts of a city. Smoke bleeds into the sky ahead. At the far end of the highway a red and white tower lifts above a long building of the same red brick and white stucco. Ffoulk yells into the mike, and the lead tank charges for it. The streets are eerily empty, and Hector wonders where the residents have gone. To death camps, like the one he and Patterson came across?

The tank smashes through a low wall, sending blocks of granite flying, and brakes to a squealing, rocking halt in front of the building.

It's been burned, gutted by fire and shells. Black eyebrows of smoke stain the white stone above the windows. Palm trees lie like pick-up sticks. Chunks have been blown out of the portico, leaving windrows of shattered brick and plaster. No one's around. "Dismount," Ffoulk yells, and they spill off and form a cordon, setting up machine gun posts in front of the building. "Come with me," she snaps at Hector and Patterson, and makes for the entrance.

The empty, echoing hallways are sooty with smoke and carpeted with thousands of cartridge casings. Blood splotches the walls. Used bandages litter the floor of an abandoned aid station. They jog after Ffoulk until she finds a stair leading up. This seems less damaged than the front of the building, though the stench of powder's still thick and broken glass from the shattered windows grates under their boots. They cover each other as they ascend.

Flight after flight . . . at the sixth landing Hector staggers. His head swims. He can barely drag one boot up after the other. Despite the break at the aid station, weeks of fatigue and terror are catching up. He centers his carbine's optical sight on Patterson's back. With an effort, grimacing, he manages to slide his finger off the trigger.

At the eighth flight he halts and bends over, trying to breathe. His legs shake. Isn't he supposed to be in better shape than this? But it's not his body that's going. It's his head. For an endless moment he's filled with utter terror. But an instant later he can't feel anything at all. Not fear, not dread. Nor any concern for his fellow marines.

Something tickles his throat . . . trickles down inside his blouse . . . he gropes a hand into his battle dress . . . tiny hard seed-shapes slip through his fingers. Falling like drops of hardened blood. Small deep red plastic spheres, little rubies.

Mirielle's rosary. The string's rotted, broken. "No," he whispers, and bends, grabbing uselessly for the beads as they fall and bounce crazily. "Fuck. *Fuck*," he mutters as they scatter and roll away, eluding his stiffened fingers in the tactical gloves, hopping like escaping crickets down the stairwell.

"Ramos!" Ffoulk, leaning over the rail above him, stares down.

He straightens from the rolling beads. "Guarding your rear," he mutters, then can't help emitting a short bark of laughter. What would Whipkey have said? *It would take a whole squad to man that perimeter.* Yeah, that's what Troy would've said.

Troy Whipkey. From South Florida. Killed on Itbayat Island by an antipersonnel drone.

He rubs his face against the rough plaster of the stairwell, relishing the pain as his skin abrades. Images and feelings jumble in his brain. A kaleidoscope of broken glass. Broken memories. Kisses from dead lips. Orietta. Clay. Whipkey. Bleckford—

"Staff Sar'n't! Get the fuck up here!"

He straightens, and shoves off the wall. Stands panting, staring down from a window. To where a second file of armor is appearing at the far end of the avenue. One of the Marine Abramses creeps out from a side street. The turret swings. Steadies.

With a terrific bang and a streak of light like a meteor's an antitank round goes out. It beams down the street and the lead incoming tank explodes. From the far side of the avenue other dazzling streaks lash out, accompanied by terrific bangs.

Pei is arriving, ahead of schedule.

"Ramos!" Above, Ffoulk is screaming. He flinches, and double-times up the stairs.

THE last flight, and they emerge, out in the open now, here at the top of the tower. The view is dizzying. They're *way* up here. The wind feels good, though. The lieutenant's pulling something from her pack. Shaking it out. It's red and white. And blue too. He should recognize what it is, but doesn't. The colors are pretty, though. It's bright, and clean, and new.

Ffoulk is clambering up onto a ledge. Above it stands a flagpole. A red cloth streams from it in the wind. The diminutive officer gropes for it, but her hands fall short. "Fuck," she mutters, then turns. "Ramos, can you reach this? Get up here. Pull this fucking rag down."

"You want that down, Lieutenant?"

"What I just said, isn't it? You still fucked up, Ramos?"

"I—"

"Never mind. Just—yeah. Do it. Haul it down."

He steps up on the ledge, reaches, and snags the downhaul. It's lashed with some complicated knot that takes some clumsy picking at to loosen. But at last the flag descends, slides down, and falls over him in folds of scarlet and yellow. As he fights free Ffoulk grabs the tattered cloth, stuffs it into her pack, and hands him the red and white and blue one.

"Hoist that," she snaps.

Then makes a strange ejaculation, a puff of meaningless sound, as her head whips round. She bends at the waist, then collapses. Past her he glimpses Patterson, gone pale under the dirt, aiming her phone at them.

Belatedly he realizes what's happened. At the same moment Patterson yells, "Sniper! Get down!"

"I gotta hoist this," he yells back, struggling with the colored cloth, looking for some way to attach the snap hooks on the halyard. His eyes work, but his brain doesn't engage. He stares down stupidly at the bundle in his hands.

There—a brass ring. He snaps the head onto the downhaul as a second bullet goes *whack* into the concrete beside him, blasting out a chunk and covering his arm with gray powder. Whatever they're shooting, it's heavy caliber. He can't imagine where they're firing from. Unless it's that blue skyscraper over there, but that's nearly a mile away. "*Somebody's* fucking good," he mutters, groping to attach the foot of the flag. He sways on the ledge and barely manages to pull himself back vertical with a savage yank on the halyard. If he loses it up here, it's got to be two hundred feet down to the pavement. More shattering blasts from below tells him the tanks are still fighting it out. A machine gun stutters. Then others, but the explosions seem faint and faraway from up here.

The snap shackle clicks home. He pulls the flag free with one arm, hanging on to the pole with the other. He glimpses Patterson in the doorway, still aiming her phone. Another bullet snaps past, just missing the pole, and a hole magically appears in the flag. He flaps it free of the halyard and drops to the terrace, taking in on the downhaul, boots planted on either side of Ffoulk's body, which is still convulsing.

The flag rises, unfurling as it catches the wind. He crouches as if pummeled by a downpour, taking in the line hand over hand, until the flag jams in the sheaves at the top and streams out over the city below, bright and lively in the wind. The red stripes lick like flames against the darkening sky. He ties it off with a clumsy knot, then bends to drag the lieutenant into the doorway with Patterson.

"I sent it," the corporal yells over the renewed clatter of fire. She holds up her phone.

"Sent what? . . . never mind. She's hurt. Need a medic. Aid station." His knees are shaking so bad he can't stand. So he kneels beside Ffoulk, patting the slack face. The officer's eyes stare blankly up at the lintel. He fumbles for a field dressing. Stuffs it into the back of her skull. There's plenty of room.

Patterson shakes his arm, then whacks his helmet. "Ouch," he yells. "What the *fuck?*"

"She's gone. Sergeant! We got to get outta here. Those tanks are gonna put a shell into this tower any fucking second."

"We can't leave her."

"She's fucking *gone.* We'll come back for the body. *Now!*"

Reluctantly, settling Ffoulk's head gently to rest on her pack, he lets Patterson pull him back into the stairwell. A tremendous blast rocks the tower. Fire rattles outside, building to the crescendo of a major battle. Mingled with it is the roar of jets. The hoglike silhouette of a CAS drone flashes past, level with the window. The *Brrrrrr* of its Gatling vibrates the air. A green comet lashes past the drone, so fast the eye can't follow. Patterson keeps pulling on his sleeve, towing him down the steps. He shakes his head, muttering. "Not right. Should'a brought her along," he grunts, lurching into the wall. "Leave nobody behind."

"You're crazy fucked, Sergeant. Just keep going."

"Just keep going. Just keep going."

"Now you got it. Watch that turn. Can you cover me at the landing? *Hector!* Can you cover me?"

"Let fucking go of me . . . gotta take a shit . . ."

"When we get down. You got me? Ramos, you fucking asshole, you covering me? Jesus!"

"Never mind . . . I got you. Got you." His eyes are burning. For some reason, all of a sudden he's crying. Though he still doesn't feel anything except the hot tears on his cheeks.

Clumsily unslinging his carbine with numb, insensate fingers, he angles for a shot downward.

Staggering down together, covering each other at the corners, slowly and deliberately, they descend the staircase.

5

Seattle

THE young, dark-haired woman ran rapidly down the stairwell, grinning. The numbers worked. They worked!

It wasn't a clinical trial, of course, with a control group and actual human beings. Only virtual, run through millions of iterations by Archipelago's deep medical AI.

But so far, everything Asklepios had predicted to happen in the human body, had happened.

She stopped at the landing, unable to wait, and texted the head of her research team.

Asky confirms 80% effectiveness in gen pop, Dr. Nan Lenson texted. *Might just have effective agent. On way down 2 u.*

THE influenza ravaging first Asia and now Africa was a virus, of course. A subtype of a common avian flu. But viruses "drifted." Shuffled the decks, reassorting segments promiscuously from other strains they encountered.

And once or twice a century, you got something devastating.

"Central Flower" had emerged in Asia two years before. No one knew from where, but it had picked up a deadly gene. The CDC infectious disease team in Vietnam had estimated a 40 percent mortality rate.

Vietnamese researchers had isolated the virus, named it, and forwarded samples. The new strain produced a protein that shut down the normal immune response. Combined with the privations of wartime—reduced nutrition, long work hours, and the psychosomatic distress of worry and fear—the result could be cataclysmic.

As Nan Lenson had told her father, Dan, months before, it might actually be good that the world was at war. The lack of travel seemed to have slowed its spread. But that barrier wouldn't stop it long.

The world faced another pandemic. Like the Spanish Flu in 1918. The CDC alert level stood at Phase Six, the highest level of the disease alert system.

Glaxo and Merck had produced candidates for a monovalent live attenuated vaccine. Unfortunately, the Glaxo version hadn't panned out, and the Merck vaccine generated higher than acceptable rates of Guillain-Barré Syndrome in older recipients.

A year before, Dr. Anton Lukajs, head of Archipelago's research team, had assigned Nan to research a family of advanced antivirals. They inhibited the neuraminidase protein that locked into the healthy cell and let a virus inject its RNA. She'd used reverse genetics to investigate the interactions that made the virus so dangerous. When she'd characterized the segments, she found a unique carboxyl terminus. Mapping that structure out on the molecular level had eventually elucidated how it evaded immunity and hijacked healthy cells.

Nan had worked with Dr. Jack Jhingan, Asklepios's acolyte, to model the interactions in the body, trying to find or create a compound to block that terminus. To throw a monkey wrench into how it reproduced inside the cell. Or, alternatively, make it visible again to the immune response, so it didn't get inside at all.

Under Nan's direction, they'd tested the antivirals on ferrets, one of the few animals other than humans susceptible to influenza, isolating the subjects in the Army Level Five containment site at Fort Detrick. But without much success, and she'd concluded that the animals weren't really homologous to humans in their reactions or transmission rates.

Every approach had hit a dead end. And the virus continued to spread.

Then Asklepios had integrated a deep neural network that modeled and predicted large-molecule interactions with the body. And Nan had asked it a simple question. Simple to ask, but unimaginably complex in what it demanded of the program.

What would be the formulation of a molecule that would block the linking action of the carboxyl group of Central Flower's neuraminidase protein, while demonstrating low toxicity, high activity, high solubility, and minimal risk to patients?

After twelve hours of dedicated thought, the AI had just delivered a hit.

DR. Lukajs was in his office. One wall, all glass, overlooked the central mall. Elms and maples were scattered across green lawns dotted with pergolas, pathways, and ponds large enough to pass for small lakes. The central mall was encircled by the immense blue-glass-and-metal ring of the Archipelago campus. Four stories, two square miles, of the most advanced science in the world.

"It's derived from Cytoxan," she told Lukajs, who stood with arms crossed, looking wearily skeptical as usual, before a screen. Biochemists seldom used test tubes these days. The discipline was as dependent on computers as every other science now.

The lead virologist was emaciated, with a wispy fringe of white hair and brown age speckles like spilled coffee dotting his hands. After barely surviving radical prostate surgery, he moved with the tentative fragility of the very old. He frequently smelled of urine. A living meme of the classic nerd, he wore a white lab coat with a pocket protector, a narrow black tie, black oxfords, and plastic-rimmed glasses. Lukajs was Albanian. He'd grown up under Communism, studied in Moscow, and hated working for private industry. "Criminal profiteers," he called them. Archipelago he tolerated, since it was a congressionally chartered corporation, like the Red Cross or the NIH. In some ways he was a dinosaur. But still, he had a frighteningly acute intellect.

"Cyclophosphamide? Already I don't like it." He waggled fingers dismissively. "An alkylating nitrogen mustard antineoplastic. Activates in the liver to form aldophosphamide. Side effects: hair loss, sterility, birth defects, mutations, cancer! This is what you bring me to cure Chinese flu?"

She pushed her notebook into his hands. On its screen a colorful, immensely complicated molecule rotated slowly in a 3-D display. "It's not cyclophosphamide. It's an isoelectronic structural analog. I screened the database. It's not in the literature."

Grumbling, the lead virologist carried the computer to a slanted table, adjusted the screen, and studied it. The visual resembled an exploding star system seen by the Hubble telescope, with its color-coded strands of sugars, proteins, chains of atoms. He cleared his throat and leaned closer. Tapped the surface to stop the rotation. Then spread his fingers to zoom in on one branch of the molecule. "This is a transition state analog."

"I believe so, Doctor." Such an analog resembled the transition state of a substrate molecule in an enzyme-catalyzed chemical reaction. And the human cell responded to viral infection by releasing enzymes. "Of course, that's just the initial candidate compound. We can modify it to improve recognition and binding geometries."

He studied it for several more seconds in silence. "Hmm. Aah . . . I think I see . . . clever. The conventional approach, to sensitize the immune system to surface proteins. But this lets virus attach to the plasma membrane. Hemagglutinin to sialic acid."

"But inhibits the cell's response," she pointed out.

Lukajs mused on, as if she hadn't spoken. "The virion . . . attaches. Injects mRNA. Yes. But this inhibits the enzyme it uses to translate into protein. No enzyme activity, no protein, no genome replication." He squinted. "But what happens to the RNA then? It is still inside, yes?"

Nan said, "The cell's defenses destroy it and MHC class I pushes the debris out onto the cell surface."

Lukajs milked his tie, grimacing. "The artificial mind says this, yes? So clever it is. But it doesn't think, what happens next? Cyto-toxic T tags cell as infected with a toxic mediator and kills it. So cell still dies, in the end."

She nodded. "But no daughter viruses are replicated. Once the initial viral load's exhausted, the infectious process ends."

He glanced sharply at her. "Database search?"

"Came up empty."

"Toxicity?"

"Worrying, but we could pretreat with amifostine. Reduce the hematologic damage, but still get the antiviral efficacy." She caught his frown before he could object. "Or maybe not amifostine. Something like it, though. We could run virtual trials on pharmacophores. Like I said, to bump up the binding geometries. Hundreds of them. Or thousands! The system's that fast."

"It might be worth trying," the old man said grudgingly. But she'd watched a light grow in his eyes as he examined the molecule. Grasped what the drug might be trying to do.

"I'll start writing it up for Drug Discovery," she said. Started to turn away. But found her arm seized.

"Just a minute, Dr. Lenson. No. You will not publish this."

She looked down at his hand on her upper arm until he released it. "Sorry. A transgression of social norms," he muttered.

"Don't we want priority?"

"You don't recall who are we working for here. A responsibility to—how do you say—the 'customer.'" Lukajs wrinkled a bulbous nose.

Outside the window, a buffeting wind thrashed the trees. Leaves leapt up, whirling in the gusts. She crossed her arms. "I don't understand your reluctance, Doctor. This may save many lives."

But the elder scientist was shaking his head. "We need tests. Protocols. Clinical trials. Far too soon to publish. Who says it cannot be toxic? Word of computer? We will be laughy stocks."

"Meanwhile, let people die?"

"Is not pandemic yet."

"Maybe not here, Doctor. But millions are sick in Asia."

"In Asia." Lukajs gave a nearly imperceptible shrug.

But the next moment he held out a hand as if to take it back. "I did not mean. No. Far beyond social norms. What I meant—we will proceed. You will meet with pharmas. Produce test quantities. Plus any isomers. I will advise the board to set up trials. Alert BARDA we might have candidate for production." The Biomedical Advanced

Research and Development Authority contracted for drugs in public health emergencies. "But you are correct about the ferrets. Not useful subjects. Perhaps we can obtain access to better."

Ferrets? For a moment she drew a blank. Then had a bad feeling. "Better subjects—what does that mean?"

"Perhaps, from the government. Volunteers only, of course." The old man smiled, reached out to pat her, but paused his hand halfway. "When time comes, we will share credit. Is your discovery, yes?"

"Actually, it was Asklepios's." But a glow ignited at the thought. She was still only a junior researcher. After the war, funding would be far harder to come by than it was now. A success like this—again, assuming the mechanism of action worked as predicted—could make her career. Could let her pursue some of her own ideas, like inhibiting other enzymes. The ones that allowed cancerous cells to evade apoptosis, for example.

"So we are agreed?" Lukajs looked out the window, down at the tiny figures far below. At researchers strolling or tossing softballs, kicking soccer balls, taking a break from work. "We do this the right way. We will not jump the rifle. We will not post to journals. You work with the pharmas to produce. I will have Dr. Jhingan set up the trials. And when they are successful and we publish, you will both receive co-credit with me. We are agreed?"

He held out a hand, age-spotted, trembling slightly; and after a moment's hesitation, she accepted it.

6

Xinjiang Province, Western China

THE four men huddled elbow to elbow around a fire beneath a gigantic rock. It crackled and wavered, the dry brush snapping like distant riflery. The stars glittered above them, wheeling toward morning. They were nursing tiny cups, blowing on the strong hot tea to cool it before taking sips. A brass pot seethed on a tripod over the coals.

The mountain valley stood above the town, which lay on the single paved road that circled the central desert. In summer, flocks of goats and sheep would pasture up here, but now it was just rock and snow and here and there a dried bush. From time to time a mujahideen uprooted one from between the rocks, brought it over, and dropped it on the fire. Around loomed black, razorlike ridges, impenetrable ravines, a bitter, racked Mars-scape that lay buried in deep shadow in the starlight.

Beijing had responded to the assassinations and propaganda of the Independent Turkistan Islamic Movement, and their raid on a hidden facility in the Taklimakan Desert, by sending a new internal security general to the West. An Uighur himself, the ruthless Marshal Chagatai claimed descent from the Mongol Khans. He'd quashed dissent in Hong Kong with thousands of executions, shuttering the municipal government and imposing martial law. He'd addressed Xinjiang on the radio, warning of the harshest retaliation for any further acts of terror.

ITIM would answer his threat this morning.

For the past week, three hundred guerrillas had negotiated those ridges, climbing by night, led along goat-paths and over precipices by local guides. Each muj had labored under a heavy load of weapons and ammunition. Dozens of carriers followed them—mostly women, Han and other ethnicities, captured in raids and impressed as slaves—tottering under huge sacks of rice, corn-and-apple loaves, dried goat meat, naan bread, blankets, firewood, and more ammunition.

Now they were here, and this morning it would begin.

All four men were bearded, wearing the pajama-like shalwar kameez and pancake-like mountain hats. Heavy sheepskin vests and coats kept them warm, and also reduced their visibility to drones, which scanned these mountain fastnesses in infrared.

The youngest, Nasrullah, was ITIM's supply guy. As such, he was also the main go-between linking the rebels in the mountains to their contacts, suppliers, and recruits in the lowlands. Nasrullah had set up the network in the town whose lights, sparse though they were, glittered coldly far below. In the chill air distant generators droned a monotonous song.

The second man's wrists stuck out from his too-short cotton sleeves. His black mustache had a white streak. A pistol belt held a military-style automatic engraved with a dense calligraphy that recounted his ancestry and his devotion to Allah. This man's name was Guldulla, but "Tokarev" was his battle name.

The third man was older, shorter, more compact, white-bearded. He said little but gazed out watchfully from under shaggy brows. Abu Hamid al-Nashiri had fought for many years in many different countries. He'd been tortured, declared dead, resurfaced somehow, been recaptured, and spent years in an American prison before being recycled out into a fresh war. Now he fought under a new name. Qurban, "The Sacrifice."

The fourth man's dirty-blond beard was going gray. Scars radiated from a potato-like nose like ejecta from a lunar impact crater. His blue eyes were cold as frost, and his bronzed, exposure-roughened skin was seamed like a coal face. He wore the same threadbare shalwar kameez as the Uighurs, the same flat cap and sheepskins, but draped over his shoulders was a worn, ragged blanket, the sort that might have been issued to a prisoner of war. His long hair was braided under the hat. A strange riflelike device was propped against the rock within reach of his right hand.

This man was American. A Navy master chief, Theodore Harlett Oberg.

The four spoke in low voices in a pidgin Han, interspersed with expressions in Uighur as well as certain English phrases Oberg had introduced. Such as "machine gun" and "ambush."

A few yards distant, out of earshot, other mujahideen squatted among the rocks, cradling AKs and RPGs.

From time to time the American checked a cell-phone-like device. He rotated it carefully, glancing up at the sky.

Teddy Oberg shifted, favoring his twisted left foot, which was lashed into a titanium brace. He was still a SEAL, but after nearly three years in the mountains, could hardly remember it. Just as he could hardly remember growing up in California, or the cop he'd been dating in LA, or that he'd wanted to make movies once.

All that was gone. Blown away like poppy pollen on the winds of war.

After breaking out of a POW camp, he and two other escapees had stumbled down out of the Pamirs to witness a mujahideen attack. The rebels had taken them captive, dragging them along when they withdrew. After a jolting ride in the back of a pickup, they'd been shoved into a hidden cave to be judged. And nearly executed.

Teddy had managed to save them by saying he was with the CIA, and could provide aid for their revolt.

Since then, he'd been working to make that lie a reality. Organizing and training insurgents was what a Special Forces A-team typically did. But he seemed to have landed the job, since it was wartime and he was here. A raid to the westward had taken out a major pipeline and power line leading down to Pakistan. A second excursion to the east had ruined a computer center in the Taklimakan Desert with a CIA-supplied electromagnetic pulse device.

There'd been setbacks. Losses. But each year the insurgency had grown, with more effectives and wider networks. The Independent Turkistan Islamic Movement harked back to an earlier resistance the Han had crushed. But also forward, to the promise of a union of all the Turkic peoples, and their liberation from the overlords in Beijing.

This morning they would take the next step on that road.

A shadow loomed between them and the stars. It hissed, "We are ready to move, Lingxiù."

"This will be a day of blood," the youngest man murmured.

The older ones nodded. "Han blood," Tokarev said, patting his pistol.

"Some of the Faithful will die as well," Qurban added.

Teddy nodded, stroking his beard. "True. But it must be done."

"I agree," said the Arab. "Otherwise the Godless will continue to oppress us."

Teddy pushed to his feet. The others stood with him. He fumbled at his neck, pulled night vision goggles over his eyes, and thumbed the stud. The world lit in shades of verdigris and olive. Nasrullah kicked gravel over the fire. It hissed to extinction with a smoky scent of burning sage.

Slinging the antidrone gun, Teddy blinked across black miles to a wall that blocked out the stars. The snow-covered, frowning Pamirs. Then he looked back down, toward the valley, and the peaceful, sleeping town it cradled below them. Trying to force the order out.

Once he spoke, all hell would break loose. And only Allah, blessed be His name, could know where it would end.

He'd spoken with Allah once, on a freezing night high in those mountains. Or something, some being, that had sounded very much like God. He still had no explanation for what he'd experienced. Hallucination? Visitation? Dream? Revelation? But he still remembered the message.

There is no such thing as choice, It had told him. *No such thing as chance.*

You have always done My will.

As My creature, you cannot do otherwise.

"Gai kaishile," Master Chief Teddy Oberg managed at last. Harshly. Savagely, biting the words off.

It is time to begin.

AN hour later the advance elements were in the town. They filtered in hidden under bags of wool in carts pulled by nodding donkeys. They slid in covered by shadow, flitting from wall to wall, pausing for long periods before moving again. They trudged in surrounded by flocks of goats, weapons strapped beneath the bellies of the rams. Once inside, they linked up with groups of town dwellers, already awake and dressed, and briefed them as to their assignments. The locals had been recruited not though social media or conventional communications, which the government strictly monitored, but through more ancient methods. The subterranean murmurings of the souk; laboriously composed messages, pecked out in mountain caves on ancient balky black typewriters, passed hand to hand and carried in beneath the square traditional central Asian caps. Along with more modern ones, as the rebels' raids had been videotaped, dubbed with stirring music, and converted with a running commentary of hate into propaganda masterpieces. Passed from bazaar to madrassa, hamlet to city by truckers and mullahs, the tapes had brought the message to the masses.

Slowly, it began.

A lookout post in a tower on the road in was taken out with a subdued scuffle, terminated by the swift flashing of knives. Then men with picks and bags of gravel went to work, emplacing mines.

Security cameras went black, shot out with suppressed rifles or cloaked with black felt by teenagers scaling their pylons.

Police vehicles sagged on deflated tires, slashed by women who crawled beneath them, screened by the night.

Throughout the town, in narrow alleys and mud-brick courtyards, rifles and grenades were pulled out of roofing thatch, dug up from under pavements, unwrapped and loaded. Extracted from a hundred hiding places, excreted like eggs of death.

The teams, assembled each under a mujahideen, took up positions atop minarets, on the upper floors of apartments, at hastily erected barricades at street corners.

The police station was ringed by thirty men with rifles, machine guns, and antitank rockets. Two hundred meters away a mortar team set up in a vacant bazaar tent, through the roof of which they would be firing.

By an hour before dawn, the rebels owned the crowded, older, Uighur half of the city. In the east, the ethnic Chinese slept on, in rectilinear government apartment blocks guarded by traffic gates and cameras, but little else.

The next phase was to isolate and secure the Han quarter. Teenagers slid through the night. They snipped the cables that fed power to the gates, then slipped black cloth bags over the monitors.

The generator station was taken, the engineers forced to kneel and their throats cut one by one. The school was occupied, and the night watchman swiftly and silently decapitated.

Fourteen men in black shalwar kameez padded through the school, down the hallway. Double doors at the back led through a deserted garden with concrete benches and trickling fountains to the lobby of a semiattached apartment building. The front desk was deserted. The man who should have been behind it was among the intruders. He pointed his comrades to the exits, and they scattered. Then, lifting a rifle, he smashed out the glass panel of a fire alarm, and yanked the handle down.

TEDDY stood in the middle of the square, behind a central plinth with a raised concrete railing. The monument was capped by a statuary group showing a huge Mao Zedong shaking hands with two smaller Uighurs in native costume. A halo of focused lights made it glow brilliantly. The police station loomed across the square, five stories of forbidding rose-tinted concrete topped by antennas and solar panels. On Teddy's side, screened by the group's base, one of his demo teams was packing explosive under the statues.

He checked his watch. Just about time.

The distant steady roar of the generators died. The lights on the statuary flickered, as did the others around the square. Then they winked out.

Darkness rolled across the city, plunging it into night.

The demo teams rolled out and sprinted across the square. They set up remote det Claymores outside the exits from the security headquarters, and slapped pounds of thick white explosive paste on the heavy doors. Within seconds the fuzes were set and they were scooting back into cover.

Amid confused shouting, the first shots cracked from upper windows. They spanged off the paving and zipped around the square. From around him, Teddy's trained snipers put bullets into each muzzle flash. The shooting slackened.

The explosives went off. First under the statuary, which jolted apart and disappeared in a smoky cloud. Shards of pot metal pattered down. Then the charges on the doors blew them inward in flashes of dull red light and the thud-CRACK of C-4.

Two trucks snarled into the square. Teddy caught a glimpse of the faces at the wheel: young, determined, intent. One male, one young woman. The snipers laid down covering fire as the vans tore around the demolished central pylons, accelerating with a growl of engines. Then straightened, aiming for the blown-open entrances.

Two massive detonations shook the city. In a cloud of smoke and dust, the whole front of the station collapsed into the square. Dragon tongues of fire licked up the interior. The snipers stayed busy. Each time a figure emerged from the flames, showed itself at the sheared-off front, or tried for an exit, they nailed it mercilessly. The Claymores cracked when groups of two or three emerged. Before long dozens of corpses in the black uniforms of the security forces littered the pavements.

Nasrullah lifted his gaze from a brace of cheap walkie-talkies sewn into pockets in his sheepskin coat. "The power house is ours . . . radio station is ours. The school. Team leader asks . . . twenty-one teachers in custody. Fifteen men. Six women. What is to be done with them?"

Through a numb mouth Teddy said, *"Paishè suoyou zhèxie."*

Shoot them all.

"Tamen shì women de dírén."

They are our enemies.

Nasrullah looked away, but relayed the order.

Tokarev jogged out from a side street, leading a rifle team. A fat, short Uighur panted and coughed in their midst. Mucus drooled from his nose. His hands were zip-tied behind him. "The mayor," the rebel explained.

Oberg shrugged. "What's he doing here?"

"He says he is one of us. An Uighur."

"So what? He's a collaborator. Shoot him."

"He says he's on our side. Swears he provided information."

Teddy glanced at Nasrullah. A frown, a shake of the head. "Shoot him," Teddy said again. The official stared stupidly from face to face, then burst out bawling. Two young men kicked him in the backs of the legs, forcing him to his knees as Tokarev drew his pistol.

Leaving them behind, Teddy jogged awkwardly down the main thoroughfare. The crippled leg jabbed him with shots of agony. Men and women parted before him. The crowds were gathering. They smashed the windows of vehicles, shattered the windows of the Han shops, wrestled out bolts of cloth and boxes of food and drinks. A shop owner protested, trying to defend his goods. Four men beat him to the ground and began kicking him, shouting epithets, as others heaved bricks through his windows and began helping themselves to cookware and appliances.

The looting had begun. Good. A resident with a closetful of illegal loot was halfway to joining the Resistance already.

A local woman bent double before him, coughing as if to eject her lungs from her chest. Snot drooled from mouth and nose. But she plodded on, dragging one end of a gigantic crate of colorfully labeled infant formula.

He glanced up to note the stars were going. The mountains were still black buttresses, but the sky was graying.

The rebels owned the city. But only for perhaps an hour. No matter how great the surprise at the security station, he had to assume they'd gotten off some sort of message. The district's quick reaction force would be on its way, with heavier weapons and far more men than the guerrillas could stand against.

But before that happened, he had a task to perform. One that was, in many ways, the whole point of the raid.

He emerged onto the second square. A broad flat paved area, set up as a marketplace on holidays and weekends. It was ringed by deserted booths and tables, flimsy sheds with rolled-up awnings. Ahead, as he limped forward, parties of rebels, accompanied by townspeople, were emerging from the streets, debouching into the square. Prodding with rifles, they pushed others ahead of them. Men, women, children. The captives' faces were sallow with fear. Most were Han, but not all. Some had the flat Turkic features of Uighurs, but they'd lived long in the Han quarters.

"Servants of those who deny God," Qurban muttered, beside him.

The old fighter had come up beside him without a sound. Teddy studied his bearded face. No sign there of pity. Just that stare of hatred.

Nasrullah joined them. "The sickness is in the city."

"I saw."

"Some were too ill to leave their beds. We took care of them before we left."

Teddy nodded. Sometimes you had to leave your feelings behind. This operation had a larger objective. A twofold aim, actually. He stole a glance behind him, to where Nasrullah was directing the camera teams. Seizing the town would demonstrate the power and reach of ITIM. But more than that, it would send a message to this new general, Chagatai. Triggering the violent, Tiananmen-style crackdown from Internal Security that would turn all the Turkic and Uzbek populations— from Azerbaijan, Kazakhstan, Kyrgyzstan, Turkmenistan, Uzbekistan, and above all, "Chinese" Turkistan—against Beijing for good.

Weakening the regime from within, as the Allies hammered on the doors from without.

To achieve that end, unpleasant actions might be necessary.

He cleared his throat and nodded to a teen. The boy spoke into a radio. Seconds later, a distant *thunk* sounded. Then, after the period of a drawn breath, another.

The flares burst high above the square. Their fierce magnesium light threw sharp-edged double shadows from each of the helplessly milling men and women confined in the middle of the bazaar area by ranks of rifle-pointing rebels.

"Hand your weapons over. Then bring us that table," he told his men. He said it in Uighur, then in the simplified Han. But many still looked puzzled. Tokarev spoke sharply, backing him up. At last they fingered their weapons, then, grudgingly handed them over.

To the townsmen. Some of whom were already armed, but others accepted the proffered rifles and pistols with grim smiles, grabbing them eagerly with both hands. A rough-looking bunch: swarthy, almost all in the traditional four-cornered caps, a few even wearing the forbidden beards, in worker's coveralls or ragged shirts and trousers. Some carried cudgels or knives. Probably criminals, along with the workers and unemployed. No doubt a hard core of true-believer Islamists among them too. Well, you worked with what you had.

"And ammunition," Teddy prompted, and his mujs reluctantly produced loaded magazines from their pouches.

ITIM could not be held responsible for what was about to happen. Or at least, had to be able to assert deniability, even as everyone understood what must have really gone down. The same way the Russians had staged nonattributable attacks in Ukraine and the Baltics and Finland.

He nodded to Tokarev. The lanky rebel climbed onto a rickety sales table the others had dragged over. Tucking his pistol under his arm, he cupped both hands to his mouth. Sentence by sentence, Teddy fed him his lines, to be shouted out in Chinese.

"Do you wish your daughters to live? If they are virgins, yet strong, let them come over to us."

The Chinese women began to howl. They saw what was coming. Families clung together, wailing. The fathers understood too. Some held their daughters more tightly. Others began prying the girls' fingers from their mothers, shoving them toward the grim-faced rebels. Who opened their ranks, funneling them toward the women slaves, who quickly led them out of the square.

Guldulla turned to the women among the townsfolk next. "We are not monsters. If any among you want children, take them now. Babies, toddlers. Take them now."

Qurban raised his arms and his voice. In guttural Arabic-flavored Uighur he shouted, "If Allah did not send you children, today truly He has granted your wish, praise be to Him, the beneficent, the merciful. Raise them as your own, in the Faith. And women, veil yourselves. Be modest and do not transgress. Men, you are free. Grow your beards, and do not defile yourselves with tobacco and beer."

The flares fell behind the buildings, guttering out in long drifting tentacles of white and yellow sparks. One parachute drifted down among the captives, emitting a sizzling smoke. The Chinese stirred like a wind-ruffled sea. The wailing rose and fell. The captives screamed as new flares detonated light over them. One by one, small children were pushed or carried out of the mass. The older kids were shoved stumbling across to the outstretched arms of townswomen. Infants were simply laid down between the two groups, on the cold pavement. Now and then a townswoman dashed out, uncovered a tiny face, hesitated, then picked up the child and retreated. One baby lay crying weakly. Snot or pus covered its eyes and face. None of the Uighurs picked that one up and it lay there, mewling like a sick kitten and waving tiny fists.

"Those who have taken children, leave now," Teddy told Guldullah in his prison Han. Tokarev repeated the command in Uighur.

Shading his eyes against the glare from the flares, Teddy peered around once more, making sure all was as it should be. The video crews stood ready atop vehicles. The snipers were stationed at strategic points, in case any of the townsmen they'd just armed decided on a change of allegiance. More flares detonated, doubling the brilliance of the scene and the inkiness of the shadows.

He jerked his head, and Guldulla jumped down. Qurban seemed to want to stay, but Oberg yanked him around by the shoulders and gave him a push. Nasrullah and the other rebel leaders fell in behind them as he paced away, away from the restive assembly, from the scowling, gesturing townsmen, who'd begun yelling curses at the Chinese. Some of the Han screamed back, but most simply waited, bleakly silent, clinging to each other with chalky faces. He headed off down a side street, until the square at Kanayi, Xinjiang, western China, was out of sight behind them.

Master Chief Theodore Harlett Oberg walked stiffly ahead, away, favoring his crippled leg. He did not turn back, nor look over his shoulder, as, behind him, the firing began.

II

NO FLAGS
ARE FAIR

7

The South China Sea

DAN scrunched tensely in the little passenger seat, hardly daring to look back as the ship fell astern. The electric motors whirred composite blades into black disks. He was alone, except for two lightweight torpedoes slung on the cargo points. No pilot. And no semblance of controls in his cramped bubble cockpit.

The ship shrank to a gray dot. The machine tilted forward and gathered speed, skimming two hundred feet above a gray-green sea. He fought panic. Since being shot down in a helo during Operation Recoil, he liked flying a lot less.

Twenty minutes, he told himself. Only a twenty minutes' flight. You can stand that.

The Harveys—UHARVs, Unmanned Heavy Aerial Resupply Vehicles—were recent arrivals in the fleet. Developed from General Atomics' close air support UAVs, they were intended to eliminate the lengthy, dangerous procedures for ship-to-ship resupply and personnel transfer. Instead of hours of straight-line steaming a hundred feet apart, any ship with a pad could transfer ordnance, parts, personnel, and ammunition to another. Or receive resupply from shore, if it was within range. The Harveys had enough lift to tote a full-sized Alliance missile booster.

No pilot . . . but the takeoff had been smooth enough. A quick run-up of nearly silent motors, then a gut-wrenched launch straight up off the flight deck. A canting, a rapid climb . . . and now he was fleeing west sixty fathoms up, clutching the handholds and trying to talk himself out of screaming aloud. If they went down, Harveys were supposed to float. It wouldn't be like trying to fight his way out of a flooded, sinking, inverted helicopter, boots kicking at doomed, wounded men strapped helplessly into litters . . . He shuddered, trying to push that horror out of his mind.

But he couldn't help remembering a twist of white smoke tipped by white fire. Then a bang, the fuselage lurching, falling—

A slim black needle was threading the waves far below. A Hunter USV, sanitizing the sea around the carrier. So he was almost there . . .

"Barbarian actual, this is Barbarian," sounded in his earphones.

"Barbarian" was his own former CTF 76 call-sign, reactivated when he'd taken command of this far larger task force. He clutched at the familiarity of his deputy's voice. "Barbarian actual here. Hey, Fred."

"Welcome back, Admiral. Hold you ten mikes out. Hang on . . . ship has visual."

Franklin D. Roosevelt's self-defense lasers doubled as powerful reflecting telescopes. It didn't add to his sense of security to know a two-hundred-megawatt pulse laser was zeroed on him as well. One miscue and he'd be burnt out of the sky like a gnat hitting a bug zapper. He breathed in, then out. Trying to take his mind to a happy place . . .

A pinprick on the horizon. It pushed up rapidly, growing into an eye-puzzling array of gray flat slabs, then suddenly, a ship. A supercarrier, powering majestically through gray-green swells. It left a flattened, nearly waveless superhighway behind it on the China Sea. He white-knuckled it through the approach as the drone lined up behind the carrier, selected a landing point, then descended.

Something hissed. He tensed, but the autonomous brain did not fail. The great gray deck, covered with the angular outlines of stealth UAVs and F-35s, slowly extended to blot out the sea. A jostle, a triple thump, and he was down.

A small group waited by the island. His staff. DEPLANE, the touchscreen read. A green light flashed and the windscreen unlocked. He slid it back and the wind hit his face, fierce, hot, thick. Smelling of burnt JP-5 and the sea.

ENZWEILER trotted into the elevator behind him, making it a close fit. The door sealed. Dan grew heavy, then light. "Video teleconference starts in fifteen," his chief of staff said.

Dan nodded, glancing at his Seiko. He'd spent the morning visiting his COs. This afternoon would be the final confab with the component commanders, the generals and admirals in charge of the Indonesians, Indian, and Vietnamese forces that—along with the US and Australian core units—comprised Task Force 91 and the invasion fleet. "I have time for the staff, right?"

"If we keep it brief. Oh, and Commander Naylor wanted to know was it okay if he sat in. His clearance arrived, by the way."

Dan smoothed his hair back. Hardly anyone wore caps aboard the carrier. Captain Skinner was a monomaniac about foreign object damage, and the low-mounted engines on the UAVs made it even more critical to prevent FOD. "Who?" he muttered, then remembered. PACOM had assigned a young reservist, one Lynwood Naylor, to his staff as a historian. Before the war he'd been a curator at the Navy Museum in DC. The guy had terrible posture and was rail-thin, but aside from a case of bad breath he was so unobtrusive it was easy to forget he existed. "For the staff conference? If he's really cleared." He took another deep breath. "Just keep him the fuck out of the video room afterward, okay?"

The doors opened and Dan stepped out. The air-conditioning was a freezing wall. Faces turned toward him. Everyone stood. He gestured them down. "Carry on, please. Let's get this started, I have a VTC in fifteen."

Enzweiler, Kitty Pickles, Sy Osterhaut, Donnie Wenck, Hermelinda Garfinkle-Henriques, Amy Singhe. He'd told BuPers he wanted people he knew for his staff. People who'd tell him the truth, without truckling to the stars he wore so provisionally. Without the truth, he couldn't make the right decisions. Mistakes were inevitable. But anyone who cared more about his career, his impression, or his ego, than the mission, was undependable. Untrustworthy. And ultimately, useless. Dan had fired men and women, hating to do it, but knowing ruthlessness saved lives in war. They could find other jobs, and maybe the experience, realizing they'd fallen short, would change them for the better.

He might have to fire someone today. He hoped not. But it might be unavoidable.

The briefing started, with Tomlin, the WTI, briefing on the final exercise with Sea Eagle, the multi-domain battle manager they would depend on to fight a sixth-generation engagement. "A rigorous, broadly scaled warfighting checkout," Tomlin was saying. "We networked eight nodes across five hundred nautical miles and three national platforms, demonstrating robust network management and maintained secure voice, data, and video connectivity against Cyber Command's Red Cell."

Dan tried to keep his mind on the brief, but found himself drifting. No. Had to concentrate. As a flag officer, he no longer carried a weapon, the way he had as a junior officer, or at the Tactical Analysis Group. He no longer directed a warship in combat, as he had as a commander and captain.

These days, he planned joint operations. Not nearly as dramatic. Briefings. Discussions. Simulations. Translating Fleet's, Indo-PaCom's, and JCS's intents into a plan that could be executed with the available forces. Managing risk. Insuring against the unforeseen with alternate courses of action. Which meant long hours poring over briefing books, orders of battle, intel on enemy capabilities, and maps. Reviewing the drafts his planners produced. Scheduling tests and exercises to iron out weaknesses. Deconflicting operations. Bounding the theater engagement problem. Puzzling over possible enemy ripostes, and how to guard against them.

Not nearly as dramatic as combat.

But this was his fight now. Commanding the commanders.

Time-sensitive crisis planning, in the face of a dangerous threat and inadquate logistics.

He bit his lips to concentrate as Enzweiler outlined the overall situation. The fall of Taiwan had put optimism into everyone. But the mainland still lay ahead. Even if they were invaded, the Chinese could hold out for years. Vietnam came to mind, and the titanic struggle China had carried on against the Japanese before and during American entry into World War II.

But he couldn't worry about that. That was for Blair to think about, and the administration she worked for.

He only hoped they were taking it seriously.

"Admiral, TF 91 is beginning the sorties from the various embarkation points. There'll be no single rendezvous point and no concentration en route. We'll pick up the various force elements between D minus seven and minus five. Transiting to a position off the Spratleys, we will conduct two practice landings to add experience to the amphibious elements and supporting forces. Meanwhile, the rest of the task force will restage at Cam Ranh Bay, then proceed to the amphibious oparea."

Dan lifted a finger. "I think we're up to speed on the big picture, Captain. I'd like to hear what Commander Garfinkle-Henriques has for us on the supply situation."

His J-4 shuffled notes and cleared her throat. "Sir, the *Mount Hood* event set our timetable back almost six weeks, and we still haven't fully recovered. We've made intense efforts to restock ammo from CONUS and other sources, but we'll still be almost twenty-five percent below the original planning points for the operation."

Don nodded. Even now, no one was sure what had triggered the detonation aboard the ammo ship. Maybe no one ever would. It would join the long list of inexplicable maritime disasters, from the *Maine* to the *Cyclops* . . . He blinked, realizing they were all watching him. He definitely had to get some sleep. But there wouldn't be much opportunity en route . . . "Okay, two questions. One: are the practice landings going to be properly covered against attack? And, two, will we have the fuel and ammo in the pipeline to sustain a protracted land battle? I asked those questions before. So far, the answers from Log Force don't make me happy.

"Bear in mind, we could face a major battle off Hainan. I want adequate fuel. At least double what we calculate as necessary. And we have to support the forces once they're ashore. I won't pull back and leave people stranded, like Frank Jack Fletcher did at Guadalcanal."

Garfinkle-Henriques swallowed. "*Double*, Admiral? LogForce is planning based on a fifty percent reserve."

Dan had read Admiral Turner's report on the capture of the Marianas, the closest analog to Operation Rupture he could find numbers on. "We've got a long trip to the objective, Hermelinda. Not just fuel for ships, but hundreds of small craft, drones, the USVs, air cover . . . I'd rather have double what we need than fall ten percent short."

The commander looked conflicted. "Sir, remember, preparations for this started two years ago. Two million tons of fuel to Australia. Two hundred tankers chartered. I can try to scrounge more, but frankly, sir, I doubt we'll get it. Our instructions from Fleet are to economize. Refinery capacity back home—"

"I know, crippled by sabotage. Cyber. And riots. But what about the Indonesians? Brunei?"

"Brunei produces crude, but they don't refine—"

Dan said, "In War II the Asiatic Fleet burned Brunei crude. Can modern gas turbines run on it? Look harder at regional supply. If we need more tankers, contract for them." He checked his watch. Five more minutes. "Check thoroughly and see me tonight. Let's move on to ammo."

"As I said, the picture's not good, Admiral. A third of our smart ordnance went up with *Mount Hood*. The Taiwan battle had priority for new weapons. A major effort to break out older stockpiles, but they're largely GPS-guided."

He nodded. "But that's been down since the outbreak of the war. No retrofit kits?"

"They went to Taiwan."

Dan frowned. "Has Admiral Custer been helpful, Hermelinda? You shouldn't be having to dig this out yourself. Logistics Force should be doing most of this for us."

His supply officer glanced down at her notes. "We're not, um . . . getting a lot of cooperation from that end, sir."

So Rupture was sucking left hind tit on ammo as well. Strapping advanced fighters and UAVs with dumb bombs meant more sorties per target, more exposure, higher loss rates. And more fuel consumption, adding to an already stringent fuel budget. But he couldn't do anything about that either, apparently.

Lee Custer just wasn't working out. Resentment at Dan's elevation over him, or plain lack of application? It didn't really matter. Tolerating substandard performance wasn't the way to roll. Not when so many lives depended on it.

Which left one more sticking point. He nodded to a champagne-blond, dark-skinned captain with a dolphin pin on his coveralls. He'd asked for Andy Mangum as his staff submarine liaison. An Academy classmate. They'd worked together before off Korea, then again in the Indian Ocean, when Mangum had been CO of USS *San Francisco*. "Andy, what about those submerged missile batteries? They clobbered Tim Simko when we went in for the raid. Tell me we found them all."

Mangum spread his hands. "I can't guarantee, *all*. But we found four with the autonomous USVs and plugged in some Mark 48s. As far as we can tell, your route in to the beach is clear."

"I'm willing to accept some risk. But we'll have our guardian angels in the basement?"

"You're covered, Admiral," Mangum said. "We've accounted for every PLAN submarine still active. These still in port, we have Hound Dogs waiting at harbor exits." Hound Dogs were autonomous torpedoes, with an added helping of cunning and silence. They crept into harbor channels at drift speeds, sank to the muddy bottom, and waited for a specific sound signature. When it came, they ballasted up, started their propulsors, and homed in.

"Sir, it's time." Enzweiler, beside him.

Dan got up, nodding to them all. "Cross any Ts, dot any Is. Remember, no operation will go perfectly. The enemy gets a vote. But we need enough margin to persist and overcome." He sounded stuffy even to himself. Started to explain, then thought: *Shut up and let them get to work.* He caught an unfamiliar face in the back, and wondered who it was before he remembered: the reservist. The historian.

He nodded again, forced a smile, and followed his deputy toward the VTC room.

THE component commanders' teleconference was already rolling. Four screens, each showing a face. The backgrounds all much the same: the drab interiors of ships or tents. In the background, men and women before terminals. Only the Indonesian marine's backdrop was different: the airstrip outside Brunei; a corner of the headquarters prefab at the edge of the picture. "Good afternoon, all," Dan said. "Admiral Daniel Lenson, US Navy, Task Force 91."

"Major General Triady Isnanta, Korps Marinir."

"Admiral Ramidin Madjid, Indonesian Navy."

"Admiral Vijay Gupta. Commanding Indian Navy operations in the South China Sea."

The fourth man was new. Dan had met the Vietnamese ground force commander at Cam Ranh. But this guy was pudgier, with what looked like an old burn seaming the side of his face. "Um, we were dealing with General Pham Van Trong."

"The corrupt running dog Pham Van Trong has been exposed as an enemy of the people. I am his replacement. General Dao."

"Oh. Um, well, welcome." Seriously? A purge, now? "Has his staff read you in to the operation? We're depending on you for the western prong of the landing."

"I regret to say our regular forces may not be available. Much depends on the present battle."

Dan opened his mouth to protest, then closed it. The bloodiest engagements of the war so far had been fought in northern Vietnam, where Zhang's armies had pushed to Hanoi and beyond, to reimpose "historic" imperial boundaries. The fighting had been desperate from the start, and earlier that year the Vietnamese had reeled back under a massive ground offensive. The other Allies had only been able to supply limited help, mainly ammunition, weapons, and fuel through Cam Ranh port, and an Air Force bomb wing with fighter support and security elements out of Da Nang. The first raid on Yulin, Operation

Quadrangle, had been designed—at least in part—to relieve pressure on the Vietnamese by forcing the Chinese to pull back forces to defend their own coast.

But this guy was threatening to subtract fully a quarter of the operation's ground troops from the equation. Dan restrained himself from scratching the prickle of sweat along his scalp. Stay cool, he reminded himself. "General Dao. Hanoi—I mean, the Central Military Commission—made this commitment. We planned on that basis. We depend on—"

"You will have troops."

He frowned. "We will? But—"

"But they will not be front-line troops. All our regular forces are engaged. You will have southern militia. People's self-defense forces are mustering. They will embark at Cam Ranh and conduct training aboard ship." Dao looked off-camera, then back. *"If this is not satisfactory, Vietnam cannot participate in Operation Rupture. We are fighting for our lives along the Ho Chi Minh line."*

Which was he guessed where they were holding the Chinese, south of Hanoi. He stifled a scowl—his left prong would be weak, green troops against beefed-up defenses—but saw no alternative. "I understand your situation.—General Isnanta?"

The squat Indonesian sounded glad to announce his news. *"As agreed, Indonesia is providing an expeditionary force of three marine divisions. Each has three combat brigades complete with combat and administrative support. The US Marines are providing training in amphibious operations. The US Army is providing reconnaissance, air support, and heavy artillery. Our preparations are on schedule. Our troops are embarking now."*

Dan asided to Gault, "Ask Colonel Osterhaut to sit in on this, sergeant." To the remaining screens he said, "Admiral Madjid, Admiral Gupta, I hope you can report the same readiness."

To his relief they both nodded. The Indian said that their newest carrier, *Vikramaditya*, would be added to the already committed destroyer and submarine escort component, strengthening protection of the transiting invasion forces. Dan briefly considered adding it to his own central strike force, but decided to keep it Japanese and American for interoperability. Anyway, the more air cover the lumbering transports had, the better. "Excellent, Admiral. We will welcome her and her accompanying tanker support, assigning them to TF 91.3." A hint he hoped Gupta took aboard, that India couldn't add ships without pushing fuel into the pot as well. "And Admiral Madjid."

He didn't remember the Indonesian, but apparently the guy remembered him. From the long hot days of the Tiny Nation Task Force's wandering transit of the Sulu Sea. Madjid had been a midgrade officer back then. Now he headed up the amphibious ready group transporting Isnanta's marines to battle.

TF 91 would be built from three expeditionary strike groups. Two would be centered on US assault carriers, *Hornet* and *Bataan*. Madjid's would be centered on *Makassar*, *Surabya*, and *Adelaide*, now guarded by the Indian carrier, along with Indian and Australian destroyers and submarines.

Dan called up a slide. It was marked TOP SECRET in red, and keyed so each receiving screen showed only a portion of the force's track. Need to know, even at the general officer level. "The transit to the objective will keep the invasion components dispersed and combat power distributed to the maximum extent possible. This, to minimize detection and the possibility of nuclear strikes, the way the Chinese destroyed our carrier battle group in the opening days of the war. All components will exercise emission control.

"The Indonesian group will leave Brunei on D minus 5. They will restage at Spratley Base, then transit to Paracel Base. A practice landing will take place at Woody Island on D minus four. Two days reembark and restage, then advance to the final assembly area via a route now being sanitized by Allied submarines.

"The Vietnamese group will leave Cam Ranh Bay on D minus 4. They will transit to Paracel base and carry out a practice landing on D minus three.

"If preparations are detected for enemy spoiling attacks, the rehearsal landings will not be carried out.

"The main group will arrive off Hainan on D minus one and carry

out heavy strikes to suppress resistance at the landing points"—
he toggled to a map of Hainan—"Here, and here. They'll cover the
landings on D-day and resupply thereafter. Once General Isnanta is
established ashore, I'll transfer command to him as CLF. He will direct the ground battle in cooperation with our Vietnamese allies and
other elements."

On his screen, the Vietnamese general raised a hand. Dan nodded.
"General Dao."

*"We must insist on one thing. From the Central Committee it-
self."*

"Yes, General?"

*"No action must be taken against the Chinese Party. Obviously
those involved in aggressive war must be removed from office.
War criminals must be punished. But the rule of the Communist
Party must be preserved. To do otherwise would invite chaos.
As the United States saw when you dissolved the Ba'ath Party in
Iraq."*

And it might call the continued rule of the Party in Vietnam into
question too, Dan thought, but of course couldn't say. He bobbled his
head; Gupta grinned. "General, that's far above my pay grade. General Isnanta will take what steps he deems necessary to govern once
the island's liberated. I assume, by imposing martial law. Whether
there'll be elections or multiple parties after that will be a political
decision by the combined heads of state.

"Let's not forget, we have to win this war before we can discuss
what the world will look like afterward. And I'm afraid that's all I
can offer you right now, General."

WHEN the screens went blue he sagged in his chair. Dragged a hand
over a wet hairline. Sat with his head empty, staring into the azure
light.

"Sir?" Gault, behind him. "Uh, sir? You eaten today?"

Dan flinched, and stood. Looked at his watch again. "Uh-huh . . .
I mean, no."

"I could have them send up something."

"Thanks, that's all right." He straightened, hands to his back. His spine popped audibly. "I need to spend some time with real people."

THE carrier's mess decks weren't exactly cavernous, but they were still noisy. They smelled of food and steam. Dan edged a green fiberglas tray along stainless rails. Meat loaf. Potatoes. Green beans. "Cherry pie, Admiral," said a smiling server. She flipped a slice onto a plate before he could refuse, then capped it with butterscotch ice cream. Dan took the plate with a smile, though he had no intention of eating it all.

He carried the tray out into the echoing crowd of coveralled men and women and selected a table at random. Brown and black faces turned, blinking in surprise. Then hesitated, clearly uncertain whether to stand. Sergeant Gault took the next table over, angled so he could keep an eye on his charge. Dan sat quickly and nodded. "Hello, everyone."

"Admiral." Mutters eddied out from their table as others craned to see.

"How's everybody doing?" he asked them.

"Oh, we good, sir."

"Tired, but we're hangin' in there."

Their expressions were questioning. Probably they wanted to ask the same questions everybody had. News got scarce in wartime. Those with phones had had to turn them in before the task force sailed. Ship's company only knew what their skipper, their division officers, their chiefs, saw fit to pass on. The gaps were oakumed with rumor. "Anybody heard any good scuttlebutt?" he tried.

A heavyset, freckled petty officer with tightly braided hair squinted at him. "Heard we going up to China. That right, Admiral?"

He chose his words carefully. "It's a major operation, all right. Can't say where. But we need to be ready to fight. Yeah."

"We got to do what we got to do," the petty officer said. "Get this over with." The others murmured assent.

The meat loaf was crusty on top, moist and tender inside; it fell flakily apart under his fork. As far as he could tell, it was the same cut everyone was getting. "This is tasty. Chow always this good here?"

They nodded, seeming to agree, but bashful. As if an internet celebrity, or movie star, had suddenly sat down among them. Oprah, or Tom Hanks. But one bright-eyed woman sitting opposite kept staring. He gave her a grin as he started on the pie.

"Admiral . . . they say you got the Medal of Honor."

He lifted his eyebrows. "That was a long time ago."

"How'd you get it, man?" the heavyset petty officer said eagerly. The table stirred, all eyes turning to Dan again.

"It was just before Desert Storm." Seeing the blankness in the younger sailors' expressions, he added, "The first war with Iraq. When Saddam Hussein tried to take over Kuwait. There was a report of some kind of WMD hidden in Baghdad. So they sent in a team to investigate." He stopped there, but six attentive faces begged him to press on. "Uh, well . . . we managed to take it out. But everyone didn't make it back. See the Marine over at that table?—his brother fought a rearguard so we could escape. And an Army doctor with us, she died later from the stuff we found."

"What'd you find?" the petty officer said.

"Nothing good," Dan sidestepped, since the mission had never been declassified. "Let's just say it was too dangerous to leave in a dictator's hands."

"Speaking of dictators. What're we going to do to Zhang?" another enlisted woman asked. "When this is over."

"Not up to me." Dan shrugged. "If he's still alive, I'd hope, a trial."

"Like Nuremberg," the bright-eyed woman said.

"Before we hang him," the heavyset NCO added grimly.

"Coffee with that, Admiral?" As he'd expected, the chief in charge of the mess had gotten word he was on deck. Dan said sure, thanks. "Anybody else want some?" he asked the table. "Master Chief here's buying for everybody."

They all broke into laughter at the senior enlisted's abashed scowl.

EIGHT levels up, he washed his face in a spartan flag stateroom—he owned a much larger suite under the flight deck, but this cramped cubicle was handier to the flag bridge—and melted onto his rack.

Seventeen and a half minutes later—and he'd actually slept, a brief period of total unconsciousness timed by some obscure circuit in his brain—he roused again, dry-shaved, pulled on fresh coveralls, and went back to the VTC space. He set up his notebook and the printed op order for Rupture, handy so he could reach for them, but out of the field of view. Then waited, looking at the Ninth Fleet seal on the single screen. A spread eagle and anchor superimposed over the numeral nine, with a blue backdrop of the South China Sea.

Precisely at seven the seal faded to the interior of an office. Dan recognized the Bunker at Pearl, Fleet headquarters. Deep underground, it had survived the nuking of Honolulu that had finally finished off the old *Savo Island*. The seat was empty.

Two minutes later, a short officer in crisp summer whites slid into it.

Dan had worked for Bren Verstegen when the three-star had been the Indo-Pacific Command operations deputy. They'd toiled in obscurity deep in Level 2, two flights down from ground floor of the headquarters at Camp Smith, to plan Quadrangle, the first strike at China's soft southern underbelly. He'd never exactly known how he registered with the vice admiral. The CNO, Dan's reluctant rabbi Niles Barry, might have foisted him on Verstegen. The small man aligning his papers fussily before the lens gave no outward clue.

Finally he looked up. *"Admiral Lenson."*

"Admiral Verstegen."

"Is Rupture set to sail?"

"Sir, we have significant shortfalls. And a personnel change I need to recommend."

Verstegen glanced away. *"I know about your shortfalls. No one out here has all they want. Or in the Gulf, either. But you have enough. Are you ready to proceed?"*

This wasn't starting well. And what did he mean about the Gulf? Dan said, "Sir, every operation in this war has eaten ordnance and fuel at twice the rate the old allowances specified. I know the pipeline's tight. Production's tight. But I don't want to take a hundred and thirty thousand troops and sailors into harm's way without giving them the tools they need to prevail."

Verstegen looked away, seeming to ponder his words. *"Was it Mount Hood?"*

"That didn't help. But not that alone."

"You were senior officer afloat. The responsibility for that catastrophe lies at your feet."

"Sir, I don't deny that. But if you believed someone else could have prevented it, I wouldn't still have this task force."

"All right, Admiral." The little officer's tone went steely. *"What's your recommendation?"*

Dan took a deep breath. "Postpone the operation."

Verstegen looked down at his papers. A moment passed. *"Again? For how long this time?"* he said softly.

"Four more weeks. To let me organize more fuel. And for you to get us more missiles. My J-4's drafting a message outlining our shortfalls."

"You want to postpone Rupture another month."

"Yessir. We need to own this fight from the start, if it's worth doing."

They stared at each other eye to eye. Dan didn't want to make it a pissing contest, so he dropped his gaze first. At last Verstegen turned away. He leaned to one side and whispered to someone off-camera. A keyboard rattled.

"That'll have to go up the chain. We'll need time to evaluate our options. The Vietnamese are insistent we start on time. The Chinese are pressing them hard. Let me give you some of the background."

"I'd appreciate that, sir."

"Intel thinks this offensive in Vietnam is a Battle of the Bulge– type last gasp. The Chinese army's hollowing out. Famine. Lack of supply. And now, desertions by minorities and draftees tired of the war. They're sick. Inflation's starving their families. If the Viets can stop them there, while we invade Hainan, this war may be over."

Dan said, "I understand the need to move, Admiral. But if we get our tails kicked, either at sea or once our four divisions are ashore, what's that do to support for the war?"

Verstegen sighed.

Dan said, "Sir, I'm trying to wear two hats out here. Warfighter and logistics. I feel confident we can win against whatever the enemy has left. We have air and missile coverage. But I need two things."

"What was the second?"

"I believe my logistics commander is . . . overextended."

A gentle word, but one any senior officer could interpret. *"Custer?"* The fleet commander frowned. *"Hard to believe. Lee's always been a charger, in my experience."*

"Sir, I can only judge by what I see. So: If the Chinese are really weakening, another month will weaken them further. It'll free up more time for training. This is a multinational force, and our Vietnamese are only militia. They're going to arrive pretty much totally untrained. Four weeks will let ammo and fuel catch up too."

"And what do you recommend in regard to Lee?" A touch of frost. Was Custer one of Verstegen's golden boys? Was that what he meant by the "charger" remark?

Dan lowered his voice, though they were alone on the VTC. "I've lost confidence, sir."

Lost confidence. The damning phrase that once pronounced could not be taken back. Command was a privilege, not a right. You didn't need a specific charge to remove an officer from command. It was enough to doubt his ability to right a situation, lead his organization, act with decisive effectiveness whatever the challenge.

No officer had a career after that.

But in wartime, hard choices.

Verstegen said, *"And replace him with who?"*

Dan had expected this conundrum. "Sir, I don't have anyone in mind. Jenn Roald, if she was available. But I doubt she is. Maybe his deputy could do a better job, and not have to start from square one."

Verstegen was obviously pondering. *"There might be a smarter way around this, Admiral."*

"Sir?"

"Another operation's gearing up to the north. A major one. JCS planned on both taking place simultaneously. Synergy. Making Zhang split his remaining forces. So delay in the southern theater would be . . . perilous.

"The best solution might well be to have Lee Custer replace you. And you take over his billet in Logistics Force."

Dan tensed his jaw, trying to disguise what felt like a punch to the plexus. He'd figured that might be Fleet's response, once they got down to brass tacks. If Rupture had to go ahead, even without assurance of success. For political reasons, or strategic—it didn't really matter, at his level.

He said calmly, "Sir, I'll gladly accept that decision. If Indo-PaCom wants it that way. Lee's senior to me, after all. But from where I'm sitting, no matter who occupies this seat after me, postponement's the right option. Until we have the wherewithal."

"I'll have to get back to you, Dan. About both issues—the postponement and the . . . personnel matter you raised. Meanwhile, give us an alternate timetable. No promises. Minimal changes. But what you think needs to be done."

It was the first time Verstegen had ever called him by his given name. A good sign, or not? He decided not to worry about it. To leave it in the hands of the gods.

The lofty deities who wore many stars, far above his own position in the machine.

We got to do what we got to do. That's what the petty officer had said on the mess deck. It was true all the way up the line. Seamen, petty officers, officers, admirals . . . all the way up to where the buck stopped. And there too? Yeah, probably there too.

A curt nod, and the screen went blank. Dan sat for a while, wishing he hadn't eaten the pie and ice cream, curdling now deep in his gut. Then got up and headed to Flag Plot, to start revising the plan.

8

Taipei

THE blues were too tight, the pants too fucking long. They weren't Hector's anyway. The white REMF public affairs captain bitch had thrown them at him and Patterson. Ordered, "Shuck those dirty rags. Put these on."

His "dirty rags" were the utilities he'd battled through the mountains in, rode tanks in. "They're what I wore raising the flag," he muttered.

"You're not wearing 'em today. Get a shower. Get those blues on, Sergeant. You too, Corporal," she snapped, wheeling away and slamming the door.

The headquarters staff had taken over the Hyatt Grand. Yeah, he thought bitterly as he peeled the filthy fatigues off, stepped out of them, and padded naked toward the shower, they'd brag all their lives how they'd liberated Taipei all on their own.

Did he care?

No. He didn't. About that. Or about anything.

Ffoulk was dead. Clay was dead. Pretty much everybody from the old platoon.

Including one C323. The Last CHAD was a Corps legend now. As, apparently, Sergeant Hector Ramos was himself.

Patterson was examining her filthy bra with disgust. A cursory knock, and the captain leaned in. "We ready yet?"

"One more second, ma'am." He buttoned his stock, straightened the blouse. The best-looking uniform in the services. But in the mirror, the eyes that stared from above it seemed to be looking back from Hell.

He glanced at the door, bent to the discarded rags, and felt in the cargo pockets. Came up with a brown bottle. He popped an anti-PTSD pill and drained the pint to wash it down. He'd just two-pointed it clanging into a shitcan when the door jerked open again. He blotted his mouth hastily.

"Are we ready? Finally?"

Patterson said, "Yes, ma'am. We are."

"Finally. Then let's go."

THE floor the hotel lobby was particolored marble, from which great pillars rose to a white-domed ceiling. Spiral chandeliers hung dark; power was still out. The walls were scarred and pockmarked from bullets, but the Chinese had apparently used it as officer housing, and so largely spared it the destruction widespread in the rest of the city.

The ceremony had been hastily planned, but the networks were here. Fox, CNN, BBC, Patriot, all the alphabets. Hector joined the other awardees to the left of a podium, where two soldiers were still chipping off the remnants of the red-star-and-banner device he guessed had replaced the Hyatt crest.

They draped a Pacific Command flag across it as an Army officer stepped to the podium. He glanced at a cell, then barked, "Attention."

Two men strode in. One was in American uniform, a tall, rangy general. The other was Asian, in greens, with shoulderboards and a peaked hat. The American wore battle dress and Hector shook his head inwardly. Why couldn't they have just given him a fresh set of those, instead of these ill-fitting blues? The US general, whose name he didn't catch, introduced the Chinese, a Taiwanese named Li Shucheng. He then gave a quick overview of the campaign, winding up with the capture of the capital.

"Unfortunately, the enemy commander, Lieutenant General Pei, escaped to the mainland during the final phase of the campaign. But all in all, the Allies have caused the enemy over a hundred thousand casualties, and bagged over three hundred thousand PUCs—I mean, POWs. Though not the most rapid victory, thanks to stubborn resistance, it is one of the most impressive ones in the history of warfare. Which the US Marines, along with their Army and Air Force comrades and the brave Nationalist forces under heroic General Shucheng, share the credit for.

"Not to say our challenges have ended. We inherit a civilian population with a ruined infrastructure after it was rolled over by two violent military campaigns. The locals are, to a large extent, starving.

"But that is no detraction from a truly audacious incident, when three fearless Marines scaled the central tower of the President's Palace under heavy fire. Three went up. Two came back. This intrepid feat has captured the imagination of the world. Let's go to the video."

A huge screen flickered on. Hector watched from a trillion miles away as Patterson's shaky video began. The sounds: the bluster of the wind, the popcorn crackle of battle, the occasional louder boom of tank guns.

Ffoulk is standing on the ledge, pointing. A pan up at the Chinese flag, streaming in the wind. Then Hector struggles with the downhaul, his lips moving, but none of his curses audible.

The flag collapses, draping him like Batman's cape. He fights free. Ffoulk stuffs it into her pack, then hands him the Stars and Stripes. She snaps an order.

Then her head whips sideways in a mist of red. She folds and collapses.

That was the sniper . . . who'd kept firing the whole time he'd been trying to get the fucking flag up . . . Hector squeezes his eyes shut, unable to watch. The world sways. The PAO digs her knuckles into his ribs from behind. A sigh eddies from the audience. Must be that last shot Patterson took, of the American flag streaming out high above the captured city.

"Corporal Emily Patterson. Sergeant Hector Ramos. Front and center."

His eyes snapped open. He and Patterson stepped out, wheeled, marched to the center of the lobby, and turned in unison into a right-face, confronting the general.

Who took a moment, studying a paper.

He said, "I will now read the citation.

"The President of the United States takes pleasure in presenting the Silver Star Medal (Posthumously) to LaRhonda S. Ffoulk, Lieutenant, U.S. Marine Corps, for conspicuous gallantry and intrepidity in action against the enemy as part of Expeditionary Forces, U.S. Marine Corps Forces Pacific Command, in support of Operation Causeway. Following the rapid seizure of a vital avenue of approach into the city of Taipei, Lieutenant Ffoulk and her Marines occupied the building known as the Presidential Office. With disregard for her own safety, Lieutenant Ffoulk exposed herself to tank, machine gun, and sniper fire in order to provide suppressive fire facilitating the evacuation of the wounded Marines. She had just pulled down the enemy ensign and was preparing to hoist the American flag when she was mortally wounded by enemy fire. Lieutenant Ffoulk's aggressive actions and bold leadership were critical in quieting enemy resistance and assuring the population they had been liberated. By her courage, leadership, judgment, and complete dedication to duty, Lieutenant Ffoulk reflected great credit upon herself and upheld the highest traditions of the Marine Corps and the United States Naval Service."

Hector squeezed his eyes shut, trying not to replay it. But already in his mind it was the video, not what he'd seen himself, high on the central tower. He felt sick to his stomach. His fingers twitched. He needed another drink. Just one more, then maybe he could hold it together.

When it came his turn and his own citation had been read, he took five steps forward and halted. The general's nametag read FAULCON. Hector tried to hold his breath, so the guy wouldn't smell the whiskey, as the tall officer pinned on the gaudy red white and blue striped medal, then stepped back and saluted.

"About . . . *face*," someone murmured, and Hector snapped around and marched back, to take his place in the ranks once again.

THE Word had been that the platoon would get a week's R&R, but that quickly got countermanded. They would load up on MRAPs and Oshkoshes and convoy south that afternoon. Somebody had to guard three hundred thousand prisoners. So nobody would be going on R&R for a while.

He did get a chance to call home. The lieutenant set it up, along with a fresh set of Cameleons at last. That made him feel a little warmer toward her. Though he still didn't feel much of anything, really. Except that fucking nausea.

"Hello. Mirielle? Is that you?"

"Who's this? . . . Oh. Hector?"

"It's me. It's me."

"Are you all right? You sound . . ."

"Borracho, I know. I had a couple."

"But you're okay. You were on the news."

"Yeah, did you see us raising the flag?"

"Yes. Oh, yes, everyone saw that. You're a hero. You're famous."

"Never mind that. It don't mean nothing. Hey, you see my mom, right? She okay?"

"She's fine, Hector. She's proud of you. The medal and all."

"That's good she heard. Give her my love." The line hissed empty for a few seconds. Finally he said, "Is that fucker Mahmou' leaving you alone?"

"Mahmou'? He's not at the Zone anymore. He left. After somebody beat him up and stole his stuff . . . was that you, Hector?"

"Me? Shit, no. I'm a man of peace." He squeezed his eyes closed, tried to keep the shaking out of his voice. "Just wish I was home. With you."

A pause then, low, *"I do too, Hector. You still got . . . you still got my picture?"*

"Oh yeah."

"And my rosary?"

"Your rosary . . . no, I lost that. The string broke. On the stairs . . . Look, they're calling me. Rejoin the platoon. I miss you, Mir."

"I'll send you another one. I miss you too, Hector. I wish we could make plans. But you know. What we said, last time you were home.

"Please stay safe. Vaya con Dios."

He wiped a hand over his face. It came away wet, but he couldn't feel whatever was making him cry.

NO one knew why it was called Camp Rocky, but the name fitted the place. Anyhow, that probably wasn't its real name. A valley in the mountains, almost a ravine, with steep slopes already blasted bare of trees by bombs or artillery, and now lined with barbed wire. Niegowski, one of his three squad leaders, said he'd heard it called Shanshuilu, where the Chinese had kept their own prisoners. But remembering the camp he and Patterson had seen farther south, Hector didn't believe it. If the slants had held prisoners here, there would be mass graves.

"Okay, get them debarked," Lieutenant Hawkshadow told him, studying his tablet. "First POWs arrive tonight. We want OPs, lights, and sensors out, MGs dug in by then. Show 'em a firm hand from the get-go."

Hawkshadow was Lt. Ffoulk's replacement. He was older than she'd been, moderate height, dark-skinned, sparing of words. Previous enlisted, which could be either good or bad. Hector guessed from his appearance and name he was ethnic Indian, Native American, though they hadn't gotten personal enough yet to really know each other.

The platoon debarked the trucks to face a line of waiting machines. They stood at ease, dull olive camo on their surfaces brightening and darkening as the clouds chased shadows over the hills.

Hector walked the ranks. Their oculars followed him, then snapped back to eyes front when he looked in their direction. These were the new D model. Unlike 323, the CHAD he'd left manning the machine gun during that desperate battle on Hill 298, these had a sleeker, less overtly mechanical appearance. Their heads were even smaller than the Cs.

Hill 298.

Dug in on a terraced ridge, in the rain, in the mountains, with only the hilltop above them. Tangled jungle two days before. Now blasted down to matchstick trees, exposed rock, and raw orange harrowed mud, glittering with steel fragments and ammo casings . . .

No, he thought, balling his fists. Then opened them, trying to breathe slow, in, out, in, out. He extracted a container from his blouse pocket and shook out another anti-P. They didn't seem to block the memories themselves, which were vivid as ever and just went on and on. But they did seem to numb his mind. Kill his feelings.

Suddenly realizing Hawkshadow had been calling his name, Hector shook himself back to the present and trotted over. "Sir?"

The officer studied him, frowning. "You okay, Sergeant?"

"Fit to fight, sir."

The lieutenant looked unconvinced, but finally just said, "Okay then. I'm going to pass on what I got from Higher. Right now, we have to feed and guard three hundred thousand starving troops. Plus they pretty much used up or destroyed any food stocks to keep the civilian population alive. The submarine blockade didn't help, either."

"Copy that, sir," Hector said. The same situation the general had outlined at the hotel.

"They estimate there'll be nine thousand slants in this camp alone."

"Nine *thousand* . . ."

"Military plus civilian internees. Locals who cooperated with the mainlanders. They have to be interrogated, sorted out, see if it's safe to release them. To contain them we have two platoons of Marines, two platoons of friendly militia, and the CHADs." Hawkshadow walked along the barbed wire; Hector paced him.

"Sir, we're not trained for this. Guarding POWs. Interrogating prisoners. I had maybe five minutes on how to treat captures at SOI."

"I know. The Army's promised us a military police unit. The . . . 728th Military Police Battalion. But I don't see them yet. So it's OJT . . . just keep things battened down, and cope until the doggies show up. Oorah?"

"Oorah, sir."

"The CHADs rotate back to the recharge station on their truck every twelve hours with minimal walking, every six hours if they march patrols. They're programmed to handle their own reliefs and pass on standing orders, so you don't have to do that. Chow and bar-racks for meat people will be at the eco station."

"The eco station, sir?"

"Down in the far valley." Hawkshadow pointed over the hill be-yond the wire. "This place was like some kind of Jurassic Park. There's an army medical team coming in too, for us and the prison-ers. There's an OP layout on your tablet. Modify it if you see better positions once you get eyes on the ground. Catch up with the other platoon sergeant and work out your guard details. Once more: Show a firm hand from the get-go, and we won't have problems later on."

Hector nodded and started to walk away, but Hawkshadow called him back. "One more thing. Sergeant. You getting rock happy?"

"Rock happy, sir?" Hector frowned. "I don't know what that means."

The lieutenant said patiently, "It means, are you still with us, Ser-geant? Because it doesn't look to me like you totally are."

"No sir. I'm on deck, sir."

"Getting enough sleep?"

"No sir."

"Taking your P meds?"

"Yessir."

Hawkshadow studied him a second longer, then leaned in. "You're a two-island Marine now, Ramos. Combat certified. That means your people look to you for how to act. I want your head in the sunshine. Not up your ass. And yeah, I smell that booze on your breath. I don't want to smell it again. We clear?"

"Aye aye, sir. Very clear."

"Good. Now let's get this installation nailed down. They hand us shit, we make it smell like Chanel. But a force ratio this lopsided can go south in a heartbeat. These people have given up, but that doesn't mean they're not dangerous. That's why I said, show a firm hand from the get-go. Firm hand, Sergeant."

Hawkshadow nodded then, as if to dismiss him.

Hector wondered if he should salute, and finally didn't. And what did "a firm hand" really mean?

He looked along the ranks of robots again. They gazed back with attention, but without expression. Without emotion.

If only he could stop remembering. Like them. Do what he was told, and instantly forget.

He thumbed out another pill, and swallowed it dry. But it caught halfway down, and seemed to stick there, burning a hole in his throat.

THE first trucks rolled in just before dark. By then the Marines had OPs out and machine gun pits started. They had sensors deployed, and mine warning signs planted along the wire, though no actual mines yet.

Hector stood by the main gate area as the POWs straggled in. They weren't short, like the troops he'd fought in the mountains. These guys looked well fed, not combat worn at all. They didn't appear defeated, though they'd been disarmed. They met his eyes. A few gave him half smiles, as if to say *We're not done with you.* Civilians were with them too, the internees Hawkshadow had mentioned, Hector figured. These were in worse shape, bedraggled and shamefaced. Some, bruised and tattered and limping, looked as if they'd been beaten up recently.

Hector put Milliron's squad on duty first, setting up the watch rotation, and sent the rest back to the center to rest. But he stayed on, supervising the digging of the gun pits, T-shaped positions with the primary field of fire down into the ravine and the secondary covering the gate area.

He dropped into one pit and flipped up the cover on the M240, pretending to inspect it, but actually just wanting to lay hands on its cold alloy. The Pig. His old friend. With him since boot camp, since SOI, on two invasions.

He wished he was just a gunner again.

A little before dusk three prisoners climbed up from the ravine to where Hector watched at the main gate. Two were uniformed. An older guy wore a gray suit without a tie. Hector unslung his carbine, but they stopped a few yards downslope, on the far side of the deadline. "What do you want," he yelled.

One yelled back, in pretty good English, "To speak to officer in charge."

"I'm in charge. What do you want?"

"Establish a cadre. We will help you manage our men. In exchange you deal with them through us. Also, we are hungry. When will we be fed?"

Hector called the lieutenant, while keeping the prisoners behind the yellow poly rope strung forty meters downslope, parallel to the barbed wire. "Sir, got three slantie zeroes here. They want to set up a cadre, they call it."

Hawkshadow sounded like he'd just woken up. *"Tell them, to-morrow."*

"Aye aye, sir. They say their people are hungry, too."

Hector glanced downhill to see other men climbing the slope behind the trio. Many others. Hundreds.

"I'm working that. Tell 'em they'll get MREs tomorrow, same as us."

He called to the shadowy figures, "You'll get rations tomorrow. Same as us."

"We demand to speak to camp commander," the older man said.

"Go back to your tents," Hector told them. "All of you. We'll discuss it tomorrow."

"We don't have tents for everyone. Half our men are out in the open. Without shelter. Without food. We protest this inhuman treatment. Against Geneva Convention." The civilian turned and started shouting to the prisoners in Chinese.

The others were still climbing, filing into ranks behind the leaders. A growing mutter, a growl, rumbled from the crowd. A searchlight beam from one of the trucks swept the front rank, leaping their faces forward from the growing dark.

"Shit," Corporal Karamete muttered, coming up beside him. "Hector. Look."

The prisoners were carrying sticks, rocks, sharpened branches. From the bomb-shattered forest. He told her in an undertone, "Get us some reinforcements. Get the CHADs on line." Then called Hawkshadow again. This time, the lieutenant sounded like he was already awake.

A motor roared on the far side of the hill, climbing up from the valley where the eco station and its parking lot lay. The Oshkosh crested the hill and braked, slewing. Hawkshadow jumped out and hiked over. He cradled a helmet in one arm, but was unarmed except for a pistol. "Report," he snapped.

Hector brought him up to speed in three sentences. The Chinese stood immobile, but the crowd behind the leaders began a chant. Obviously something they'd learned before, maybe a marching song. Yeah, it had a cadence.

"I'm going down," Hawkshadow said. He stripped off his pistol belt and thrust it into Karamete's hands. "Don't let them cross that line."

"Sir, don't take this off. And let one of us go with you—"

She tried to give it back, but Hawkshadow refused with a hand-chop. "Take it," he snapped. Reluctantly, she accepted. He handed Hector his phone. "I'll be right back. If I'm not, notify Battalion. Oo-rah?"

"Oorah, sir. Did you tell them what was going on, sir? We gonna get some reinforcements up here, like, ASAP, right?"

"They're all still at the parade. We're all there is."

Parade? Hector thought. What the hell? A fucking parade, when they had nine thousand POWs locked down here? But before he could voice the protest Hawkshadow was striding away down the slope, the heels of his combat boots digging into the shell-plowed soil.

Karamete frowned. "This is a bad idea."

"You got those CHADs coming?" Hector said. "And the rest of the platoon?"

"Second squad's mustered, Sergeant. Behind the crest. CHADs are mustering. And don't forget, you got two MGs covering the gate."

He glanced back to note the line of machines and the weapons they held. Thumbed his phone, and called up their command app. Muttered, "Detail: Lock and load."

Lock and load, the confirm read. Behind him bolts rattled as they stripped cartridges off magazines, snapped safeties on. Unfortunately he wasn't sure sending the CHADs down there was smart. They were programmed to detect humans with weapons, execute an algorithm to identify them, and engage those tagged as enemy. If they had any kind of crowd control setting, he didn't know it. He told Karamete, "Get me more lights. Or a helmet. I can't see shit up here."

"Here's the lieutenant's helmet."

Hector settled it over his head and turned on the Glasses. But the night vision was busted, or below spec. It came up in a puke-green-and piss-yellow boil, with shit contrast. Through the shifting, foggy murk he could barely distinguish Hawkshadow as a figure surrounded by the slightly shorter Chinese. Behind them secthed the crowd, which seemed to be growing increasingly restive.

A rock flew over the deadline and thudded at his feet.

In the piss-green seethe, a lifted cudgel.

"On me," he yelled to the rest of the gate guard. He unslung his carbine and started jogging down the hill. Into the valley . . . he hurdled the yellow deadline and glanced back to make sure they were following. Karamete, Milliron and his squad were behind him, but that was all. The CHADs stood immobile, watching.

"Want me to bring 'em down?" Karamete said, low, urgent.

"No. I can't command them like this. Have them stand fast." He faced front again.

But now he couldn't see Hawkshadow at all. The whole bottom of the valley was a writhe of green-lit forms, rushing here and there, apparently all carrying rocks and sticks. Where had the lieutenant gone? Check his tablet loc—no, he'd handed that over.

Go down and find him? Unwise. They'd be surrounded, and either beaten up, or have to kill prisoners by the dozens. Maybe by the hundreds. But they'd still be overwhelmed, their weapons taken, the gate forced, the POWs streaming out.

A firm hand.

He held up a closed fist. Karamete passed *"Halt"* over the tac circuit.

He clicked on it too. "Post One, Post Two, fire mission. To the east. One long burst, over their heads. I say again, fire mission, to the east, one long burst, over their heads. *Execute.*"

Fire lashed out in a solid-seeming beam of bright green, arching like a deadly rainbow as the tracer zipped across the valley and blasted up the ground on the far side. The chatter of the guns was deafening even through the helmet. *Die goddamn you die. Die goddamn you die.* The machine gunner's mantra for timing a burst. "Repeat," he told the gunners. "Then lower your sights. Stand by for fire mission."

When they fell silent after the second burst the crowd had parted, sullenly, but the way downward lay open.

To where a form lay supine. But another prisoner was bent over it. For a second Hector couldn't see what he was doing. Leaning on a stick? Then he did. The guy was holding something. A suicide charge. The pale thing in his outstretched hand, the detonator.

A firm hand.

Before he knew it, the lit circle of his reflex sight framed the bent-over silhouette and the carbine jumped against his shoulder. He didn't even remember taking the safety off. Only that when the muzzle flash ceased dazzling his Glasses the prisoner was crumpling, sliding to the torn-up, boot-scuffed earth.

Karamete shouldered past his frozen offhand firing stance. With no more thought than before he averted the muzzle from her and thumbed the safety on.

Then followed, forcing his steps, staggering like Frankenstein's monster. He slipped on the muddy slope and almost fell, but recovered himself, staggered up again, and half slid, half stumbled the rest of the way.

To Hawkshadow's limp body, and the prisoner's beside him. The crowd had backed off, but they were still waving sticks and shouting, if anything, more violently and threateningly than before.

The roar of surf in his ears. Men wading toward him through the water. Water red with blood. His hands shaking.

He tried to pick the officer up, but he was too heavy. Drag him, then. "Give me a hand here," he grunted. "Or if you—no, never mind, I'll get him. Cover me, though. Shoot them all if they come at us again."

"Sergeant—"

"What, Corporal?"

"I think he was trying to help."

Ramos stared down at the man on the ground. Half his abdomen had been perforated, horribly mangled by the tumbling bullets. His guts hung out, and he was craned back, convulsing, wide-open eyes fixed on Hector's even through the seething murk.

A pop above them. Flarelight blanked the goggles, carving shadows into the torn soil. He tore the goggles off, to see what the Chinese had been holding. It was a medical pack. The pale thing in his hand had been a bandage.

He started to lift the carbine again, not really understanding what he was doing. Then Karamete was pulling it from him, dropping the mag, jacking the live round out of the chamber. She all but threw the rifle back into his defensively raised hands. He mumbled, "I thought—"

"Yeah, well, maybe you had the wrong sight picture." She grabbed Hawkshadow's other arm and they began tugging him uphill. But before they got three yards four of the D models were striding downslope. Ranging themselves around the body, they lowered themselves with that strange hydraulic slippage that always looked so inhuman, linked hands, and lifted the sagging body.

Only it wasn't a body, but a wounded man. Hawkshadow stirred and flung out his arm. His gloved fingers lashed Hector's cheek like a challenge. Karamete ordered, "Take him to the eco station. Aid station. ASAP."

In a hollow voice one of the CHADs repeated the command.

"What's going on here?" A steely voice from a bulky shadow striding downhill. The tone alone said mid-grade officer. "I'm Major Deutschmann. Seven Twenty-eighth Military Police Battalion. Who's in charge here?"

Hector turned his face away. After a couple of seconds Karamete said Lieutenant Hawkshadow had been, but that he'd gone down alone to speak with the prisoners, who were presenting grievances. Now he was wounded, but they hadn't seen how. One of the prisoners had been shot.

The major shook his head in disgust. "He went down alone? After Koje Island? I won't say he deserved what he got. But that's not procedure, not with POWs. Look . . . we'll take it from here. Just hand over command of these Ds. Both of you, and the rest of you Marines, you can go back to your hootches. Or wherever. They're shipping you out. For Korea, I guess. But don't come back here." He glared down into the valley. "Grievances. And they beat up an officer? We'll see about grievances."

HECTOR went back to the aid station with the lieutenant, and stayed until the corpsman said he was stabilized. Battalion was sending a dustoff. He needed another pill. He kept patting his cargo pockets, but each time they were still empty.

They're shipping you out for Korea. He was pretty sure that's what the major had said.

The corpsman kept looking at him. "Sergeant. How long you been shaking like that?"

Hector extended his hands. Yeah, they looked bad. "Pretty much since Taipei," he muttered.

"Might be CSR," the corpsman said. "Combat stress reaction. You been feeling okay? Panic, anxiety, depression, hallucinations? See stuff that isn't there?"

"No, nothin' like that," Hector lied.

"You're not getting flashbacks? Feeling bad about something you did?"

The Pig jackhammers his shoulder as other guns along the beach open up too. He traverses, picking out clusters of wading figures. Geysers of white spray burst up. Those who still carry rifles throw them away, raise their hands too. They cry out, pleading, but he keeps firing. Under the relentless impacts they wilt, spin, drop, sink back into the sea. The water turns red beneath the silver mist. Screaming. Cries. The other guns fall silent. Someone grabs his shoulder. But he shakes it off and keeps firing.

Behind a walking wall of gray-white antitargeting smoke an army of huge green cockroaches lumbers up the slope.

Gun flashes winks from their muzzles. Whistles blow. Laser beams probe like antennae through rainfog and gunsmoke. Helmets bob behind the beetles. Cheers carry on the wind. The Marines yell curses back.

The flag descends, slides down, and falls over him in folds of scarlet and yellow. As he fights free of it Ffoulk grabs it and stuffs it into her pack. She hands him a red and white and blue one. "Hoist that," she snaps. Then makes a strange whisper, a puff of meaningless sound. Her head whips around, surrounded by a pinkish halo like that of a stained glass saint.

He snapped his head up, trying to focus. The medic frowned. "Want to lie down awhile, get some shuteye? We got a spare bunk here in the tent. Nice and quiet and dark."

"What I could use is a drink," he said. "Any of that medicinal brandy, or whatever?"

"We don't give out alcohol," the medic said. "But I can issue something to calm you down. No problem, that's what you want. Off the books. No record."

He didn't need calming down. He needed . . . he didn't know what exactly. To be somebody else. He rubbed his face so hard he felt the skin come off. No. That was somebody else's face, burned, sloughing away . . .

He stumbled out of the tent. The corpsman called after him, but he didn't go back.

A lightless time. He wandered, groaning aloud. Flashes of vivid images. He must have thrown his helmet away then, though he didn't miss it until later.

Sometime after he found himself at a low block building, lightless, that he only slowly recognized as the eco center. He tried the door. Unlocked. He went in, then flinched, startled, whipping around, aiming his carbine instinctively. A dinosaur . . . no, some kind of frog, only a hundred times bigger than life. A plastic model. But it loomed menacingly in the dim light. It moved . . . no it didn't . . . it had teeth . . . shit.

Korea. Another battle. More horror and killing.

He looked at the carbine again. Sniffed the muzzle. It still smelled of powder from the valley. From when he'd shot a man who'd only been trying to help . . .

An idea struck him. He stalked the corridors until he found the room he was looking for. A window shattered, smashed in by the butt of a carbine. A door clicked open.

Glass glittered in the light of his flash. A clear fluid surrounded bizarre shrunken forms, reptile embryos, snakes, insects, amphibians in the unlikely colors of a fluorescent rainbow. Beneath the counter, ranks of chemicals . . . he unscrewed the cap on a carboy and sniffed.

He carried the jar back to the lobby before taking the first swallow. The neat alcohol, nearly two hundred proof—or maybe it was actually ether, the label was in Chinese—seared the membranes of his throat like napalm. He choked, gasping, reeling, coughed and snorted, barely able to breathe through the fumes. He waited until the fire died, drew a deep breath, and took another sip.

It hit in seconds. He slumped-slid down into a corner filled with darkness. He huddled there, looking up at the frog monster. It loomed threateningly, ready to leap. His head spun. Another sip, another coughing fit . . . He set the carboy down, leveled the carbine, and flicked off the safety. The optic powered up with a faint high buzz, barely discernible above the hiss and roar already in his ears. His finger trembled on the trigger.

Then he reversed the weapon.

He set the muzzle under his chin, and closed his eyes. The raw alcohol would take the pain away. The guilt. The suffering. But when he was sober once more, the horror would still be there. Waiting.

But he could end it.

No more killing.

No more terror.

No more of this awful feeling of doom.

Hell? The priests said so. He'd be judged. Condemned.

But even eternal flame might be more peaceful than this.

"You're a two-island Marine," he muttered drunkenly. *Your men look up to you.* Duty, he had duty . . . the Corps . . . but he wasn't up to this. Wasn't right. His head . . . his brain . . . felt . . . fucking . . . *broken.* Something in there was shattered. Through the cracks, the horror was flooding in. And the pills only made it worse.

He set the rifle aside. Fingers scrabbling desperately, he extracted a slip of photo from his combat wallet. *Mirielle.* But her features were blurred, the colors had run together with rain and sweat and wear. Even with the flashlight, he couldn't make out her eyes.

He set it aside, propped it facing him on the frog's pedestal, and picked up the carbine again. Settled it between his legs, and set the powder-smelling muzzle once more beneath his jaw.

Crouched there, shivering, panting, Hector Ramos wavered between life and death.

9

The Karakoram Mountains

DEEP in these remote caverns, the air was humid and somehow denser than out in the open. Water dripped. Echoes reverberated. Lanterns hissed, radiating light the color of copal. A fire crackled in a groove in the wall, sending aromatic smoke eddying toward where bats twittered and squeaked far above. A shortwave radio ranted, turned down until it was barely audible. Worn carpets and low tables of rough wood were scattered across the eroded limestone floor. Ancient Buddhas lay shattered, faces gouged away. Wall engravings were scarred by bullets. A crushed mass of ancient parchment shoaled the corners. Black banners hung behind a stone lectern, and a battered scimitar leaned against it.

Once Teddy Oberg had been judged from that lectern. Now he led hundreds of fighters, and unnumbered thousands followed his bidding throughout western China.

Yet not without opposition.

"Chai," a girl whispered behind the seated men. Brass tinkled as she set down a tray. Barefoot, she was sheathed from crown to dirty toes in black cloth, save for a slit for her eyes. One of the Han taken at Kanayi. She was slight, frightened, twelve or thirteen. Teddy had never asked her real name. He called her Dandan, after an earlier girl slave. As he'd trained her, she poured a cup for herself first, from the same pot, and drank it off. Stood trembling, holding her hand to her no-doubt-scalded mouth.

Teddy stroked his beard, fondling her absently from behind with the other hand. After some moments he pushed her away, leaned in and took one of the tiny blazing-hot turned-brass cups, holding it with the tips of gloved fingers. Despite the fire the air in the cave was close to freezing. Guldulla—"Tokarev"—sat to his right, his breath a white plume. Nasrullah, their spymaster, squatted to Teddy's left.

"Report," Teddy said.

Nasrullah gestured to a young Uighur who sat a few feet away, legs crossed, cradling a small coffer. He set it in front of Teddy. Accepted a teacup, yet did not sip. He stared at them with wide eyes.

"Tell the Lingxiù what happened," the spymaster prompted.

The muj cleared his throat. He spoke in Uighur, which Teddy could follow by now, though he didn't speak it fluently. "Respected sir. The governor was well protected. Bodyguards. Escorts, when he traveled in his car. Guards outside his home. We observed for many days. Then a friend told us to watch the side of his office in the city. The exit the workers use, those who clean up and serve the meals for the officials.

"He left by that back gate and we followed. Once or twice a week he leaves the office in mid-afternoon to visit a widow who runs a duoba shop. She locks up and they go into the back."

Teddy nodded. Duobas were the traditional embroidered Uighur hats. He reached for a pot of honey and stirred some into the aromatic chai. It was a green tea, from Jiangxi.

"We promised her life and those of her children if she cooperated. She wept but agreed. We remained in the back room until he visited again. She rang a bell to warn us. When he came in, we were ready."

The boy presented a cheap phone and thumbed up a photograph. The severed head had a startled expression. Blood surrounded it on a rumpled-up pink bedspread.

"What did you do with it?" Oberg muttered.

"Displayed it in the marketplace. Later the Han troops came and removed it. But by then many had seen."

"And the widow?"

"Killed, with her children. As collaborators. Also displayed in the market."

"You have done well," Teddy told him. He reached into his vest, into the hidden pocket beside the holstered Makarov with the safety off. He counted five shining Krugerrands onto the carpet. Each was worth twice the annual income of an average worker. The boy gawked down at them.

"Share them with your comrades, the brave mujahideen of Urumqi. Tell them your leaders are generous. Tell them they have served their people well." Teddy waved to the guards standing a few paces off. "Go now. Rest, eat, and receive more of the rewards ITIM reserves for the bravest of its fighters." The boy bowed and got up, leaving the box in front of Teddy. Teddy flicked a finger at it, but didn't touch it. Dandan came forward from the shadows, and spirited it away as Nasrullah beckoned to the next man in line.

One after the other, their agents reported assassinations, car bombings, suicide-vest attacks against the government and those who collaborated. Others reported on ITIM's self-financing efforts, primarily moving high-value low-bulk Afghan exports down into the lowlands. Some of the spies arrived coughing. They reported sickness in the towns. Deaths. But also a heavier Internal Security presence, with patrols, roving drones, and counterassassinations. Prominent Uighur lawyers, doctors, and clerics had been rounded up and sent east.

Teddy nodded grimly, knowing what that meant. Camp 576, where he himself had toiled and nearly starved.

The audience ended. Teddy grunted, hoisting himself awkwardly from the cushioned nook where he usually sat, his back to the cave wall. His injured leg flamed. He eased it within the brace, stretching the warped muscles and pain-racked tendons until they cracked. He limped back and forth, shaking it off. He'd have to sit again in a few hours, for the talk with the leadership. Then again that afternoon, when their CIA contact arrived.

But first they had to get a few things straightened out.

IMAM Akhmad's white beard fell to his waist. The end lay curled in his lap. The old man's eyes were cloudy, but cataracts didn't seem to keep him from reading the Koran. Or maybe he'd memorized it by now. He must have learned it from some local cleric in his youth; his Arabic pronunciation was worse than Teddy's. Never spry since Oberg had known him, over the last year he'd grown feeble. Slaves had to support him when he tottered about. These days he seldom left his side cavern, and spent long periods of time alone praying, or maybe just staring at the stained walls in the flickering light of a single candle.

Now the old man welcomed them to his retreat with a graceful flexing of long fingers. "Come to me, my sons," he mumbled through a toothless mouth, coughing. His left hand was tucked under his robe. His right groped toward a dish of qiegao: slices of a cake made of stewed sugar, minced nuts, dates, raisins, and figs. Akhmad seemed to live on candy: chocolates, White Rabbit milk candies, sugared fruit, puddings, all prepared for him by his slaves.

Before Teddy could react, Qurban, the former al-Qaeda chief, settled himself at the right hand of the sheykh. They faced Teddy, Nasrullah, and Tokarev across the desserts and an ornate little samovar which bubbled over a Sterno flame.

Okay, round one to Qurban. Teddy handed the imam the box the assassin had given him. Dandan had cautiously opened it to reveal neat rows of Chinese chocolates in gold foil. The old man smiled, but set it aside. They chatted, Teddy restraining his impatience. The elder had to broach the conversation first.

"What brings my sons to visit an old man?" the imam finally muttered, wiping his nose on a stained sleeve.

Guldulla said respectfully, "Reverend Sheykh, events are pressing. We must discuss our leadership before the American arrives."

He blinked at Teddy. "But al-Amriki is already with us."

"We mean, the American from outside," Qurban put in.

The old imam blinked again, looking blank. Was he out of it? Going gaga?

Teddy, Guldulla, and Qurban were currently sharing the leadership, in an uneasy triumvirate led, or rather figureheaded, by the old imam. A respectable Islamic insurgency had to be headed by a cleric. Unfortunately, the sheykh seemed to be losing his grip.

Teddy watched Qurban's hands as he passed tea around. As far as he could tell, he hadn't slipped anything into it. As they sipped, Nasrullah presented the news from the lowlands. The authorities were responding to the massacre, and the rising insurgency, by prohibiting prayer other than in approved mosques, prosecuting those who wore beards and veils, and dissolving those madrassas that did not slavishly follow Beijing's line.

"This is very evil of them," Akhmad mumbled, fumbling in the dish for another slice of the sweet cake.

Nasrullah said humbly, "It is not all the evil they have done. Marshal Chagatai has ordered in another interior security division from Hong Kong."

"Chagatai . . ." the old man's voice trailed off.

Tokarev said, "The general who shot a thousand people in Hong Kong. He is an Uighur, but he kowtows to the Hans."

The old man bobbled his head, but his beatific expression didn't change. Nasrullah went on. "He has begun roundups and mass executions. There are rumors chemical weapons were dropped on Kanayi, which is being called Town of the Dead."

The old man mumbled, "Kanayi . . ."

"Where we raided, and punished the Han," Teddy supplied.

The old guy didn't seem to be following the conversation. Actually, he seemed much more interested in his snack.

Qurban cleared his throat. "Revered Sheykh, may this humble one contribute?" After a moment the former al-Qaeda fighter spread his hands. He said in flawless classical Arabic, "Honored sir, forgive my forwardness. No more than al-Amriki al-Oberg, am I one of your clan. Yet long have I fought on the side of the Faithful. Multitudes have fallen around me. Still, by the will of Allah, Blessed be his name—"

All four men mumbled, "Blessed be his name."

"—by His will alone, have I survived to carry on the struggle. I have not the military training of our American friend." He nodded to Teddy, smiling. "Nor can I merit the confidence you repose in your fellow tribesmen, the brave Guldulla called Tokarev and the cunning Nasrullah who carries our message to the people.

"Nevertheless, I have seen great movements defeated before. They never completely die, as they are dedicated to the Faith. But they suffer setbacks. Become complacent. And sometimes are betrayed, by members who appear as stone but are merely salt within."

He didn't so much as glance at Teddy, but Oberg tensed. What kind of treacherous, underhanded shit was this asshole up to?

"I fear we are at the crossroads of decision. The Han have a Final Solution in sight for the Turkic peoples. Beijing is growing desperate. This Chagatai arrives with hands dripping with blood. We must take measures."

He paused, and they all looked to Akhmad. Who sopped up a bit of sweet sauce, sucked on his fingers, and gazed over their heads. Finally he mumbled, "What is it that you propose, Hajji al-Nashiri?"

"Honored Sheykh, far be it from me to suggest guidance."

"Please, go ahead," Teddy broke in. In Arabic, just to remind everyone Qurban wasn't the only guy around who could rattle it off. Plus, his ass was going numb on the thin blanket. Nothing under it but wet rock, if the seeping dampness was any clue. Drink tea, chat, drink more tea . . . being a rebel and a guerrilla wasn't a bad gig, but this part sucked.

Qurban nodded. "Two things must be done. First, this marshal must die. If our clever friend here," he nodded to Nasrullah, "can arrange the assassination of a governor, surely he can give death to this bloody general."

The old man held up his cup. Above them bats twittered. A dollop of dung splattered down onto the blanket. A slave reached to brush it away. Another refreshed the sheykh's tea.

"And the second?" Guldulla prompted, when the old man didn't answer.

"We must recast the mission of ITIM," Qurban said. He stroked a gray beard, shorter than Akhmad's, but longer than Teddy's. "So far we have been promoting a political, democratic, secular rebellion. I understand that the Independent Turkistan Islamic Movement revives the name of an earlier resistance. I also understand its promise—to unite all the Turkic peoples. Not just from China, but from Azerbaijan, Kazakhstan, Kyrgyzstan, Turkmenistan, Uzbekistan. Yes. That is a powerful message.

"But we must be realistic. It must change."

"To what?" Teddy said, but he knew the answer.

"It is simple. We must pronounce jihad. Turn this rebellion into a sacred battle, of the Faithful against the godless. This will unite us with the fighting House of Islam throughout the world."

"Daesh, al-Qaeda, Boko Haram," Teddy said. "You mean, like them?"

Qurban turned a gentle smile to him. He said politely, "The one you call The Sacrifice has fought under many banners. Yet it is always the same banner. Nothing must be exalted over Islam. We must fulfill Allah's will as revealed by the Prophet, blessed be his name. We will bring all the faithful of the world under the sacred law. We will subject the polytheists to obedience and destroy the atheists and idolators. Is this not how you, honored Sheykh, have governed your fighters?"

Addressed directly, Akhmad merely belched and closed his eyes.

"I will speak, if that is agreeable," Teddy said. Guldulla and Nasrullah nodded; the old sheykh looked away; Qurban smiled.

"I am not saying the hajji is wrong. His first suggestion, the assassination of the marshal, is good. Removing this devil will strike fear into the Han, that such a high one can fall, like the shattered idols in our cave.

"But pronouncing jihad . . . this is a different matter. It detaches us from many supporters in the urban areas. Those who hate the Han, but who are educated. The merchants. It places us in company with some whom even much of the Umma abhors. I fear most of all that it may cost us the support of America. Where most of our weapons and ammunition, as well as other supplies, originate."

He stroked his beard. Just like one of them . . . "I am open to reason, and to the sheykh's command. Whatever he decides, that will I execute. But I warn against this second step. I warn against it most sincerely."

The imam looked at Nasrullah, who turned his hands upward, abstaining. At Guldulla. Who hesitated, smoothing his mustache. But who finally shook his head. "There are good arguments on both sides. This matter merits more thought. But as Qurban and the Lingxiù both have said, it is for the sheykh to decide."

Akhmad closed his eyes. With an audible spatter, another dona-
tion from the bats hit the hem of his coat. A slave mopped at it, but
the old man didn't seem to notice.

When he opened his eyes again, they were clouded, rheumy, but
seemed to see beyond the cavern, beyond the mountains. Maybe,
all the way to the Seventh Heaven. He patted each of their knees in
turn. Smacked his lips, and reached for another sweet. Masticated it,
while a little drool stained his beard.

Finally he murmured, "I agree with noble Guldulla. This merits
thought. I will ponder all you have said. May Allah grant me wisdom.
Go in peace." He waved a flaccid hand, and one after the other the
men in front of him rose, and bowed, and left the cavern.

"VLADIMIR" arrived that afternoon, on a donkey, with an escort
of mujahideen and pack mules. Nasrullah patted him down and relieved him of his pistol.

The Agency field officer had Slavic cheekbones and a nose like a
thin-blade knife. His short beard was black. His hooded eyes were
bloodshot from the altitude. He stripped off a heavy greatcoat and
insulated gloves to reveal a tactical vest, a maroon turtleneck, and a
now empty holster.

They shook hands as Teddy tried to reorient his brain to English.
It seemed to have left his skull, to no longer reside on his hard drive.
Finally he managed, "Good to see you."

"Good to see you too, Teddy."

"Vladimir" was a cover name, of course. He said he'd been a Ranger
before joining the CIA. Teddy didn't know his real one, though the
guy seemed to know everything about him. From his Team files, of
course. Plus records of his other missions.

Which all seemed so long ago . . . like the movie he'd never made,
back in LA.

Vladimir jerked a thumb at one of the mujs, and they began wrestling crates off the mules. A crowbar was applied to wood, and
with considerably splintering and banging a green-wrapped bundle
emerged.

Teddy cradled the rifle, running his gaze up and down the stock. "M40."

"Marines were getting rid of them. I put in for five for your snipers."

"Optics?"

"In the side compartment."

"Yeah, this'll reach out and touch 'em. What else you got?"

"Ammo. Stingers. Batteries, night vision, flu meds."

"Meds, excellent. We've had a shitload of sick lately."

"This stuff should help. Experimental. The latest and greatest. But keep close tabs on it. We wouldn't want this to get to the Hans."

Teddy said he copied that, and that they might as well go on up to the cave.

THE agent looked keenly about as they threaded the men sitting on the stone floors. Some were cleaning rifles. Others swayed and chanted: a Koran class. And some were sleeping, arms thrown over their faces; come in from guard duty in the surrounding mountains.

Teddy bent double and scuttled into the side cave reserved for him. A tight little space, but with only one entrance he felt more secure when he slept. Dandan bustled about as they settled on carpets. He snapped, *"Chai. Choy va nonni olib kelish."* She bowed and withdrew.

Vladimir's gaze followed her. "That's a different kid, isn't it? What happened to, um, Dandan?"

"Fell off a rope bridge in the mountains. But you can call her Dandan too."

"I see. How old's this one?"

"Fuck if I know. Who gives a crap?" Hey, he was remembering. At least, how to flip somebody off in good old American.

Vladimir said mildly, "Just making conversation. And how's the imam? Akhmad?"

"He's . . . getting on. But still on top of things." A white lie, maybe, but why rock the boat. Especially when Mr. al-Qaeda was angling to be next in line. "Okay, enough foreplay. Let's talk about what you can do for me."

"What I can do you for right now was on those fucking donkeys. But I've got a message you need to hear."

Dandan set down the tea tray. Teddy waited while she poured herself a cup and sipped it. He eased his bad leg out in front of him and poured a cup for the Ranger, then for himself. Though he didn't touch his own, having drunk more than enough tea during the sit-downs that morning. "Shoot."

"That reminds me," the agent said, "how about we start by getting me my Glock back?"

"Soon's we're done here. So what do I 'need to hear'?"

Vladimir looked grave. He tapped the Bukhara between them with a gloved finger. "This is from up top. You have to cut back on targeting civilians. The IEDs are okay. The assassinations of cooperators—we never knew about that. But the massacre in the town, the Agency disavows."

Teddy cracked his knuckles, getting angry. WTF, over? "Disavow. What the fuck's that mean? Besides, that wasn't us. That was the townspeople, taking their revenge. But, shit, wasn't that what you tasked me with? Pull the Internal Security divisions west? Well, another one just got ordered in."

The agent nodded. "And that's appreciated. But nothing like Kanayi ever again. Copy? Your insurgency's growing. Hurting Beijing. But it can blow back on the Allies, if the news gets out we're promoting ethnic cleansing. I need a roger. This is serious, Ted."

Teddy nodded. "Message received. But we're getting pressured out here. Do you know what the Han are doing? They've installed facial recognition systems throughout Xinjiang. Tracking the native Uighurs. Public spaces. Markets. Roads. When they spot a suspect on a facial match, they raid at night and shoot his family. Not even a summary trial, they just leave them in the house for the neighbors to clean up.

"The latest is they've sent out some hot-shit, hell-raiser new general."

"Chagatai," Vladimir put in.

"You know?"

"Marshal Chagatai claims descent from the Mongol Khans. He

was in charge of restoring 'law and order' in Hong Kong. We don't have hard numbers, but probably over twenty thousand dead."

Teddy nodded slowly. A serious opponent, then. Despite what some liked to believe, sometimes ruthless repression, the mass infliction of sheer terror, actually tamped down a rebellion, if carried out thoroughly enough. "Uh, we got reports of gas being used on one of the Uighur towns. Possibly, Kanayi itself. To punish residents for massacring their Han neighbors, I guess."

"That's not the only bad news, I'm afraid. Have you seen any patrols, any drones up here?"

Teddy shrugged. "Just the usual sweeps. So far we haven't been targeted. Why?"

Vlad told him that the Hunza, the tribe downhill and west, had been bought off and turned against the Allies. "By the Iranians. An offer they couldn't refuse. So now they'll be pushing up along the road from Azad Kashmir into your territory."

Teddy reflected dourly on this. So ITIM would be pincered, with enemies on both sides. Then did a double take. "Wait a minute. So how'd *you* get here? If the Hunza just flipped?"

The operative just rubbed thumb and index finger together, in the universal symbol for a payoff.

Teddy thought aloud, trying to remember his insurgency doctrine. "Okay, then, we're being isolated. We get boxed in, surrounded, they're gonna localize us. Then drop some big bunker-buster and bang, we're history.

"That means we need to get out of here. And not just to another hole in the wall. We need to go to the next stage."

"Mao's three phases?"

"We already did the base area phase. Now we need to expand. Go to the cities, or maybe, in this case, the hamlets. Gather popular support, which shouldn't be too tough, considering how hard the Han's cracking down. Then, take on larger units. Build this to a full-scale rebellion, with forces down in the lowlands taking territory."

"Fine. You want to grow this thing, we're ready. More gold. More weapons. What else?"

Teddy eased his leg again, wondering if he should run Qurban's proposal past him. Jettison the ITIM idea, uniting the Islamisists and the secular rebels, and go straight to hard-core jihad. But he didn't think it would go over very well. Not after how that strategy had played out in Afghanistan.

"Deep thoughts?" The agent helped himself to a cookie.

"Forget it . . . If what you're saying about the Hunza, they're gonna outnumber us. And they know where we are. Remember, *you* brought those two guys here. Leonardo and what's-his-name."

"True." Vladimir nodded. "A mistake, in retrospect."

"So we're gonna *have* to vacate the premises. Relocate."

"Okay. To where?"

"Due respect, but let me think about that. I prepped two other caves as hide sites, but like I say, we need to get out in the population." Teddy pondered a little longer, then added, "but if we gotta leave here . . . maybe we can exact a price."

The agent cocked his head. "How so?"

"Need to think about it some more . . . maybe, some kind of ambush."

They plotted over tea and cookies, and came up with the beginnings of a plan. The rebels would set up a false-flag IED school in the valley. Nasrullah would put out the word through his contacts that they needed recruits to build devices. But some he would involve would be known enemy collaborators. Instead of executing them, ITIM would employ them as channels to feed false information to the Chinese.

Teddy liked the idea. "With luck, we could tempt this Chagatai in. He's under pressure from Beijing to close down the insurgency. How could he resist being in at the kill?"

"Maybe. Considering his profile. He's a take-charge leader. Executes people himself."

"My kind of guy." Teddy gave it a beat, then grinned.

The other smiled back, but reluctantly. "Okay, so you get him here. Then what?"

"We blow the cave. The whole fucking complex. A massive charge up there with the bats. They'll be sweeping for radio detonation, so we leave a suicider behind to fire it. Blow the whole thing down on him. Meanwhile we scatter, setting up cells to spread the insurgency."

Vladimir nodded slowly. "We could get behind that."

"Can you get us four, five hundred kilos of C-4?"

"You'd have to promise positive control. We don't want this stuff getting into the wrong hands."

Teddy nodded. Just what the guy had to say to satisfy the legal beagles down the line when, inevitably, some ended up blowing up somebody who at the particular moment wasn't on the target list. Or mowed down a bunch of civilians in a truck bomb. But there was no way to infuse weapons and explosives into a war and not have some go adrift. Hell, even some SEAL units had had guys stealing shit, C-4 and radios and goggles. "Absolutely. Lock and key. Mission checkout only."

The agent stretched. He got up, bent over to avoid the low ceiling, and smiled. "How about me seeing the sheykh now?"

Teddy got up too. "I think he's at prayer, but I'll check."

Vladimir halted in the exitway. "Oh. Before I forget. A message from your old girlfriend."

"My . . . girlfriend?" Was this code for . . . ? "What girlfriend?"

"In San Diego. Didn't you have somebody there?"

He remembered then.

Mulvaney's Gingernut, a fake-Irish pub across from the Del Coronado. A sign out front: *Why do they call it tourist season if we can't shoot them?* Nothing to show it was a Team hangout, unless you counted the Harleys and jacked Jeeps and even the odd full-sized Hummer.

The bar had smelled like beer and corned beef and hot grease. It was full, SEALs, old-fart retirees, Viet vets, and people who came in to tour the zoo. A lot of women. Frog hogs, the operators called them. In a way it was annoying. On the other, wasn't it what every man wanted?

On the back patio, drinking what he'd promised himself would be his last Harp before getting back to the base. The late afternoon sun falling through the trees, warming his face as he lifted it, seeing only blood red through closed eyelids.

She'd spoken first. "Fresh meat," her opening words to him.

Muscular thighs, slim waist, the hard core muscle of her torso. Dark hair. Tight jeans-clad legs wrapped around the base of the stool. A bulge under her left armpit that wasn't tit.

Salena Frank had been with the sheriff's department in Vista. A smile that made you see what she must have looked like as a little girl in braids. And later, her drunken blond friend fingering herself in the bed next to them. And the pink plastic toy rabbit she'd handed him after. Telling him he was now an official San Diego Sheriff's Department badge bunny.

It all seemed so long ago and so . . . American. "We didn't actually have anything going," he told the agent. "A one-night stand."

"Didn't sound like it, from what she said."

"I already told her the guy she knew is dead."

"She doesn't seem to think so." Vladimir took a worn, creased envelope out of his tactical vest, and handed it over.

THE old man's guard confirmed he was asleep. "Let's get you settled in," Teddy told the agent, and led him to the guest quarters, which was a down bag in a side cave. A blanket served as a curtain, with a rug for prayer. A plastic bucket for piss and two bottles of drinking water completed the furnishings.

"I'm gonna have one of my own guys sleep outside. Oh, and here's your Glock back." He handed the weapon over butt first.

Vlad surveyed the room. "Rough, but I've slept rougher."

"We can provide *some* comforts." Teddy beckoned a dark-clad figure from behind him. Her thin fingers were locked in front of her. Her downcast eyes were the only part of her visible through the black chador. "Loula'll keep you warm. Got smoke, too, if you want to try a pipe. From Helmand."

The agent passed on the opium, but without a word gestured the girl over to his sleeping bag.

Teddy went outside. He sat on a rump-worn rock near the entrance, close enough he could duck in if they got a drone warning. He fingered the envelope thoughtfully.

Back then he'd wanted to make movies. Then the world had gone to hell, and since then he'd been sucked into one hot spot after another. Until the raid, and the capture, then torture and prison camp . . . Yeah, a lot of rapids under the bridge.

Over time, you changed. And remembering what he'd thought before was important, and cool, and would make him happy . . . made it all seem . . . pretty fucking shallow and pointless. So what if *A Teddy Oberg Production* was projected for a second on a big screen? So what the fucking fuck?

He'd had a vision, on a mountain.

Since then, nothing had been the same.

Now he served Allah. And was in turn served, by his mujahideen. And slaves. Like Dandan and Loula.

But he was still making movies. Sort of. In a way.

There was a hidden camera in the side cave. When the agent left, Teddy would retrieve it himself. Just for leverage, either with the Agency or Vlad personally, in case he ever needed it.

Espionage and guerrilla warfare weren't about playing fair.

He toyed with the still sealed envelope for a few minutes, then finally limped inside again. The fire was glowing coals. He threw on a few more sticks—wood was scarce in the mountains, and had to be husbanded—and laid the envelope on them. It smoked. The edges curled up, turning brown. Writing showed for a moment through the crisping paper. Then the rectangle burst into flame.

He watched it burn until it was nothing but crumbling char.

ONE of his mujs found him outside sometime later, in the dark. "Al-Amriki!"

"Do not call me that," he told the man in Uighur. "I have said before, I am one of you now. The only American here is the one asleep inside."

But the man only waved him to silence. "Come quickly. Sir. It is the sheykh."

When he got to the old man's cavern he had to push his way through the throng. Guldulla was standing over the imam, holding a hissing gasoline lantern. The sheykh's slaves were crouched a few paces away, trembling, hiding their faces. A guard stood over them with an AK.

Teddy bent over the old cleric. Those rheumy eyes stared up sightless now. The dirty hand was still outstretched toward the dish. He felt for a pulse in the neck. Behind him, someone murmured. He ignored it. Probed again. Nothing. The skin was already cold.

He straightened, and murmured, *"Inna lillahi wa inna ilayhi rajiun."*

To Allah we belong, to Him we return. The murmuring grew. Teddy glanced around at them, and that silenced it. Mostly. "What happened, Tokarev?"

"As you see," Guldulla said. He gestured at the candy, at a teacup that lay on its side, at the brass pot. Teddy bent to peer into it. Empty.

They had to cajole the elder woman to talk. Teddy was surprised to learn she wasn't a slave, as he'd assumed, but an Uighur, and the old man's lawful wife. Apparently the only one, though he could have had as many as he liked.

The younger, of course, really was a slave. The older woman suddenly began cuffing her, screaming at her. The young woman cowered silently, head shielded beneath a black-clothed sleeve.

"Someone must die for this outrage," said Qurban, appearing almost magically from the crowd, which edged apart to give him space. "Who has done this? Someone must die."

Teddy caught sight of Vladimir, at the back. He beamed him a scowl, hoping he got the message. *Get out of sight. Don't get mixed up in this.*

"The sheykh was very old," Teddy said.

"It was the sweets," the hajji persisted. "Do you not see? He died pointing to them." The crowd murmured, passing the observation from mouth to mouth. "Either in the Han chocolates, or the qiegao. Or perhaps the tea."

Teddy ruminated, stroking his beard. It *could* have been poison. A quick-acting one. But the question of murder or old age was secondary. Just now the rebels were looking to him and Guldulla. But if they didn't act, the al-Qaeda zealot would take over. He was already muttering to certain young men in the crowd. Voices were rising, dissatisfied, suspicious.

"The young slave," Teddy pronounced. The crowd quieted. "Her name?"

"The Han she-dog is called Bubu," the wife spat. "Kill her!"

Teddy picked up the dish. Silently, he held it out to to the girl. She stared at it, horrified. He shook it, offering it as to a dog. *"Názhe ta. Chile ta,"* he said.

Take it. Eat.

She stared around again, terrified, then understood. She grabbed the dish and began stuffing candies under her niqab. The crowd murmured. Teddy seized her face scarf and threw it back. Chocolate stained her lips. Brown eyes blinked fearfully. Then closed as she reached for another handful.

When the dish was empty she covered her face again and stepped back. The crowd sighed. Teddy shook off his sleeve and ostentatiously consulted his watch. Minutes went by. The girl stood erect. Still trembling, but erect.

"How do you feel?" he asked her at last.

"I am perfectly fine. I did not poison him," the girl muttered through clenched teeth.

"There was no poison," Teddy announced to the crowd. Hoping they'd forgotten the teapot, since he'd done his diversion with the candy. "The sheykh was long in years and honor. Allah took him to his bosom, blessed be His name. There is no one guilty."

They wavered, murmuring. Finally Qurban stepped forward. "We have no imam now. But I will say a du'a."

Teddy nodded. Gave him a "you have the floor" sweep of one arm.

Lifting his hands in the shape of a begging bowl, the old fighter intoned, in flawless Arabic, "As the Prophet, peace be upon him, said at a funeral: Allah, have mercy on him. Forgive his sins, wash him with snow, clear him of his sin as a white shirt is cleaned of dirt. Give him a house better than his home on earth, a family better than his family on earth, a wife better than his wife on earth, and spare him the torture of hellfire. In Allah's name, Amin."

"Amin," they all echoed. Qurban shot Teddy a narrowed look, but said nothing more.

As Teddy thought, *Fuck. The bastard just dog-whistled the religious right.*

Slowly, the crowd dispersed.

VLAD left the next morning. Their farewell was edgy. Vlad told him again ITIM had to cut back on the civilian losses. Teddy promised to, again. At last the CIA man mounted the donkey, tossed a salute, and rode off down the valley.

As soon as he was out of sight Teddy retrieved the camera, popped out the chip, and hid it in his cave. Had to start packing soon, if the Hunza were coming. Fortunately that wouldn't take long. His drone rifle, his bedroll, his weapons. And Dandan, to carry everything.

When the old sheykh's funeral was over, Teddy, Nasrullah, Guldulla, and Qurban sat down together in the cave.

Teddy kept his face serene. With the scars, of course, he always looked terrifying, but he tried to smooth his expression to placid acceptance.

It had been poison, of course. The old man might have been half blind, but from his wife's reaction, he'd been hale enough to be actively porking the Chinese babe.

One of the three sitting with him was most likely the killer.

Guldulla, of course, was the likeliest successor to the sheykh for overall leadership. Teddy had always figured him for a straight shooter, but ambition couldn't be ruled out. Nasrullah, the spymaster, ran the asset who'd brought the gift chocolates. The girl had eaten some, but only one would have had to contain poison. And Qurban had been with the imam earlier, drinking tea. Nothing easier than to drop a little something into the pot.

Before he could speak Qurban raised his hand. "May I?"

Teddy looked to Guldulla, who hesitated, then nodded.

"I have fought in many lands, but I am not an Uighur," the Arab said smoothly. "I will happily follow the leadership of our brave commander, Lingxiù Teddy al-Amriki, friend from over the seas, who has joined the Umma of the Faithful."

Teddy forced something he hoped resembled a modest smile. A great opening move. One there was only one response to. "I appreciate the honor, Hajji. And I too have fought in many lands. But neither can I lead you. ITIM is a movement of the Turkics. It should be led by one." He nodded to Guldulla. "Like Tokarev. Brave in battle, wise in counsel. Also, the second most handsome of us."

They looked disbelieving, then got it. There, a chuckle or two. Good.

"Yes, a wise proposal," the ex-al-Qaeda fighter said.

Guldulla stroked his two-tone mustache. "I wish we weren't discussing this. But we must. You would acknowledge me as commander? And the Lingxiù as our military chief?"

Qurban bowed to the ground. "You will be our honored *amir al-mumineen*. The Commander of the Faithful. All I ask is to be allowed to lead the prayers."

Teddy kept his eyes on the rug. He didn't believe a word of it. The guy was dying to be alpha wolf. Had made that plain since he arrived.

Raising his gaze, Teddy said evenly, "Of course, the hajji must lead our prayers. There must be peace between us, and understanding. Let us trust one another, go forward together, and strike the enemy as one fist."

Their eyes met across the carpet, and Teddy Oberg understood.

No matter what was said aloud, sooner or later, two of them would have to die.

10

Anacostia, District of Columbia

B LAIR paused on the sidewalk after stepping out of the car, as the escorting vehicles slewed in. Her guards muttered into headsets, aiming short rifles at possible ambush points as they trotted toward overwatch positions.

Black SUVs had preceded and followed her through the scruffy, narrow, nearly deserted streets of Southeast DC. After the bombing in Indianapolis, all federal officers Executive Schedule III and above had to be escorted by the Federal Protective Service. But these guards wore black shooting gloves, ballistic helmets, and short jackets embroidered with Velociraptor Systems' snarling dinosaur head. More and more, it seemed, private security was taking over what had once been basic government functions.

And milking away profit instead of providing services . . . *Anyway.* She brushed back her hair, deciding to worry about that later, and handed the documents she'd been reading to her aide. "Stay with the car, Erika. And boil this down to talking points. I'll try not to be too long."

Striding forward and lifting her gaze, she marveled at the antique crenellations of the old building. Its central structure rose to a five-story Gothic red-brick tower. So like the Smithsonian . . . The sun threw dappled shadows through the maples, and a breeze from the direction of the river stirred the sunny drops of light like golden flakes in a vodka martini.

A vodka martini . . . sounded good, actually. "Really, such a nice day," she muttered. At the very least, she was getting away from briefings and screens for a few hours.

The Government Hospital for the Insane—later called St. Elizabeths Hospital, without an apostrophe, for some reason—dated from before the Civil War. Midwived by Dorothea Dix, this gloomy brickpile had specialized in treating, or at least confining, patients with mental disorders. During World War II the OSS had tested truth serums and mescaline here. Ezra Pound had been locked up inside. The CIA had conducted experiments here too. The shady, tree-dotted campus still served its dual functions of treating insanity and housing intelligence activities. The eastern half held a high-security facility for the criminally insane. The western hundred acres, including the original building, was owned by the federal government. The Department of Homeland Security and its daughter agencies were being moved here, into the refurbished hospital and other, new buildings. Some of which were still under construction, to judge by the trucks, cranes, and hoardings, the torn-up, muddy street.

"Ms. Titus?" A fresh-faced young woman waved. "The chief of staff's office is this way. Please follow me. But your people"—she glanced at Blair's bodyguards—"will have to stay out here."

SHE'd sought this meeting for weeks. Operation Causeway, the liberation of Taiwan, had succeeded, though at a heavy cost. To judge by the administration's press releases, and their echo chamber in the controlled media, victory was in the air. But as the undersecretary of defense for strategy, plans, and forces, she'd been privy to disquieting reports. Which she now planned to surface with someone she'd once known well.

Or thought she had. But these days, you could never be completely sure of anyone.

To her surprise, once she got past the nineteenth-century facade the interior was modern. White walls, white tile floors, white overheads, still sour-milk redolent of fresh latex paint. The aide led her past a checkpoint, waving off the guards. Funny, that the DHS, supposedly in charge of security for the whole country, with nearly half a million personnel, didn't even wand her. But maybe that was a good sign.

Into an elevator. Spotless. Stainless. New. Another corridor, and on into an office with a breathtaking view of what looked like all of the Southeast District. And in the distance, the cupola'd snow-mountain of the Capitol.

"Blair Titus. How great to see you."

"Nice to see you too, Sol. This looks much more comfortable than Nebraska Avenue."

Laughing, Solomon Bischoff, chief of staff to the secretary of homeland security, came around his desk. They shook hands warmly, the old-pols' two-handed grip. "Yeah, six hundred million in congressional funding, another matching six hundred through GSA. We'll get this done. ICE and CBP, the Coast Guard and everybody else right here. No more chasing around the city. Long overdue."

She and Bischoff had been lowly GS-9 analysts together at the Congressional Research Service, ages ago. They'd had dinner together a couple of times, gone dancing, but nothing had clicked. They'd stopped seeing each other before she'd gone to work for Senator Talmadge, and then she'd met Dan. Since it had been so long, she'd looked Bischoff up on LinkedIn and Google. Since the CRS, he'd gone from researching hedge funds into setting them up, leveraging a modest family fortune into major holdings in FANGs and defense stocks. His nomination hearing had featured a partisan grilling over the extent of his divestitures, and at last he'd been disapproved for the deputy position. Instead he'd become chief of staff, which didn't require confirmation, but by all accounts he still made the decisions.

"You look great, Blair, just great. Not a day older."

"All this gray says differently. You're married, right? Kids?"

"Daughter and son." He'd gained weight and lost hair, but still had the same crooked smile. Actually, he kind of looked like Dick Cheney now. "You're married to that Navy commander, right?"

"He's an admiral now. In the Pacific."

"Really? Good on ya both. Yeah, I followed your campaign in the *Times*. I'd say I was sorry you lost, but really, we needed a fiscal conservative in Maryland. Whatever his . . . sexual preferences. And all in all, you can do more for us at Defense." He showed her to a chair. "Coffee? Tea?"

"Coffee. Thanks."

"Alexa: coffee. Large. Two, please."

"Coming up, Mr. Bischoff."

Blair was surprised to hear an active digital assistant in what she hoped was a secure office. But no doubt DHS had anticipated any possible leaks. Sol settled behind the desk. "Usually we don't do things this way. It's the old memo, meeting routine. Not that I'm not glad to see you! But I assume this is about defense business."

"In part. So thanks for the meeting. In my position, I get wind of developments across the country. And some of them lately disquiet me. From the point of view of workforce morale, primarily."

"Ready," Alexa said.

Bischoff got up and fetched the brews. "Cream? Sugar?"

She took cream. They sipped and were silent for a moment. Then she murmured, "Shall I continue?"

"If it impacts defense research, production, I need to hear it," he said. "Absolutely."

"All right, then. Some of my scientists suspect their offices are being monitored. That some of their assistants even report back to you."

He sighed. "I'm not privy to the specifics, but I wouldn't deny it. This is wartime, Blair. The enemy continually probes our cyberdefenses. Tries to intercept communications. You were on that plane that almost hit Los Alamos, correct? Someone slipped that Trojan horse into the flight control software. And they're still out there. So I shouldn't have to convince you of the danger."

"But . . . are you monitoring their families? Their personal computers?"

Bischoff shrugged. "If they give us reason to. Really, Blair, if we can penetrate their data clouds, the enemy can too. Rest assured, when we find a hole that could be exploited, we notify the agencies concerned."

She touched her lips lightly with a knuckle. Proceed carefully,

Blair. "Um, some of that's justified, Sol, I'm sure. And maybe we can justify drafting and expropriating anyone found without documents. But I also hear you're using the Defense of Freedom Act to round up political opponents. Are there really black prisons in Kansas and Indiana?"

Bischoff's eyebrows went up. He snorted. "Fake news, Blair. There's nothing like that going on. Rationing's working perfectly. Okay, scattered riots and minor looting here and there—but isolated, minor issues. This country's marching forward together."

Right, in lock-step, she thought. "And the Loyalty League. They aren't suppressing peaceful dissent?"

"The Leaguers are solid citizens," Bischoff said. "They accepted our confiscating their private weapons without objection."

"Which were then returned to them under federal deputization."

"The Mobilized Militia is constitutional. The Supreme Court says so. What's your objection?"

"That only League members got the weapons back. No one else."

"Because we can count on them." Bischoff shrugged again. "The M&Ms do useful work. Guarding defense plants. Enemy alien and D class ethnicity camps. The Zones of Concentration. And I'll underline once more that it's conducted under the president's war powers as granted by the Constitution. Passed in the DOFA, implemented in consultation with Congress, and approved by the courts."

"Yes, but—"

"Here's how it works." Bischoff sat forward, spread his hands. His tone went earnest. "Our fusion centers at DHS identify persons and organizations that may become inimical to the war effort. Oppositionists. Active seditionists. Hostile ethnic elements. The first step's the watch list. Once on the list, there's no employment in sensitive positions, no firearms, computer, or car purchases, no driver's licenses, and limited access to travel. Second step, the members and their families are taken into custody. They're assigned to remunerative, productive work in public-private partnerships, in locations that assure their security."

She tilted her head. "That *may become* inimical?"

"The exact wording of the Freedom Act. Or would you rather we left them at large until disaffection progresses to active treason? Work slowdowns? Sabotage? Bombings, like Indianapolis?" His face was turning red. "You do know there've been over three hundred domestic bombings so far this year? More than any year since 1968. If we hadn't kept the lid hammered down, some parts of this country would be in open revolt."

Perhaps that was true. But Blair couldn't help reflecting that this was how other governments, some of them infamous, had explained away their mass clampdowns, their targeting and elimination of anyone who disagreed. "Well, Sol, I'd feel more comfortable with some of these measures, if I really could be sure it was only for the duration."

"I see." Bischoff swiveled away to look out his window. The trees were a nearly solid canopy, a speckle of gold and green stretching away down to the Potomac. "Can I share my feelings about that? We've known each other a long time. I think you know you can trust me."

"Of course I can, Sol. I'm just not sure about some others in this administration."

"Including yourself?" He chuckled, then turned serious. "This country has been heading down the wrong road for a long time. Remember De Bari? His fucking firefighter buddies . . . his mistresses . . . it's been us against them ever since. And nothing ever got done, you know?"

She had to agree, at least in theory. "It's true, very little ever seemed to happen."

"And why? Because if any of our many problems actually got solved, there wouldn't be money flowing in anymore to push the ball this way or that. We were stuck at top dead center for a long time. Until this president."

"So what are you actually saying?"

He grimaced. "I'm saying, we can't go back to that kind of . . . free-for-all after this war. We have to march together, to get anywhere. And if that means snipping off the fringe elements, the nut jobs, the activists, well, so be it. The broad middle path, that's where this country has to go. All together. Forward as one."

Forward as One was that month's slogan. Taught in the schools, postered on billboards, flashed on every computer screen, repeated every five minutes on every talk and news show and government-approved blog. "Forward as one," she murmured.

"That's the spirit!" Bischoff beamed. "And seriously, Blair, if you want to keep playing . . . you need to reconsider your own position."

She gave him her most polite smile. "What exactly do you mean, Sol?"

He ticked points off on his fingers. "You're a smart girl, but you're still rooting for the wrong team. The president sees you as a holdover from the previous administration. Yeah, you're effective, hardworking. You contribute to victory, I guess. But really you're only on board because of Ed Szerenci. He brought you in, and he's the guy keeping you there. Now, this is only to be perfectly frank with you about what I hear. So when Ed goes in the dumpster, you'll go too."

"Is he headed there? I hadn't heard that."

"Nobody lasts forever, sweetheart. There are those who blame him for this war."

Blair couldn't contradict that; she'd been one of them, though she didn't think so now. Or at least, saw his share of blame as smaller than she once had. "So what are you telling me, really?"

Bischoff rolled his eyes, as if any fool could connect the dots. "Cross the aisle, Blair! You're pro-defense, right? Move from the right wing of your party to the left wing of ours. There's only really going to be one left after this war, anyway."

She said carefully, "But that sounds like what we're fighting, Sol. In China. Iran. Pakistan. The other one-party states."

Bischoff smiled. "History, Blair. Remember yours? Someone's raised the same old alarms in every war we've had. They called Lincoln a tyrant. Wilson, a dictator. When Roosevelt ran for a fourth term, they said he was becoming another Caesar. And FDR ran concentration camps too. Remember that."

Blair had to nod. "I do. Touché."

"If we're all rooting for the country, we need to work together. To win this war, then rebuild bigger and better. Forward as one?"

She almost said "As one," but stopped herself at the last moment. "It's certainly one philosophy, Sol. But I've always believed that the more noise and fuss, the more things are working the way they're supposed to. That when everything's quiet and serene, usually it just means someone's getting away with something."

The soft voice from the little speaker said, *"Time for your call with the secretary, Mr. Bischoff. I'll dial."*

"I used to believe that too." Bischoff gazed out the window again. "Back in high school. But seeing the way we can actually get things done now, it's changed my mind. Come over to us, Blair. Look to the future."

He cleared his throat. Pushed up, and came around the desk. He was shorter than she now. Had he always been? She couldn't remember. But the way he put his hand on her arm seemed all too familiar. He murmured, voice husky, "And, you know, we used to be—close. Your husband. You say he's . . . away?"

She took her arm back, out of reach. "Yes. He's overseas. Fighting."

He looked away. "Uh-huh. Sure. Well, just thought I'd ask. So, was there anything else?"

"I guess not." She stood, and suddenly wished for gloves, so she could pull them on. Or some other sweeping gesture, to draw a line. "I guess not. Thanks again for the meeting, Sol. If you can ask someone to see me out, I'll get off your desk."

HER aide briefed her on the report as they drove the narrow streets to the Suitland Parkway, then headed back toward center city. She made appropriate noises, but found it hard to concentrate. She tapped her knuckles to her lips as she stared out the green leafiness of the parkway. They tore across town on 695, through a ghostly emptiness where traffic had once roared. Before the refineries burned and the Cloud exploded. Before war had desolated the economy, and chopped the country apart like a cleaver.

She was wrestling with her angels.

In 1860, Secretary Cameron of the War Department had empowered Francis Blair to tender the command of the Union Army to Bobby Lee. His son Montgomery had served Lincoln as postmaster general, and his sons had continued the tradition as lawyers and politicians and generals.

By her generation, the connection was tenuous, but she'd always cherished that history. Public service was a family tradition. She'd hoped to continue it in the House.

Only now, was it still a tradition she should continue? Or would it be better, more honest, to quietly resign?

On the pro side: she'd be out of a government that seemed increasing focused on suppressing dissent. And Bischoff had reiterated a point she'd heard before: that politics were "different" now, that the old checks and balances were obsolete, wasted effort. A unified country . . . the phrase sounded good. But there was no way to unify a political entity as huge and varied as the United States. That had once been seen as a source of strength: that so many different interests, ethnicities, political viewpoints, could swear allegiance to one flag and Constitution, and, for the most part, get along.

Also on the pro side; spending more time at home, with her cat Jimbo and maybe, one of these days, with Dan. If everything worked out, if he made it home . . . this war had to end sometime. Didn't it?

Against resigning: now and again, she might serve as a moderating voice in a Pentagon that seemed increasingly hawkish as the tide of war turned. And how long would she actually feel fulfilled, at home with the cat, a cup of tea, and Jane Austen on audiobook?

She made a face. If she knew Blair Titus, not very long.

Her little motorcade turned off 395. Pros, and cons. Should she stay, in hopes of moderating Szerenci and the generals? Or resign, and try to salvage her reputation for a postwar run for Congress?

She touched the damaged ear, winced, shifted on her seat. Her bad hip flamed, as it always did when she spent too much time sitting. A reminder that America still had enemies other than China. That someone had to fight back. Defend the country, whether its enemies were without, or within.

"Be realistic, Blair," she whispered to her reflection in the window. It was too late for a postwar run. The antiwa wing of her party had tarred her unmercifully for participating at all. They'd never support her candidacy; she'd be slaughtered in the primary.

She didn't want to stay. But if she left, she'd be out in the cold.

There were no black-and-white answers. Not at her level.

"Also, Blair," the aide said, softly, as if unwilling to interrupt her brown study, "you got a call from overseas. From Ireland. No name given." She passed over a slip of paper.

Blair recognized the number. Liz McManus, from the previous year's UN meeting in Dublin. But she couldn't call back right now. And probably, if she replied at all, ought not to do so from an official phone.

She sighed as the car coasted to a halt for the security check at Lafayette Square. And put off the decision for one more day.

THE West Wing portico, once again. The same Walmart-style concrete planters, so cheaply and badly made she shuddered every time she saw them. She bent to a reader for a retina scan as the Marine guards patted down her aide. Then, surprising her, turned to her. "You too, ma'am."

She lifted her arms, staring at the ceiling as hands ran up and down her sides, felt the small of her back, and investigated, briefly, between her legs. Well, well. This was unexpected. Had some new threat been detected? Was the president becoming even more paranoid? Or had Sol passed along some kind of warning about her? She checked her watch, worried she'd be late. But at last she and the aide were shown through.

The Roosevelt Conference Room. She'd been here so often, during so many crises. This was the second meeting of the Szerenci-named Hostilities Termination Working Group. Today she would present the results of her DoD/State joint working group, and maybe, just maybe, some way forward might emerge. She got coffee, looked at a tray of pastries, but made a deliberate turn away. More and more often, rich, heavy foods made her feel ill.

The usual suspects were assembling, this time without the deputies who lined the walls in the meetings across the river, in the more capacious Tank. Heavyset, slow-moving Helmut Glee, the Army chief of staff. Gray, birdlike Absalom Lipsey, Joint Chiefs Operations. Rolling in in her wheelchair, Dr. Oberfoell, from the Office of

Cyber Security. Admiral Nick Niles gave a terse wave from across the room. Beside him was Jim Yangerhans, in command in the Pacific, Ricardo Vincenzo, chairman of the Joint Chiefs, and the bent back of Leif Strohm, the sickly, often absent secretary of defense. Blair crossed to shake Strohm's hand and ask about his health. That courtesy accomplished—she worked for him, after all, though Szerenci seemed to think otherwise—she nodded to the CIA rep, Tony Provanzano.

Then, as if attracted by some magnetic force, heads turned toward the door. Where a tall, gaunt, dark-skinned woman in a dark blue suit, red bow, white shirt, and dark skirt had appeared.

Dr. Swethambari Madhurika—"Swethi," as the mainstream media called her, or "Sweaty" to *Mother Jones* and the *Daily Kos*, before they'd been shut down—was a rarity in American politics, a first-generation immigrant. Her upswept hair was a dark, flat black. She carried through the forbidding look with one concession to femininity, large pearls at her ears. Arriving from India as a child, then practicing as a neurosurgeon, she'd built a biotech company that had IPO'd at two billion dollars. She'd entered politics in Florida, to become the first Hindu governor in the country. She'd built a reputation for ruthless pruning at HUD, cutting the staff by twenty percent while actually reducing homelessness, at least before the war wrecked everyone's plans. Her predecessor as White House chief of staff had self-destructed in a sexting scandal.

"The president asked me to sit in," she said in a husky timbre. She took a seat at the side of the table. "I won't be chairing. That will be the national security advisor. But we're hoping for concrete options. To move forward, together, and get this war behind us." She glanced at the empty chair at the head of the table. "And where is he?"

Szerenci appeared in the doorway just then, looking rumpled. "Helicopter was delayed," he muttered, and took his seat. He greeted everyone, then turned to Blair. "The war termination study. Ms. Titus, d'you want to kick off?"

She flipped open her folder. "The heads of state meeting in Jakarta outlined what the Allies would consider a satisfactory settlement of hostilities. That may or may not include what we typically think of as victory. A lot will depend on how far the enemy leadership's willing to go before admitting they can't continue the conflict.

"To reach that goal, while bearing in mind the necessity to avoid massive civilian casualties, and set the stage for a durable peace, the heads of state approved plans for the final military phase. With China and North Korea weakening, a decapitation strike was approved for Korea, with the possibility of a follow-on invasion should conditions warrant. The Indian army has taken Gwadar. Operation Rupture, the invasion of Hainan, will be under way shortly.

"Thus, a military solution may be in sight, if two of the opposed Powers—Korea and Pakistan—can be knocked out or persuaded to surrender. Iran can be dealt with later; we think they'll ask for terms once China capitulates. In the Gulf, we would lift the blockade and ease sanctions in exchange for cessation of hostilities and admission of UN or NPT teams to inspect for WMDs."

She took a breath. "That is, a *military* end is in sight. But that brings up new questions, that did not apply in any previous conflict. For what insight history and theory can bring to that issue, Professor Kevin Glancey, of Stanford."

She'd warned the historian to keep it to three minutes, and he nearly made that deadline. The thorniest problem, he said, remained. "There's no protocol for war termination between nuclear powers. Much less, for the goals the administration has set forth—regime change, stabilization, and regeneration under a democratic government. As Blair pointed out, what we used to regard as 'victory' may no longer be possible. And even if we achieve it, the results could be catastrophic."

He flicked a finger, and a graph appeared on the wall. "Note the steep, nearly asymptotic rise of risk as territory and allies are lost on one side. As that side is more seriously threatened, the possibility of escalation increases.

"The limited number of Chinese strategic missile submarines have already been sunk or bombed to uselessness in port. Our air defenses hem in their bomber force, which was never designed for penetration of robust defenses. The stumbling block remains: his land-based missile force. A cornered Zhang will be tempted to employ them to set red lines, to demolish Allied forces or US cities, or to essentially freeze the Allied advance in place."

"None of this is new," Szerenci observed. "You said the same thing at our last meeting. Unless you're telling us something useful, we're wasting our time here, Kevin."

Blair brushed her hair back over her damaged ear and hardened her voice. "The net here is perfectly clear, Ed. Unless and until we can disable those heavy missiles, the best we can hope for is stalemate. Not victory. Not peace. But the American public doesn't do stalemate. No matter how many people DHS puts behind barbed wire, we can expect the antiwa movement to grow."

The White House chief of staff lifted a hand. "Then . . . Blair . . . how *do* we end this war? Because to me, it sounds like you're saying we actually can't?"

No one stirred. Until Szerenci sighed. "Blair's put her finger on it, Swethi. Unless we can take those heavy missiles off the table there's no viable path to termination of hostilities with the central antagonist."

"And if we don't, or can't, disable them? Then what?"

Blair said, "Either a full-scale invasion of the Asian mainland, or return to the status quo ante bellum via an armistice."

"And renewed war in ten years, when the enemy recovers. Both impossible choices," Szerenci said. "Are we agreed on that?"

A hesitation, then nods and murmurs of agreement around the table.

Madhurika inclined her head as well. "All right. Both alternatives are unacceptable. So how do you plan to disable these missiles? Without bringing on central nuclear war?"

Dr. Oberfoell stirred in her wheelchair. "We discussed this at the last meeting. War Eagle may be able to disable command and control, now that Jade Emperor's toast. At least, we can slow their reaction time."

CIA said, "We're exploring an alternative with one of the senior generals. But to be frank, we doubt this will resemble the scenario in Iraq, where the regime largely crumbled from within."

Blair exchanged glances with Szerenci. She'd briefed him on her meeting in Dublin, just to be safe. He'd grumbled, but hadn't taken action against her. But neither, apparently, had he mentioned the other side's feeler to anyone else. She tensed, though, as he tapped a pencil on the table.

He said, "We've fought this entire war from a position of escalation inferiority. Which is why I've always advised the president against use of nuclear weapons. Even when they were used against us. Cost and danger rises with each rung up the ladder. And since Zhang had dominance, goosing the counterescalatory spiral meant we lost. Until now."

Szerenci turned his head, speaking now across the table directly to the White House chief of staff. "The president knows about the EP Heavy. Bigger than any previous ICBM, with four hardened earth-penetrating warheads of twenty megatons each. Accelerated on the way down with a Trident engine, the penetrators will punch through two hundred meters of granite. The harder the rock they encounter, the more destructive the shock wave they generate."

Madhurika said dryly, "So you can destroy China's strategic missiles in a first strike. You *think*. STRATFOR *thinks*. So the operative word is *maybe*. And we still have to be ready for an all-out nuclear exchange after that.

"So if they've squirreled anything away, mobile launchers we don't know about, or have a missile sub lying low we missed somehow—"

"There'll be risks," Szerenci said. "Of course. As I've said before, let's rid ourselves of illusion. That's how this war will end. With a nuclear exchange. The professor's told us, more than once: it's the only way it *can* end.

"But that's still my recommendation, and the recommendation of this working group."

He started to get up, and Madhurika's brow furrowed. She nodded to the chairman of the Joint Chiefs, to the secretary of defense. "Ricardo. Leif. You agreed to this?"

"I see no alternative," General Vincenzo said softly. "Unless we want to go into Asia, and fight it out there. With casualties possibly in the millions."

Beside him the secretary of defense coughed into a handkerchief. He nodded silently, suffering clear in his eyes.

Blair shuddered. Was about to object when the chief of staff said, "Assuming we do as you say, Ed. Then what happens?" She leaned in, looking at an Air Force general halfway down the table. The head of Strategic Forces. "Can you shed some light on that?"

The four-star cleared his throat. "Well . . . we used to play that scenario, in the old Global Thunder wargame. Back when we *did* have escalation dominance."

"The results?" Madhurika asked, sounding skeptical.

The general said soberly, "Every scenario we played went full central nuclear exchange."

"And your opinion of a first strike? Can we really take out those heavies?"

"It will be risky."

"Agreed. But, possible?"

"No one can answer that," the general said. "Ma'am. Too many unknown unknowns."

Madhurika pushed back from the table. She looked down it at Strohm. "Leif, you and I need to go in and see the president." She rose, and after a moment the secretary of defense, coughing, haggard, obviously near death, rose to follow her out.

AT home that night, in the house in Arlington, Blair carried her tea into the library and sank into the leather recliner. Dan's easy chair. Which he'd occupied all too seldom since they'd bought the house, though he'd built bookshelves . . . bought these books . . . she sipped and contemplated them. By now she knew what he liked. Every birthday and Christmas, the shelf grew a few volumes. Nonfiction, mostly, about history and faraway places, science and archaeology. But here and there, a novel too. Plus a whole shelf of stories of the sea. Marryat. Cooper. Melville. Conrad. De Hartog. Wouk. Reeman. Beach. Searls. Cornwell.

Would they really retire someday? Slippers, a crackling fire . . . It was hard to imagine. Neither of them were the type to sit around and relax. They'd both been made in some queer way, that forced them to hammer their heads against an obdurate world. Over and over again.

But now and then, maybe, they could make a dent in it.

There was the matter of her debt, too. Rampant inflation was softening its impact, but she still owed nearly a million dollars on her House campaign. Perhaps Archipelago or Zuza would offer her a board position. Or she could go into university administration . . .

The cat came in while she was fretting. "Jimbo, c'mere," she muttered, scratching the arm of the chair. Black and white, very fat, he seemed to think about climbing up to her lap for a moment, but gave up the effort and curled at her feet.

Forcing her to bend and lift him up. She stroked his back absently, sipping the tea now and then as it cooled. Contemplating, once again, her dilemma.

Stay, or go?

As if unwilling to confront it once again her mind gave her: Dublin. She'd never returned McManus's call. She sighed and reached for the phone. Then hesitated, hand hovering in midair.

Are you monitoring their families?

If they give us reason to.

But Szerenci knew the Chinese had contacted her. If this was what she thought it might be. He would back her up, if questions were raised. At least, she hoped so.

She glanced at the wall clock, then decided.

"Yes?" A sleepy voice.

"Hello. Ms. McManus? I'm returning your call."

Liz McManus, the Irish rapporteur and chairperson at the UN conference the year before. A former teachta dála, a congresswoman in American parlance, she'd led the Labour Party before retiring. *"Blair . . . oh yes. It's . . . six AM here, you know."*

"I'm really sorry, Liz. I just couldn't call before now."

"I understand how it can be. Believe me." A silvery chuckle, and her voice became more alert. *"You recall our conference in Dublin."*

"I do."

"We've evolved the monitoring team arrangement we set up last year. It will now be the the International Commission Against War Crimes and Genocide in Asia. Our next meeting will be in

Zurich. On the tenth. Do you think you could make room on your schedule?"

"Um, let me check my calendar." She called it up. Yes, two days free. Well, not free, but she could reschedule. "Yes. It might be possible."

"The handsome young man you met before may be there. And I understand he's still interested in you."

A misdirection, of course. The "young man" had been a member of the Chinese delegation. Their chat in a Dublin pastry shop had been inconclusive and off the record, but it *had* been a contact. A reaching out.

And if a back channel could be opened, it might offer a way forward. A way other than the full-scale nuclear attack that Szerenci, and now apparently Madhurika, were no longer just contemplating, but being driven to. Not by any excess of aggressive instinct, but by the inexorable logic of war.

Of course, it might also expose her to accusations of treason.

But given the stakes, a personal risk was worth taking.

"Are you interested? I can set it up. With him. Can you get to Zurich? If so, leave the rest to me. I know your friend Miss Salyers will be there, from your State Department. Perhaps you could attach to her mission?"

Ensconced in the comfortable chair, she lifted her hand from petting the cat. And was unsurprised to see her fingers trembling. Jimbo pushed his head into her palm, wanting more. Eyes closed, purring. Her palms were sweating. A hinge of history? Or the biggest mistake she would ever make? She had to force herself to say, "Um, I think so, Liz. I'll call Shira tomorrow. And see what can be done."

11

13°, 12' 46" N, 133° 46' 43" E; the Sea of Japan

H AMPTON *Roads* is on the screen, Captain."

"Very well." High on *Savo*'s bridge, Cheryl turned from contemplating the slow heaving of the Pacific at dawn.

Podded electric motors were driving them through an oil slick. It undulated languidly in the glinting sun, weaving tapestries of rainbow over the new cruiser's hull.

She frowned, stretching, easing her spine with fists pressed to her lower back. Could be a slow leakage from a wreck. Or from a subsurface well, abandoned with the outbreak of war. Or a sunken submarine, trapped and blasted apart in the deadly undersea minuet of sub against sub that had marked the conflict's opening months.

She stretched again, hearing disks pop, hoping *Savo Island* wouldn't add to that toll. She reached for a phone, then paused. New ship, new comms. Crossing instead to her seat, she swung up into the CO's chair, and pivoted a terminal into her lap. High-side chat, relayed via nanosatellite, was more secure than voice, and wouldn't betray their position.

Which lessened the chances of any missiles headed their way, as they approached the combat zone for the always tricky turnover of responsibilities. She spoke into the mike, watching the text scroll. The ship's AI was parsing each sentence. Testing whether her orders conformed to doctrine. If AALIS judged a communication out of bounds, or violated security, it would highlight it and sound a warning. If she sent it anyway, a copy went automatically to Higher.

Matador: to Monitor
Hold your bearing 285 60 miles

"Matador" had been the old *Savo*'s call sign, reassigned at Cheryl's request to the new cruiser. "Monitor" was USS *Hampton Roads*, a Tico-class that had stood missile watches in Westpac since the start of the war. Cheryl could have used her task group call sign, "Tangler," since she commanded the convoy, but judged it simpler to converse using the ship designator.

Monitor: to Matador
Have you as well, reciprocal. Plus four other contacts

Matador: to Monitor
Other contacts frigate, tanker, supply, tug. Request actual for
turnover

Monitor: to Matador
Stand by

Of course the ops specialists and combat systems controllers in CIC had been in touch. The two ships' Aegis systems had been linked for hours as *Savo* crossed the last degrees of longitude to their rendezvous. But there were the traditional courtesies to be exchanged, and maybe some local knowledge.

Monitor: to Matador
Actual on line. Hey Cheryl

Matador: to Monitor
Hi, Omar

Monitor: to Matador
Wish we could do this over a beer

Matador: to Monitor
Concur. Maybe someday. We are on scene RTR. Anything needs to
    be passed CO to CO?

The lines of glowing type unspooled rapidly from there, as if the other skipper was cutting and pasting from a prepared turnover statement. Before moving north to her current station, *Hampton Roads* had covered the Marine-Army landing on Taiwan, shielding it from ballistic missile attack. Moving north to the Sea of Japan, she'd guarded Tokyo and begun assembling intel for the upcoming strike. A list of shore missile batteries, radar sites, command nodes, and pre-identified mobile launcher locations had come in via a separate message, as well as being downloaded to *Savo*'s combat system over the nanonet.

A phone talker called, "Captain, CIC: USV holds intermittent contact bearing zero eight five, sixty thousand yards from own ship. Preliminary classification, marine life."

"Keep an eye on it," she muttered, typing.

Matador: to Monitor
Thanks. Any surface/subsurface threat activity in surveillance
    area?

Monitor: to Matador
Sporadic out of Busan

Matador: to Monitor
Anything from Russkis?

Monitor: to Matador
Heavy air activity attributed to announced exercise "Muscovy."
    Helicopter activity at Klerk training range in Primorye. Recon

flights over SOJ at least once a day out of Kamchatka. Usually
SU-24s

She scratched at an itchy patch under her collarbone, frowning.

Monitor: to Matador
Also of note. Via uncovered comm channel with the Russians.
    A General Yevgeney Sharkov keeps protesting what they call
    "intrusive radar probes." I told him we were operating in normal
    ABM scanning mode. But you know the problem

She did indeed. Any ICBM launched from either north China or
North Korea would overfly Russian territory during its boost phase,
before arching out to sea on its looping trajectory toward North
America. Adding a diplomatic problem to the already daunting technological issues. She hesitated, wiggling her fingers over the keys.

    "CO, CIC: Contact at zero eight four identified as whales."

    "Very well," she muttered. If only there were some way she could
tell the poor creatures to clear out, that very soon this whole sea
could be a radioactive soup. She clicked her screen to tactical, and
checked the formation.

    Savo and her shotgun escorts, USS *Sioux City* and ROKS *Jeon-
nam*, the other warships, and the tanker, tug, and containership
they escorted were paced and flanked by aerial drones. Autonomous Hunters loaded with sensors guarded their flanks against
submarines.

    Although, since the great battles in the central Pacific, few enemy
submarines were still at large. Blockaded and penned in, her navy
battered to pieces, China was smoldering. Dangerous, but no longer
pushing outward, as Admiral Lianfeng had once planned for his Second Phase Offensive.

    Now it was time to start kicking in the doors.

    The biggest ship she was escorting was an expeditionary trans-
port. It toted fuel and hovercraft in the hull of a civilian supertanker,
with a flight deck for helicopters, Ospreys, and F-35s. It would serve

as a floating base for the smaller units it accompanied, Sealift Command Spearhead-class catamarans. Austere but fast, they were built to support deep strikes by special forces. The hospital ship, converted from a Carnival cruise liner, and the tanker traveled within a protective screen.

Which it now would shed, as she transitioned from convoy commander back to the antiballistic missile role, under the operational control of Seventh Fleet.

"I'll be in the Citadel," she said, and headed for the elevator.

SHE stopped at her inport cabin, dry-bolted an antihistamine, and rubbed cortisone cream into her hands and under the neck of her coveralls. The skin there was erupting, red, bumpy, and peeling. The itch was maddening. If she let herself, she'd scratch down to bloody bone. Even four applications a day barely kept it under control.

When she settled in at the command desk, the left-most display had the geoplot up. She glanced back at the VR helmet racked behind her, but decided to stay with the bulkhead screens for now.

To the west, the eastern coast of the Korean Peninsula was freckled with rugged mountains. To the east lay Honshu, the main island of Japan. To the north, Korea butted up against a tiny slice of Russia, right at the seacoast. And farther north from there stretched the enormous, valley-furrowed wastes of Asiatic Russia, degree on degree of latitude reaching nearly to the Pole. To the south, Taiwan was out of *Savo*'s organic sensor range, but visible through the data feeds.

She watched for the next two hours, occasionally interjecting a suggestion as Mills, her exec, disentangled the steaming formation. The tug and hospital ship headed south, accompanied by most of the USVs. The transport, tanker, and the Fast Transport EPFs headed for a Japanese port, escorted by *Benfold. Savo Island* and *Sioux City* continued for Ballistic Missile Oparea "Aleph," where they would rendezvous with *Hampton Roads* and her escort for the turnover.

The comm officer came by with AREPS data. She studied this carefully, asking him the occasional question. AREPS were like weather reports for sensor propagation conditions. They decided the port after panel needed a groom. Meanwhile she kept up with the nanochat, shuttling between rooms but mainly keeping tabs on the pri channel, which kept her in the loop with Fleet, local task groups, and the building strike group. Her other prime link was with Colorado Springs, Fort Greeley, and Tokyo via the GMD Combined Missile Defense network.

An hour out from the official relief, she checked her watch.

Time for the conference.

There hadn't been a physical sit-down for Operation Chromite, since Pearl was still digging out from the damage and Guam was too dangerous to group ships at. Earlier in the war, Allied communications had been compromised by Chinese intrusion and spoofing, aided by a master AI. But of late the word had gone out that the enemy AI had been crippled, though with no further explanation, and that nanochat and nanovideo communications were secure again.

The Skype-like screens in the little video teleconferencing space next to CIC would have to serve. They were bandwidth-limited, with a low refresh rate, but gave at least the illusion of others in the room.

She beckoned to an enlisted at the ABM consoles. A small, meek-looking young woman who seemed too cherub-faced for the insignia on her collars. "Terror, I mean, Petty Officer Terranova, I'd like you in on this. In the VTC, now." Then she called the ops office, asking the operations and comm officers to join her as well.

IN the little VTC space, chairs in front of a large display. Terranova, at the coffeemaker, asked if anyone else wanted a cup. Cheryl shook her head, getting ready to take notes.

But the teleconference opened with a junior briefer instead of the operations deputy. *"The admiral's been delayed. I'll fill in with a refresher,"* she began.

Mills sighed and sat back. He, Terranova, and Branscombe took out their cells—they all had skin-of-the-ship service—and began scrolling through their in-boxes. Cheryl resisted the temptation. If anyone had to pay attention to the big picture, it was the CO.

"After the nuclear attacks on USS Roosevelt *strike group,"* the on-screen briefer said, *"Our antimissile capabilities were relayered. But the strike on Pearl Harbor showed there were still holes holes in our coverage. We scrambled to make it more robust, but our production base is still crippled by cybersabotage, strikes, and antiwa activities. Technological challenges remain as well."*

A chart of the western Pacific came up behind the briefer, like a met chart on the Weather Channel. *"Our forward-deployed ABM Afloat ships are the first barrier between the enemy and the homeland. They're tasked with detection, cueing, and reporting track data to the Combined Missile Defense system. That's aggregated with information from our allies, the nanosatellite network, and the SBX seaborne early warning radars. Alerts and data go to the Midcourse Defense interceptors in Alaska and California, and to the THAAD and Patriot batteries that protect major West Coast cities."*

Cheryl took out her own cell. This was a PR backgrounder, not a pre-operation brief. Why were they wasting time on this? Oh yeah. The admiral was late.

A video of ships under way replaced the briefer, but she continued. *"Currently in theater are* Hampton Roads, Monterey, *and* Monocacy, *the last Ticonderoga-class antimissile cruisers. Along with the ABM-capable later-flight Burkes, USS* Lyndon Johnson *and* Michael Monsoor, *and the Japanese ABM-capable destroyers of the Kongo class, they've been relieving one another on station, turning over at one-month intervals. However, both ships and crews are operating at reduced states of readiness and lower than desirable manning and ordnance levels."*

Beside Cheryl, Matt Mills uncrossed his legs. Cheryl cleared her throat and lifted a hand. "I don't see *Savo Island* on your list, Commander."

The briefer nodded. *"You will the moment you take station, Captain Staurulakis. Your increased radar range, and your wide net of deployed and networked sensors, will be very welcome. Along with a fresh crew as we begin the operation."*

"We're glad to help, but when are we going to get to that?" Crisper than she meant to make it, but she let it hang.

The briefer looked off-camera. *"Oh . . . The J-3 . . . here he is. Thank you for your attention. And best of luck. Here is Admiral Enders."*

The Seventh Fleet J-3 was bull-chested and gray-mustached, of a vintage with Cheryl's former commanding officer, Lenson. *"COs and other senior officers, welcome,"* he said. *"You've all studied the plan. We suffered a lot of damage here, but enough capacity survived in the Bunker to generate it. It'll entail risk, and we anticipate losses, but we think it'll work.*

"Make absolutely sure relevant personnel are clear on all three phases: approach, strike, and withdrawal. A frag order will go out in about six hours. Last-minute updates. So I'll limit myself to general remarks and cautions.

"Chromite will be our major attack on Korea. The second big raid on the Asian mainland, and an all-out attempt to knock one of our most dangerous enemies out of the war. We'll put the Marines and the special ops teams ashore and support and cover them until they're ready to retire. It will be kinetic. And bloody. But it has to be done.

"At the very least, even if we miss the prime targets, we'll reassure the exiled government of the Republic of Korea that the Allies haven't forgotten them. And the captive population of South Korea that, eventually, we will come to their rescue.

"At best, we knock one of the Opposed Powers out of the enemy coalition. In any case, we should pull mainland Chinese forces to the north, distracting them from an offensive being planned elsewhere."

Cheryl nodded. Where "elsewhere" was going to be, exactly, she didn't know, and didn't want to.

"The major difficulty in striking Korea has always been their ICBM force. It's not large, but they've threatened us with it for years. We backed away from dealing with it, since they threatened launch on warning. But since we've got the forces generated and in theater, the administration's given us the go-ahead to take it out for good.

"We'll depend on a tactic called AEI, autonomous early intercept, to inhibit their strategic strike capabilities." A computer animated

video replaced the J-3, a contractor logo still visible in the lower corner. *"In advance of the strike force, a swarm of Trugon UAVs controlled by uprated Marauder drones and microsatellites will blanket the battlespace with a sensor net. Once they detect launch, either by visual observation of the launch platform or the infrared booster plume, they pass the information up the kill chain. If detection occurs early, a modified Hellfire takes it down in the boost phase. If not, cueing will pass to USS* Savo Island, *in the Sea of Japan, for a shoot-look-shoot engagement in the pre-apogee arc of trajectory. Past that, it will be up to ground-based interceptors in the United States."*

Petty Officer Terranova leaned over. She murmured, "Ask him about Space-X, Skipper."

She blinked. "About what? No."

"Come on, Skipper, ask. There's somethin' up the-ah in a low polar orbit, and it's big. Radar signature like the side 'a a barn. It has an orbital number and it's in the NORAD catalog, but the-ah's no other parameters. Nanochat from back east, scuttlebutt about somebody lofting a private interceptor."

She said unwillingly, "Cheryl Staurulakis, sir, USS *Savo Island.* Admiral, we're picking up a large unidentified object in polar orbit. Can you give us anything on that?"

"No," Enders said. *"That's a firm neither-confirm-nor-deny. Clear enough, Captain?"*

"Yessir, we copy," she said, shooting a furious glance at Terranova. She quirked her eyebrows and slid down in her chair.

Another officer, in a box on her screen, raised a finger. Enders acknowledged him with a nod. *"General."*

"Quick question. What's Moscow's take on this? Some of the locations we're tasked to hit are only ten, twenty miles from the border."

"And the prevailing winds blow north," Mills muttered, beside her.

Enders glanced off-camera. *"Jack, want to take that? Mr. Byrne is one of our civilian advisors."*

The scene panned to a sun-tanned, stunningly handsome civilian in short sleeves. Despite herself Cheryl couldn't help staring. His features were perfectly regular. But his eyes were hidden behind tinted glasses.

Byrne said, *"Moscow's warned us they won't look kindly on military actions close to their border. But will they intervene? Tough to judge intent, but the consensus of the community is they won't, unless we actually infringe on their airspace. The Russians are making major money out of this war. Selling aircraft, radars, ordnance, to replace Chinese losses.*

"But Zhang's growled at them too, in the past couple years. Threatened to take back territory China lost to the tsars. Essentially, blackmailed them into providing weapons on credit. There's no way he could've paid for what he's been buying. We wrecked China's economy."

"Like they wrecked ours," Terranova observed sotto voce. Mills made an impatient *keep it down* gesture at her.

Enders put in, *"The frag order I mentioned directs all aircraft, drones, and ordnance to hold south of the 42nd Parallel. Well clear of the border."*

Byrne added, *"And we've advised General Sharkov backchannel that's what we intend to do. No answer seems to equal no objection. So as long as we can stand clear . . ."*

Cheryl didn't want to comment again, but had to. "If we have to intercept a launch, it may be over Russian territory. Or their territorial sea, west of the Kamchatka Peninsula. Has that been raised with this Sharkov?"

Byrne looked to the admiral; Enders looked down. Finally the latter muttered, *"That'll be a decision for Higher."*

What the hell? She couldn't help it; her tone rose. "Sir, we won't have time to check in. I'll have maybe fifteen seconds warning. Can you please furnish some guidance?"

"We'll get back to you on that, Captain." Now Enders's tone was frosty.

She caught Mills's warning glance. Well, to hell with it. If they didn't want to back her up . . . she'd seen how Dan Lenson operated. Do what you have to do, worry about consequences afterward.

"I'd like to end with a caution," Enders said. Beside him, Byrne

and the Air Force general nodded agreement. *"This is direct from Indo-PaCom himself. This will not be a rollover. This enemy's been indoctrinated for three generations that we're devils coming to enslave them. We can expect suicide attacks. Mass assaults. Maybe, weapons we've never seen before. Stay alert, observe the rules of engagement, keep us informed."*

The central screen went blank, showing only the Command logo of an enraged eagle, its cruel beak facing west, its outstretched wings shadowing half the globe. One by one, the feeds around it blinked and went dark.

Cheryl blinked too, caught herself scratching, and snatched her hand away.

"Time for turnover, Skipper," Mills said. "And for COMOPS."

"Set the ABM watch, XO," she told him. "And let everybody know what the admiral said. This won't be a walkover. We've got to bring our game to this one."

"You should tell 'em yourself, Skipper. Get on the horn and tell the crew."

She grimaced, acknowledging he was right. They needed to hear it from her.

After all, their lives would be in her hands. If she made the wrong decision, or just as bad, the right decision two seconds too late, everyone aboard could die. Instantly, or slowly, in the weeks to come, in the slow agony of radiation poisoning.

Or even worse: If *Savo* failed in her mission—if she and the entire complex system of systems backing her up and supporting her failed to intercept the weapons an unpredictable despot had aimed at the homeland—hundreds of thousands would die back home.

The responsibility weighed in her gut like a wintry-cold rock. Was probably what drove her neck to ache, her very skin to itch, flake, and burn, rebelling against the weight of how much they depended on her.

But there was no evading it.

For good or ill, she was the Captain.

12

Seattle

THE Archipelago campus drowsed in a heat wave. No one strolled the shaded pathways. No one had spread blankets, to picnic down by the ponds. Below Nan Lenson's window, the treetops were turning brown. Without rain for weeks, the greensward was desiccating as well. A silver rain pulsed in one quarter of the square, jetting water over the victory garden some of the junior researchers had put in, yet it too was wilting. The tennis courts baked in the sun, empty of players. How many months since she'd held a racquet . . . At the far end, almost obscured by the trees, an empty carousel rotated, its decorative mirrors flashing in the sunlight.

Nan turned from the view toward the two men who'd just brought her a sealed envelope. They weren't military, though they wore uniforms. Blue, with a gray wolf's-head patch. The manila envelope was striped with red, and stamped TOP SECRET. "We'll need a signature, Doctor," one said. When she handed their tablet back they nodded, the taller one glancing at her legs. He thanked her gravely and they left.

She examined the envelope. Addressed not to her, but to Dr. Anton Lukajs. She unsealed it anyway. They were on the same team, after all.

She read through the cover sheet.

And smiled. A victory, but in a different battle than the current war.

Though she really should read the entire report—and intended to—just scanning the summary told her the most important fact.

The new drug worked.

It didn't have a formulary name yet. So far they just called it LJL 4789, after Dr. Lukajs, Dr. Jhingan, and herself. With unpleasant, occasionally fatal side effects, cyclophosphamide wasn't what you wanted as an antiflu drug. But Archipelago's massively powerful AI had suggested a subtle reformulation, adding a complex molecule to interrupt the virus's reproductive cycle.

And it had worked. The first cells the virus infected would still die, of course. Like most influenza strains, Flower infiltrated via nose and eyes. The virions reprogrammed the cells that lined the respiratory system. This triggered the primary immune system to produce cytokines and chemokines—proteins that attacked viruses. Meanwhile, the secondary immune system was designing custom T cells primed to destroy that specific invader.

This secondary response triggered the fever, chills, and congestion the sufferer noted. But the virus proceeded more stealthily, subverting the body's cells in a steadily accelerating chain reaction.

If the T cells and cytokines won the race, the patient lived. If they lost, he died. But the virus itself, a selfish gene if ever there was one, lived on, sprayed out by the millions with each cough, sneeze, or secretion.

LJL 4789 blocked the neuraminidase protein, limiting Flower's ability to replicate. The patient would still fall sick. But the body could clear up the damage much faster. And most likely, since the T cells would activate, be protected against reinfection from then on.

A magic bullet? Not quite. Asklepios had predicted low toxicity, high activity, and high solubility, all necessary to enhance delivery within the body and minimize side effects. But the drug's heat sensitivity meant it would break down rapidly in nonrefrigerated storage. Not to complete uselessness, but it would reduce biochemical activity.

Still, all that aside, the reviewing authorities had judged it worth testing.

And the results had just come in.

THE old man was outside, under one of the arbors, invisible from above. A small bottle and a glass sparkled beside him on the bench.

Artificial bees buzzed from flower to flower. The tiny drones were programmed to replace the ranks of natural ones decimated by lowered protein percentages in pollen—a consequence, researchers said, of increased carbon dioxide in the air. The lead virologist sat quietly, staring into the distance. His wispy white hair stirred in the hot breeze. He looked more emaciated than ever. A drone hovered before his eyes, inspected motionless, age-spotted hands, then moved on about its business.

"Dr. Lukajs."

"Dr. Lenson." He bowed courteously and made room on the bench. Gestured at the heat-blown roses drooping above them. "Do you know, my grandfather used to sit like this, a glass of wine lasted all afternoon. Debinë, he liked. A sweet white wine. This from California, it does not taste as well. I did not understand back then how he could sit and do nothing. I wanted to act, to study, learn, work for the People. He would just smile at me." Lukajs waved away a real bee, or a drone that looked like one. "Now I understand him, I think. I would offer you some but only the one glass."

"That's all right, sir. We have test results. From Dr. Jhingan."

"Ah, the study." A shadow shaded the old man's pale watery gaze. "You will tell me? My eyes tire from the screens, these days." He poured himself another tiny glass and sat back, eyes sinking closed.

She read, "'This study describes the results of a chemotherapeutic strategy for Central Flower subtype virus infection in humans. A combination of the primary agent and a pretreatment regimen to reduce hematologic damage generated increased survival rates in test subjects. In controls, challenge with an infectious-level dose of the highly pathogenic, wild-type North Vietnamese strain resulted in uniform infection, 42% of whom progressed to death in less than one week.

"'In contrast, over 84% of treated subjects were asymptomatic for one month, with no detectable virus after one week. Of the remaining treated subjects, 15% progressed to infection but recovered, and one patient died.

"'These findings demonstrate that LJL 4789 is effective against the specified virus infection in human subjects.'"

She paused, waiting for his reaction. But he didn't speak. The wineglass glittered untouched beside him.

At last he murmured, "'Forty-two percent of whom progressed to death.' This makes you smile?"

She cocked her head, confused. "The mortality rate tracks with what CDC reported."

"So nearly half of the controls died."

"Yes, Doctor."

"We infected them, in the tests. They would not have died otherwise."

She bent her head, feeling it like a sudden icicle thrust under her breastbone. Understanding, now, what he was referring to. She'd known it too, but had suppressed the fact somehow. Denied it, even to herself. "Uh, yes. That's right."

"And who were these subjects?"

"Dr. Jhingan says they were volunteers."

"From the camps, yes? From what you call the Zones."

She didn't answer. Couldn't. She waited as he blinked off into the distance.

"So we are not so unlike *them*, in the end," he said softly, as if to himself.

AFTER a discussion of the results, the afternoon meeting proceeded to an overview of the way forward. No one mentioned the deaths of the control subjects, or the conditions in which the tests had been carried out. As if they'd made a tacit agreement to overlook that unpleasant topic.

Mike Consiglio, their program manager—Lukajs was the team leader on the medical side, but he avoided administration—wore a white coat, probably to make him look like a doctor, though he wasn't. Some kind of medical administration degree out of Purdue. He laid out the milestones. Peacetime procedure included filing a new drug application, with review by a team of physicians, statisticians, and pharmacologists from CDER. This would be short-circuited now. BARDA was cleared to begin trial production, which would be subcontracted to manufacturers. Consiglio portioned out tasks to the rest of the team: developing labeling, dosage forms and guidance, production oversight.

He smiled at Nan. "The first batch will be produced by Qwent Pharma, over in Tukwila. Dr. Lenson, would you act as our liaison?"

Nan frowned, chasing an errant memory. "Mike, isn't . . . wasn't the Qwent plant the one FDA sent a warning letter? About contamination from the pesticides they make?"

Consiglio looked away. "Phosphamides are a pretty common ingredient in insecticides. ThanaPest. B-110. It breaks proteins, I understand, like LJL does."

"Don't meddle with the biochemistry, Mike," Dr. Jhingan said. But grinned, to take the edge off.

Consiglio said, "But since that warning, the production lines have been hived off in a separate area of the plant." Nan started to protest, but he waved her silent. "That's why we picked a nearby facility, Doctor. So we could keep a close eye on things like that."

"They were also lowest bidder, yes?" Lukajs put in.

"They say they can grow production tenfold within two months. If that doesn't work, AstraZeneca and Roche are gearing up too. The target is a hundred thousand doses in two weeks, a million by the end of next month, scaling up to ten million a month. Based on CDC rate-of-spread estimates, even if Flower hits the US at full lethality, we should be able to save over eighty percent of the population." He eyed Nan. "If you see a problem once you inspect, let me know immediately. Further questions?"

There were none. Consiglio flipped to the next paper on his clipboard. "All right, a related question. About whether we publish."

"Do we *publish*?" Lukajs burst out. "Of course! What kind question is that?"

"A delicate one, Anton, given our funding stream. Merck and AbbVie are pushing for publication, massive production, and wide distribution. On humanitarian grounds. And those of profit, of course. But remember, under the Defense of Freedom Act industrial profits are limited and subject to confiscation."

"What's DoD's position?" one of the younger team members wanted to know.

The project leader faced him. "They advise against. They gave me as an example, the restriction on distribution of penicillin during World War II. To keep it secret from the Germans."

The team exchanged glances. "I didn't know we'd done that," Nan said. She turned to the old scientist. "Dr. Lukajs?"

The old man bent his head and didn't answer. Well, he wasn't going to be any help. She said evenly, "Well, I think we should publish. What about the Africans, Europeans? Indians? We already have reports of a locus of infection in Delhi. They have a huge generic industry. Are we providing this information to them?"

"That's not in our hands," Consiglio said.

Nan shook her head. "Whose is it in, then, if not ours? The discoverers publish."

The manager smiled. "I'll make this simple, Dr. Lenson. We're barred from releasing *any* information about this drug without specific permission. Under the penalties set forth in the DOFA for defense-specific intellectual property."

"This isn't a weapon," Dr. Han said. Nan looked at him; he was usually so silent.

Consiglio pointed at him. "Doctor. You, *specifically*, are enjoined from *any* communication on the topic. As someone in a D-classified ethnicity. I would expect anything you say, record, or transmit to be monitored." He looked around the table. "And I hate to say it, but that applies to everyone here. Each and all of us could be prosecuted for disclosure of classified information relating to national security. Everything about this drug, and the tests, is top secret. Including the fact it exists.

"Jenny will bring the forms around to sign. Just to make clear everyone understands."

"I will not sign," Lukajs muttered, but Consiglio ignored him. As if the chief of the team—the winner of the Warburg Medal for molecular biology—Had. Not. Spoken.

WHEN they broke up she went back to her desk. The research offices were open plan. Privacy was a long outmoded concept at Archipelago. She opened her email, but instead of keyboarding hovered her fingers over it, staring into the blank template.

Her first impulse was to reach out. Ask for advice. But from whom? Her dad was in the middle of the war. Hadn't answered her last two emails. Even when he did, sometimes it took days. She couldn't bother him with this. And probably shouldn't get him involved, if she did something illegal.

Should she go public? Up until now, the threat had been banishment to the Zones. But now people were being shot for treason. For anything deemed to be "impeding the war effort." The first execution had been carried live on the Patriot Network last month. A defrocked priest who'd cut through a fence and sliced a tire on a fighter plane.

And she'd just been served with a warning against disclosing the very existence of the drug, let alone its chemistry or efficacy.

Well, what about Blair? She was well connected. Actually, a member of the administration, though she'd come to it from the opposing party. Which was now far from power, with anyone who mentioned it favorably online immediately piled on by paid trolls, flagged by DHS, added to the List, and probably due for a "friendly visit" by the local Loyalty League.

No. Not the Honorable Ms. Titus. She was part of it now.

She felt ashamed for even thinking it. But the country was splitting, like a malignant cell. Its always-present legacy evils metastatizing. The way it had been during Vietnam, she'd read. But that had been long before she'd even been born.

She rubbed her face, a gesture she only seconds later remembered had been a tic of her dad's when confronted with some painful decision. Such as whether to punish her for riding her new bike through a stop sign, the summer she'd stayed with him and Blair.

No. It was up to her.

She had to decide on her own. To "adult," as her friends at school used to put it.

Okay, as Lukajs always said, formulating the question correctly was half the answer . . . Was withholding a medical treatment from

a hostile power defensible as a means of war? She remembered Consiglio had mentioned penicillin, and went online to check that out.

A few minutes later she nodded, closing Firefox's Incognito window.
In World War II, the very existence of the antibiotic had been kept
secret from the enemy.

According to the news, today the Allies were fighting hard somewhere in Asia. Hundreds of thousands of troops were risking their
lives. Including her dad and his friends. The woman who'd been his
second in command had his old ship now. Once she'd wondered if
Staurulakis and her dad were getting it on. She really doubted it. But
the way they'd looked at each other . . . No, forget that, she was avoiding the issue.

So. Cooperate, or resist? Sometimes you had to swallow your misgivings. Toe the line.

But . . .

Her dad. He'd disobeyed orders sometimes. When he thought they
were wrong, or that he could accomplish the mission with fewer
casualties. But knowing him, he'd thought about it first. Thought
deeply, and reasoned it out.

Something he'd said once. *The right way isn't always the easy
way. But nobody else can tell you the right one. That, you have to
figure out for yourself.*

And: *It's only when you stop doubting that you can be certain
you're wrong.*

She shivered, realizing how difficult it must have been for him all
these years, to have lives depend on what he decided.

The way so many lives might turn on what choice she made now.

AN hour later the department secretary brought the security forms
around. But by then the younger members of the team were coordinating by text to meet out on the quad.

They convened near the heart of the campus, by one of the pergolas. The carousel was playing oom-pah-pah music, the carillon ring-

ing out, echoing from and imprisoned by the vast enclosing circle of the building. But Nan felt nervous. On edge. The tiny drones kept up a steady buzz all around them. They were supposed to be for plant pollination. But she had no doubt some had different purposes. Fitted with cameras. Facial recognition. Microphones. Maybe even video-to-speech. Archipelago had AIs that could lip-read.

The younger members of the team looked to her. Crap, she thought, biting her lip. How had *she* become the leader? Of this mini insurrection?

"Let's take a ride," she said at last. Then turned, and led the way to the noisy, cheerful carousel.

III

WHO FIGHTS
FOR FREEDOM

13

The Sea of Japan

TWENTY-four hours straight so far, locked down in *Savo*'s Citadel. Relieved, when Cheryl absolutely had to take a break, by Mills, or one of her tactical action officers.

Over the days on station the darkened cavern of the Combat Information Center had seemed to expand, to swell, growing larger than a hull could possibly contain. Cheryl's own consciousness had expanded too, each time she settled the helmet over her head, plugging in to the artificial overmind that contemplated a hemisphere like an antecreational God brooding over the landless ocean.

Hanging in the air, her avatar looked down on a virtual world, created and reinterpreted by an intelligence far greater and infinitely faster than her own.

The large screen displays were still up. But she didn't need them. The helmet/headset weighted her shoulders. Screens dominoed her eyes. A fan streamed cool air on the back of her neck. She could check own ship status as well, from the condition of every space and pump to the remaining weapons in the deep magazines. Developed from the helmet-mounted displays of fighter planes, with enhancements by Oculus and Sony, the VR screens before her eyes showed the entire battlespace, as sensed by satellite, ground-based radar, and her own ship sensors, deconflicted and reinterpreted as to threat level.

She floated in space, contemplating like Zeus an enormous blue tabletop scored with latitude and longitude lines and layered with shaded altitude readouts. With a flick of her eyes radio and radar transmissions appeared in coruscating curtains of delicate jade, violet, and indigo, wavering and fluttering like a Van Gogh sky. Neutral, friendly, and hostile contacts registered in standard symbology, though she could toggle to downlinked video from drones, or direct view when they were in line-of-sight range. If she glanced down she could see "through" the hull, to the irregular, rocky bottom over a thousand fathoms below.

She was barely conscious of her ass in the chair, of her hands resting lightly on the armrests.

Over the horizon, the strikes were going in.

The missiles had launched first, some from *Savo* and the other surface ships. But the majority had been barrage-fired from Ohio-class SSBNs off the coast, and attack boats USS *Arkansas*, *Idaho*, *North Carolina*, and *John Warner*. Slipping in low, accelerating to hypersonic speeds, they'd drilled in on antiaircraft missile batteries, intelligence fusion centers, power plants, radio and television stations. But most were concentrated on two points: the sole over-the-horizon radar the North Koreans possessed, outside Wonsan, and their command centers in Pyongyang.

She watched entranced as rapidly pulsing bright ruby trails marched inexorably down. Descending from exoatmospheric trajectories, three warheads preplaced in orbit by Delta IV Heavy boosters were burning their way downward. Both the Chinese and Russians had been notified minutes before. But along with that, the approach angles had been calculated so as to make it obvious that neither nation's core strategic forces were being targeted.

They were over *Savo* now, converging inexorably on the Hermit Kingdom's most vulnerable points.

Mills's voice in her ear. "Standing by to go Shitstorm proof."

"Do it," she said into the throat mike. "EMPcon Charlie. Come to optimal course. Slow to ten. Make sure the rest of the formation rogers the warning. *Jeonnam. Sioux City.* Double check all UAVs are on deck, shut down, and hangared. All USVs submerged below sixty feet."

"Already put that out, Skipper." Was that a hint of irritation in his voice? Well, better to micromanage a bit, than leave her people exposed to what was about to happen.

The pulsating red lines stretched relentlessly onward.

The ship tilted beneath her. The world whirled as *Savo* swerved on her heel to course 095. The results of the tests off Kauai, during their workup, had been clear: this class would ride out an electromagnetic pulse best bow-on to it. This course pointed her directly at Wonsan. That city, hub of the eastern coast's defenses, was almost three hundred miles distant. But even that far away, *Savo* would feel the effects.

The pulsing red line had almost reached its target, the mountain command post just east of Pyongyang. She scribed a distance and ran the numbers in her head. One minute remaining. Back to the throat mike. "All right, XO. Shut her down."

The displays before her eyes flickered and died. She boosted the helmet off her shoulders. At the same moment the large screen displays at the front of CIC went dark. The consoles behind her powered down, the fans whirring off to silence. The air-conditioning hissed to a halt, leaving only the creaking of steel in a seaway. The distant thud of a hatch being dogged. A strange, lonely, haunting creaking, like the baffled protest of an abandoned mansion buffeted by the wind.

"*CIC, DC Central: EMP condition Charlie set,*" the old-style 21MC in front of her reported. It reminded her to reach down and shut off her own Hydra, her portable radio, and power off her cell. Probably protected already by the Faraday box of *Savo*'s hull, but why take the risk.

She looked at her watch. Just about *now* . . .

The overhead lights flickered, shading a deep blue for just the fraction of a second; then came back on to bright white. With a muted clicking, relays cycled like crickets in the fall. "Heavy EMP pulse," called the petty officer at the electronic warfare console.

She whipped her head around. "You were supposed to be offline—"

The petty officer looked startled. "Uh, that's from the detector, Captain. It stays online during Charlie."

"Oh, right. Sorry." She looked at her watch again. The first burst, right on time. The second should follow any moment now.

The weapons, predicted theoretically for years, had only recently been achieved. By an ad hoc team of nuclear program retirees and fusion experts, gathered at Lawrence Livermore after the labs at Los Alamos and Sandia had been laid waste by cyberjacked jetliners.

A nuclear-pumped electromagnetic pulse bomb.

She'd been briefed about this before leaving the States. Not in detail, but enough so that the commanding officers could protect themselves, and understand what would be happening ashore.

Along with blast, heat, and radiation, nuclear detonations produced stupendous waves of electromagnetic energy. The enormous gamma output "ruptured" the earth's magnetic field. Traditional nukes only converted about one percent of their energy into the pulse. But Sandia had reverse-engineered the most massive bomb the United States had ever produced, the 1950s Mark 15, and modified it to convert half its fifteen-megaton yield into electromagnetic disruption.

At three locations, over Wonsan, Pyongyang, and the northern mountain complex that Intel estimated sheltered Kim's deployable ICBMs, the action she'd heard called unofficially "Operation Shitstorm" was going into effect. Over the space of two minutes, every unshielded circuit in North Korea—every transmission line, radio, generator, radar, anything else that used metallic wiring—were being subjected to a power surge of tens of thousands of volts, at an amperage so massive it would jump air gaps, fry electronics, even melt transformer windings inside their casings.

"Second pulse," the EW operator announced over the command net. *"Less pronounced than the first. Call it as more distant."*

"That'll be Pyongyang," she told Mills. "One more, and we're home." A wave front hammered by that much energy would penetrate hundreds of feet of rock, short-circuiting missile guidance systems, launch equipment, even the starter wiring of the logging trucks the NKs depended on to haul their transporter-erector-launchers out of the tunnels for firing. But they had to be carefully timed, to avoid frying their own microsatellites as they swung overhead. Sizzle one, and their battlespace picture would be degraded. Electrocute two or three, and Chromite itself could be at risk.

The seconds ticked by.

"Nothing?" she yelled across the space.

The operator shook his head, pale-faced, sweating.

"Fuck," she muttered, scratching furiously at her armpit through the coveralls.

"Let's give it another minute, Skipper," Mills said in a low voice.

She snapped, "I don't need fucking *talking down*, XO. The terminal body has to have hit by now. Something's obviously gone wrong."

"Sorry, Captain."

She regretted lashing out at him, she was sleepless and irritated, but he'd just have to let it pass.

He said, not meeting her gaze, "Roger, CO. Um . . . high-side chat just confirmed blast three isn't coming off. Warhead malfunction. Seismics registered low-order detonation only."

All right then. She raised her voice, setting aside the helmet, which she'd cradled on her lap during the blackout. "Shift to EMPcon Bravo. Forward array back online. Power back to the magazines. Reset the ABM watch. Let's get AALIS back up, get back on our mission."

But she didn't have a good feeling. Two devices had worked as specified. But the last, and the most vital to mission success, hadn't.

The decapitation raid on Korea had just become enormously more difficult.

Now its success might depend on *Savo Island*.

OVER the next hour, she watched the raid unfold on the displays, accompanied by a psychopolitical offensive by the ROK government in exile. As soon as state television went off the air, prerecorded messages blanketed the country from Allied transmitters. From the Yalu to Pusan, they warned the population to stay indoors, not to report to work or duty, that liberation had come and Korea was being reunited under a democratic government. A wave of Harops had gone in next. The Israeli-produced drones lingered over suspect sites, searching for any remaining radars and destroying them as soon as they radiated.

Gremlins and Trugons had followed. Drones, dispensed from C-130s and C-17s from outside the range of any still unsuppressed antiaircraft sites. The swarming UAVs had been tested in the raids on the Chinese coast and in combat with the Marines on Taiwan. Whenever a military vehicle moved, whenever an aircraft taxied out from its hidey-hole, they darted down to attack. Marauder drones with Hellfires orbited over areas identified as hide sites, alert for the IR glare of missile boosters.

The assault unfolded with incredible swiftness. After an hour, Cheryl's displays showed large segments of the coast crosshatched green . . . safe-fly zones, where nothing larger than small arms would threaten Allied aircraft.

Then the planes went in. US Air Force F-22s and F-35s, and JASDF Mitsubishi F-15Js, F-2s, and X-2 Shinshin stealth fighters, were joined by the seven squadrons of ROKAF F-15s and FA-50s that had sought refuge in Japan after the fall of Seoul. Navy and Marine fighters from the jeep and strike carriers concentrated on the landing zone, blasting everything with low level runs.

The bombers followed. The first wave, lancing deep into the northern mountains, dropped Deep Digger bombs, penetrators that literally burned through rock and soil into tunnels intel had identified as likely locations for the hidden Korean retaliatory capability.

The second wave had obliterated the palaces and bunker complexes where Kim Jong Un was expected to hide. Others had spread terror and death along the old DMZ, blasting apart the artillery batteries that had intimidated the Allies for so many years with two-thousand-pound smart bombs. South of that demarcation, SEALs, Deltas, and Republic of Korea special ops teams were blowing bridges and mining highways, trapping the occupation forces of the North Korean army deep in South Korea.

Cheryl was getting up to pee when the surface console operator called, "Surface contacts, emerging from the harbor."

She sighed, and settled the helmet back on.

She hovered in midair, three hundred miles off the coast, but able to zoom in on any point in the country. Her gaze took in the whole peninsula now, all quarter-million square kilometers of Korea.

Up to the 42nd Parallel, where the display showed General Sharkov's heavily armed divisions, deployed along the Russian border.

AALIS's disembodied voice murmured in her ear, *"Small craft emerging from Wonsan harbor."*

She zoomed in. Six, seven small contacts were slowly departing the breakwaters. *"Probably diesel-engined,"* Chief Terranova said on the command circuit. *"So no ignition systems to disrupt."*

"Jesus. Seriously? *Fishing boats?"*

"Guess they have their orders," Mills said. "Doubt they'd have anything aboard heavier than an RPG, though."

So, a group suicide mission. But one she couldn't just ignore. She switched to the formation circuit. "Hungry Ghost, Hungry Ghost, this is Tangler, Tangler, over."

"Hungry Ghost" was *Jeonnam's* call sign. Appropriate, since it was manned by the surviving crew of a ROKN frigate sunk in the Battle of the Taiwan Strait.

"This is Hungry Ghost, over."

"See the hostiles sortieing from Wonsan?"

"Roger, Captain. We hold those contacts."

"Move to a position to intercept. If their radios still work? Try to persuade them to turn back. If they won't, sink with gunfire. Stay alert for midget submarines, more suicide attacks, drones. Don't move too fast, I want to send USVs with you. Over."

The accented voice acknowledged and signed off. Seconds later, *Jeonnam* peeled off from station, heading toward the beach.

She passed the information to Sonar and ASW, and got two AI-enabled undersea vehicles dropped through *Savo's* central well. Once they were speeding after the destroyer, she returned her attention to the northern reaches of the peninsula.

Savo's powerful phased array scanned it thirty times a second. She was getting feed, too, from the Marauders that cruised the valleys and the MICE microsatellites that flashed past in low orbits, each handing off the surveillance mission to the next as it rose above the horizon. From the Air Force AWACs that was even now angling in closer to Chongjin, in the north.

All collected, fused, and displayed in her helmet. Her eyes flicked from one callout to the next. No human brain could assimilate all this. No human intelligence could sort through so much input, and react quickly and correctly to the one piece of data that meant an emergent threat.

But the ship was backing her up. Sifting through the terabytes of data streaming over the networks.

An insistent pressure from her bladder recalled her to where she'd been headed before all this started . . . turning the watch over to Mills, she unsocketed from the helmet and uncrimped a stiff back from the chair. Then staggered, catching herself on the seat back as CIC reeled around her. The dim space seemed insubstantial, indistinct, an unreal shadow-cave after the omniscient reality of the Network.

For a moment her mind staggered as well, as she gripped the hard edge of the seat and tried to master the disorientation. Which was more real, flesh and blood and atoms, or the digital simulacra that more and more reflected how battles were managed? Were not both of them only surface manifestations, mere surfaces to a deeper reality?

No, she reminded herself. There was a stratum beneath appearances.

A reality in which people's loved ones, husbands, wives, sons, daughters, died, shot down.

Just like someone else's loved ones were dying ashore now, under American missiles and bombs. *That* was the reality.

"Y'okay, Skipper?" Terranova, concerned. Taking her elbow.

She cleared her throat. *Deep breaths, Cheryl.* "Um, yeah, thanks. Just thinking."

"You looked . . . like you needed to sit down. Shu-eh you're all right?"

Cheryl nodded. "I'm fine, Terror. Be right back. Just need a head call."

SHE escaped for a few minutes to the narrow cramped airliner-style head beside CIC. Peed, remembering only then to turn her Hydra back on, in case the TAO needed her for some fresh crisis. Washed her face. Considered, and peeled her coveralls down to douse her armpits as well. A sniff test. Better, but . . . Send somebody to her cabin for a fresh set? Maybe. If this went on too much longer.

She blinked at a too-pale, strained-looking visage in the mirror. She couldn't obsess over casualties ashore. If Chromite went as planned, it would bring peace a long step closer.

Peace. It seemed like heaven. A long-ago Golden Age when you didn't have to know where the nearest blast shelter was, and carry a gas mask at all times. When you didn't have to leave your cell on to be ready for a Homeland Security warning text. Didn't have to watch everything you said, and who you said it to. When you could say what you liked about politics, and not be accused of being an ass-symp and taken in for "counseling."

It occurred to her then that she hadn't eaten lunch. Or breakfast, either. Someone had come by with a tray, but she'd waved him off. Well, there were breakfast bars and hot coffee in the sonar shack. That should keep her going a little longer.

Maybe even, until this was over.

BUT the landing itself was delayed. No reason given, but the spearheads still orbited twenty miles off the beach, overheaded by heavy combat air. Finally the order came over the command net. The special ops teams headed in aboard Ospreys. Lagging them, deployed in an arrow formation, were the fast catamarans and LCACs, loaded with Marine light armor. Overheaded by Marauders, Gremlins, and carrier air, they hit the beach to hold the exit door open while a combined ground and airborne force made a furious dash eighty miles inland.

Kim's father had built a remote mountain stronghold at Mount Paektu, a gigantic volcano near the border with China. Over decades, the regime had turned it into a sprawling redoubt of tunnels and underground fortifications.

Unfortunately, they were off-limits to nuclear or even heavy conventional bunker busters. Swiss geological experts warned that the volcano was still spasmodically active. Too great a shock might trigger a full-scale eruption, bringing on something like nuclear winter and massive crop failures over most of the Northern Hemisphere.

So the Kims had chosen well. But with most of the NK army now sucked into the occupation of the South, the Joint Chiefs had calculated that a surgical strike stood a reasonable chance of taking down the command structure, possibly including the dictator himself.

At least, that was the plan. As the trooplifters headed inland, escorted by fighters and attack helicopters, Cheryl tried to keep her attention on her own role. Stand guard, defend Japan and the other Allies, and the homeland, against retaliation. That was *her* mission.

Jeonnam reported back that they'd warned the fishing craft heading for *Savo* and *Sioux City*, received no response, and sunk the lead two with gunfire. At which point the other fishermen had turned south and headed away down the coast.

Fleeing. And the right choice, she thought. Their hammering diesels had been impossible to overlook, their scanty armament a risible nonthreat. Even if they were burdened hull-deep with explosives and manned by suicidal fanatics, they'd never have gotten close. Not that North Korea had any shortage of either—explosives, or fanatics.

But she couldn't help donning the helmet again now and then to monitor the beachhead elements as they crept inland, securing roads and heights. Sealing a perimeter against counterattack. Creating a safe zone damaged aircraft could retreat to, along with developing a lodgment in case the Koreans buckled after their leadership was decapitated. Helicopters and LCACs shuttled in artillery and ammunition. Close air support UAVs circled ahead of the ground element, eliminating opposition, while deep strikes cut bridges on the Chinese side, in case Beijing was tempted to intervene. The Ospreys hopscotched ahead, dropping parties to seize bridges and passes.

So far, they seemed to be making good progress.

She scratched violently at her neck, where the helmet rested. It seemed to be irritating her skin, which was already prone to rash. Sighed, and told the TAO to call instantly if he needed her. "And by instantly, I mean if anything at all happens out of the ordinary. Bad news doesn't improve with age. I'm going to see if I can get my head down, at least for a little while."

"Best of luck on that, Captain. Wish I could join you," Mills said, with a tired smile.

At her console a few feet away, Terranova snorted. Mills reddened. "I mean—I didn't mean—!"

"I know what you meant, XO. Forget it." She felt like giggling. Laughing insanely. God, she was tired. She couldn't think of anything to add that didn't sound ludicrous. So she just sighed, and undogged the door.

THEY were on the beach again, at the bonfire. Alone together there, this time. The steady wind from the sea whipped the coals into white heat in the moonless, starlit dark. Sparks snapped and whirled up into the night. The surf crashed with a long, dull, withdrawing roar.

She and Yeiyah. His skin like smooth brown leather, so soft-looking she had to caress it. A tattooed dragon in blue and green writhed down his arm in the firelight. Muscle bulged, and tanned fingers gripped her shoulders like iron clamps. She pulled the blanket over them as he drove into her. Dug her head back into the sand, gasping, as the stars far above almost went supernova in her belly.

Almost, almost, *almost* . . .

But never quite. She could get only so close, and then, it didn't seem to happen . . .

He lifted his head in the firelight. No. It wasn't Teju. It was Eddie. Only there was something wrong with his face. His breath stank of decay. When he pulled out of her and rolled away, it felt as if something remained. She looked down. To see it had come detached, rotted out of him, was still sticking out of her . . . and it was *beeping* . . . oh my *God* . . .

She bolted upright, eyes blasted open, to near-dark. Red numerals blinked *0300*. She was in her at-sea cabin, and the phone beside her bunk was going nuts. She tried to shake off the dream. It was too horrifying. Too *real* . . . she grabbed the handset desperately. "CO," she rasped.

"Skipper, TAO. Call for fire from Underwood."

"Underwood" was the fire coordination center for Chromite, back in Japan. "Go ahead."

"They want Tomahawks on an armored concentration north of Paekam."

She struggled up on an elbow and clicked the bunk light on. Stuck her toes down, searching for her boots. She was still in her smelly coveralls. Shit, fuck, she'd meant to change . . . "Paekam . . . what . . . where the fuck's that?"

"It's a blocking force. Holding the Strykers up at a pass through a ridge. They need a laydown ASAP."

She zipped her boots. "Get a package rolling. Be right there."

The dream shredded, evaporating into confused wisps as her mind lurched ahead. Into what her task group had left in the magazines, flight time, preparations for launch. She started to grope after it, then shook her head. Why bother? They didn't mean anything, dreams. They were less than nothing . . .

UNDERWOOD requested an immediate laydown of sixteen TLAM-Ds, which expended the last of *Savo*'s land attack inventory. That left her with only the Alliance rounds and enough Standards for self-defense, plus the railguns and lasers, of course. The Tomahawks were on their way within eight minutes, along with five more from *Jeonnam.* AI-enabled models, once in the target zone they would seek out armor on their own, distinguish enemy vehicles from the Marines' Strykers and Abramses, and dispense submunitions to destroy them.

Aboard the old *Savo*, each launch had vibrated the ship and shaken dust out of the overhead. But now, deep within the Citadel she couldn't hear the faintest echo or tremor as they roared out of the magazines, oriented themselves, dropped their boosters, and headed off. Only the video from the deck cameras showing gouts of flame venting from the redirectors, then stars climbing into the night, proved they were indeed on their way.

"Sonar reports engine noise bearing zero eight eight."

She cleared her throat, knuckled her eyes, and got up from the command desk. Crossed to the blue curtain that traditionally walled off the sonar stacks from the rest of CIC. Pushed them aside, to reveal a small balding man leaning over the chairs of two younger petty officers, like an aging high priest over his acolytes. Before them screens streamed marigold lines. They marched steadily top to bottom, a mysterious hieroglyphic only the trained eye could make any sense of. "Chief, what've we got?"

Chief Zotcher glanced up. "Skipper. Something out at roughly zero nine zero."

"Those are fishing smacks," she told him. "*Jeonnam* sank two and the others are skedaddling."

One of the petty officers placed a finger on the screen. "See it? There's a tone."

Zotcher said, "Use the K filter." To Cheryl he added, "We have those, yeah. Broadband, small-boat harmonic signatures. Off the engine and prop, mainly. Typical four-stroke, six-cylinder marine diesels. But there's something else there too."

She glanced back at the displays in CIC. The gaggle of small contacts that were the fishing boats had slowed. They were trailing out into a long line, but still heading south along the coast. "Something else. What?"

"We're not sure . . . a bathtub pattern under what we think is the fishing boats. But on the same bearing, so it's hard to separate out, even with analysis.—Move the window, show the Skipper the Fourier."

She stood watching marigold waterfalls march up the screens as Zotcher prattled on about grating lobes and covariance matrices. Not for the first time, she reflected that the chiefs could probably run the ship without officers aboard at all. At least until they confronted the administrative requirements . . . She interrupted his search. "I don't see it."

The petty officer hissed. Zotcher hopped from one foot to the other, pointing. "Right there. *There!* See it?"

"I don't, but I believe you. So what is it? Biologics?"

"I can't tell you that, Captain, just that it's multiple low-energy contacts, with low bearing drifts. Biologics come in at a higher frequency."

She scratched between her fingers, considering. Low bearing drift meant the source was headed either for or directly away from the receiver. "Does *Sioux City* have it? Did you get a cross-bearing?"

"She's only got the towed 20. They're not picking this up, but they don't have our whiskers." Meaning, the supersensitive passive detector rods lined along the keel. "Uh, I'd recommend getting our bloodhounds out there, check this out. Captain. Just to be on the safe side."

"Both our USVs are inshore with *Jeonnam*. Just get me a range," she told him, and turned and pushed her way back into the main space. Worrying, now, that her resources were being drawn down to the danger point. She could send a drone out along a line of bearing, but it would be slow and largely limited to video coverage. Could launch a helo, but that might constrain maneuvering for at least a few minutes . . . She glanced at a wind direction indicator. Actually they were pretty close to a launch envelope.

"Let's get Bedsores out there. Come right till we have wind. Vector him out along zero nine zero, on sonobuoy and ELINT run," she told the TAO. The lead helo pilot was compact, taciturn, and apparently born without the need for sleep. He spent most nights playing board games in the hangar with several of his similarly addicted maintainers. Hence, naturally, the nickname.

The TAO nodded and started the ball rolling.

FORTY minutes later their TLAMs reached the target area and began crisscrossing it, dispensing munitions over the enemy armor and bunkers blocking the pass. She kept checking the nanochat and was happy to see the land commander's praise of their effectiveness.

When the announcement came they'd broken through a muted cheer bounced around CIC. Not long after, the symbology showed the lead elements on the move once more. They pushed through the pass, hooked left along the ridge, then turned right for the climb up the mountain. Their final destination lay six miles ahead: the tunnels and bunker systems of the dictator's last redoubt. A second surge of refueled UAVs and fighters orbited overhead, taking out bunkers, concealed batteries, and firing points along the road with Hellfires and JDAM bombs.

Cheryl couldn't help marveling. Chromite had seemed like a bridge too far, a victory of wishful thinking over the reality of the North Korean will to resist. But to judge by their progress so far, the operation just might succeed.

Surely killing one of the enemy dictators, and knocking one of the Opposed Powers out of the war, would go a long way toward ending it.

She was actually feeling optimistic when one of the UAV symbols popped red. A line unrolled on the nanochat board.

Locus: to Matador
Disturbance reported on surface Lake Chon

She frowned. Chon was the jewel-like pool cradled in the caldera of the volcano. Similar to Crater Lake: an immense spread of water walled by precipitous mountains. A disturbance? Maybe . . . it was erupting?

Half a second later the alert-script cuing buzzer went off at the AALIS control station. Chief Terranova called over the racket, "Launch cuing! Simultaneous cuings from MICE and Locus."

"Confirm from UAV," said the controller, behind her. "Video."

Cheryl snatched for the helmet. Her hair snagged on the cable. She jerked it free, tearing strands out by the roots, and powered up. The screens lit. She toggled to overhead from Locus, the Marauder that had sent the alarm.

Rugged, snow-etched mountains fell to a blue, lovely, wind-rippled surface. For a moment she stared, puzzled. What the fuck, over?

The camera lurched, canted right, and refocused.

On a patch where that placid blue was being torn apart, erupting into foam and smoke as above it a fiery lance climbed skyward.

Beside her Mills, probably seeing the same feed on his screen, breathed, "That's a JL."

CALLOUTS flashed beside the video of the climbing missile on Cheryl's own screens. Terranova called, "Profile plot, designate Meteor. Very rapid climb rate. Consistent with solid-fueled first stage. Size and acceleration profile . . . consistent with sub-launched IRBM. Passing angels five. Identify as SLBM. ID as hostile."

Sub-launched? But there couldn't be submarines in an inland lake.

There could be submerged *tubes*, though. Linked with command nodes through deep tunnels . . .

"Take as target," Cheryl said into the throat mike.

"Roger, ma'am . . . have lock-on . . . computing trajectory and IPP."

Beside her Mills said urgently, "Their sub-launched IRBM. Reverse engineered or copied from Chinese JL-1. Range . . . red book guesses at a thousand kilometers. Unitary missile. Single warhead. But . . . I don't know, this looks . . . *bigger.*"

"Presumed thermonuclear," Cheryl added through a suddenly dry mouth.

The video froze, canted, then recommenced. A mountain filled the field of view. Then the lake surface again, boiling once more. A second blunt-nosed torpedo-shape burst up through smoke-stained spray, ignited its booster with a silent clap that spread blast waves across the water, and began to climb.

But as the video canted again, violently, a flame-tipped cone of white fire entered the frame from the right. It dwindled rapidly as it chased the rising missile into the crystalline sky.

The two fires merged and vanished in a ball of yellow-white flame, followed by an immense cloud of dirty smoke. Pieces emerged at jagged angles, still afire, looping and tumbling before falling back into the seething, steaming lake.

She toggled from video to radar. The vibrating brackets of AALIS's tracking. Readouts showed a rapid climb rate, altitude angels fifty. "Meteor Bravo splashed. Meteor Alfa, nearing pitchover," Chief Terranova noted.

They had a problem. She toggled from screen to screen, thinking rapidly as a third missile burst out of the lake and climbed. Another Hellfire chased it, but fell behind and at last staggered down out of the sky to detonate against a mountainside.

"Meteor Alfa, gathering horizontal velocity," AALIS's neutral, ungendered voice informed her. *"Stand by . . . pitchover. Meteor Charlie, locked on. Solid lock both contacts."*

Two targets now. They wouldn't get an impact point or an inter-

cept angle right away. Once she had a firm impact prediction, Terranova could set up to fire.

A unitary target—meaning the warhead didn't detach from the
main body of the missile—presented a huge radar return. But Cheryl
also had to consider range, speed, and geometry. If the target was
too far to the south, the intercept probabilities went down. If it was
aimed north, they rose. Best of all was a head-on shot, the classic
reentry phase intercept, but she doubted they'd get that. One seldom got an easy shot at a ballistic missile. And they had no idea how
many more lay poised at the bottom of that lake. Or when Dictator
Kim would decide to push his famous red button again.

Not that she wouldn't whack that mole if she had to. Just that she
might have to expend more Alliances to get an assured kill. Without
all that many rounds to start with. "I need an IPP," she snapped. "First
target's coming out of pitchover. Let's get it, I need it *now, people!*"

"Looking at the angle. Extending the arc . . . Target is . . . Tokyo."
Terranova's soft voice was as unconcerned as it would have been if
the thermonuclear had been dialed in on the South Pole.

Cheryl toggled to the IPP screen. The GCCS underlay on which it
was imposed didn't show populated areas as such. Just black circles
with town names. But the way they clustered as they approached the
largest circle of all made it plain how many millions lay beneath the
lifted sword.

In the streets, sirens would be wailing. Cells would be streaming
text alerts, directions to the nearest shelter, warnings to take cover
immediately.

But even with the sirens, the texts, the shelters, hundreds of thousands of Japanese would die.

The AOU shrank, widened, then contracted again as AALIS re-
calculated, matching its projections with the Network's. But it never
budged from the middle of the Tokyo plain.

Okay, Cheryl. Stay cold. Execute the prefire checklist. Toggling
to the intercept template as AALIS set it up, she contemplated the
geometry.

The missile's closest point of approach would be southeast of
their assigned station. If she launched quickly enough, they could

catch it in the postboost phase, while the sustainer engine was firing and it wasn't yet at maximum velocity.

Move farther south, out of her box? They didn't have enough time to gain a better angle for the shot, but if more surprise packages emerged from Mount Doom, even a few miles southing might improve their P sub K. She snapped to Mills, "Come around to two zero zero, XO. Flank speed, thirty-five knots."

He was bent forward, frowning at the display. "Pass to the bridge, or execute from here?"

"Suit yourself. Just get us around and kick her in the ass."

The compartment heeled slightly. Something clattered back by the ASW plot. Without shafts or the conventional huge spinning screws aft, propelled instead by electric motors in rotatable pods along the hull, the cruiser pivoted and accelerated without a shimmy.

"Hitting thirty," the TAO told her a couple of minutes later.

"CO, Air control: Helo reports sonar contact bearing 085 true, 21,000 yards Mother."

"Mother" of course was *Savo Island.* Cheryl rogered, intent on the still climbing radar contact that was Meteor Alfa.

Headed for the biggest city on the planet.

Thirty-eight million people. She remembered that. From somewhere.

The Japanese had layered missile defense. Patriot Advanced Capability, Aegis Ashore with Standards, and an independently developed multi-object kill system based on the SRB-A3 solid rocket booster. She assumed they were seeing the same picture she was. But she owed them more than an assumption. She typed rapidly:

Matador: to Grandstand
Confirm MDA, Tokyo informed ICBM en route generated IPP Tokyo

Grandstand: to Matador
Affirmative. But if you can intercept do so soonest. Reduce risk to
    population as much as possible

She nodded, understanding. Taking it down early would drop it in the Sea of Japan. A hell of a lot better than raining radioactive debris on one of the most densely populated areas on earth.

Matador: to Grandstand
Will do our best

She glanced down, searching for the red Launch Enable switch. Then remembered: that had been aboard the old *Savo*. Now AALIS ran the entire launch protocol, once a target was designated to the system. Cheryl could veto a launch, up till the boosters ignited, but that was all.

More and more autonomous with each software flight, "Alice" was now all but independent of human decision making. The ontologists had discussed, the designers had designed, the Navy had approved. The ship would think more quickly and more correctly than humans under pressure. It tracked the target, tested itself, ran last-second operability checks on individual rounds, and calculated the chances of a successful intercept twenty times a second, until the parameters optimized.

Then it would send the signal.

"This is Savo Island. Designate target Meteor Alfa. Three round salvo, one from forward magazine, two from aft," the ship's detached gender-free voice intoned in her earbuds. *"Initializing missiles 2, 4, and 7. Testing . . . testing complete. Missiles ready. Standing by to fire."*

"Steady track," Terranova called. "Still accelerating. But it's gotta be close to sustainer burnout."

Cheryl was taking a deep breath when a discordant chime sounded. Zotcher burst through the blue curtains. "High-speed screws," he yelled. "TWS has torpedoes in the water, bearing one zero zero. At least two. No pings. Bearing zero eight zero."

"Bridge, TAO," said the officer next to her instantly. "Execute turnaway—"

"Belay that," Cheryl snapped. "Belay that, maintain course and speed!" The inertials on the missiles required the launch platform on a steady course for at least sixty seconds before launch.

The external cameras on the helmet gave her faces turned toward

her in CIC. A close-up of the TAO's strained features as he acknowledged. "You can slow to ten," she added, "and get the CATs in the
water. As soon as missiles-away, we can—"

"*Two more torpedoes in the water,*" a sonar petty officer's voice
came over the comman circuit. "*Total four. All running hot. Sound
like CHT-02s. Wake-homing guidance.*"

She scratched furiously at her neck, fighting a sudden, dizzying
sense of dejá vû. Then realized: No. It's wasn't dejá vû.

This was identical with the exercise scenario they'd played during
workup, off Hawaii. Dual threats, missile and subsurface, simultaneous and unexpected.

And that exercise play had ended . . . with a torpedo slamming
into *Savo's* stern.

"Activate Rimshot," She snapped. "Hold off on decoys. Stand by
on CAT."

Unfortunately, Rimshot, the magnetic foxer, wouldn't spoof a
wake-homer. The bubble decoys confused active homing torpedoes,
but once again, wouldn't deflect the weapons charging toward them
at sixty knots. The Countermeasure, Antitorpedo, was her last resort. It would home in on and detonate beside the enemy fish.

But she still only had the single brace of four CATs. She hardly
noticed as her nails dug into the itching sores between her fingers.

They might still catch a break. Wake-homers were usually fired
from astern of their target. They zigzagged up the path of disturbed
water a ship left behind. They had a secondary passive sound-homing
capability, but with her podded Teslas *Savo* put much fewer decibels
in the water than a ship with conventional screws.

But fired from ahead, as they'd been in this case, they'd most
likely pass by *Savo*, detect her wake, behind her, then U-turn and
home in from astern.

And whoever had fired them was still there, ahead. But why
hadn't sonar picked them up? She touched her throat mike. "Sonar,
CO. Chief, why didn't we hear the archer?"

"Low and slow . . . and masked by those fishing smacks. Blade
noise square on the same freq spectrum."

"And from the same bearing," she said, understanding now. The fishermen hadn't been the threat at all. They'd been masks, to cover the approach of something more dangerous. Probably, some of the midget submarines Intel had warned about.

Maybe they'd all been too dismissive of this enemy. Both of his resolve, and his craftiness.

"Captain, we need to turn away," the TAO said.

"Negative. Where's Bedsores? I mean, Red Hawk? I mean, Dagger 02?" Their helo was still out there. It carried homing torpedoes, cocked to track and kill. "Vector him toward home plate. ASW, drop at Sonar's best guess of range."

She toggled off that circuit and back to ABM. Less than a minute had passed since her last look, but the climbing missile was higher above their radar horizon. She scratched viciously at her wrist. Sweat trickled down her neck under the helmet. Three minutes since initial cuing. AALIS was computing intercept points. But with a crossing engagement their firing window would be tiny. Even the uprated Alliances could miss. The terminal interceptor depended on kinetic collision, actually slamming into the target. It could fail too.

But if she held off too long, nothing would be able to catch up as gravity increased the velocity of the falling reentry body.

And then, Tokyo . . .

She couldn't think of that.

"*Two more high-speed screws,*" Zotcher said over the circuit. "*Total six in the water.*"

And she had only four CATs.

She closed her eyes.

Savo was doomed.

The enemy had won. Snuck in under aural cover, then swung for the groin. And in a few seconds, the punch would connect. Heavy, explosives-packed weapons, sniffing the sea like hunting hounds. Closing from astern. And finally, crashing into the hull . . .

A flash of her old CO, Lenson, intent at the command desk, in situations as tight as this . . . how frosty he'd always looked . . . surely he'd never felt this intimidated, or unsure. The guy had self-confidence she could never match. And the unorthodox brilliance to come up with tactics that left the enemy flatfooted in left field.

And just then, in remembering him, one last thing she could do to save her ship occurred to her.

She recoiled. To do it would condemn her to obloquy. Subject her to court-martial.

But it had to be done. To save her ship, her crew, and their ability to keep fighting.

Reluctantly lifting her arm, which felt like it weighed tons, she toggled her throat mike to task group command. "Sandman, this is Tangler," she murmured.

Sandman was *Sioux City*, the frigate pacing her a mile off *Savo*'s quarter.

Tangler was Cheryl herself, commanding the task group. Including the two non-ABM-capable escorts.

"This is Sandman, over."

"Tangler Actual. Immediate execute. Break. Flank speed, cut left, cross my stern at two hundred yards. Stand by. Execute."

"This is Sandman. Say again, over."

She repeated the command and got a roger. Feeling cold, she shivered.

She'd just condemned others, in place of herself.

No. Not in *her* place. In place of her ship, and the weapons and sensors it carried.

It was the inexorable logic of every game, from chess to war.

Sacrifice the lesser, to protect the greater.

Just as her old *Savo* had been sacrificed once, to protect a carrier.

Now only the new *Savo* stood between Japan and destruction.

Sioux City would have to be the sacrifice.

She sighed, feeling like she'd held her breath for half an hour. Toggled to the ASW net, to see Dagger One winking on and off five miles to the southwest. *"Mark on top Datum. Fish in the water,"* its pilot reported. *"Will orbit and drop number two."*

"CATs triggered," the ASW officer said on the same circuit. *"CATs away."*

"All engines stop," Cheryl said. The cruiser would coast on, driven by the sheer momentum of nearly twenty thousand tons of steel. But with her wake dissipating, and with a more attractive target, the frigate, crossing behind her.

Luring them away . . .

To chase *someone else* down instead . . .

She pushed her horror aside and hit the mike again, this time the internal command circuit. "Alice: initialize three more Alliances. First salvo will be, three missiles on Meteor Alfa. Second salvo, three rounds on Meteor Charlie." She'd get her interceptors out where they could do some good, at least. Even if her last parry failed, and *Savo* too was hit. Even if she and her escort both went down.

"AALIS aye. Initializing Alliances one, three, five. Two, four, and seven standing by to fire. Magazines in 'operate' mode. Three-round salvo on target desig Meteor Alfa. Second salvo, three rounds Meteor Charlie. Warning alarm forward and aft. Safeties and interlocks disengaged. Standing by for CO's command."

"You have permission to engage," she said, enunciating it in the distinct, clear tone you had to use talking to voice recognition software.

"Acknowledge weapons free. Stand by . . . missile two away. Missile four away. Missile seven away. Alliances one, three, five, and six initializing. Stand by for second salvo, target Meteor Charlie."

No roar, no rattle, not this deep in the hull, but she followed the fiery plumes toward the horizon on the video feed. "Very well."

"Permission to engage Meteor Charlie."

"You have permission to engage Meteor Charlie."

"Acknowledged."

She toggled to nanochat and sent:

Matador: to ALCON
Under wake-homing torpedo attack. Ordered Sandman to cross my
    stern to absorb. Accept full responsibility.

In her earbuds AALIS said, *"All missiles away. Salvos complete. Tracking. Stand by for intercepts."*

Cheryl sat shaking, unable to respond. Her fingers left bloody prints on the command desk. She squeezed her eyes closed. She'd done all she could. All she fucking well could.

Now they'd all just have to live with the consequences.

14

Zurich, Switzerland

THEIR driver, a jolly, flatulent older gentleman with unruly gray hair like Einstein's, talked nonstop on the way in from the airport, in a fast German-accented patter Blair found hard to follow. They were three in the back of the limo: herself, Shira Salyers, from State, and one Adam Ammermann from the White House. He'd been added at the last minute, and she was pretty sure what his function would be.

For some reason, she'd expected Zurich to be in the Alps. But it was surrounded by forested hills, not mountains. But at last the driver pointed ahead and she peered out the tinted windows and saw them: distant, hazed blue-gray with distance even in this clear, high air, but definitely tall, snowcapped mountains, many miles away.

They'd arrived along with diplomatic missions from other countries. The Swiss had assembled them into a motorcade, preceded and trailed by bright red police cars. "So if anyone wants to know who to hit, they shine a light on us," Salyers remarked, beside her in the backseat of the black Volvo S90.

The State rep was about Blair's age, slender, small-boned, African American, with a piquant face. She was whip-smart and a riveting speaker. They'd represented the US together once before, in Dublin.

Ammermann was silent, looking out the window. He was a tall round-faced man in his early forties, whose smile rang the tiniest bit false despite Hollywood-perfect teeth. He wore a blue blazer and gray slacks, with the blue and gold White House Staff lapel pin.

The cortege broke up as the hill-cupped city opened, sprawling down along the valley and widening as the Sihlquai met Lake Zurich. "I giff ze der quick tour?" the driver bellowed back. "You will want to see the waterfront, der alte stadt, apartment Lenin lived in, ja?"

Ammermann snorted. "You can skip Lenin."

The driver chuckled and turned onto a street that wound alongside the river. Stone-paved walks bordered a broad, gray, fast-moving stream. It rippled white as rocky rapids furrowed its surface. Ducks paddled hard to breast the current flowing out of the lake. The banks were vertical walls of ancient masonry, pinning the river firmly to its course. They passed a soaring gray stone church. Then another. "Calvin. Melanchthon. Zwingli. You know these, ja?" the driver said, as if he'd heard them preach himself.

A blue and white streetcar trundled by. They slowed to view a cunningly wrought fountain, bronze filigree arching over a statue of someone Blair couldn't quite make out. "You can drink from any fountain in the city," the driver said, as if he'd laid the pipe personally.

All the cars were new. All the buildings looked freshly washed. The pedestrians were well dressed, and walked fast as New Yorkers. A scooter whined suddenly past, threading the lines of cars, its rider's face invisible under a full-face black helmet. Ammermann, on that side, flinched back, then looked sheepish.

They cruised past the waterfront, which was thronged with hundreds of the most expensive boats Blair had ever seen. Only a few were out on the lake, though, which stretched into the distance, its far end lost amid the mountains. "It really is quite beautiful," Salyers murmured. "We should try to visit the old town. The shopping has to be terrific. And *I'd* like to see where Lenin used to live, myself."

Ammermann turned his face away but said nothing. Blair guessed he wasn't into shopping. Or Communists.

The motor hummed as they began to climb. They passed huge nineteenth-century stone mansions that looked as if they'd started as minor palaces, then become the headquarters of banks. The grade steepened. The driver pointed out a funicular railway that ascended the mountain. "But will take the back road, ja?" he chortled. Blair and Shira exchanged eyerolls.

Birches replaced maples as the road wound upward. The homes became more palatial, set back farther from the road.

As the car rounded a final turn, both women blinked.

A fairy-tale castle revealed itself. It looked as if an Alpine chalet had interbred with a Moorish fortress. Multi-tiered spires needled the sky, rising from steeply pitched slate roofs. Four men were grooming the box hedges in front of a wide downsloping lawn. On the other side of the street golfers paced and swung across an immaculate greensward. Past them the mountain fell away to overlook all Zurich, the glittering stretch of lake, and beyond them the now clearly visible jagged peaks of the Alps.

"Der Dolder Grand," the driver announced, sounding as complacently proud as if he'd built it himself. "Eighteen ninety-nine. Art Nouveau. But sehr modernized. Sie hast comt to the best hotel in Zurich. Maybe in die world."

"This isn't how DoD travels," Blair muttered to Salyers. "We're more like Hyatt Regency. At best."

"The surest way to lose in a negotiation is to look as if you can't afford to play."

Ammermann snorted. He seemed about to vent a retort, but didn't. He muttered in German to the driver, who guffawed. When they parked he went around to open the trunk for the uniformed porters at the porticoed entrance.

Shira opened her purse, but the driver waved her off, pointing up. At the sky? Blair had no idea what that gesture meant. That the God of Zwingli and Calvin would provide? That didn't sound like what she remembered of their doctrines. Mainly, that you were either Chosen or Damned, and there was absolutely nothing, really, you could do about it in the end.

THEIR room was opulent as well. She marveled again at how diplomats managed to ensconce themselves in luxury, and present it as essential to representing their countries. Salyers turned the huge flat screen TV on, and flipped until she found a news channel. It was in Italian, so Blair could only catch a word here and there. But they both stopped unpacking and stared at the screen as gray jets flashed across gray clouds, followed by the billowing smoke of a strike. A map came up, wheeled, the camera zoomed in. Then a picture of the obese and grotesquely coiffed North Korean tyrant, pendulous jowls sagging as he ran greedy fingers over the curved cowling of a missile. Text crawled beneath the video in a chyron.

"Can you read that, Shira?" Blair said.

"I think it's saying . . . he's dead. Or maybe deposed—I'm not sure what 'deposto' means."

Blair tried the news on her cell but got nothing. She had bars, but no service. "Fuck," she muttered. This happened every time she went overseas. Well, she probably shouldn't be using a personal phone here at all.

Salyers was looking down at her own phone. "He's missing, presumed dead. Possibly shot by his bodyguards. That's all so far."

"That's official? Or commercial news sources? They don't always—"

"State. Confirmed by CIA."

Confirmed that it was a rumor, or confirmed that he was dead? But of course Shira wouldn't know. Probably no one would, until an actual body turned up.

THE reception that night was in the Gallery, catered by a hotel restaurant reputed one of the best in Europe. Its floor-to-ceiling windows opened on a stone-flagged terrace that overlooked the lake far below. Blair had dressed carefully, a black scoop-necked dress with Louboutin heels and a two-strand necklace of royal amber.

She remembered a previous reception, in the Throne Room in Dublin Castle. Tonight, much like then, elegantly attired women and nattily dressed men mixed and chatted. She glimpsed Liz McManus, the Irish delegate who'd invited her, deep in conversation with a petite woman in a sari. Then spotted a dignified African gentleman, late seventies or early eighties, gray tufts seeded like rows of corn across an otherwise naked temple. As their gazes met he bowed slightly.

"Is that him?" Salyers murmured, above the hubbub.

Blair nodded. She'd briefed Shira about the contact in Dublin. The old African had slid a message to her beneath a cup of tea. Acting as go-between for the Chinese. Whom Blair had then met, at a pastry shop, for a curiously contradictory conversation.

Salyers had subjected her to a good half hour of alternating reproaches—on how she hadn't pressed for concessions, elucidated credentials, set up a follow-up meeting—and then advice—about how to respond to a diplomatic feeler in an informal setting. The key takeaway had been how dangerous such a contact was, how cautiously it must be handled. "Above all, don't commit yourself, or us," Salyers had warned. "You don't have the power. More critically, you don't have the trust."

Blair had nodded. "Okay."

"Remember this. A private feeler serves three functions. One: as a signal. Two: it can permit concessions on the other side. And three: it serves what we call a 'screening function.' The way you respond to the contact gives both parties the opportunity to earn trust. How do you earn it? Mainly, by not leaking.

"You can't negotiate if you don't trust your adversary. At least, to some extent. Since they contacted you again, that demonstrates some confidence. Possibly," Salyers hesitated, "and I may be wrong about this, but perhaps because they think you're linked to what could be seen these days as the peace party."

"Linked to . . . Shira, I've never advocated peace without some kind of permanent settlement. We don't have to have a victory parade. But we need to fight long enough to make it clear to the Opposed Powers they're beaten. And there has to be regime change. Progress toward democracy. Otherwise"—she thought of Szerenci— "We'll be doing this all over again twenty years down the road."

So now she nodded, and drifted toward the old man as Salyers headed in another direction. He smiled and bowed again, a twinkle in his eye.

Of course, she'd looked him up. "Minister Madubuike. How nice to see you again."

He looked over her shoulder, still smiling vaguely. Barely flicked his gaze across her face; then turned away.

She halted, unsure what was going on. Then noticed more and

more of the delegates drifting away from her. And from Shira, who stood still in the middle of the floor, puzzled creases faintly engraved between her eyes.

To test it, she went to the refreshments table. Here, not really to her surprise, cheese ruled. It poured from heated pots, down gleaming stainless spouts, to uncoil over breads and meats, noodles and vegetables. Fondue reigned supreme, apparently. And the smells were terrific. She hesitated in front of a simmering pot.

"It's a moitié moitié, I think." A familiar voice.

She glanced up from the bubbling pot to find McManus studying her across the table. "Liz. Hi. What's going on? It's like we have on some kind of diplomat repellent."

McManus was in a severe violet sheath, with modest heels, perhaps to deemphasize her height. Picking up a spoon, she helped herself to the slow waterfall. "Gruyère, along with a nice creamy Vacherin Fribourgeois. Should go great with a dry white." She nodded toward a side table where several men were laughing, nursing tiny glasses. "And the Swiss like to follow it with a shot of kirschwasser. Want to make friends? Stand by the drinks table."

"I'm not really here for that, Liz. About the Chi—"

McManus too turned away, all too abruptly. Blair frowned. She looked down the front of her dress, but there didn't seem to be any wardrobe malfunctions. Glanced sideways at her face in a pier glass. Nothing in her teeth.

Then why was everyone avoiding her?

The realization came accompanied by a chill.

The outcome of the International Commission Against War Crimes and Genocide in Asia had already been decided. Like the prepackaged statements at the end of the heads of state meeting in Jakarta, which had been written and agreed on by all parties weeks before the principals flew in.

Suddenly Ammermann was standing beside her. A late arrival, and given his contemptuous references to the UN during the flight, she was surprised to see him here at all. Maybe the two glasses of clear liquor he carried were the answer. "For you," he said, extending one.

She pretended to sip while casing the rest of the reception. A few faces she half recognized. Others, she knew from the briefing book Shira had sent. "What have you heard about Korea?" she asked him. "About Kim?"

"CNN says his bodyguards shot him. Like with Indira Gandhi. But I don't trust anything they say. We'll wait until it's confirmed."

Salyers joined them. "Wait for what?"

"Confirmation. The president will want to anounce it himself." Ammermann looked Blair up and down. "Anyone asked you to come over to our side? Join the Patriot Party? Oh, wait—shouldn't have let that cat out. But now you know . . . we're changing the name. To be more inclusive of those who want to join us. Forming the first truly united party. So we can march forward together."

Blair forced a half smile. "Yes, I've been approached. But I haven't made that decision yet, Adam. When I do, you'll be the first to know."

"You can still be a rising star." With a catlike smile he snagged a canapé from a passing tray. "Man, look at all this fucking cheese. Enough to clog you up for a month."

"Excuse me," she said, suddenly feeling the jet lag hit. Her head swam, and after only two sips of schnapps. She dragged herself across the parquet, heading at an angle toward a tightly cliqued group clustered near the exit to the terrace. Four Asians, all in dark blue suits, three wearing the heavy black plastic-rimmed spectacles affected by their leader. The premier, president, generalissimo, and chairman, the ex–Second Department spy who'd set half the world on fire: Zhang Zurong.

Her gaze crossed that of the youngest-looking of the delegation, and certainly the slimmest. Also, this time, the only one not wearing the heavy glasses. Their eyes met for the merest fraction of a second before they both dropped them.

Xie Yunlong . . . Yun. Who'd met with her one-on-one in Dublin, pursuant, obviously, to his orders, since he'd related what he had to say as if memorized word for word.

But she didn't stop. Simply kept her face front and her stride unbroken. Even as she replayed that shutter-flick of mutual recognition, musing over it as she crossed the terrace to stand overlooking the sloping stretch of green that fell toward the golf course and woods.

Twenty yards below, Swiss police in dress gray stood ten meters apart, facing the jadeite glitter of the lake. Each with a submachine gun slung under one arm. Farther down the driveway, at a road block, some kind of armored vehicle was parked across the access.

Yun had looked ill at ease. Slumped, as if disappointed. Or as if he'd just gotten bad news. Standing to his right was the deputy minister, Chen Jialuo. The elder statesman had been holding forth, gesturing with a kirschwasser glass.

To his left, bending to the shorter Chinese, deep in the conversation and obviously listening carefully, had been another white-haired, older man she didn't recognize. But he wasn't Asian. And now, revisiting the glimpse, she realized that he'd worn the blue-white-red flag of the Russian Federation on his lapel. What had Shira said, on the plane . . . about how at an event like this, everything had meaning. Everything was a message.

Was that a message, then, that the Russians and Chinese stood together?

She glanced back to see Salyers still alone, cupping one elbow with a hand and looking both proud and lonely. No one was stopping for a chat with her. And again, that premonitory chill caressed her spine.

"Could we all gather here . . . those on the terrace, could you come in please . . . Thank you." McManus, alone at a small podium. She didn't seem to need a sound system. "There on the terrace, please come in. Thank you.

"Good evening, and welcome." She smiled at the audience. "This meeting will continue the work of the United Nations conference on possible human rights violations and war crimes in south Asia and the Pacific. That conference, which set up monitoring teams to report and substantiate or dismiss charges of war crimes by the warring parties, was judged a resounding success. It has been extended, to now become the International Commission Against War Crimes and Genocide in Asia. Unfortunately, no continuing resolutions have been adopted in the Security Council, since two permanent members vetoed them. That is, the United States, and the People's Republic of China."

She went on for a few more minutes, about how if the international community looked away, no one could expect the combatants to respect human rights under the pressure of war. At one time Blair would have snorted, confident that only the other side would have a problem with that. Lately, though, a lot of her complacency about American virtue had . . . eroded. And not just because of one administration, or one party.

But enough of that, Blair . . . she tuned back in to hear McManus wishing the attendees a pleasant evening. "Tomorrow we'll gather in the Grand Ballroom at nine sharp for our introductory report from Dr. Abir al-Mughrabi. As many of you know, he is a former Appeals Division judge, International Criminal Court at The Hague, and has acted for the prosecution for crimes of civil war and genocide in Lebanon, Rwanda, Afghanistan, and Syria. He'll be accompanied by others from our monitoring teams, returned from the front lines. Join me up here, please, the team members! Let's give them all a hand for their dedication to the cause of international peace."

Blair was applauding too, when her iPhone chimed. She hastily set her glass on a side table, and checked the phone, surprised. It hadn't worked earlier, how could it accept calls? But then she saw it wasn't a call, but a text. The little cartouche pulsed on her screen, then dimmed. Brightened again once, then faded for good.

It was gone. But not before she'd read it. Four words only.

Vladimir Lenin's. 2100. Alone.

A quick check on her room computer confirmed what the taxi driver had said. Lenin and his wife, Nadezhda, had indeed lived in Zurich during his exile from Russia. The apartment was at Spiegelgasse 14. She started to enter it into her Maps program, but decided not to. The fewer records, the better. But it was too far to walk, and she didn't want to take a taxi. They too kept records. She decided not to tell Shira about this second contact. If it went sideways, why tar both of them?

She thought for a few minutes. Then took two hundred-dollar bills out of her stash, and headed for the elevator.

• • •

THE little engine buzzed in her ears. The machine wobbled more than she liked. She braked again and again, keeping the scooter to a speed she felt comfortable with. The fenders were battered, but it was high visibility yellow. The high beam was bright. That was good too, since dusk was falling as the Vespa descended the mountain, purring through residential streets with expensive homes set back on carefully groomed lawns.

She was nearly alone on the road. That too was fine. She'd hadn't been on a scooter in years. Since her dad had gotten her a Honda for her sixteenth, so she could putt-putt around the back roads of Maryland. But the skill came back fast. Like riding a bike. The groundskeeper she'd approached had been happy to "loan" it to her for a couple of hours. "A little sightseeing," she'd explained, handing him the money folded small.

Riskier than a taxi, sure. But it felt exhilarating, swooping down toward the darkening city over silken-smooth Swiss pavements. Amazing what one could do in terms of infrastructure when you didn't have to spend 40 percent of GDP on a war. She kept her head down, hoping the too-large, slightly smelly helmet and face shield concealed her features.

But the exhilaration ebbed. She felt more apprehensive as the scooter swooped downward, as the shadows deepened and the streets narrowed. It was getting cold too, as the wind whipped her coattails and felt inside her blouse. Should have worn a sweater . . . other mopeds buzzed past, whining as they powered into the climb. Choosing a side street, she pulled off, doused engine and lights, and waited, watching the road behind her. But no one was following. The street was empty.

Shit. What the hell was she doing? She was no spook. No Jason Bourne. Clandestine meetings weren't supposed to be how undersecretaries of defense spent their time.

But once more, when she set her own anxiety against the possibility of forestalling the horror Szerenci seemed all too ready to risk, she had to push on. She kicked the engine back to life again and pulled out, giving the little putt-putt more throttle. The streets became cobbled, twisting alleys. She pulled over again, unfolded the map the front desk had given her, and pored over it in the light from a shop window.

A sign: *Spiegelgasse*. A narrow chink of alley. Good idea, the Vespa; this wasn't wide enough for a car. She blipped the gas and turned in. The too-small tires juddered and skidded over rounded cobblestones. Then it widened, to a little plaza. A minuscule square, with benches, trees, grass. Another sign: *Plaza Casa Lenin*. She steered to a bike stand, hit the cutoff, and killed the engine. Struggled with the center stand, and finally got the machine up on it.

Lights flashed at the far end of the plaza, downhill. She lifted the helmet off, fighting the chinstrap. She debated leaving it with the scooter, but finally tucked it under her arm, like a severed head, and walked carefully, over the slippery cobbles, down toward the lights.

Xie Yun stood beside a table on the terrace of a small café. She didn't see a car. Maybe he'd walked, or taken the funicular. But she didn't like the man beside him. At all. She halted dead. Almost turned on her heel and walked away, uphill, back to the Vespa.

He was tall. White-haired. In a dark topcoat.

The Russian she'd seen chatting all too intimately with the deputy minister.

She took a deep breath and let it out. The café was filled with chatting couples. A public place. Nothing would happen to her, at least not here. She'd listen to what they had to say. That was all.

Yun bowed slightly as she approached. He looked more haggard than the first time they'd met. Less well fed. Shadows under the eyes. He offered the same limp handshake as before. "Mrs. Titus."

"Yun." She nodded. "And who's this?"

"My name is not necessary, Ms. Titus. Call me Dick, if you like."

Seen up close, even by the dim light from the café, the Russian wasn't as old as she'd assumed. His hair wasn't white, but a very light blond. Once more she debated. Would it be wiser to walk away? And once more, she steeled herself. Dan was taking more risks than this daily, of a stray missile, a torpedo. The least she could do was hear them out.

"What is it you wanted to tell me?" she muttered.

"Let us sit down," the Chinese suggested.

He led them to a table inside, in the back. A waiter brought a menu in four languages. Yun asked for the brownie and tea. The Russian shook his head, stony-faced. "Nothing for me." She refused too, arms crossed.

When the waiter left she leaned in. "We aren't here to nosh, Yun. Don't you have pastries in Beijing? And why's this guy here?"

"Moscow wants to facilitate an armistice," Yun said.

Blair sat back, gobsmacked. So surprised that for a moment she could not respond. The Chinese went on. "Our friends have acted in support of the People's Republic in many ways. The latest is the sale of three hundred Sukhoi Su-35 multi-role fighter planes, to replace the losses sustained in your strikes. They will strengthen our southern defenses. You can confirm this with your intelligence organs.

"But as the war becomes more critical, the danger to all concerned increases. Thus, we would like to make an unofficial inquiry."

She shrugged. "We've set forth our proposals. At the Jakarta conference."

"Regime change? Unconditional surrender? Those terms are not acceptable. And will never be accepted, as long as China lives."

She shrugged and looked away. Let him dangle, and see what he said next.

Yun glanced at the Russian. "Then we have both a warning and a question. The warning is, do not underestimate the sacrifices we are willing to make. Chairman Zhang will destroy the world before he accepts defeat."

She nodded. That had been conveyed over and over, by Shanghai Sue and Beijing's official statements. "Message received. And the question?"

Yun glanced at the Russian, and lowered his voice still further. "A hypothetical. What would be form of government if the regime were to change? Would current Party leaders and generals retain their positions? Or would this be like Iraq, the army and party dissolved? Would generals be tried as war criminals?"

"And what would be the position of the Allies on war debts owed by China to other nations," the Russian murmured.

Blair tried not to show the thrill that shot though her. She dropped her twined fingers beneath the table, lest a tremor betray her. There *was* a clique opposed to Zhang. They wanted guarantees. And the Russians were getting involved simply and purely because they'd advanced billions in weapons and energy credits, and wanted to be sure they were paid. Follow the money!

This was momentous. She had to convey some measure of accommodation. But how could she manage it, with a crippled and frightened State Department? She certainly couldn't commit the US to anything on her own.

Then she remembered what Shira had said. Back channels built trust. "I've held it very closely, that we're in touch," she told Yun. "I hope you have too."

His mouth set. "Indeed I have."

"Can I have some hint of who you represent? Who you're speaking for?"

He looked down at his half-eaten brownie. Picked it up, then put it down. Shook his head in silence.

The Russian hitched his chair closer. "The US must realize it would be insane to invade China. So you can't end hostilities that way. Your war aims included evicting the Chinese from the South China Sea. You've done that. Retaken Taiwan. And set the country's development back twenty years. At enormous expense, crippling your own country. What more do you want? Honolulu is gone. Your urban areas are boiling with revolt. End it. Negotiate."

"I'm not saying we wouldn't talk. But this isn't the place to bargain," Blair said. "And I'm not the one you should be discussing this with. Make a proposal. Openly. In the United Nations. Or tomorrow, at the conference. Would the deputy minister be open to doing that?"

Yun froze in his chair. He worked a finger around inside his mouth. Blair stared at him. After a moment he muttered, "I think I had broken a tooth."

The Russian frowned. "Our president will support an armistice proposal. We will even propose one. But it has to include debt guarantees."

"You want America to back the debt China incurred to fight us?" Blair waved it away. "Impossible. Anyway, how much are we talking about?"

"Unless it was a secret agreement," the Russian said.

She turned to Yun, who was still probing his mouth and looking worried. "What would satisfy your principals? If they were presented with the chance for an armistice?"

He spoke right up, as if primed for this question. "The Party must continue to govern. Senior military leaders will be allowed to retire. No prosecutions. No trials."

She opened her mouth to say "No way," when the waiter appeared. *"Ist hier alles in Ordnung? Möchtest du mehr Tee?"*

"Nein, danke," the Russian said, clapping a few francs down on the table. *"Behalte das Wechselgeld."* The waiter scooped them up and left. When they were private again Blond Hair said, "We will propose the armistice as soon as you are ready to talk. The signal will be the debt guarantee. No guarantee, no talks."

She stared him out, but finally had to drop her regard. Why were the Russians steering this scooter? "I'd still need a number. To even present the proposal to the administration."

The Russian shrugged. "Very well. Eighteen hundred billion dollars US."

"Good God," Blair muttered. Even with wartime inflation, it was an unimaginable sum.

He spread his hands. "So much less than you are spending on this war! And bear in mind, China will do the paying. The US is only guaranteeing the loan.

"You don't have to answer now. Just convey the idea." He glanced around once more and rose. "You can contact us through your Irish friend."

Hard-nosed terms, for certain. But it *was* an offer. "And if Chairman Zhang refuses to discuss peace?"

The Russian said, deadpan, "It is very sad, what happened to the leader of North Korea."

Yun did not meet her eyes. He rose, looking deflated, and made as if to follow the Russian out. At the last minute he turned back, gaze pleading. "Please, please, when you pass this on, do not mention names. We would be shot. It is known how many leaks your government has. We will *all* be shot. Do you understand?"

Blair nodded, and he stumbled out, still holding his mouth.

She stared after them, feeling light-headed. Woozy. Could it be possible, they might end this shambles short of a nuclear exchange? Szerenci would lobby against it. He wanted war to the knife. But it *was* an opening. A pathway to peace, however narrow, steep, and rocky.

Outside, in the street-lit square, rain slicked the rounded cobbles. Passing the anonymous-looking building where Vladimir Ulyanov had plotted revolution and tyranny, where the barely started twentieth century had aimed itself at the deaths of millions, she slipped and nearly fell. Fitting the key, pressing the start button, she reminded herself to be cautious heading back. Uphill on wet asphalt, at night, in the rain, on those tiny tires . . . it wouldn't be as easy as coming down.

Take it slow, she told herself. Be vigilant.

One wrong move, on that glassy, black, too-slick surface, and it could well be her last.

15

Northern Xinjiang

T HE village sprawled amid rolling foothills, beneath mountains whose snowcapped peaks floated like the tents of the gods. The sky was cloudless, not blue but a sullen, scorched brownish white. To the south, just visible in the distance, lay the desert. Its brutal, serrated corrugations swelled away to the horizon, and the thin cool wind that blew in from it abraded like a sanding disk.

Teddy Oberg strolled through the bazaar, flanked by personal guards and trailed by other rebels. One carried a video camera. Another, a device with a cloaking app that replaced their faces with those of approved citizens on the security cameras that festered like polyps on steel poles every hundred feet. They were wrapped in heavy robes against the sand and dust. They all had rifles under their wraps, except for Yusuf. He was a recent recruit, a heavily bearded, reticent, hulking twenty-something who claimed a technical education. Teddy had trained him to use the drone rifle, which he toted charged for instant use.

Teddy himself still carried the Chinese carbine he'd picked up last year. The bullpup design looked weird, but he liked it. No recoil, fast follow-up shots, easy to hide, and a great optic sight. They had hundreds of thousands of rounds of ammo, looted from supply trucks and burned-out police stations and scavenged off dead Internal Security troops.

The cadre had come down from the mountains after the imam died. This was the next phase of the insurgency. Blending with the population, gnawing out the overlords' infrastructure from within. In this particular village, the first guerrillas to enter had beheaded the mayor and the police chief, then shot their families and any Han residents misguided enough to remain. The government had bulldozed the mosque; the rebels reopened one in the former police station. Now the townspeople smiled and bowed to them in the street. The women covered their faces and stayed indoors. Other than that, Teddy had kept everyone's heads down for a while, until they could close the trap on Marshal Chagatai.

ITIM was growing. There were cells in all the villages now, and recruiters in each of the scores of concentration camps the Chinese had set up to corral their restive minorities. Not only did thumb drives and DVDs circulate in every bazaar, smart young men and women were hacking the cyber infrastructure the Chinese had gridded over the province to detect "terrorists." Using a CIA-furnished software tool, they spoofed the spyware every smart phone carried. They jammed and misled the facial identification systems that were supposed to identify security risks and predict terrorist actions. Now Qurban's sermons played on the Chinese equivalent of YouTube, registering to the authorities as droning presentations on livestock management. The Han police and troops had to travel in armored vehicles. On foot, they were vulnerable to knifings, shootings, or simply being dragged into alleys and beaten to death.

And he'd laid a trap.

Tomorrow, it would be sprung.

Nasrullah's opium-for-jade traders had spread the word. Surreptitiously dropping a clue here and an oh-so-casual reference there, in the hearing of collaborators, that the IEDs tormenting the authorities were coming from the high valley. A lab, a testing ground, and a school for those who built and planted them. From one of their embeds, a Uighur who served the security forces as a translator, they'd learned Chagatai had taken the bait. Under pressure to end the insurgency, the counterterror general was planning an assault. Even better, he planned to be in on the raid personally, arriving in his helicopter for an inspection and photo op as soon as the rebel base was secured.

Teddy paused, there in the bazaar, to look down at a blanket. Along with the usual brassware, plastic bowls, and cheap battery-powered fans, he'd spotted a strangely shaped hemisphere of grooved wood, half hidden, since the merchant was sitting on it. *"Assalamu äläykum,"* Teddy said, bowing.

The old guy bowed so deep over his wares his beard curled in his lap. *"Wä-äläykum ässalam,* honored chieftain Lingxiù al-Amriki," he mumbled, gaze downcast.

They all knew who he was. Bad? No, good. To know was to fear. To fear was halfway to recruitment. Nasrullah was squeezing the bazaaris and shop owners. Taking half of what they made for the Cause. Using them to help distribute low-volume, high-value imports from Helmand down into the lowlands, then farther east into China proper.

"What is it that you have there, under you?" Teddy asked him.

The old man looked frightened. Reluctantly, he brought it out and handed it up, butt first.

A Mauser broomhandle. The Bolo model, with the stubby barrel. Teddy racked the bolt and an ancient, green-corroded cartridge reluctantly ejected. Making sure that was the only one, he reversed the pistol and peered down the barrel. Pitted, but the lands still visible. He turned it over. The markings were faint, almost obliterated. But it seemed to be a real Mauser, unlike the Chinese and Spanish copies you ran into in out-of-the-way places in Asia. "Where did you obtain this?" he asked the old man.

"Sir, sir, I apologize. I did not know we were to turn in weapons—"

"That was the Han order. Not ours. Only oppressors disarm those they would rule. You are loyal?"

"Oh yes sir, yes sir. Three of my sons are with you. And a grandson—"

"This is good. So, the pistol . . . ?"

"My father's brother bought it from a shepherd. He found it on the mountain. With some bones." The old man cast a frightened glance at Teddy's guards. "Please, sir, accept it. As my gift. Will you not sit for tea? I will have my wife—"

Teddy didn't need more iron to carry, and doubted he could find ammo if he did, but the camera light was on, the video guy crouching. He thumbed a gold Krugerrand from his belt and dropped it on the blanket. The merchant's eyes widened. The cameraman backed off a step, swinging to zoom in on the coin, then on the merchant's face. Teddy reversed the pistol and handed it back butt first. The merchant accepted it reverently, bowing over and over. *"Xäyri xosh.* Peace be with you," Teddy said.

He could already hear the narrator in his head. *"ITIM leaders are peaceful men. Generous to those who are loyal. Resist the Han and bring freedom to all Turkic peoples."* Folding his hands, Teddy tried his best to force a scarred and forbidding countenance into a friendly, approachable smile.

VLADIMIR was due in that afternoon. Teddy hadn't seen his CIA handler since the night the imam had been poisoned, but the promised shipments had arrived. They included six hundred pounds of C-4 plastic explosive, with primacord, fuzes, and remote detonators. The explosive had come up by donkey, the detonators separately. The supply drones had flown low and at night through the mountain passes, landed to drop their hazardous loads, then vanished once more into the dark.

Since the passing of the old imam, Teddy, Guldulla, and al-Nashiri—the ex-al-Qaeda fighter who now called himself Qurban, "The Sacrifice"—had shared leadership in an uneasy triumvirate. Headed, for the sake of appearances, by the Uighur.

But it couldn't continue. Teddy had realized that as he'd knelt beside the imam. Guldulla—Tokarev—he trusted. The mustached fighter dealt openly. His only aim was to eject the hated Han from his homeland.

But the al-Qaeda man wanted more. Abu-Hamid al-Nashiri's fanatics followed Qurban himself, not the Uighur, much less an American foreigner. Only the link with the CIA, and the supplies they provided, gave Teddy the upper hand.

How long that would last, he had no idea.

The school was two stories, cheaply built of concrete blocks by the government, and taken over by the rebels, who'd dismissed the students when they'd infiltrated two days before. Usually they blew up the schools and shot the teachers, but just now they needed a hideout and rallying point. Not to mention a hospital; the cafeteria had become a medical center, for rebels wounded in the last operation.

The room he entered now was a command center. Hastily set up screens lined the walls. Cables pastaed the floor. Notebook computers nestled on laps, their operators cross-legged on colorful rugs with geometric evocations of gardens, flowers, trees, fruit, and birds. Clamps tapped the high-tension line outside town, evading the consumption algorithms that otherwise would alert the army something new was drawing power here. He walked the space as images flickered, as lines of software lit intent young faces. One screen showed the activity of Marshal Chagatai's wife's personal cell. Another monitored communications with the helicopter-borne interior security unit that would carry out tomorrow's raid.

Regular combat units had electronic warfare and signals intelligence sections. Teddy wanted cyber specialists, linguists, and codebreakers. Most of all, he needed signals intelligence. He wanted the ability to spoof, jam, spy on, and ultimately bring down enemy communications, drones, and surveillance.

This rebellion would be fought in cyberspace as much as with rifles and rocket grenades.

Not that they hadn't been expending a lot of those as well. He'd reserved two hundred pounds of the C-4 for IEDs. The old cave actually *was* a school, but each day the completed devices had been packed out. And each day, he'd reduced the number of students, replacing them with volunteer fighters.

They probably wouldn't make it out. But they knew that, and had embraced martyrdom.

One of the young women caught at his robe as he passed. She wore a blue headscarf patterned with butterflies. The Hajji Qurban had demanded they be in full hijab, but Teddy had vetoed that. He liked to see their faces. After a protest, the ALQ veteran had given way with his usual tranquil smile.

"I do not understand what I am reading." She showed Teddy, but it was in Chinese and he wasn't up to recognizing more than a couple of the ideographs. He got "internal security" and "special artillery" but that was all. "What's the problem?" he asked her. Thinking, Damn, she's got nice lips.

As if sensing his attention, she looked down. "This unit they mention is not in the table."

They actually had the Southwest Frontier's Table of Organization, listing and describing every unit assigned to western China. A convert to Islam had filched it from General Chagatai's helicopter, scanned it, and returned it the same night. Teddy had wanted to know how committed the guy was—if he could steal a manual, surely he could plant a bomb—but he'd already been rotated out. Still, they had plans for Chagatai . . . he refocused. "It's not in the TO? What's the unit title?"

"The 103rd Special Counterterror Unit."

"Infantry? Cyber? What?"

She said it might be artillery, but couldn't really tell. Only that it had been deployed the night before to a code-named location.

Teddy stroked his beard. Since they didn't have the key to the code, no telling where it was. Most likely, though, close to the cave complex. Mountain artillery? Part of the strike force the marshal was putting together to hit what he thought was an IED school?

A rebel appeared in the doorway. "For you, Lingxiù," the man said, extending a slip of paper. The rebels didn't use digital communications themselves. Only paper, or more often, simple verbal codes.

Teddy unfolded it. Nodded.

Vladimir had arrived.

The agent was being held in a hut outside the village. Teddy debated going there, but decided bringing him in was the better course. That way he could see what the Agency's money was buying.

THEY embraced, awkwardly, but more easily than the first time, a year before. This was the third visit by the man they knew as

Vladimir. He looked different, and it took Teddy a second glance to make out why. "What happened to the beard?"

The agent shrugged. "Hurt my credibility in the Agency."

"It helps your cred here, bro."

"I'll work on it." He clapped Teddy's shoulder. "You're looking good, though. How's the leg holding up?"

They chatted as he led the way to the schoolhouse, but Teddy's handler fell silent when they entered the command center. He stared around, then whistled. "Impressive. I had no idea."

"You can't run an old-fashioned insurgency. Not against the Chinese."

"I see that, I see that. And, wait, what's that—a typewriter?"

"Can't embed spyware in it. Can't be intercepted. We use it to type five-letter code groups."

"Fascinating, Look, we should get you to do a piece in *Studies in Intelligence*. How to run an insurgency in a cyber-hostile environment—by Theodore Oberg."

The name sounded weird, as if it had been his in some previous incarnation. But it wasn't anymore.

He was the Lingxiù.

But he couldn't tell this guy that.

So instead he took the agent's hand and led him into the cafeteria, which was filled with wounded and groaning men attended by hastily trained medics. Into the armory, where weapons were being repaired. He showed him a drone they'd jammed and recovered when it fell from the sky. Vlad kept shaking his head and exclaiming.

Until finally they were in Teddy's own room. Actually, the janitor's closet. Dandan had fixed it up some, but it fitted his image as the ascetic, luxury-spurning battle commander. Had to think about shit like that if you wanted to lead a rebellion. They settled on the carpet, and the girl brought tea and crackers. Teddy was settling in for another tea-and-chat session when a dull concussion tinkled the cups on the tray.

Vladimir tensed. "What was that?"

Teddy had half risen when a second, much louder detonation rattled the mop buckets. He grabbed his carbine, jumped to his feet,
and rushed out.

In the control room the guys and girls were still working away,
heads down. Damn, Teddy thought. I got me some serious operators
here.

Then the first shell came through the roof.

It exploded in the cafeteria. The whole school rocked. The second
landed just outside, in the playground. Teddy caught the flash. But
even as he ducked under a desk and the window blew in, he was
thinking: That wasn't high explosive.

"What the fuck," he muttered as a billowing mist swept off the
playground and filtered through the shattered window. Other detonations shook the ground and the air. Other shells, but only a few
went off with the ear-shattering crack of high explosive. It wasn't a
crushing barrage. More like a carefully spaced scattering, some near
the school, others farther away.

Then his eyes stung. Vladimir seized his arm. "It's gas," the CIA
agent yelled. He yelled it again, to the room, in Chinese.

They began screaming and jumping up. "Save the computers,"
Teddy yelled, and laptops slammed shut and plugs were yanked from
extension cords. "Into the basement!"

"No!" Vladimir shouted. "It's chlorine. Chlorine settles. Get them
outside. Disperse and fight. That's all we can do."

"It isn't *all*," Teddy yelled back. His throat burned. The faintly
green vapors were almost invisible, but breathing them was like
drinking bleach. He could feel his lungs dying. His sight swam in
tears. He picked up a discarded headscarf from the floor, tied blue
butterflies over his mouth and nose. "Follow me."

The air outside was choking, smoky, filled with screams. Shells
were still falling all across the town. This was a big attack. A house
exploded across the street. The upper floor lifted for a fraction of
a second, then disintegrated into a cloud of the dried mud it had
been molded from. The ocher dust mingled with the green mist rolling through the streets, darkening the air, turning it the ominous
reddish brown of dried blood. The townspeople were running like

ants. They carried children, coughing and sneezing. Some fell as he watched, to lie convulsing and kicking, hacking a bloody foam at nose and mouth.

"Get on the rooftops," he yelled to a passing family. "The gas settles." The father sneered at him, spat a curse, and pushed past.

Vlad, beside him. "Helos," he said through a muffling sleeve, and pointed.

Teddy wheeled, and saw the familiar shapes. He unslung the carbine and checked the magazine. Inadequate, but all he had.

The gunships came in first. Z-10s, in their trademark tight formation. Behind them, staggered at different altitudes, the bulky, carpenter-bee lumberings of the troop carriers. But with something under them he didn't recognize. Floats?

The gunships banked and went in. He couldn't see what they were firing at, but the oddly pedestrian stutter of miniguns drifted down from the sky.

"You should have given us those Stingers," he said.

Vlad grimaced, admitting Teddy was probably right. Then yelled, "Gas dispensers."

The lead pair of transports tipped into a shallow descent, and banked outward, one left, the other right. A silvery mist trailed out behind them, whirled and spread by the rotor wash as it descended, encircling the town.

Teddy nodded, pointing the carbine up, but not firing. They were far out of range.

The Han weren't just after the rebels. Though they were the main target, no doubt.

They were going to kill everyone in town.

Chagatai had struck first. And neither Teddy's cyber team nor Nasrullah's spies had warned them.

Qurban lurched out of the scrum fighting to escape the school and collided with them. He recoiled, then grabbed both Americans and dragged them after him toward the bazaar.

Teddy resisted, then gave way and ran with him. They weren't getting out; the wall of gas and strafing the Chinese were building around the town was locking them in. The only alternative was to go to ground, endure, then kill as many of the black-clad troops as possible when they landed. Go down fighting.

As they emerged into the square a toadstool of flame and black smoke rammed upward to the north. Teddy couldn't see what it was, but Qurban's walkie-talkie crackled like a brushfire with rapid Arabic. "One of the black birds has fallen," the squat hajji yelled back. He made a ninety-degree spin move and pelted full tilt into another alley. Teddy and Vlad sprinted after him. Standing in the open didn't seem like a good tactic, with the gunships lining up for another strafing pass. A ripple of shells exploded behind them, tearing the marketplace apart into screams, blood, wreckage, and smoke.

Qurban's back-turned face. An open mouth in a gray beard. "One of their helicopters crashed. An opening. To the north. We must go up."

Apparently "up" in this context meant scrambling up a ladder to the rooftop. Here in town the flat roofs were separated only by a few feet, enough to jump. They scurried helter-skelter over the rooftops, boots skidding on terra-cotta tiles and corrugated iron. In the alleys below the mist swirled. The dying littered the streets, flopping like beached fish. When they had to descend a staircase and cross to the next roof, Teddy tried to hold his breath, but sensed fluid building in his lungs. He wheezed and coughed until he retched, doubled over, but still couldn't clear his airway.

A black silhouette flashed above them. He dashed away snot and tears with a sleeve, unlimbered the carbine, and fired out a magazine, the butt pressing his shoulder, leading his target by eye. As he'd expected, his bullets made no visible difference. He jammed in a second magazine and resumed scrambling across the roofs.

But he was tiring. Losing it. Didn't seem to be able to get enough to breathe, no matter how hard he panted.

As the slope rose the homes began spacing out, becoming separate compounds. The three fugitives were on the ground now, retching and stumbling. A pyre of black smoke rose ahead. Qurban was headed right for it. Teddy noted the direction of the plume at the same moment Vlad screamed not to go that way. "Go upwind. Upwind! Whatever's in those belly tanks is in that smoke." The hajji hesitated, then nodded.

They circled the crash site. Bodies in black uniforms lay crumpled around it, smoking or on fire. One struggled to rise, and Teddy put a double tap into his back. Around them other rebels, some with rifles, most without, struggled through the brush and rugged shallow ravines. Trying to filter out. A gunship circled. As he'd trained them, everyone froze in place. It seemed to work. The ship droned past, gaining altitude.

Qurban gained the shelter of a hole in the ground, and Teddy and Vlad tumbled in with him. They coughed and panted. Vlad blew drooling strings of red-tinted snot into the dry soil. "Well, that was unexpected," he muttered.

Teddy bent over, gripped with uncontrollable laughter at the same moment he was racked with coughing spasms and an overwhelming desire to barf. He hacked and guffawed. Finally he wiped both hands down his slick, filthy face. "Sorry."

"Teddy, this is a fucking disaster," the CIA man said. "Somehow they knew this was your HQ."

"Not my HQ. Distributed operations."

"Well, they knew we were here. Unless you think this was a random attack on a Uighur village?"

Teddy said he didn't have any idea. But then, remembered the detection of the special counterterror unit. Maybe artillery, the headscarved girl had said. What had happened to her, anyway? And Dandan, was she still back there? Well, bed slaves were expendable.

Vlad persisted. "They knew you were here. Or anyway, that a leadership node was here."

"Maybe they were tracking *you*," Teddy said. "That's possible too. Right?"

Small-arms fire crackled from back in the town. The high-pitched snapping of the Chinese rounds, answered only now and then by the lower-pitched barks of AKs. Teddy coughed again, not feeling much like laughing now. It sounded like the Chinese were shooting anyone left alive.

Vlad said, "I doubt that. The leak was probably from within your organization. Who wasn't here today?"

"I did not see Nasrullah," Qurban put in. He blew his nose in his fingers and slung it into the soil, then reseated the magazine in his AK and cast a glance skyward. "But we should move. The black devils will be combing the village. Counting the bodies of the Faithful for their masters in Beijing."

Teddy checked the sky too. Clear. For the moment. The transports must have gone back for a second wave. "Let's move," he grunted, and scrambled out of the gully.

THEY had a rally point to the north, between the village and the pass out of which they'd descended to the lowlands. Only a scatter of stone shepherds' huts, with half-dug-out caves leading back into the mountain, but he'd stocked it with food and ammo for just such a contingency as this.

A chill was descending, walking down out of the high ravines, as the leaders convened that night around a shielded fire. The rest of the surviving rebels were getting their heads down in another hut.

Teddy. Guldulla. Qurban. Vlad.

And Nasrullah, the youngest. Their link with the lowland traders, and their chief spymaster. He'd shown up two hours after the attack, explaining he'd been held up while making the final arrangements for the ambush at the old cave site. "Which is still on, yes?" he asked, warning his hands at the fire and ignoring the chilly reception the hajji, in particular, had given him.

"I don't know." Teddy was suspicious too. Vlad sat a few feet off, keeping his counsel. "If our HQ got blown, did our trap for the marshal?"

The younger man spread his hands. "The charges are planted, yes? The arrangements are made. It is too late to stop."

Teddy had to agree. Reluctantly. If there was even a micro chance to terminate Chagatai, they had to take it. He turned his cell on and called up the app that gave him remote viewing of the cave mouth. Yusuf, his tech guy, had set up six cameras. They showed the uphill approach to the valley, the sky overhead, and two views of the cave entrance. The interior cameras, when he toggled to them, showed the interior of the main cavern, with its toppled statuary and the carefully arranged paraphernalia of bombmaking.

And far above, packed into the bats' holes in the cave roof, four hundred pounds of plastic explosive.

But if their location had been given away, maybe their trap had been blown too.

He kept toggling between the sky screen and the one showing the valley. Anyone invading had to come either by helo or on foot. But nothing stirred. The dusk deepened, and the fire crackled.

Finally Guldulla stirred. "They aren't coming." He looked around at the fire-lit faces. "They knew."

With a smooth, practiced movement, Qurban drew a pistol from under his sheepskin coat. Nasrullah had only an instant to gaze into its muzzle, just long enough for his eyes to widen.

The bullet threw the Uighur spymaster's head back. Qurban fired twice more, so rapidly it was all one burst, into the groin and chest. Nasrullah was dead before he sprawled backward full length on the sand.

A wisp of powder smoke drifted on the breeze. The fire crackled. Nasrullah's legs twitched, spasmed. Then, slowly, the tremors died away and the corpse lay still. The old hajji clicked his safety back on. He slid the pistol away again as the others stared at him in horror.

"You had no right to do that," Teddy sputtered at last.

Qurban said coldly, "He was the traitor. That is plain."

"Why 'plain'? If he tipped off the marshal, why would he show up here again?"

"To continue his treachery. That is obvious."

"It could have been someone who worked for him. One of his spies."

"Then he was incompetent. In any case the punishment is the same." Qurban drew up his legs, in their ragged trousers, and glared around at them. "When will you learn you are leading a jihad? There is no room for mercy here. A whole town died. Because of him? No man can know. But all will see that we execute justice. If he was innocent, Allah will welcome him. If he was guilty, he will burn in Jehannum. There, let that be an end to it."

Teddy glanced at Vladimir, who looked shaken. The agent, though, didn't speak. So he had to. He turned to Guldulla. "Tok, you're our leader. Our judge. Not this guy. Whatever he thinks."

But the Uighur was gnawing his mustache. "I agree, that was a hasty trial."

"That wasn't a *trial*. That was murder."

"True. It was done too quickly. But 1 cannot bring him back, Lingxiù. Nor can you. And perhaps the hajji is right. Perhaps he *was* a double agent. Working for the Han, while pretending to spy for us. Was it not he who told us Chagatai would be there? And he did not come." Guldulla sighed, and nodded heavily. "Perhaps it is best to let this pass quietly. He was cleaning his pistol, and it went off. But . . . someone will need to take his place,"

"Yusui," Qurban put in. "He is skilled, and trustworthy as well."

Teddy shuddered inside. He hadn't realized the big technician was one of his enemy's young radicals. And he'd been beside Teddy all day, a knife's-length away.

But the gray-bearded terrorist was turning to him now. Putting his hand on Teddy's knee. "You too, al-Amriki. Do you agree, the traitor had to die?"

Teddy hesitated, looking into those gray-blue orbs. Mustering his own will to meet them. He'd liked Nasrullah. Trusted him. The kid was into some hinky deals, sure. Trading the fat-marbled jade of Xinjiang, silver and gold and surplus weapons to the Pashtun for opium, and opium back east for weapons and information and money for bribes. He probably had dirty hands . . . but you couldn't run an espionage network with clean ones. And his own palms weren't exactly pristine.

But now . . . replace him with one of Qurban's minions?

The strategy was clear. First Imam Akhmad, then Nasrullah. Step by step, the professional jihadist was liquidating the original leaders. Taking over the rebellion. Remaking it in the blood-stained image of the evil he'd served before.

Teddy had no doubt he himself was the next target.

Beneath his tunic, he wrapped his fingers around the hand grip of his Makarov. Watching Qurban's shoulder in the flickering light. Waiting for the intention movement. Across the fire, he glimpsed Vladimir's fingers snailing toward his own gun.

But the hajji didn't move. And after a moment Teddy forced himself to say, "I agree with our leader. The traitor had to die."

THEY slept in the hut with the others that night. But Teddy couldn't sleep. His lungs burned. He couldn't catch his breath. So he kept one hand on his thin-blade and lay listening. Maybe a drowse toward morning, but every snore and crackle as someone turned over in the straw startled him awake again.

That last time he woke, someone was crouching over him. The blade whipped out, and he stabbed up with every bit of force he could muster.

To have his wrist caught, and the blade twisted harmlessly away. "It's me," Vladimir whispered, lips touching his ear.

"What do you want?"

"I'm leaving. Come outside."

The thin dim cold of morning. The mountains were black cutouts against gray sky. Stars still glittered. His CIA liaison sagged to perch on a stone. A Zippo click-clanged open, followed by the rasp of the striker wheel against flint. "Want one?"

"No, I . . . okay." Teddy accepted the smoke. The first inhalation triggered the burning in his chest all over again, and he stifled what felt like his lungs convulsing. He hastily passed it back. "You leaving?"

"Need to get back. Need to turn over something. And orders."

Gold clinked as Vladimir laid a soft bag in his hands. More Krugerrands. "To keep things going," his contact said. "You can bounce back from this."

"I thought we had Chagatai. But he outsmarted us."

"Not every operation succeeds. You rebuild, and move on to the next."

"They killed everyone in that town. Everyone."

"Like Lidice. I know. Chagatai will stand trial after the war."

"Do you see now? I was right about that al-Qaeda son of a bitch."

"He's an inspirational speaker. He's built your numbers."

"He's turning it into a jihad."

"If that's what it takes to force Beijing to the table, we can deal with it later. By then you'll be out of here. But before you leave, we have one more tasking."

He slid his cell out of his pocket. After a hesitation, Oberg withdrew his as well. A faint note chimed as they synced.

"What is it this time?" Teddy muttered.

"We're calling it Operation Jedburgh."

"Go on."

"We've identified a heavy missile base northeast of the Taklimakan. There's a contingency plan to take it out with nukes. But it'd be less risky if we could do it with a ground assault."

Teddy didn't like it. "*Less* risky? Not for us. Take out a launch site . . . that's gonna be heavily guarded. Special sensors. Special troops."

"Your people destroyed Jade Emperor."

"We took seventy-five percent casualties."

"This mission could end the war. I'm serious. It's that important." Vladimir's voice went urgent, cajoling. "Once you hit the base, we'll pull you out. We've discussed this with the Teams. You've spent long enough out in the cold. A well-deserved rest. Promotion to warrant, with pay backdated to your capture. A training assignment, back in San Diego. Where Salena lives, right? Then medical retirement, if you want it. Or if you don't, a senior position with the Agency. Special Activities Division."

Teddy tried to visualize what the guy was talking about. Back to the United States? When he'd only found meaning out here, in the mountains. Found God, or something enough like Him that his fucked-up, wasted, cunt-chasing life finally seemed to make sense.

There is no choice. There is no chance.

There is only My will.

Was this His will?

Shielding the glow, he thumbed the phone on. Flicked through the map, then the plan. His heart sank. "You're asking for all the effectives we have left."

"It's that important."

Important? Or an extermination strategy, a suicide mission designed to snuff out the rebellion? A fucking missile base . . . he'd have to lie to his guys. They wouldn't see the point. His leadership was shaky enough now.

Finally he murmured, "You wouldn't even give us Stingers. And you saw what those gunships did to us. Sorry, I can't sign up for this one, Vlad."

The other didn't answer for a time, just sat, an immobile shadow. Finally he murmured, "I got to take a piss. Be right back."

THE satellite channel was clear tonight. The agent waited, shivering in the cold, while his call went from the monitor up to those he reported to. He blinked up at the coldly shining stars. One was probably the tiny satellite that was bouncing his voice around the world.

Finally his supervisor came on the line. He muttered, "Mister P, this is Andres."

The news didn't go down well. *"Can we really count on this guy's loyalty?"* his supervisor asked. *"Is he going native on us?"*

"Give me one more chance to turn him around. He wants MAN-PADS."

"Forget it. No Stingers to insurgents."

"He took major losses from gunships yesterday. He won't do it without them."

"I'm not going up the line with that."

"Then he won't take the mission, sir. And I can't say he's in the wrong. The Chinese decimated his people from the air. He had no way to fight back."

Silence. Voices, in the background. Then, finally, *"We'll have to disavow."*

"Is Jedburgh that important?"

"Important? Yeah. It's crucial. So . . . if that's what it takes. A limited number. On loan. With the short-life batteries. So they can't go rogue on us later."

He trudged back to the hut. Squatted, again, on the same rock. The black silhouette of the rebel leader waited opposite him. Oberg coughed hard, an agonizing sound that was more like a retch. Vlad's lungs ached too. He couldn't help thinking of all the villagers. Gassed to death.

They had to bring Zhang down. If they had to make sacrifices to do it . . .

"I got you Stingers, Master Chief," he muttered. "They didn't want to release them. But they will. For this one mission. There'll be more gold too. Guns. Medical supplies. Eavesdropping equipment. Even your own recon drones, if you want them."

The SEAL's silhouette remained still. Silent. As if pondering. Finally he murmured, "And this mission will end the war?"

"Yes."

TEDDY sat motionless, thinking it over. He hacked and spat. Closing his eyes, he flashed back on the terror of the flight over the rooftops. The corpses carpeting the streets. Exterminated by their own government, and any survivors murdered.

No. It wasn't *their* government. Just brutal oppressors, who massacred them because they wanted freedom. Maybe not the CIA's brand of freedom, or America's. But their own.

If he agreed, a lot of his men would die. Or Qurban might succeed in turning them on him.

But if Jedburgh worked, it might finish the war.

Was this His will? Or the warped desires of ignorant, deluded men?

He coughed again, dreading the welling of fluid in his lungs. Well, he could pull out, if it looked too dangerous. And with more gold, guns, shoulder-fired missiles, they could rebuild from today's catastrophe. Grow the rebellion. That was his mission out here, after all. And surely that had to be Allah's will too.

But even he could hear the doubt in his voice as he muttered reluctantly, there in the dark, "Okay. We'll give it a shot."

16

USS *Liscombe Bay,*
the Eastern Sea

NIGHT, deep night, but in the infrared goggles the heat still ed- died in shimmering waves off the steel deck, griddle-hot from where the strike fighters had warmed up. The dark lightninged from strobes. It shuddered with the SHUMP SHUMP SHUMP of huge four-bladed rotors powering through the greasy sea air.

Sergeant Hector Ramos bent into the prop blast, clutching his Mickey Mouse ears. They were clamped tight, but the engines all around still battered at his brain. Behind him the platoon waited, down on one knee, gear-heavy, silent, focused on the black aircraft that squatted ahead, maws open. Half the Marines were human. The others were CHADs, in a new pairing-up Higher thought might be a better tactical mix.

At the far end of the flight deck, the UAVs were taking off.

Ahead, the vertical takeoff aircraft that would shuttle the Second of the Third in to hit the beach.

Behind, his men and women.

Second Battalion, Third Marines. He'd hit hostile beaches with them on Itbayat and Taiwan. But he was practically the only one left from those assaults, aside from a few lifers in the head shed. A staff sergeant now, but he never felt like he knew what he was doing. Embrace the suck, sure, but the enemy had cut down so many officers so fast the new ones had no idea what to do in combat.

Which left the Combat Action Ribbon vets. Like him.

The Corps had reorganized again, struggling to learn from the bloodbath on Taiwan. A squad still had three fire teams, but only six members were human. Each team was led by a human lance corporal or PFC, and built around a M240B machine gun, the new titanium-framed model with increased rate of fire. A Sensor and Robotics Controller had been added to each platoon. Hector's "sark," as everyone immediately called him, was a slim Puerto Rican named Vacante. Vacante spoke a weird Spanglish but Hector could make himself understood when they went off-line so the others wouldn't hear.

Except for the Pigs, everyone's weapons had suppressors now, plus a stabilized sight and a laser pulser built into their rangefinders that would dazzle an enemy at three hundred yards. Their jelly armor was tougher and when they moved it generated power for their electronics. Their helmets incorporated night vision, intrasquad radio, and Battle-Glass data. The heavy face shields opaqued like a welder's goggles when a laser hit them.

The nonhuman squad members were CHAD Ds, driven by an uprated AI that was supposed to give each robot the combat reactions of a Marine PFC.

Hector scratched at his eye. He'd had the face shield pushed up just for a second when out of nowhere some bit of grit or steel blew off the deck and into his eye. The more he dug at it, the worse it would feel. Fuck it, he thought. Let it fucking go blind if it wanted to. He snatched his hand down.

He was looking at the nearly invisible disk of the propeller.

For some reason, last-second maintenance probably, the VTOL had its engine nacelles turned partially down, nearly horizontal to the deck. The flight crew had a ladder up to the engine. The Marines were holding to see if it could be readied in time for the launch.

This time, for the plains of North Korea, east of Pyongyang.

The lieutenant said it would be like Inchon, except from the east. He said Kim was dead, the regime decapitated. It must have been a hell of a naval battle. They'd passed smoking wrecks of three ships on the way in, and the Marines had spent all night up on the flight deck, in case a torpedo found the carrier.

Hector had already decided: He didn't plan to survive this one.

He curled his fingers around the crucifix in his pocket. Mirielle had sent it, since he'd lost the rosary on the steps of the government building in Taipei. *To remember me by*, she'd written.

The lieutenant down-crouched beside him in the thundering dark. Hector reoriented his brain, but it felt slow, a hard turn, like steering a truck across a potato field. He'd done that when he was ten, on Mister Savage's farm. He'd felt so grown up that day. Until his too-short foot could not reach the accelerator, and the harvester had edged up on him, and suddenly hundreds of pounds of dirt and potatoes had cascaded in his open window, burying him where he sat.

Burying him . . .

"Staff Sergeant. You with us?"

"Yessir." He tried to straighten, to look alert. But who was this? It wasn't roly-poly little Lieutenant Ffoulk. Wasn't angular tall Hawkshadow. So who? He couldn't remember. Lieutenant . . . but his mind had gone blank. The pills deadened the rage. Stopped the blackouts. But they numbed him, too, made him more a robot than the mechanical shapes crouched behind him. "Yes, sir. Say again, sir? Those engines are so fucking—"

"I said, five-minute hold."

"The wave, sir, or just us?"

"Five minutes on everybody, but get ready to load. Should get the word over—"

The soft-voiced AI the troops called Wet Dream said in his headphones, *"Wave two, five-minute hold."* Hector tapped his headphones; the lieutenant slapped his shoulder and went to the next stick.

Hector looked back along the line of troops. A hand lifted. Patterson was a squad leader now. He'd gotten that for her at least. Karamete was a sergeant, the platoon guide.

And he, Ramos, platoon sergeant. Expected to lead. Expected to take them into the fight.

But he couldn't. Not again.

He lifted a hand in return, muttered, "hope you make it though this, Wombat." Then faced front again. To where, past the deck edge, a black-on-black horizon was beginning to show. Delay much longer, they'd lose the dark.

But he wouldn't be here to worry about it.

The engine roar increased. The deck shook. The other VTOLs were warming up too. Their own still had its props lowered. Was spinning up. A whirring disk, nearly invisible, though lit, in his goggles, by the infrared plumes of the engine exhaust.

Setting his rifle aside on the deck, Hector hoisted himself to his feet. He walked forward, unbuckling his pack.

Ahead, the deadly blur of the propeller.

Behind, he supposed, his Marines were staring after him.

He started to shrug the pack off.

Then stopped. Hesitated.

The platoon was watching.

If he did this, if he abandoned them, they'd die too.

So what? They were gonna anyway. Like all the others.

He stood shaking, drenched in sudden cold sweat, two paces from the whirling propeller. The wind was sucking him toward it. A mechanic looked down, mouth open in a soundless yell. Those huge blades would end all fear. All terror. Right now. It would end.

A hand clamped his shoulder. Karamete, shouting into his ear. He couldn't hear the words, but she was yanking on his load-bearing equipment. Pulling him back with violent jerks. He resisted, then gave way. Stepped back from the prop. She thrust his carbine into his hands. Pushed her helmet into his, so they were touching. "We need to vack you, Staff Sar'n't," she shouted. "You shouldn't be on this op."

"Fuck that. You just want my billet."

"Yeah . . . yeah, I want your fucking asshole billet." She guffawed. "The fuck you think you're going? You got a straw? Suck it up, battle buddy. Oorah?"

"Rah. Rah. Thought that was the word to go."

He allowed her to drag him back to the queue, but halfway there the intrasquad told them to board. He let the dread go, with the terror. Blanked his mind, and signaled the platoon to their feet.

The prop blast battered them as they lurched forward, each marine bent under a hundred and fifty pounds of assault pack, weapon, ammo, food. The flight deck crew flicked wands of invisible light, waving them to the boarding ramp. Hector had already transmitted his manifest to the loading assistant. He faced the ramp, telling each man, woman, or robot as they passed to strap in and thumbs-up. When they were all boarded, he swung himself on too.

THE flight in jolted the hell out of them. Even above the roar of the turbines Hector heard the explosions outside. The airframe jolted, tilted, shuddered. A bang outside, a rattle against the fuselage, and wind whistled through holes. Hector rode with eyes closed, fists clamped on his carbine. Thinking of absolutely nothing but the map. He'd downloaded it to his command tablet, and he could access it with the BattleGlasses. But in the mountains of Taiwan so much gear had gone diddley fuck he'd decided he needed it stored in his head too this time.

Before embarking the Marines had worked in Taipei loading the ships. No one knew how many there were total, because they came from different ports. He'd counted seventy in Taipei alone. Missiles had screamed in several times a day, forcing everyone to take cover and keep masks handy. A constant threat of air attack from across the strait. Two ships were hit going out and left behind, burning.

Operation Catapult. ROK airborne would parachute in to feint an assault farther north, but the Marines would make the main landing, with the Japanese conducting a parallel assault to the south. He'd memorized his objectives for D-day. If they could reach those, Division would echelon more forces ashore and move to the next phase: reinforcing, holding any counterattack, and transitioning to sustained combat operations. The Third would be a maneuver unit. Since this was the fighting season, with hard ground and the rice paddies drained, they'd move with the tanks, punching through and penetrating deep into the enemy's rear.

At least that was the plan. The plan had worked on Itbayat. Sort of. Hadn't gone very well on Taiwan, though. But this was a different enemy, not Chinese. North Korean. Maybe their regime was decapitated. But no one seemed to think they wouldn't fight, once the Allies hit the beaches.

The beaches. The diversion to the north was on Red Beach. The Japanese were landing on Blue. The Marines, on White. The hydrography was gradual for a quarter mile behind the high-tide point. Past that was rough ground, gun emplacements, concealed pillboxes, and dug-in tanks. The air and CAS drones had worked them over but there were probably plenty left. A mile in they would hit flat land, a river delta landfill. Possibly too soft for armor; the tanks would hook to the right. The city would be to their left. Leaflets and drones had warned the inhabitants to leave, but Higher doubted the enemy would let them. Which could mean dismounted urban operations. Regardless, they'd punch ahead on the right while the Japanese struck to the left. Past the city they'd join up again for the push on the capital. Always staying alert, this time, for a Chinese incursion on their right flank, across the border.

Semper Gumby, as the old Marine saying had it. Always flexible.

"Rampart, Iron Dream. Three minutes out," the intrasquad AI said in his earbuds.

Hector blinked. Had he been here before?

Yeah. He definitely had.

When he opened his eyes one of the CHADs was watching him, tiny head cocked, its buglike, multi-lensed oculars glittering in the gloom as if lit from within. Its identifier, stenciled on its chest, read 323. They stared at each other in silence, machine and man.

Something detonated outside, or maybe it was just flares. The airframe jolted, then rolled so far he grabbed for the seat frame. "One mike," said Iron Dream in his earbuds. Then another voice, male. "Heliteam leader, crew chief. You'll exit the aircraft facing south. The terminal will be to your right front. The fighter revetments, behind you. The ferry harbor will be on your left."

"This is Rampart 1-2, roger. Thanks for the lift."

"Give 'em hell, Rampart."

Seconds later the airframe jolted, hard, and Dream added, "On deck."

"This is crew chief: on deck, dropping ramp."

Hector had popped his lap belt and hoisted to his feet. "Rampart 1-2, load and lock. Deplane, deplane," he'd yelled.

But that was then.

This was now.

Again.

He shuddered, gripping his weapon, squeezing his eyes shut. Weren't two-island Marines supposed to be over this . . . over this fear? But it got worse every time. Not better. Worse.

While you were supposed to pretend—

Someone was shaking him. Shouting in his ear.

He opened his eyes unwillingly. "On deck, Sergeant," Karamete was yelling, bent over to screen him from the others.

Oh yeah. He was supposed to be first out. The ramp was already down. The night was flickering, so bright it blanked his NVDs. He thumbed them off, stood, yelled an "Oorah," as loud as his lungs would yield, and forced shaky legs to totter him down the ramp.

Into a flickering, noise-crammed night. He oriented, pointing his guys out to their perimeter. A shell burst a hundred meters away. The shock wave pressed his chest. His mouth was cottony. Flashes lit the hills. Line of advance . . . break through, disrupt the defense . . . fight and lead to the objective.

The air was fogged white, making it hard to see. Dust? Mist? Smoke? It didn't seem to be gas. Whatever it was made the beams flickering through it visible. His face shield blanked, then cleared. Tank engines growled to the north, interspersed with the deafening cracks of high-velocity guns. Drones whirred overhead, heading inland. A fine mist of particles fell from them.

The lieutenant was talking in his earphones but Hector couldn't make out what he was saying over the noise. So he ignored it. Skirmishers? Wedge? Wedges were easier to control. He hand-signaled the platoon into a vee of squads, each squad into a wedge of fire teams, and led them forward as at close to a trot as he could manage. The ground yielded, mushy under his boots. Puddles glinted. This must be the landfill. Too fucking flat, why were they even here? Zero microterrain. No cover. Get across as fast as possible. Patterson waved at him, pointed to an area in front of her. *Mine.*

Oh, God no, Hector thought. Flat land, and mined? Then he realized why they were skirting the road. Looking back, he realized something else. Behind him, thickset forms with narrow heads were moving more slowly than the rest.

"Rampart, Rampart One. We got a problem."

"Go ahead." Hector crouched, cupping an ear to the intraplatoon.

"CHADs are falling behind. Ground won't take their weight."

"Fuck. Uh—they're holding up the advance, we leave them behind."

"Leave them—? That cuts our effectives by half."

"They can catch up when we make contact. We got to keep moving." His own boots were sinking deeper too, almost disappearing in the muck. Shit, he thought. If this gets much deeper, none of us are going anywhere, human or machine.

The growl of engines and crack of guns to his right intensified. Armor was fighting inland along the road. The platoon had to guard their flank.

Rockets flashed above, wove, and dove into the ground ahead. The muck quaked. Fiery pinwheels rose above the flashes, and drones flickered in and out. *"Somebody's getting their asses handed to 'em,"* one of the squad leaders offered.

Hector signaled the base fire team off to the right, where it looked like it might be slightly firmer terrain. He couldn't slide too far in that direction or he'd collide with the next platoon, but maybe they were having the same problem. He tried the radio but couldn't raise them. An ominous crackle grew ahead, as they waded toward what looked like a paddy wall.

Geysers of wet muck blasted up, spattering his face with mud as he dived flat. A heavy MG. And they were out in the open . . . he rolled over, opened his tablet, and punched it in. The drones hesitated, milling around; then wheeled, merged into a swarm, and dove. The *tap-tap-tap* faltered, then fell silent.

Another two hundred meters. The paddy seemed endless. The platoon alternated rushing and dropping, in case somebody remanned the gun. Hector lay in the mud, yearning desperately to stay there, but forced himself to his feet. *I'm up.* He rushed. *They see me.* He dropped. *I'm down.* Around him the others sprinted forward in bursts, then covered the others as they in turn exposed themselves.

They reached the paddy wall, panting, mud-smeared, exhausted, but without being fired on again. The wall was like a dike, running roughly north and south, about twenty feet above the lower ground behind them and ten feet above the ground ahead. Bodies in green uniforms were sprawled around their weapons. Some were still trying to crawl. The Marines kicked their rifles away, or shot them if they wouldn't give them up. Beyond the dike to the west flat ground stretched away, stitched with small sheds and, between them, what looked like vegetable fields with stakes and nets. To protect the crops from birds, Hector figured. He'd seen nets like that growing up. In the far distance more brown mountains rose.

Karamete pulled the block out of the enemy MG and whipped it sidehanded out into the paddy. Hector fired several rounds into an antitank launcher with bodies sprawled around it, then looked again at the flat land ahead and wished he hadn't. They might need a weapon like that if the enemy counterattacked with tanks.

Well, fuck, too late now . . . should think before he acted . . . He checked his tablet. The flanking platoons had reached their objective line too. He didn't understand, it looked like they were parked out here practically in the open, but those were the orders.

"Rampart, consolidate in place," came down from Company. He pointed his guys out into a hasty 180 and started improving his position, basing it on the dugout they'd just captured. The tablet recommended his geometry of fire and it looked okay, so he got his guns digging in right and left along the paddy wall and threw OPs out. As Vacante, the sark, deployed ground sensors a kilometer to their front, Hector got on the tactical for ACE reports.

A rank of slowly marching machines caught his eye. The robots, just now catching up. They dragged mud-caked extremities through the soft soil as if they were wading. He put the word out to send one back from each squad to bring up more ammunition, and to reintegrate the rest into the fire teams as they arrived.

The drones were still buzzing above them, orbiting, dipping in, optical turrets flicking from one face to the next. Hector waved at them. It was futile, they wouldn't respond, but he was worried that with the mud covering his guys and the mist over the battlefield the things might not be able to read the uniforms. He was still waving when Karamete bent and picked up a Korean rifle out of the mud.

"Don't—!" Vacante shouted.

"No," Hector yelled, taking a step toward her.

The drone had been headed away, toward the front, but suddenly it banked. It rotated in midair and banked again, back toward her. The platoon guide froze, staring upward at it as Hector jerked forward, stumbling as the soft earth gave way, grabbing for the enemy rifle.

A jet of fire lanced down from the drone and drilled into Karamete's chest. She went down without a scream, without a sound. Or maybe it was just covered by the whirring as the other disks wheeled back, like a swarm of aroused hornets, and began buzzing to and fro over them, optics glinting this way and that.

The whole squad had rifles up, aiming at the drone that had fired, which was still hovering threateningly. "Cease fire," Vacante shouted. Hector repeated it, waving his open palm in front of his face in the cut signal. For a heart-stopping moment the humans and robots below and the hovering disks above froze, weapons trained on each other. Then, apparently, the disks decided they were friendly. They canted away and buzzed off, zigzagging in erratic but probably closely coordinated patterns to reconnoiter the fields,

Karamete lay still conscious, blinking up. One of the squaddies pulled her jelly armor away. It revealed a charred hole in her chest. There wasn't any blood. Just black char. Hector took a knee. They looked at each other. "Gloria," he said.

Her lips twitched, but she didn't say anything. She looked away from him, up at the sky. Then closed her eyes.

Hector whirled away and fired out his magazine toward the fields. Then the others' hands were on him. Removing the carbine. Patting his back. The world turning white, like a jet of fire. Then red. Then black.

HE woke on his back, staring up at the same white sky. Like Karamete. His brain was dead as the sky.

Patterson was crouched over him. "Hey," she said. "*Hey.* Staff Sar'n't. You there?"

"Here," he grunted, and tried to sit up.

She pressed him back down with firm hands. "The old man's online again," she yelled to someone. Then, to him, "Lieutenant says, stand to. Counterattack's forming up, in those hills."

He cradled his head. Then groped in the mud. "My rifle. Where's—"

"Sark's got it. Sure you ready for it?"

He held out a hand. She handed it over reluctantly.

"Take cover," Wet Dream said in his earbuds. *"Take cover. Gas attack. Gas attack. Set MOPP level four. Active agent, presumed VX. Set MOPP level four. Active agent, presumed VX."*

With a distant rumble fiery trails leapt up far ahead. One after the other, so fast it had to be a rocket battery. The comets arched upward, bent, then plunged. Hector tensed, then sucked a relieved breath; they were aiming over them, past them. Lasers burned the air behind the Marines, searching out the plunging projectiles. Some detonated. But there were too many to stop.

The explosions started. Behind them, back in the paddies, hollow cones of smoke, but mingled with each a silvery mist. The detonations walked forward as the rockets kept falling. Around him Marines were struggling with packs, pulling out masks and suits, ripping plastic, throwing away wrappings, stuffing legs and arms into the protective suits in an ecstasy of fumbling.

Hector tore his mask carrier open, oriented the rubber spider, and snapped it onto his face. As he kicked off his boots he tore wrappings from the one-use plastic suit that had replaced the old charcoal-lined overgarments, thrust his legs into it, his arms, and sealed the seam. The others panted and cursed, fighting their way into the suits as the barrage rolled over them. Hector sealed the hood around the mask, pushed his feet back into his boots, rolled into the bottom of the hole, and pulled Karamete's body over him as the ground quaked and the air filled with hissing steel.

Been here before. Been here before, he told his terrified mind. In the hills. Taiwan. Heavier shelling than this. You can stand this.

But it hadn't been gas then.

A marine fell screaming into the hole, thrashing and writhing. Hector grabbed him, shook him. He couldn't tell who it was through the mask. Jagged rips in the suit showed where fragments had torn the plastic.

Hector groped for an autoinjector, hesitated—he might need it himself in a few seconds—then thought *fuck it* and banged it into the guy's thigh. The other marine was doubled over, vomiting into the mask, struggling to pull it off. Hector knocked his hands away and banged him with another autopen. The guy relaxed, maybe passed out, but not fighting him anymore. Hector dragged him down into the hole as another salvo, heavy explosive this time, shook dirt down over them.

Alternating gas, fragments, HE. He had to admire the tactic even as he cowered at the bottom of a hole, clawing more dirt over them. Maybe it would absorb some of the agent. Even a pin speck would kill you, they said. He could see the shit seething in the air, a deadly mist settling on everything: weapons, bodies, live Marines, CHADs with their oculars and the air intakes for their fuel cells sealed.

"Rampart, Foolhardy, Mountain Goat, ACE reports," the AI said. Hector ignored it, trying to fucking breathe in the mask. Dizzy. Coughing. Thickness in his throat. His chest, hard to breathe. He wanted to tear it off too, but kept his hands down, fists clenched. Only now realizing he'd lost contact with his weapon in the struggle with the suit. Fuck. Fuck. Any minute now—

"Rampart, Foolhardy, Mountain Goat, stand by for enemy counterattack to your front," the AI intoned, barely audible over the whine and buzz of jamming.

Explosions were still quaking the ground. But he had to force himself to shove the body off him, scoop the dirt away. *Get out of the hole. VX heavier than air.* The guy he'd atropined lay motionless, arms flung out. Now Hector saw the torn-away foot, dangling by a ligament. He'd been bleeding out even as Hector injected him. He looted the corpse's pack for the decon kit and injectors and jammed one into his own thigh. Didn't feel the puncture, and had to look down and see a spot of blood to confirm the pen worked.

He crawled over bodies, stuck his head out of the hole, and scanned the line through the fogged-up eyepieces. Only a few forms still moved. Fewer carried weapons. Eyes front . . . a wall of even thicker white was rolling toward them. Antitargeting smoke. The enemy would come out of that to hit them. He looked around again, spotted one of the Pigs. Unmanned. Bodies lay around it. He low-crawled toward it. Silvery condensation sparkled on the cover assembly.

"Safety on 'F.' Bolt to the rear," he muttered. He slotted the charging handle and flipped up the cover. Stuck a plastic-covered finger in to check that the feed tray and chamber were clear.

While maintaining rearward pressure, pull the trigger and ease the bolt assembly forward.

"Double link at the open end," the voice of a man long dead yelled in his ear. "Free of dirt and corrosion."

He snapped the first round of the belt into the feed groove, double link leading, open side of the links facing down.

Hold the belt six rounds from the loading end. Ensure that the round remains in the feed tray groove, and close the cover assembly.

The pale shining smoke walked closer, blown on the wind. Shadowy objects moved within it, then were obscured again.

"Gun one up," Hector yelled, swinging the barrel to make sure he had traverse and elevation. Two boxes. Four hundred rounds. Spare barrel. Tool kit. Beside him one of the masked forms stirred. Built to hands and knees, and swayed into position to help feed the belt.

Hector glanced around for gloves. If he tore the thin plastic of his suit on a link, if a hot case melted through, the agent would penetrate and he'd die. He found one, pulled it on, and snuggled into the butt. Set his face to the sights.

A hot day in California. The mad-sounding old gunny with his Iraqi accent pacing along the top of the berm. *Fucking optics gonna go south on you. The internal components shift and you'll lose the zero. Grease-smear, blood on the lens, you're fucking toast. Learn the fucking irons too.*

"Fuck the queen," Hector muttered. "You the king."

He was about to press the trigger when the plain ahead of him erupted in smoke and flame. He crouched, hugging the mud as something roared overhead, shrieking and whining.

The earth tore apart two hundred meters ahead. Flashes flickered just above the ground, succeeded instantly by black bursts of smoke.

They sounded like 155s going over, but they didn't burst like any 155s he'd ever heard.

A tank silhouetted itself through the smoke, infantry trotting behind. They looked tiny and ineffectual behind the hulking machine. Hector swung and started work. The gun battered his shoulder and the bipod feet knocked dirt free. He reset them, aimed again, and fired another burst. Can't see. Mask fogging. Can't breathe. Red things swayed at the edges of his vision, like closing scarlet curtains on a stage.

But got to keep firing.

Something burst directly over the tank. A bluish flash, a dazzle of light, and the huge metal beast faltered. "What the fuck," Hector muttered into the mask. The barrel rose into the air. It halted. It wasn't smoking or on fire. Didn't look damaged. Yet somehow that blue dazzle had just . . . stopped it dead.

When he looked back at the enemy infantry, they were all down. He sent a burst their way, but then let up off the trigger, scowling. Puzzled.

"What the fuck," the guy beside him muttered through the mask diaphragm. At least, that's what Hector thought he said. Past him he spotted the upper shell of a half-buried CHAD. Its "head" was bent back at a strange angle, and a good half of the wedge-like "face" was cleaved away. Maybe nerve gas didn't bother them, but they didn't seem as adept at digging in as the meat Marines.

When he looked front again more tanks were looming, more troops trotting toward him. He resumed firing. The barrage resumed, built, climaxing to a terrifying roar as hundreds of tiny bomblets tumbled from the sky. They hit the ground, kangarooed up, and exploded. The closest sent fragments whacking overhead, and he pulled his loader back into the fighting hole, pushing his helmet down into the mud. Until they could decontaminate, a slice from a Blue frag would kill just as fast as one from the enemy. Shells rumbled in over them like a steady stream of tractor trailers on a six-laner.

He suddenly realized what was going on.

The Second of the Third was bait.

Nothing but chum for these fuckers, to lure them into the kill zone.

Pushed out to this dike on the edge of the plain so the NK would have to come across it to attack them.

Exposing them to the full weight of Allied air, and drones, and missiles and shelling from the sea.

But he still didn't get what the blue flashes were. So bright it hurt to look at them, even through the laser shields. They were stopping the tanks. Mowing down the infantry. But he didn't see how.

All he could think to do was keep as much dirt as he could between him and the killing going on to their front.

He lay there for what seemed like hours. The sky dimmed, whether from smoke or dusk he couldn't tell. Occasionally the AI would transmit an update, or Company would call for reports. Hector texted short answers on his command tablet. Dimly, through the din, he marveled that this time, comms were holding up. He could even make out, dimly, through the glimpses the sensors sent back, what was happening in the four-mile swathe of flat land between him and the mountains.

It was a zone of annihilation. Whole mechanized divisions rumbled down the road, formed up in battle order, and advanced. The steady thunder never let up. It waned from time to time, but always built again. Missiles flashed over. Now and then he could make out a darker speck: a plane or attack helo, higher up. A conveyor belt of destruction, moving ordnance to the front, chewing up steel and human flesh, then returning to rearm.

But the attacks didn't stop. They kept coming. A river, unrelenting.

He lay prone, firing only occasionally now, to conserve ammo, when he was sure of his targets. But his fear did not abate. Sooner or later, the planes and ships would run out of ordnance too. If even a platoon made it to the dike, they'd roll over the few Marines left. Another salvo of gas, a few more air bursts, and the thin green line would thin, crumple, evaporate.

The enemy would punch through.

But then . . . he'd be bogged down in the paddies behind them. A mile or more of wet, soft ground, no microterrain, not even any way, in such soft muck, to dig in. Even if the enemy broke through, he'd still be wide open from the air, from the guided munitions coming in from seaward.

But the platoon, his guys . . . they were the sacrificial lambs.
Lamb of God, who takest away the sins of the world . . .
He touched the crucifix, beseeching God to help his Marines.

MUCH later, the rumble lessened. The captain transmitted, *"Rampart, Foolhardy, Mountain Goat, stand to."*

Hector and his hole mate pushed themselves up and scanned their fields of fire. Smoke rose slowly from all around. In the gloaming he could make out piles of dead, canted, broken silhouettes of armor. A single figure staggered to and fro out there. He charged the 240, then realized it wasn't advancing on him, just staggering about. Even as he watched, it crumpled, and lay still.

Something exploded in the distance, sending popping tracers of fireworks into the air. It chattered on for some seconds, then slowly died away.

Hector pushed himself out of the hole. His arms and legs shook uncontrollably. Something soft squished in his trou. He fumbled the decon kit open and wiped the gun down. Checked his ammo. He tapped his loader's shoulder, pointed to the Pig, and staggered away. Check the line. Report. Ammo. Casualties. Report.

Most of the platoon were dead. They lay with masks on or off. Those who'd torn them off sprawled blue-faced, foam drying at nose and mouth and eyes. Those with masks on lay smeared with blood where they'd clumsily, futilely tried to patch torn suits before they died. Only a few blinked blankly up at him through the masks, or lifted shaking fists in token they still lived.

A hundred meters to the north one of the tanks had run up onto the dike before being stopped. A T-72, with bricks of reactive armor glued all over the turret. Marines lay curled around it like dead insects.

He climbed up onto its rear deck, faced into the breeze, and lifted his mask, just for a second. The air stank of bitter powder and shit and death, underlaid by a strong kerosene-y smell he figured was the sarin. Bodies and wreckage as far as he could see. The paddies behind them were cratered with shell holes.

His heart began thundering in his ears. A fine sweat broke on his back and prickled along his arms.

He fitted his mask back on and banged another injector into the meat of his thigh. His mouth was dry as the tomb. The sky seemed darker than it should be this early. He staggered as if heatstroked, wincing at a splitting headache.

Orders came down to stand by for another attack. Drones buzzed in from beachward. They landed on the dike and released their cargo: ammo, water with electrolyte replenisher, more injectors, mask filters, replacement suits. Hector set up his remaining MGs and reallocated fields of fire. He got the men digging out the CHADs, pissing the mud off their oculars, finding operable weapons for them, and placing them back on line. Both his 0352 Javelin missilemen were out of action, one gassed, the other missing, but the launcher seemed operable. He assigned two PFCs to see if they could spin it up. "They gonna reinforce us, Staff Sergeant?" one wanted to know.

Hector just shrugged.

THEY repelled another attack that night, around 0200, but it was weaker than the afternoon's. This time the tanks advanced warily, only five or six, and they pulled back as soon as a shell burst near them. The PFCs got a Javelin off but they must not have hit the right buttons because it vanished to the west, still going strong.

Higher said the enemy was losing confidence. Or maybe just running out of men and tanks. Still, the platoon stood to all night long. Hector snatched half hours of sleep in his mask between standing at the Javelin's thermal sight unit, which gave him a better view than his own NVGs. Each time he fell asleep, though, he woke gasping, his heart hammering, feeling suffocated.

THE next day dawned to an ominous quiet. Hector kept expecting orders to move out, take the hills ahead. But they stayed put. Around noon word came down that the commanding general had broadcast an invitation to the commander opposite to meet. He was suggesting a cease-fire while the higher-ups talked.

After another long tense wait the captain passed the word to stand easy. *"We're in a cease-fire status,"* he said over the net. *"Nobody knows for how long, or what, but we're to halt in place for now."*

Hector walked the line again, noting once more how many fighting holes were empty. How few of the platoon was left. None of the old dogs but him. Patterson was dead. Karamete, a blue-on-blue casualty. Vacante, the sark, had been laser-blinded and evacuated. Hector fleeted up PFCs to squad leaders, and radioed back that they'd need reinforcements if they had to keep holding here. Drones humming along ten feet above the line, spraying a chemical that smelled like limes and was supposed to neutralize the sarin.

As dusk neared again the captain showed up in person. He walked the line with Hector but said little beyond that some refurbished CHADs were on the way up.

As they got to where Patterson had died two marines in masks and gloves were working her stiffened limbs into a plastic body bag. "Hey," one said. "Can you guys help out here?"

"What you need?" the captain said, voice muffled in his mask.

"Just hold it up. Need to get a shot. This one's in pretty good shape."

The other guy was going through her pockets, stuffing whatever he found into a Ziplock. Hector knelt and got his arms under her. When he hoisted her up the mortuary guy felt down around the body. He held up her dog tag beside her face and snapped a photo with his tablet. Then inverted the tablet and held it to her neck, scanning her chip. He stood, and took another photo. "That's good, thanks," he said. "You can let it down now."

Hector squatted beside her as they zipped it up. Her face was the last to vanish. Somebody had wiped the mud off but she still didn't look good. He rubbed his cheeks, making sure to keep his hands clear of his eyes. He didn't feel anything, though.

He could see her again, standing at the top of a building, smiling at him as he raised a flag. Broken-field sprinting along the line, ammo boxes tucked under her arms. Squatting with him as they shared a vape.

But he didn't feel a fucking thing.

Karamete. Patterson. Vacante. And six more, out of twenty humans left in the platoon.

He could remember all their names. Funny. Because as the captain stood above him, Hector couldn't recall who *he* was. Something Italian? Fuck, he couldn't remember his *own* fucking name. Had to take out his Geneva ID to remind himself.

But he could see every guy and girl who'd died beside him. Remember what they looked like. What they'd said.

Weird. He couldn't remember the names of the living.

Only those of the dead.

Hector pushed to his feet, not looking back, and he and the captain moved on. Stepping over the torn-up ground, skirting the body bags, each neatly laid out by the graves registration team.

"You did well, Staff Sergeant," the captain said. "They threw everything they had at us. Three full mech divisions. But the Second held. You did okay." He glanced sideways. "How you holding up?"

"I would like to apply for a transfer," Hector said, rubbing his throat. Astonished, once the words were out of his mouth.

The officer frowned. "This campaign's over, Staff Sar'n't. Seoul's in uprising. Kim's dead. We broke the army's back. But we'll have to occupy. Pacify. We need you here."

"I want to put in for a transfer, sir."

The captain examined Hector's face. His expression changed. Became less surprised. Almost understanding. "Where would you want to go, Staff Sergeant? Training? Or do we need to evac you for CSC? I can't see inside your head, Marine. You tell me."

Hector bent over, breathing hard. Something immovable and solid and very hard seemed to be choking off his breathing. He pulled out another autoinjector, and hit his thigh with 2-PAM chloride. The spring triggered but he didn't feel any pain. He didn't feel anything. Except the weight in his chest, the inability to swallow anymore, which no antidote seemed to help.

"Well?" the captain said.

Hector said, forcing the words out past the thing crouched in his throat, "Sir. To anywhere I don't have to send my people out to die."

17

Andersen Air Force Base, Guam

THE heat was intense. Dan staggered as it hit him, nearly losing his grip on the boarding ladder. He shaded his eyes, squinting across miles of concrete thronged with planes. Bomb damage showed as dark patches, filled with asphalt. On the far side of the main strips piles of wreckage had been bulldozed up, smashed aircraft and buildings ruthlessly cleared aside, part of the squandering and detritus of war.

"Okay, Admiral?" Sergeant Gault, taking his arm. "Look a little pale."

Dan nodded angrily and shook his hand off. The Marine aide was sometimes a little *too* attentive. "Let's get to the terminal, see if the next flight's on time," he snapped. Then reeled himself in. "Sorry, Ronson, I'm . . . tired."

"You got your head down for a little while on the flight, sir."

"Yeah, but . . . yeah." He vaguely recalled disturbing dreams. Even when he could snatch two consecutive hours of unconsciousness, it didn't seem to dent his fatigue. It shrouded both mind and body. Slowing his reactions. Making him take too long over what should be simple decisions.

Not good, in a battle commander.

The terminal was a hundred yards away, over concrete so scorching it burned through the soles of his boots. Inhaling the hot, kerosene-smelling air, he forced his steps toward it.

• • •

Indo-PaCom and JCS had reluctantly agreed to a two-week push-back for Operation Rupture. Accompanied by promises of priority shipments of missiles and some additional fuel.

His request that Lee Custer be relieved had been denied. Dan hadn't been privy to the proceedings, but one of Tomlin's WTI classmates had been in the room with the VTC when Fleet had raked the logistics commander over the coals. Giving him a stark choice: Provide better support to the operating forces, or someone would be found who could.

Since then their requests for support had found more responsive ears. LogForce had set up a test of Brunei crude pierside aboard *Ma Kong*, ex-USS *Chandler*, a modifed Spruance-class destroyer sold to Taiwan years before. For two hundred operating hours her turbines had digested a desalted and washed light export blend rich in medium distillates, without excessive ash accumulation. Fourteen general purpose tankers idled by the slump in world trade were under contract, total capacity one point five million barrels. Dan planned to hold them in reserve at scattered anchorages south of the Spratleys.

He hadn't heard a word from Custer personally. They dealt through subordinates, or official messages.

But just now Dan was headed for Japan, at the request of Admiral Min Jun Jung, Republic of Korea Navy. After the elected president and his entire cabinet had been shot in Seoul, Jung, as the senior officer to have escaped the North Korean takeover, had gotten himself recognized by the Allies as head of the government in exile. Which, for Dan, entailed a long flight back to Guam, then this second, upcoming leg, Guam to Yokota.

He was only getting spotty information. Nothing was on the official news except feel-good interviews and gushing predictions of secret new miracle weapons. But it did seem the Allies were finally making progress in Korea. Operation Chromite had combined a raid with a decapitation strike. After a combined air and ground assault on his stronghold in the far north, the Leader was off the air and presumed killed. Resistance in front the Allied landings near Pyongyang had collapsed. A glacier that had stood frozen for nearly eighty years was finally melting, collapsing.

"We have to take advantage of it now, Daniel," Jung had told him

in a patched-through call. *"I asked Jim Yangerhans for you. Suffering Korea needs you. I know you will not leave her to cry out in vain."*

The orders had arrived within the hour. Dan would go with one aide. His staff would continue planning. Lee Custer would put on Dan's hat as Commander, Task Force 91.

Dan's shoulders had slumped, then lifted.

So Custer had won, after all. And Dan had lost his chance for professional immortality. Instead of the history books, as the man who'd invaded China, he would be a footnote, a spear-carrier in a side drama.

He felt less disappointed, than overjoyed at that turn of events.

FIVE hours later they descended once more. The beach flashed past. Then mile after mile of densely packed buildings, streets, the solidified encrustation of human occupation, came into view. Tokyo. The C-17 had only tiny portholes in the doors, but through one, from his fold-down seat along the bulkhead, he noted the clouds being replaced by distant green hills. Next, a radio tower, then oil storage tanks and radomes. The wheels shrieked and they were down, rolling. He and Gault unbuckled and got ready to deplane.

Jung's headquarters was posted with a hastily painted sign. Korean, and under it in English, HEADQUARTERS OF PROVISIONAL GOVERNMENT REPUBLIC OF UNITED KOREA. JUNG MIN JUN PRESIDENT. A picture beneath it showed Jung resplendent in choker whites, medals, and white gloves, a smile lighting his broad face as he saluted, gaze lifted to a Korean flag streaming in the wind.

When Dan was admitted to the inner sanctum, though, the president was in his undershirt, sitting cross-legged at a low table, chopsticks flicking among dozens of tiny bowls. Dan's first impression was that his old shipmate had gained weight. He'd always been barrel-chested, but now excess flesh drooped from his jawline. His belly bulged the thin cotton. Jung glanced up as Dan stopped in the doorway, then hoisted himself with a grunt and waddled toward him, big fleshy arms extended.

"Bro hug, amigo," he said, and wrapped Dan in a heavy-armed embrace. Dan patted his back, exchanging glances with Gault. "Hey, have some lunch. They feed you on the plane? Damn, I'm glad you could make it. We're going back. Just like you said we would. Three years. You remember Min?"

Min Su Hwang had been Dan's liaison during Task Force 76's swirling, murderous battle in the central Pacific with the Chinese submarine force. Dan shook the willowy captain's limp hand, then noticed something different. "You're an admiral," he said.

"I promoted him." Jung guffawed and dropped back to a cross-legged posture. He gestured expansively. "Bulgogi beef, that was what you always liked. And white rice. You don't have to eat the kim-chee, Dan. I know how you hated it. But you don't have to eat it to please me. Not anymore."

Dan hesitated, then settled across from him. He crossed his legs, and was immediately reminded how uncomfortable most Western-ers found the position.

"Admiral, put him in the picture," Jung said around a mouthful of rice.

Hwang sank to a graceful lotus. He said in a soft voice, "The main battle is taking place in the north. Some of our ships are support-ing the Allied invasion there. We have gathered the rest in Nagasaki Bay. From there, only two hundred and fifty nautical miles across the Korea Strait—which you know."

Dan nodded. Yeah. He'd fought there too, back when the North-erners had tried to slip a nuclear weapon into Busan.

"The ships you know, as well. You led many in our central Pacific fight together. I have done the planning for our return. But it would be helpful if you could look it over."

"Sure," Dan said. "Glad to help."

While Hwang spoke Jung's wide face had clouded. He lit a cigarette and sucked deep, waving it around as he exhaled. Said, "Unfortu-nately, we do not dispose of many ground formations. Kim dissolved the ROKA. The officers went to prison camps or were shot. The rank and file went to work battalions. Our spies tell us many have died of starvation. And the Americans say the US has no ground forces to spare, with the occupation of Taiwan and actions elsewhere." Jung shrugged. "They want me to wait. But I cannot, when my country suffers. We must rescue her. This is the time."

Goading Jung into action had never been the problem. Restraining him from a headlong Light Brigade charge into the midst of the enemy—that had been Dan's challenge during their operations in the Taiwan Strait. He couldn't decide which was harder, getting Custer going or Jung stopped. "So where will your troops come from?"

The provisional president chopsticked up ponytail radish and chewed, eyes narrowed. "We have a few. Perhaps a regiment's worth. Patriots who left the country when the government fell, or afterward, when I broadcast the call to rally to me."

"One regiment?" Dan blinked. Was he serious?

"Of course, far too few. So . . . I have asked the Japanese for an armored division. And for the amphibious lift. It is not how I wanted to return. My countrymen still hate the Japanese. For what they did to us for so many years. On the other hand, they would welcome the Americans. We will have American air cover. But no Marines. No U.S. Army.

"Therefore, Dan, my old friend, I want you beside me when I lead the way ashore. Two heroes, allies and friends. From there we will proceed north, reconstituting the forces of freedom for the liberation as we go."

Dan fidgeted, shifting his legs, which were already cramping. A division and a regiment didn't sound like a lot to take on an army, even a weakened one. And "reconstituting" sounded risky too. On the other hand, Napoleon had returned from Elba nearly alone, and rallied enough troops to make it a close call at Waterloo. Obviously Jung fancied himself in the same mold. "Um . . . when did you plan to land?"

"We sail at midnight." Jung gazed into the distance with lifted head. Dan suddenly noticed an unobtrusive little man in gray across the room. He was taking pictures, moving about silently on tiny, high-arched, stockinged feet. A striking Asian woman in pink lipstick stood there too, communicating with the photographer via silent gestures.

"Holy . . . there's not much point in my looking at your plans, then." Dan coughed, fighting a tickle from the smoke. "I thought you needed my advice. Landing beach, strategy, breakout, support, comms—"

"That is what I told the president," Hwang said softly. "But he insists."

Jung said, "The air strikes will begin tonight. Busan would be the most convenient point at which to land. But the Northern forces realize that too. They have fortified it with heavy defenses. The naval bases at Cheju and Sinseondae as well.

"Therefore, we will land at Gwangyang. A large commercial port. It is well sheltered, with a channel depth of fifteen meters at low tide. If we capture it undamaged, we will be able to offload directly onto the container piers and push inland."

Jung beckoned and an attractive young woman in a loose combat uniform knelt to spread a chart on the floor. Hwang clicked a laser pointer in the shape of a pink mouse. He briefed the order of sailing, the assault lanes, and the order in which the special forces would secure the port entrance. "We will not have the fire support for heavy preparatory fires," the chief of staff murmured. "We must count on the cooperation of the dockworker's union, which we have organized into resistance cells. From there, the railroad leads north."

"North, to victory," Jung pronounced, and lifted his chin. Smoke curled up from the cigarette.

Winstons, Dan remembered. Hwang was staring at him, expression bland, yet still somehow questioning. He rubbed his face, covering his misgivings with a sip of hot tea from the tiny porcelain cup the uniformed woman poured for him.

The operation looked reasonable. *If* you had four divisions in the assault, and a couple more in reserve. With only one-plus and no reserves, they were begging to get their tails kicked back into the sea. If he was honest, it looked like a recipe for failure.

Should he say so? He couldn't decide. Couldn't decide if Jung was a deluded buffoon or quite simply one of the few truly great and historic figures he had ever met. Or perhaps those two things were the same thing, and only Fate and Luck drew the distinction afterward.

A few feet away the little man in gray squatted, aiming his camera at them both.

IN the end Dan recommended that they have a fallback plan for withdrawal if enemy resistance proved too heavy. And, just as he'd expected, Jung waved it away. "There is no point," he said mildly. "We won't need it."

They flew out of Tokyo that evening in a Japanese Air Self-Defense Force V-22 and boarded *Sejong the Great*, Jung's flagship, that night.

The destroyer was massive, a cruiser in all but name. Aegis-equipped like the Arleigh Burkes, but over a thousand tons bigger. Capacious, modern, and with deeper magazines than comparable US classes, they also had a large suite of flag quarters that Jung occupied with the attitude of a medieval ruler in his keep.

Dan had been impressed with the Koreans back when he'd operated with them. He'd seldom seen better sailors, with more can-do attitudes. Maybe Jung was just the average Korean writ large.

Instead of adjourning to those luxurious spaces, however, Jung went to CIC. He was uncharacteristically quiet, replying in monosyllables. Dan took the hint and found a seat at the end of the command table, facing four large-screen displays.

US submarines had wiped the board clean of the antiquated North Korean diesels in the first year of the war. The Japanese, Hwang muttered, had guaranteed transit across the strait, since their ground forces were involved. They were embarked on Hyuga- and Oosumi-class LSTs and what the JSDF called "helicopter destroyers," though they were more like small carriers. Hwang said the Japanese navy suffered a lot of damage during the campaign to retake the Senkakus and Okinawa. Their marine force had island-hopped down the Ryukyus chain on their own. Their troops were battle-hardened and their ships ready to fight. Another plus would be the foothold the US Marines now held far to the north. That might attract the enemy's mobile forces, draining them from where Jung planned to land.

Dan could only hope resistance would be light.

THE transit took five hours. They exited Hiroshima Bay, threading past Tairajima and Hirado Islands, then sortied into the open sea. Dan sat in CIC, drinking the coffee that Jung ordered specially for him—it didn't seem to be a staple in this navy—and tensely watching the screens. The symbols for friendly air stitched the southern edges of the peninsula. The Japanese and US air forces, taking down any remaining fighters and what defensive installations could be identified. As they neared, two hostile contacts sputtered outward from antiship batteries Intel had missed. Japanese missiles swiftly batted them down.

Hour by hour, the coast grew closer. The minesweepers went in first, escorted by patrol craft backed by missile frigates. Dan discussed hypersonics with Hwang. Intel said the Russians had sold them to Pyongyang—Mach 7 missiles that flew too fast for older antiaircraft systems to track—but no one had seen them yet. Ballistic missiles were a possibility too.

They stayed alert, but no more threats appeared. When the main body altered course for the channel in, it was almost dawn.

The prospect of landing in daylight didn't seem to faze Jung. He sat Buddha-serene in his command chair, chain-smoking, only now and then shooting a question in rapid Korean to Hwang or to the ship's CO, beside him. Dan kept wondering why he himself was needed. He didn't seem to have a job, or be expected to do anything. And he didn't speak Korean. Was it just for appearances? He reflected uneasily that that was pretty much what Jung had said he wanted, after all.

"We will be pierside in half an hour," Hwang said, placing a soft hand on Dan's shoulder. "You will want to prepare."

He flinched at the touch. "Uh, prepare. For what?"

"The president wants you in the landing party. You have brought a fresh uniform? Ribbons? Your Congressional Medal?"

WTF, over? "Uh, well, no . . . just khakis. But will it be secure? Aren't we going to have to fight for the port?"

"It is in our hands. The unions, the port authority are ours. There may be some slight resistance. Communist stragglers. But we are ready for them. Demolition teams from the North tried to destroy the cranes. They have been dealt with." Hwang lingered, then said again, "You will need to be in proper uniform."

Dan took the hint. He found Gault asleep in their stateroom and changed without waking him. Considered, then nudged him. "Sergeant. Need you on deck. We're going ashore."

The marine looked dazed. "Ashore . . . right, sir." He swung his boots out. He'd slept with them on, only taking off his blouse.

Dan turned back at the door. "And find a weapon somewhere."

"Broken down in my duffel, Admiral."

"Get it. They say there's no resistance, but Jung's a prime target. We need to be ready."

He left Gault assembling his rifle and went back to CIC.

Video feed from a UAV showed the lead destroyers, *Daegu* and *Gangwon*, making a slow approach to a huge commercial pier area. Nearly four miles long, it lined the inner harbor. When they halted alongside, a body of armed men, but not regular troops, emerged from containers stacked across the concrete and set up a ragged perimeter. The frigates' guns rotated uneasily from point to point, standing by for counterbattery. But there didn't seem to be anything to fire at.

Jung snapped an order. Dan caught *Shimokita* and *Kunisaki*, the landing ships. On the screen, the huge vessels drifted in to the pier. Within minutes ramps extended to the concrete and the lead tanks rumbled ashore.

Jung stubbed out his cigarette and stood with a grunt. Sweat gleamed on his brow. The uniformed woman held out a fresh shirt, and the president put his arms out. A uniform, but without medals or ribbons. Just a plain khaki shirt, open at the neck. Plain khaki trousers. Black half-Wellington boots, lovingly shined, which she placed carefully on the deck, then bent to help slip his feet into them.

"It is time," Hwang said softly.

WHEN they emerged into the dawn, fog lay over the bay. The ship seemed to hover, suspended in the clouds, between low areas of fill or marsh. The narrow strip of hoary water was cupped by green-topped almost-mountains. But the low land lining the bay was covered by concrete seawalls, cranes, warehouses, pyramids of containers, and inshore of that, a city. A frigate lay four hundred yards off.

Twisting his head, Dan caught the upperworks of the landing ships farther inland, above a low island that masked a turn in the channel. Jet engines shrieked. A CAS drone rocketed across the low island, rocking from side to side as its sensors scanned the ground below.

He'd expected a helicopter, but Jung led the way to a ladder. They descended cautiously, gripping the handrails, into a battered, listing landing craft. A dozen tough-looking Koreans, heavily armed and bulky with black tactical gear, ballistic vests, and black helmets, were already aboard. The craft surged and clanked in the chop. The official party huddled in the well as the diesels growled. The last to file down the boat ladder were a party of men and women in casual clothes, carrying black plastic cases with bright chromed clasps.

The diesels gave a throaty cough, clunked into gear, and the gray sheer salt-whitened sides of *Sejong the Great* fell away. Gault checked his carbine. He pulled another helmet from somewhere and held it out. "Admiral. Got a nine-mil for you too."

Dan weighed the pistol belt. Glanced at Jung. The president was staring away, as if into the future. Dan cinched the belt on and checked the firearm. Magazine loaded. Chamber empty.

He searched the sky again. One fighter, or attack helicopter, and they were toast out here. Hwang was deep in conversation with the high-cheekboned, pink-scarved, rose-lipsticked woman who'd supervised the photography the night before. Today, in a black leather jacket and beret, she seemed to be directing the civilians.

The engine roared, going to speed. Dan couldn't see over the high bulkheads of the well deck. He sagged to a squat and closed his eyes. The pistol wasn't enough to reassure him.

Sometime later, Gault shook him awake. He came up with a snort. Had been dreaming about a booth, some kind of sales booth, outside the White House. He'd been scrubbing the walls with bleach and cleanser. While arguing with someone about Dostoevsky, who'd come by earlier. "Eah," he grunted.

"Admiral. Your Korean buddy, he says to get ready."

He creaked to his feet. The gritty, rust-stained deck was steady under him; they'd reached the inner harbor, apparently. The troops were mustered in front of the ramp. The civilians had opened their cases, revealing fitted foam cutouts where delicate machines had nestled. The tall woman in the pink scarf was shrieking at her crew over the clamor of the engines. Dan caught what he suspected was gunfire in the distance. "Just fucking great," he muttered, exchanging glances with Gault.

The sergeant charged his weapon and checked his safety. Dan loosened his pistol in the holster and wished he had one of the protective vests. The black-clad bodyguards returned his gaze flatly, with no trace of expression.

"Gyeong-go! Jin-iblo-eseo dwilo mulleo seo!" shouted the lead woman. Hwang craned above the other heads, caught Dan's eye, and waved him back.

With a grating roar, the bow rose. The sudden deceleration sent everyone staggering. One man dropped his camera, and was subjected to a renewed dressing-down from the lipsticked woman.

She was interrupted mid-diatribe by a sudden flood of light as the bow ramp dropped away, slamming down hard into wet sand. Dan crouched, clearing his holster, expecting every moment a shower of machine gun bullets. The troops charged off, shouting, boots thundering on the dented metal.

The producer wheeled and marched after them, signaling her crew to follow. They scrambled off behind her, jumped off the ramp, and ran up the slope.

Jung stood alone now, in the center of the ramp. Hwang, glancing back, beckoned Dan to join them. To the right Dan made out the cranes, the piers, the gray upperworks of the LSTs. Ahead lay white sand rising to scrub, and beyond that the red roofs of what looked like beach cottages. The PR team was spread out in a ring inside the larger perimeter of the black-clad special operators. The latter faced outward, weapons ready; the former inward, toward the landing craft.

Jung turned his head. Up close his face was shiny with sweat. "You have never truly believed in my destiny, Daniel," he said.

"I'm not sure I believe in destiny, period, Mr. President," he said. Then wondered: Why am I suddenly calling him that?

"But we each have a fate, my friend. If we doubt, it will abandon us. But if we believe, work for it, it will make us great. You too have one. Do not doubt it. Fight for it."

"It's time, Mr. President," Hwang said. "They are ready for us."

Jung nodded tightly. He hesitated for one more second; then stepped out as if given a "Forward, march" command, and strode down the ramp. He stumbled as his boots plowed sand, but kept himself upright, powering forward. Toward, Dan saw, an orange plastic disk in the sand some fifty feet up the beach.

Dan suddenly understood. Jung was playing Douglas MacArthur. This was a PR event. He almost rolled his eyes, but to be honest he felt too pumped to mind. Maybe Jung really had a "destiny." Or maybe seeing him stride ashore would inspire his countrymen to resist.

If it helped end the war, it was worth putting up with some theatrics.

The producer was shouting orders as she backed up the slope. She spotted Dan and pointed at him. "To right of President. That's good. Gun is good. Hold gun out more. That's good. Like that." The cameras circled. Above their heads a lens glinted from a camera drone, hovering a hundred feet up, staring down. At a shout from the woman a crewman ran up and planted a microphone on a stand in front of the disk.

Jung strode up to it and halted. He glanced down, positioning himself on the marker, then thrust his hands into his belt. He looked up, lifting his double chin, narrowing his eyes. The wind ruffled his black hair. Dan stood awkwardly two steps away, holding the pistol away from his body. The chamber was still empty, but he was ready to rack it and shoot.

Jung began speaking. His tones rolled out. Deep. Booming. Grandiloquent. Dan didn't follow the Korean, only got a word here and there. Like "America," when Jung turned to him and beckoned him forward. Placed a heavy hand on his shoulder. Dan lifted his head too, and tried to look inspired as the troops unwrapped flags and jammed the hafts deep into the sand. The blue and white of the United Nations. The Stars and Stripes. And the red/blue yin/yang of the Republic of Korea. No Rising Suns, he noted. The Japanese were going to be left out of this piece of showmanship.

A snap, and sand spurted up between Jung and the cameras. The pop-*crack* of a distant shot. The troops wheeled, and began ripping out automatic fire. Dan couldn't see what or who they were firing at. Somewhere over by the piers.

He leapt in front of Jung, arms flung wide. And then, shouldering him aside, Gault was there too, the pair of them human shields in front of the president. Who didn't cower or hit the dirt, though his voice shook as he called commands. The video crew threw themselves down but kept filming, some lenses pointed at the distant piers, others at Dan and Gault and Jung.

The black uniforms closed in, grabbing them, hustling them up the beach. At the last moment, as he passed it, Dan bent and in some inexplicable impulse jerked the orange tee marker out of the sand and stuffed it into a pocket. They climbed to the dune line, boots slipping in the loose shifting soil. On the far side was a road, black SUVs, a police car, and a yellow utility truck, strobes on and rotating.

Dan followed Jung and Hwang as men in dark business suits and identical blue ties stepped out of the SUVs. They arranged themselves in a line, a welcoming party, and bowed as one, as Jung slogged up to them. His pants legs were wet and his boots coated in sand but that didn't seem to slow him down. He nodded coldly as they held their bows. A driver jogged around to open a door.

Dan made as if to climb in after Jung, but one of the black-clad security guys grabbed his sleeve. The soldier pointed to the second vehicle, then held out his hand. Another trooper was trying to wrestle Gault's carbine away from the unwilling marine.

Dan stared at the waiting glove for a moment, then understood. He handed over the pistol and trudged back to the second car as the suited men climbed into the first vehicle after the president.

He stood looking back for a moment before he got in. On the beach, the media crew were repacking cameras and broadcasting equipment. The tall woman, arms akimbo, was yelling at them as they furled the flags. In the harbor, low wisps of white fog twisted across the water like mooring lines under strain. Troops and combat vehicles were streaming out of the landing ships. A few bodies lay at the base of the cranes, as if they'd been thrown off.

Destiny? Or stage management?

Strategy, or luck?

He stared for another second, imprinting it on his memory. Then ducked, and slid into the car.

IV

THE FIRES OF HELL

18

Task Force 91,
the South China Sea

THE new screens weren't blue. The human factor engineers had decided blue light caused macular degeneration. In the darkened compartment phosphorescent greens and reds and yellows glowed above the ranked workstations.

The Combat Direction Center aboard *Franklin Roosevelt* was sprawling compared to those Dan was used to aboard destroyers and cruisers. Other spaces opened off it, like side branches in a cave system. One led to his own flag bridge.

He liked to get up and walk around. Chat with the people manning the consoles. A flag officer had to be careful, though. Captain Skinner was casual about it, but Dan wanted to respect the skipper's prerogatives.

He stood alone, arms crossed and chin propped on his fist, studying the screens.

He'd returned from Korea, after two days trailing President Jung in his triumphal procession north, to find Custer unwilling even to meet with him. Until in a video teleconference Yangerhans had reamed them both out in no uncertain terms. *"Lenson will lead TF 91. Custer, you'll wear the Logistics Force hat again. If the two of you can't work together, tell me now, gentlemen, and I'll put officers in your chairs who can. Do I make myself clear?"*

"Yes, sir," Dan had said.

After a second's hesitation, sullenly, Custer had assented as well.

And Dan had resumed command.

Now the rehearsals were over. The plan he'd worked on, in one form or another, for over a year, was executing. Hundreds of ships had sortied from across the South China Sea and even farther afield. Their various courses were gradually converging into loose formations. Scattered across the sea, yet knit together by invisible threads of data. The whole immense machine was grinding forward across the darkened ocean, through the sky, supported from space, bringing to bear against a weakening enemy the greatest assemblage of force ever seen in these waters.

China's expansive claims in the Spratleys, reefs built up into artificial islands a thousand miles to the south, had been isolated and rolled up in the first weeks of the war. The Paracels had fallen later, to a joint US/Vietnamese invasion force.

Now it was time to lay the scourge of war on their adversary's homeland.

The screens showed mainland China to the north. TF 91's target, the large island of Hainan, was separated by a narrow strait. The broad plains inland gave back little radar return, but the net of sensors and lookdowns that microscoped the enemy coast were in continual motion. It was probably the most heavily surveilled area on earth right now. As the drone swarms went in, Operation Rupture Plus approached its climax and goal. To make clear to the enemy his homeland was no longer a sanctuary.

And, Dan fervently hoped, end the war.

"Admiral, Skipper wanted to make sure you had these." Captain Enzweiler, his deputy, was offering a flak jacket. A flash hood was made up inside it. "With your permission, he's going to general quarters in five mikes."

"He doesn't need my permission, but make it so." Dan went through the habitual motions with his mind elsewhere. He bent to fold and tuck trouser hems into his socks. Pulled the flash hood over his head, and shrugged the bulky vest over his coveralls. He accepted the mask carrier from the deputy and unbuttoned the flap. They weren't gas masks anymore, but compact, self-contained oxygen-breathing gear that gave the wearer half an hour in smoke, gas, or oxygen-depleted atmospheres, and even underwater, as long as you weren't over thirty feet down. The flash hood would go underneath his VR helmet.

He surveyed the busy, crowded, dimly lit compartment one last time, recording it in his memory. No matter how it turned out, this day would live in history. Survivors would be recording oral histories for decades to come. Studies and books would be written, documentaries and movies made, about the hours ahead. Probably some based on whatever notes Naylor was making. Dan caught sight of the reservist now and then about the ship, unobtrusive but industrious, interviewing pilots, crew chiefs, Intel weenies, anyone he could dragoon for a chat. Each maneuver of the invading fleet, each reaction of the enemy would be discussed for generations in command and staff courses. Thousands of men and women would live or die according to the decisions of the commanders. The fates of two empires would turn on them.

For a moment doubt gnawed. Maybe Custer was right. He wasn't right for the job. He'd screwed up before. Maybe he would again, and sailors and marines would die, the Allies topple in defeat.

He sucked a breath. No. He had the experience, the staff, the plan, and the forces. He had enough fuel now. Over a million barrels of burnable light crude in reserve south of Woody Island. He could have used more ordnance, but the delay had let several more shipments arrive, rushed out of the new factories in the Midwest. He should have enough, if his commanders showed restraint. As he'd advised them, in a face-to-face VTC the night before.

So there was nothing really to do now but wait. Wait, and obsess, and worry.

Oh yeah. He felt up to that.

A few hours later the first air strikes returned. They touched down above him, a faint thunder and roar as they went to afterburner hitting the flight deck, in case they missed the wires. Strike UAVs, mainly, but accompanied by networked fighters to control them over their targets.

But he was no longer there.

He floated above the battlespace, consciousness magnified a thousandfold in the virtual reality helmet. Another avatar hovered near: Lieutenant Tomlin. His young WTI had spent the hiatus digging into the preexisting plan, ideating new tactics based on the way the Chinese had maneuvered in previous battles, and running them against a Red Cell back at the Naval War College.

Hovering together, they gazed out over a flat sea far below. A smooth, featureless blue, without waves, currents, or winds. A digital simulacrum that he couldn't risk accepting as reality. Other figures hovered at various altitudes. His commanders, his COs. Latitude and longitude lines scored the surface, but he could see all the way down to the sea floor far below. In the distance, radar and laser beams flickered in all shades of the spectrum.

He visualized *forward* and his avatar glided north, toward the battle. Here the air seethed with purple, green, red, blue. Fighters and UAVs wheeled and engaged in silence. Missile symbols crossed trails in a complex and deadly knitting and purling.

Sea Eagle, the tactical AI, whispered to him, feeding him information and advice. Most of which he let pass without comment. His air and screen and antisubmarine commanders would react to individual threats. He wanted to stay above the battle, sensing its rhythm, alert for the unexpected. Of course, if the enemy really pissed in their Cheerios, he'd have to get involved then. To retrieve the battle. And if he couldn't, to pull back.

He didn't want to think about that, about retreating, but it was his duty. Unlike Jung, *he* had a withdrawal plan, and had directed Tomlin to game it out with the AI as his opponent. A couple of times it had gotten ugly. But they'd ironed out the glitches: exit lanes, conflicting fires, crossed routes of retreat. He was fairly sure now that at least into D plus Two he could pull everybody back in a combat reembarkation. It would be as confused and tragic and brutal as Dunkirk, but he should be able to extract most of the landing force. If things went to shit after Plus Two the reserves would have to insert and hold the line while the first waves were withdrawn. And it would be the ground commander's responsibility then, since once the force was established ashore command transferred to him.

To General Isnanta. In the virtual reality, the Indonesian marine floated miles distant, above the shore, looking down.

Dan was about to "call out" to him when the tactical AI spoke again. *"Final data on losses, first strikes: loss rate twenty-two point three percent,"* it intoned in his headset. *"Additional damaged to the point of mission kill, nine point three percent. Further breakdown available on request."*

Dan exhaled, gut cramping. That emotionless voice carried no hint of the gravity of what it conveyed. A twenty-plus-percent-loss rate was catastrophic. It put the whole operation in doubt. "Uh, Sea Eagle, check and confirm."

"Data . . . checked and confirmed. Update: damaged, nine point seven percent."

The numbers were trending in the wrong direction. Up on the deck, and aboard the three other supercarriers and five assault carriers supporting the invasion, those planes and UAVs that had survived were refueling. Rearming. Unlike the great battles of 1944 and 1945, the landings of this war weren't supported by lines of battleships belching smoke and projectiles. Without air support, the ground troops would be mowed down.

And judging by the numbers so far, the enemy were more than ready to meet this assault.

Tomlin turned his head. *"Admiral. Those figures are three times the estimated loss rates."*

"I realize that, Lieutenant. What I could use is some explanation why."

"Advanced antiaircraft missiles. Hypersonic. Extended range."

"Russian-supplied."

"Yes sir," Tomlin said.

The statement hung between them. Dan wanted to rub his face, but found his hands stopped by the smooth outer shell of the helmet. Moscow had sworn piously to stay neutral in this war. But at every opportunity to turn a profit, they'd undercut the Allies. Sold advanced weapons to Iran, North Korea, Pakistan, and China. Jacked up the price on natural gas to Europe, since Mideastern supplies were cut off. Suborned and funded protofascist elements in the Baltic states, Ukraine, Poland, Finland, Germany, and the US. An extension of what they'd been doing even before the war, in what hardly anyone called "peace" any longer.

It was the world Orwell had envisioned. A Hobbesian war of all against all, where one nation's loss could only be another's gain.

But maybe it had always and only been that way. Maybe the dreams of world peace, world government, were only that. Dreams.

He shook his head angrily. Keep your mind in the game, Lenson. No philosophical excursions today. "We're moving in," he said, and toggled to the brain-to-text function of the helmet. He thought each word distinctly, hard, and watched them appear as a running banner beneath his video. ALL CARRIERS, SCREEN UNITS, AND ASSAULT SUPPORT MOVE FORWARD FROM ASSIGNED POSITIONS. He thought Send and snapped to the AI, "Implement two-hour hold on H hour."

"H-hour delayed to 0730. Notifying all units."

In the distance General Isnanta turned his head in Dan's direction. Dan waited for an objection, but the distant figure only stared, arms crossed. Waiting.

The WTI said, *"Sir, that will expose the carriers."*

"Got to sustain our sortie rate, Lieutenant. With fewer aircraft, the only way to do that is to shorten the range."

"But they might have ballistics left. Or hypersonics. If we lose a carrier—"

"They're built to take it," Dan said between gritted teeth.

He didn't like it either. But for this whole war, JCS had held the carriers back. East of Hawaii the first year, for fear of ballistic and submarine attack. Outside the second island chain the second year, except for one raid on the base complex at Ningbo. Husbanding them, like a retiree afraid of losing his investments. The one positive outcome was that their aviators had acted as training cadres, using the years of risk aversion to generate nine new air wings. Meanwhile, the small boys—submarines, destroyers, frigates, cruisers, plus a few jeep carriers, merchantmen hastily converted with flight decks—had taken the battle to a dangerous enemy.

The bottom line: It was time the supercarriers finally ventured in harm's way. He said grimly, "Get me numbers. How close do we have to approach to generate the same target-effects rate as originally planned."

"You'll need to close main body to within a hundred and twenty miles." The cool voice of the AI, which had apparently interpreted that question as directed to it.

Up, Dan thought, and rose thousands of feet, smoothly, dizzily, as the sea rolled out a slaty digitized blue beneath him. The battle drew closer. A flickering maelstrom of tinted light, silent but crackling with energy. Coruscating veils of electromagnetic radiation pulsed and wove. Lasers drew pencil-lines. Contacts flickered like dying fireflies, then went dark.

"Second support strike, loss rate thirteen percent," the AI said.

Less, but still far too heavy. But the enemy, too, must be running out of ordnance. Each successful Allied sortie degraded his defenses. *A close-run thing,* his memory retrieved. Wellington, at Waterloo. *Hard pounding this, gentlemen.*

Let's see who will pound longest.

"Keep moving in," he told the AI. "Flank speed consistent with launch and recovery courses. Release holdbacks on ammo expenditures. Empty the magazines. Retain close-in self-defense only. Ditto with the screening units."

"Sir, I don't advise that. You were telling them last night to conserve. We need to guard against—"

"Not now, Lieutenant."

Tomlin vanished, meaning he'd taken off his helmet. Gone off the matrix. Dan rose higher, until mainland China pushed up behind Hainan. He zoomed in, searching for evidence of reinforcements, for new formations of fighters and attack aircraft arriving to back up the defenders. But only an occasional meteor trail showed units being brought forward. The enemy was fighting, but not reinforcing.

Which meant there were no more reinforcements available.

He just had to keep pounding, then. Until his own magazines

were empty, his own aircraft expended, his own forces exhausted. At which point, if his adversary's will remained unbroken, he would counterattack. Dan would lose the battle, and probably the carriers as well.

Hard pounding, gentlemen.

ONE hour later they were forty miles closer.

And the losses were climbing again.

Twenty more fighters down at sea, failed to return, or damaged and wrecked on landing. Five more ships hit. Missiles, mines, and a submarine attack on the eastern flank. Two US screen destroyers, two Tarantul-class corvettes, and one of the Vietnamese landing ships, HQ-512, were falling out of formation. The task force was leaving them behind as it ground forward. Dan denied permission for other units to stand by for assistance. Steeled himself against pity, and pressed forward.

Tomlin had returned, with Captain Skinner behind him. Dan lifted his helmet off to confront them face-to-face. "Before you say anything: We're not turning back," he told them.

The tactics lieutenant glanced to the carrier's skipper. Skinner looked wrung out, pale, sleepless. He said, "I've lost a quarter of my air wing, Admiral."

"Admiral, we planned for this," the WTI pleaded. "If losses got too heavy, we could abort."

For a second Dan contemplated it. Was he hurtling to disaster? Miscalculating, as Lee had at Gettysburg? Squandering lives in a battle already lost?

The ground forces weren't even ashore yet, and the task force's magazines were nearly empty. Billions of dollars' worth of aircraft were gone. Hundreds of lives. Was he wasting them? What was he after, anyway? Glory?

No. He didn't value that.

Victory?

He doubted it was still possible, between adversaries that could destroy each other's homeland in hours. At least, not in the sense warriors had always understood triumph and defeat.

Then what?

It all came down to pressing on.

This was the moment he'd trained all his life for. The courage to stay the course, when disaster and defeat looked you in the face.

"Hard pounding this, gentlemen," he muttered.

"Sir?" Skinner frowned.

"End of discussion, guys. We keep pounding." He cut them off by settling the VR helmet back onto his shoulders.

And the vast world within bloomed with fire and light.

HE toggled to high-side chat and relayed a brief report to PACOM. Enzweiler was sending updates back every half hour too. And the headquarters in Honolulu, and no doubt the Tank and Sit Room in Washington were getting much the same data he was seeing as task force commander. But for the moment, they were staying off the channels and off his back.

He appreciated the forbearance. The Navy had always trusted its commanders, far more so than the other services. Had trusted in their leadership, skill, and integrity.

With that, though, went complete accountability. Unlike so many other institutions, its leaders did not believe in protecting its own. The sea service was remorseless in punishing errors in judgment.

If he guessed wrong today, it would probably be better if he never came home.

He was discussing the defensive missile drawdown rate with his screen commander when buzzers sounded and alarms flashed. The cueing came from the microsatellites. Missiles in boost phase. Probably the carrier killers China had vaunted before the war . . . and used once before, to destroy the *Roosevelt* battle group. He toggled to his exterior cameras, to make sure his staff picked it up.

"CSS-5 launch cueing detected. Source, MICE. Confirmed by OTH radar Woody Island," Sea Eagle told him. A moment later,

"Launch area confirmed. Vectoring Global Hawk overhead recon-naissance. Recommend strike as soon as possible, before refire."

Dan turned to Tomlin. "Lieutenant. *Monocacy* and *Jack Lucas* will take the missiles. Can you handle the launchers?"

Tomlin looked taken aback, but nodded. "Yes, sir." He gestured in the air, and four F-22s peeled off from above Hainan and headed inland. Their callouts spun as they went to afterburner and accelerated.

"Do we have an AOU yet?" Dan asked the AI.

"Still in boost phase. Lucas has cueing, seeking track."

Dan contemplated this. He had several seconds while the missiles climbed, but not much margin after that. The question was, where were they getting their targeting, and how accurate was it. The D-26 had a maneuvering capability, allowing the terminal body to correct for a limited error in the initial aim point during its hypersonic descent. *Roosevelt* and the other supercarriers could move off a bull's-eye at thirty-plus knots, but they still advertised their locations with a monstrously large and unmaskable radar signature, both to operate aircraft and guard against incoming strikes. Both prewar studies and wartime experience had confirmed that the terminal body came in too fast for a warship to rely on repositioning.

"Barbarian, this is Democracy. Initiating Doppelganger." Skinner, reporting that the unmanned Hunters accompanying the carrier were activating as decoys. They had Nulka rockets too, plus dedicated drones that radiated on the carrier's frequencies, but the drones were untested against actual Chinese homers.

His air warfare commander: *"Barbarian, Lifeline: Lucas reports lock-on, Meteors One through Three."*

Dan said, "All screen units, stand by to squawk flattop.—Eagle, do we have a PI yet? Where are they getting their targeting? I need answers. ASAP."

He zoomed out, backpedaling away from the sputter of battle ahead. Picking up, far above, the curving tracks of the incoming missiles. They pulsated a bright orange. Hitting pitchover. Beginning the long arc that would burn them over home plate at more than fifteen thousand miles an hour.

Half a megaton. Even with a near miss, the blast overpressure would mission-kill a Ford-class supercarrier at a mile and a half. He toggled to the Air Control circuit, then the cameras on the island. Helicopters and drones were vaulting aloft. The port catapult slung a refueling UAV into the air. Skinner was getting everything up he could, and striking everything else below into the hangar deck.

Dan toggled to brain-to-text. He thought each word separately onto the chyron beneath his video. CONFIRM DECOYS CONFIRM READY TO TAKE DF26 CLOSE ABOARD. He thought it to the other carriers and the screen commander, and squeezed his eyes shut. SEND.

Then waited, as the orange trails curved over, foreshortening. Aimed at him, and those around him. He forced a slow breath. Then another, trying to calm his racing heart.

Then realized his heart wasn't racing.

He felt cold. Detached.

Above the battle, even as his disembodied body floated above the sea, watching death approach.

"Sea Eagle? Barbarian," he said.

The AI: *"Listening, Admiral."*

"If I go off-line, continue the operation." The AI was distributed. Processing simultaneously on hundreds of computers. Dan and all the steel around him could be vaporized in a direct hit, gasify in the thermonuclear fireball, but the artificial mind would carry on. "Don't step back. Don't call it off. If we backtrack, we can't win this war."

"You're asking for a promise we can't make, Admiral."

"I'm giving you a strategic order. Acknowledge and execute." He cut it off when it tried to speak again.

There was no time left to argue. Only to make a final peace with whatever governed. Fate. Mars. The God of Battles. The Lord of Hosts.

Rising as the sky blackened toward space, he contemplated for one last time the immense armada that still, in the face of grievous losses, clanked steadily forward toward its fated goal. The ragged lines of ships sprawled across the face of the sea. Two hundred miles from the easternmost screen units to the outlying hunters on the west, nearly in sight of the Vietnamese coast. Stragglers and damaged units lay motionless behind them. He couldn't spare escorts or help. Smearing a trail of wreckage, death, and wounding as he crawled ahead.

Leaving the dead like a million bloody rugs . . . The coast was surfacing over the horizon as slowly as the rising moon. A multicolored glow like blasted and burning rainbows glimmered and flashed ahead. Gaps marred the screen where ships had been torn apart, topsides smashed, backs broken, on fire, sinking. *Borgnine. Norton Girault. Warramunga. Lý Thái Tô. Yos Sudarso.*

Just as he'd drilled them, the screen units were widening their sectors to cover the gaps. But each missing destroyer or frigate meant less security for the transports, carriers, and replenishment ships. He could toggle to loss numbers on aircraft, remaining ordnance, sortie rates, but he didn't. There was no point now. He'd committed everything he had.

But the enemy was striking back hard, and not just with missiles. If Intel was right, he was sacrificing his last reserves too. Untrained pilots in ancient MiGs. The last submarines, old diesel boats, short-ranged, breakdown-prone, hastily pressed back into service.

Yet when Dan peered inland again, the airspace still sprawled empty. No more fighters coming. Which meant only the conscript armies were left. Huge, but little more than cannon fodder against the Indonesians and Vietnamese, Army artillery batteries, Air Force ground support aircraft.

And once again he gave way to that fucking questioning. Was this truly the best his species could do? They devoted their best minds, their greatest resources, to weapons. Established their boundaries by seeing who could murder most efficiently. It was mad. Irrational. Absurd. Appalling.

A Stone Age beast, armed with the powers of the gods.

He'd pondered the dilemma as the years went by and he witnessed ever more battles, from ever higher levels of command. But the incongruity had only grown. The roots of war were sunk deep. Maybe in human nature itself.

But he couldn't accept that explanation.

There had to be another way. Just as the survivors had hoped after every global conflict.

But now, they had to finish this one.

And if they could endure, they might well end it today.

Miles distant, a tiny figure hovered. Dan steered toward it. The landing force commander was gazing down at a ship. Clots of black smoke billowed from its foredeck. One of the Indonesian transports. But it was still under way. Still bulling ahead, welded to its assigned course and station.

"General," Dan said. "How bad?"

Isnanta turned a grim face. *"No one knows where the missile came from. There are many dead. But I think the ship will survive."*

"We're all taking heavy losses. But so is the enemy. I propose to press on."

"Just put us ashore," the Indonesian said. *"Put us where we can fight. That is all I ask."*

Dan nodded, and looked up.

Far above the atmosphere, orange trails bent downward. Toward him. Gathering speed. Beginning to glow, as they reentered the atmosphere.

Monocacy reported lock-on. Then, seconds later, *"Birds away."*

"Admiral!" Tomlin again, this time shouting, gripping his arm. "Sir. *Block Island*'s been hit. No damage report yet. *Patrick Hart* reported sinking. *Makassar*, fire's spreading. *Kuklenski* is prosecuting a submarine contact. Two more Raptors lost. Close air support drones running low on ordnance. Catapult breakdowns on *Stennis*, unable to launch further strikes. *La David Martin* and *Rafael Peralta* report 'winchester,' defensive ordnance exhausted."

Dan surveyed an entire sea on fire. A blue arena where exhausted, reeling boxers staggered in for the final confrontation.

He remembered the boxing ring at the Academy, under the iron arches of Macdonough Hall, when they matched each midshipman against the one he hated most. The smells of old leather, rancid sweat, and wintergreen ointment. The creak of ancient canvas. The muffled grunts as the final blows were exchanged.

Let's see who will pound longest.

19

Hainan, China

THE heat was intense. The ship had baked in the sun all day, and now that it was night, the steel deck radiated that heat back out.

Hector Ramos couldn't help wondering how it would look to the seeker of an antiship missile.

The invasion force had gotten under way the day before, and immediately scattered. The major said there were submarines below them, drones far above. And now and then you could spot one, a dark speck, way up there in the blue. But most of the time it just felt like the three ships, *Makassar, Surabya*, and one distant destroyer, floated alone in a vast and hostile ocean.

Hector lit a kretek. He hadn't smoked before, but one of the Indonesian officers had offered a pack of the sweet clove cigarettes and now he couldn't do without them.

Since he was a three-landing Marine now, Division had approved his transfer. With a black mark for instability, probably, but . . . whatever.

He was still a Marine. But he wasn't *with* the Marines anymore.

At least, not the U.S. Marines. He looked back at his troops. They were lined up two and two across the deck, grunting and yelling as they went through hand-to-hand drills.

Smaller than most Americans, though pretty much Hector's own size, the Indonesians still appeared tough. Their rifles looked like a cross between an M-4 and an AK. Their other gear was new to him too. The sergeant said a lot of them were Papuans.

Hector pretty much accepted whatever the division noncom, *serson mayor*—sergeant major—told him. Handayani was taller than Hector. Which wasn't saying much.

But they looked up to Hector too. They called him "pria tua," which seemed to be some kind of compliment.

After he'd turned down the tactical cyber-school offer, knowing there was no way he was smart enough to keep up, his orders had sent him to Indonesia. Headquarters, Third Pasukan Marinir, the Third Marine Division. Most of the officers spoke some English. So did a private named Slamet, so Hector had grabbed him as gofer and translator. The Indonesians kept asking Hector questions, since he'd been in combat and they hadn't. He tried his best to give useful advice. The language barrier was a problem, though. Not just for him; apparently not many of the troops spoke the official tongue as a first language.

His first recommendation was to get rid of the bright purple berets. The second was to get a lot fitter, and to practice moving and shooting in full gear. There'd been limited facilities in port, but he'd led the troops on runs and set up a firing range and shooting house, to give them at least some practice. They had their own squad tactics and he didn't want to confuse them. But they perked up when he demonstrated a combat glide—how to steady the sights so you could shoot as you were moving—and it got picked up across the division. He emphasized the basics, Barney-style. Communicate. Lay down fire. Keep eyes on your NCO. Hold on to your masks. Don't touch the enemy dead.

Across from them now, ranked in rows, sat dozens of CHADs. The old model, the Cs, repainted, refurbished, some pieced together from battlefield retrievals. The scrapings from the bottom of the barrel. And only enough to furnish one per squad. The Indonesians were wary of the bots. They called them "hantu" and gave them a wide berth. The best he could figure was to use them as disruptors, sending them in ahead of the human troops to draw fire so the follow-ons and supporting arms could light up strong points. He'd recommended that to the general, who'd said it sounded reasonable and put him in charge of training the NCOs in the control apps.

He strolled to the edge of the flight deck and looked down at the passing sea. He didn't want to. But he couldn't help it.

Yeah. There they were. Again.

Under the water.

Looking up at him. Some, waving. Others with their mouths moving, though he couldn't hear what they were saying. Bleckford. Breuer. Titcomb. Conlin. Schultz. Vincent. Orietta and Truss and Whipkey and Lieutenant Hern. Pudgy little Lieutenant Ffoulk. Sergeant Clay, Patterson, Karamete . . . they wanted something from him.

He stared down, wanting to make out their words, but afraid to.

He knew what they needed, anyway.

They wanted him down there with them.

He lifted one hand and gave a little half wave back. Groped with his other hand, and found the crucifix Mirielle had sent.

He held it over the water for a while, and finally let go. It dropped, vanished, sucked down into the black.

Someone came up behind him and took his other hand. Hector jerked, flinching away so violently he nearly toppled into the nets, with nothing but nylon between him and the blue-dark water slipping past below. Then he *would* be joining them, because the captain had made it clear they couldn't turn back if anyone went overboard. "What the fuck!" he shouted, before he remembered: he'd seen lots of the Indos holding hands. It didn't mean . . . anyway.

"I am sorry, Sergeant Ramos," Private Slamet said, clearly startled.

The guy was still too close. Hector bulldozed his chest with both palms, shoving him away. "Get this straight, Private. I'm not your buddy." He clutched his head. He needed a drink. But there would be no drinks until after the battle. Unless he could organize something, the way he had in Taiwan. "Uh, look. Don't go to thinking we're friends. *Mengerti?*" That was one word he'd picked up. Usually from some guy giving him a blank look when he was trying to explain something. *"Saya tidak mengerti"*—I don't understand.

"We are not friends?" The terp furrowed his brow.

"Get lost," Hector told him. "Shove off. Don't you get it? There's no point. We're both gonna . . ." he stopped himself at the last moment. He'd almost said *We're both going to die*, but that wasn't what you told anybody you were trying to lead. He mastered himself, trying to look away from the faces below. Whipkey was laughing. Fucker . . . "Don't get attached, Private. It's just gonna . . . . wreck you, when they get killed. Concentrate on hating the enemy. *Mengerti?*"

The Indonesian only looked puzzled. He stood with arms dangling, staring. Until Hector sighed and walked away.

THEY mustered after a midnight meal of rice and fish with a red sauce that reminded him of his mother's pico de gallo. Then had to wait for hours in a sweltering passageway to load up. The usual drill.

Hector squatted without thought, without emotion. The colonel had wanted him to hold back with the headquarters unit. And maybe that would have been okay for a liaison, but Hector had insisted he wanted to go in with the first wave. The officers had glanced at each other and worked their eyebrows but finally agreed. Clapped him on the back and told him apparently complimentary things, but in Indonesian so he didn't have to respond.

He didn't care what they thought. Or if he made it through this time.

Actually, it would be a relief not to.

The Indos didn't run LCACs so he loaded with Slamet's squad. Down in the well deck, yells and clanking echoing off the high dark overhead. Now it was windy, and water dripped down from above. They filed down into a landing craft that looked like a leftover from World War II. They huddled cheek by jowl cross-legged under the hulls of two huge-wheeled APCs, Hector elbow to elbow with a CHAD. The Indonesians, except for Slamet, glanced at them both, but didn't speak to them.

Hector spotted their machine gun, and held out a hand. After a glance at his squad leader, who nodded, the gunner pulled his mag, racked his bolt, and handed it over.

The weight was reassuring. As heavy as the old model 240 with the steel receiver. Belt-fed. A hefty handle to change barrels with. He didn't want to give it back. But finally, reluctantly, let it drop from his hands back into the gunner's.

"You're the king," Hector told the gunner, then to Slamet, "Tell him what I said. Translate. The machine gunner, he's the king of the battlefield. Infantry, they're the queen, but the king fucks the queen. Got it?" The private looked doubtful but rattled it off. The rest of the squad looked shocked, then chuckled uneasily.

Hector blew out and glanced at the CHAD. Its oculars were examining him curiously. What was it thinking? Oh yeah, they didn't think. Didn't feel. Or see the faces of the dead, like it was Día de los Muertos every night.

"Must be nice," he whispered.

He looked at the oculars of the others. The humans. Nothing going on there either. Robots made of meat. Or maybe that was just him, a meat robot named Hector Ramos. Who'd seen too much to feel anything ever again. A burned-out fuse in an old house like his mom's. Rented from Mr. Tankard. The old round glass ones that turned black when they burned out. Did his eyes look like that? Burned out. Nothing behind them.

He sat with the rifle he'd been issued across his lap, swaying with the roll of the ship. When the fuck were they splashing?

They'd given him the transfer, but the captain said it wouldn't look good in his record after the war. Hector had stayed silent, not wanting to say that didn't matter. There would be no "after." He groped for Mirielle's cross, then remembered: he'd dropped it overboard. Fuck, why had he done that? Maybe its power had kept him alive. A sudden jolt of panic terror left him sweating. Then it too vanished, sucked back into the massive numbness.

At long last he felt the craft lift. Water surged around them. They rolled, only a little, but enough to know the ship was flooded down. The engines whined and started. They settled into a dull roar and smoke choked the air. The marines coughed. A few broke out masks.

The sky appeared. A black lid slid back to expose the stars. The landing craft took on a sharper roll as it hit open sea.

The engine droned on, hour after hour. Now and again water spattered up and rained down. He licked salt from dry lips. It mixed with the blood from a deep crack in the middle of his lower lip. Here and there bright stars swayed overhead, like scratches on the night. How fucking far out were they? He tried to figure out how far they'd come already, but couldn't multiply in his head. The old problem: numbers. They'd issued him a combat cell, a gimcracky thing, but since it was in Indonesian he couldn't access it.

Around him the Indos began to retch. Great: puke and hot sauce. Rice and fish on the deck. Like that movie about Private Ryan. One guy was barfing into his mask. Hector jerked it out of his hands. "You're gonna want that, once we land," he yelled, then wondered why he bothered. He shrugged, handed it back, and crawled to his tire again.

The men opposite—there were no women in Indonesia's assault divisions—took on the same look he remembered from other landings. Some joked and chattered. Most withdrew, looking inward. A few fingered worry beads. Others nervously, mindlessly checked gear, or picked their noses. A few were asleep or pretending to be.

He stared into nothingness, and it reflected his mind.

AT last, a far-off rumble. Faint at first, it slowly grew. Jet engines, or maybe rockets, screeched overhead. Shells howled and crumped.

He knew that rumble. Those sounds.

The hymn of War.

He checked his rifle again, and met the unblinking oculars of the C opposite once more. It hadn't looked away from him the whole time. Mindless. Thoughtless. A thing. He envied it. He closed his eyes and waited for the shell to hit. Like the one that had wrecked their LCAC on Itbayat, killing most of the Marines aboard. Leaving him wandering memory-less until he'd come to on the beach, not even remembering how he'd escaped that flaming pyre.

The grumble grew into a continuous thunder. He couldn't see what lay ahead, but he could imagine it. The fiery trails of missiles going in. The flashes along the line of coast. Smoke billowing up.

The darting and swarming of the drones. Shell bursts, the searching beams of lasers, and the smoke trails of incoming rockets as the enemy fought back, intent on wiping out the invaders before they set foot in China at last.

He lay propped against the tire as his ear tuned through the barrage of sound. Picking out mortars. Heavy MGs. So they were close now, and this enemy was throwing everything he had against the first wave.

The serson mayor bent and waved five fingers. Hector passed it on. He checked his rifle one last time and adjusted his jelly armor. The Marines had let him keep it, instead of the old-style Kevlar the Indos wore. He eyed the front ramp. A single shell, and no one would make it ashore.

With a jarring, rasping *chhhnkk*, the craft lurched, throwing them all forward. The engines rose, strained, but nothing happened.

The troops cast frightened glances at each other. The serson mayor bent, and shouted something to them.

"Fuck," Hector muttered, fearing the worst.

The engines declined to idle. The transmission thudded, then strained again at maximum RPM. Trying to back off. But the deck under them didn't move.

They were aground. A big fat motionless target for every gun on the beach.

Handayani bent to him. Yelled over the rumble, which reverberated now terrifyingly close, "We are no float. What we do?"

"Debark," Hector yelled back. "Get off boat."

Beside him Slamet was yelling too. Handayani sucked air, looking startled. Then his face closed. He nodded, once, and vanished again.

Above them the engine of the personnel carrier cranked, cranked, then fired with a muffler-less bellow. The marines scrambled out from under its iron belly and fastened themselves along the bulkheads. A klaxon honked, cut off, then cawed again. Hector unsnapped the flap of his mask carrier and gripped his rifle, staring forward. Feeling nothing, except that his legs were shaking.

Ahead, light. Flickering color. The rattle of machine guns. The crack of bursting shells, merging in an unending growl that seemed to grow from heartbeat to heartbeat to a crescendo of mind-battering noise.

The personnel carriers roared and eased forward between the ranks of infantry. The deck lurched with the shifting weight, and for a second Hector wondered if they'd buoy up off the reef once they unloaded. But the craft settled back again as the lead APC, venting a cloud of black smoke, charged down the ramp and sank immediately up to its thrashing wheel hubs in a dark surf. It lurched and wallowed, clawing its way toward the shore.

Hector looked out then, into the maw of Hell.

The whole coast was on fire. The first light of dawn showed gray against black, but the burning glare cast writhing shadows across the sea. The pounding surf was heavy. Six feet, maybe eight. High and dry, the landing craft blocked it directly in front, but to either side it surged in toward the beach in snowcapped rollers that broke and foamed as if huge serpents were battling beneath them. But weirdly without sound. No sound at all, the roar was so loud. Concussions vibrated his chest like an emergency room doctor pounding on it, trying to bring him back from the dead.

The second APC gave a bull roar and charged forward. It cleared the ramp, hit the sea with a booming splash, and rolled to a halt, dead, the engine choked.

The serson mayor walked forward. He stood for a moment silhouetted against the gray dawn, rifle raised, yelling something soundlessly back at them.

A clatter tattooed along the bulkheads. Suddenly he whirled and fell, rolled off the ramp, and vanished.

Hector grabbed Slamet with one hand and the CHAD that had been eyeing him with the other, dragging them forward. Toward the gray light, the battering sound. Each step forward took an age. But they couldn't stay here. Another burst would wipe everyone out. The steel walls were a trap now. "Get out or die," he screamed. "Tell them, Private. Get out or die." Four steps to the edge of the ramp. Three. Two.

He drew a deep breath and jumped down into the foaming surf.

It was shockingly cold, and much deeper than he'd expected. His face went under and he struggled, choking, drowning. A hundred pounds of pack, weapon, ammo, and gear weighed him down as if four anvils were strapped to his back.

Then the jelly armor inflated, automatically buoying him up. He shrugged off his pack and ditched his helmet and entrenching tool. Got his boots on something soft underneath him, maybe the sergeant major, and pushed off. He got a hand on the stalled APC. Bullets clanged off it, lacerating the hull, ricocheting into the landing craft, where the Indos were still crowding the ramp. Some fell. Others jumped. They all vanished under the black sea, in the glimmering surf. A few fought their way back up, without weapons, and stumbled or swam after him. Hector looked for the CHAD, but the robot had sunk like a stone. He waved the platoon forward, then faced front again.

The beach was blazing with what looked like a hundred Fourth of Julys going off at once. Laser beams searched here and there through the smoke, focused to burn out retinas and flash-sear skin. Hector clawed his way around the stalled armored carrier, ducking almost too late as the forward machine gun began firing, then began wading toward the distant beach, angling left in case the guy in the gunner's seat depressed his aim too far. He remembered his rifle and lifted it above his head, then changed his mind and lowered it to shield his chest.

Tracers floated lightly above the surf, like fiery fairies. The din built as the flashes ashore turned blinding white flecked with sparks of blue. A familiar smell freighted the wind. The stench of explosives and burning vegetation.

Two hundred yards out from the beach the sandy bottom dropped away under his boots and he went under again. This time he felt heavier. Or weaker. Underwater the sounds were muffled. Bullets went *pock* and zz*zip*. He fought free of his mag pouch, leaving him only the thirty rounds in his rifle. Came up again, gasping for air, vision hazed and burning with red floaters he couldn't tell from tracers or lasers or something damaged inside his eyes.

Shallower now . . . close to the beach . . . he turned again and saw their heads, helmets gone, most of them, black heads bobbing in the surf. Others, just corpses, each wave body-surfing the dead on toward the land they'd striven to reach in such agony in their last moments.

This was worse than Itbayat. Much worse than Taiwan. The enemy had learned from those defeats. He was putting everything into decimating the first wave, hoping that discouraged the rest, persuaded them to go to ground or retreat.

Hector staggered forward, each impossible step consuming him. The sand seethed at his knees. Then at the tops of his boots. A wave rolled in and shoved him forward, almost toppled him onto his face. He staggered on, boots digging and slipping in wet sand.

Then at last found dry ground, hard footing. He forced a last floundering run from quivering waterlogged limbs and stumbled thirty yards to higher ground. He hit the deck and hugged the sand for a long time; seconds, minutes, sucking air. Until he was able at last to breathe, get his head up again, and peer around.

To their left flank, beach houses, a development, burning fiercely, the flames squirming shadows all along the beach, smoke blowing low and dense along the surf-line. Farther away, the white towering of high-rise apartments or hotels. Now and again something exploded like fireworks, throwing green sparks and heavy black smoke. Beyond them blue flashes rippled steadily, like a string of giants' firecrackers. To the right, a rise, MG fire flickering from it. Along the beach lay a dark wave of stranded troops, a little above the high water line, like seawrack cast up by a storm. Behind them floated the dark hulks of wrecked, burning APCs and landing craft. Zeroed on by the enemy's artillery and missiles, it didn't look like a single piece of armor had made it to the beach. Above them, the threatening buzz of quadcopter drones, imminent as hornets.

Hector hoped the drones were friendlies. For the moment, at least, they didn't seem to be firing on the marines. He was timing the muzzle-flicker ahead, waiting for the belt to run out, when a cicada buzzed against his throat. He flinched away, then recalled: the detection alarm. Silent, so it didn't give away your position.

"Gas," he yelled, and the cry, in English, went along the wrack of troops. The men rolled over in the sand, pulling frantically at mask carriers, fitting black goggle faces over their own. Others, maskless, fought their comrades for them. Rifle butts rose and fell. Men scrambled up and bolted back toward the sea. The MG cut them down as they ran. They flung out their arms as they were hit, falling in splashes in the red firelight to lie at rest at last in the embracing ocean.

Hector was too occupied to care. The mask first. He snapped the soft curved rubber over his face and sucked. Tight. Ripped open the protective suit. Pulled it on in a sort of controlled frenzy. It had to go on fast. But it was easy to tear. Finally he sealed the last seam.

The belt ran out and the gun ahead fell silent. He grabbed his rifle and jumped up, or at least lurched up, and ran along the line of troops. Looking for someone, anyone, who'd gotten some weapon ashore heavier than a rifle. To his astonishment another trooper rose too and ran four paces behind him. Private Slamet, still alive, still with him, faceless in the black mask, helmetless like Hector, but with the hood pulled up over his head.

Hector found a beefy Papuan Javelin gunner with his missile and tube still bagged in green invasion plastic. He'd lost his ammo bearer, but Hector clapped him on the shoulder and signed *follow me.*

Leaving Slamet to organize covering fire, he and the gunner rushed and dropped, sweating and suffocating in masks and suits, until they were behind the wrecked pier. They rested for two minutes, panting, then worked their way toward a parking lot.

Asphalt, good. Hector kept peering to the right, looking for another bunker or post or maybe a tank, because you set up for interlocking fire, but the prep must have taken it out because he couldn't see any. The noise was still rumbling away, flashing and quaking the ground, but it had moved inland, walking ahead of them. Good.

A roar in the sky, and heavies came in, shaking the earth in russet flashes all along the beach. He reeled back off the lot and burrowed into the sand as the salvos walked over him, tearing apart his mind. He screamed into the black din. Again. Harder. He couldn't remember who'd told him to scream. The heavies in Taiwan . . . this was even worse. The noise was catastrophic. Objects wheeled through the air. Bodies. He squeezed his eyes shut and buried his face in the sand. Dirt cascaded over him. He screamed. The cicada chirruped at his collarbone. He was starting to salivate. He pulled the mask tighter and extracted two injectors from his pocket. He jammed one into the Papuan's round ass as the man lay ahead of him, the other into his own thigh. He kneaded it, distributing the injection.

When the barrage slackened his ears rang so loud it sounded almost quiet. He pushed off the dirt, along with something heavy and soft he didn't want to look at, and low-crawled up onto the lot again. The Papuan was behind him now, both men low-crawling for all they were worth.

A huge crater, a smoking hole. They skirted it, creeping from abandoned car to car, the wrecks perforated like rural stop signs, gas tanks burning with a sputtering roar, until he spotted what might be a clear line of sight to the bunker. But even on a paved surface, the backblast would highlight their position. And he was still edgy about drones. But they might get off one shot.

He squeezed his eyes shut again, then shook his head to clear them under the mask. He was weeping. Drooling. The cicadas chirruped, chirruped. Dawn was darkening back into night. His lungs felt like dishrags being wrung out. His mother's strong hands, wringing out a wet towel. He coughed, trying to get a clear breath. But fluid seemed to be bubbling up nonstop from a thick spring deep in his lungs. His hands shook violently. He dropped the rifle, groped for it, dropped it again. Dug for another autoinjector and jammed it into his other leg.

A CAS drone screamed over. For a second he thought it might be after the bunker, but it screamed on inland, weaving between burning buildings until it suddenly exploded in a gigantic fireball that sputtered with red sparks and spun from the sky in a spiraling pinwheel of white smoke lit from within as if welders were at work. Hector hadn't seen what had shot it down, but there might be enemy troops over there, ahead.

The darkness receded a little. He clawed down a halfway decent breath. Then another. The tightness was still there, but he could get air past it. For now.

Okay, the bunker . . . bent double, they rolled behind a white SUV with bullet holes riddling the doors. He tilted a side-view mirror and spotted the bunker. A line-of-sight shot into its firing slit? Even if the Javelin missed, fragments and blast might take out the gunners. If

there *was* a human in there. This could be automatic, or teleoper-
ated. Maybe overhead mode would be better. He positioned the big
Papuan behind the rear quarter of the vehicle and got him set up. He
checked their rear, slapped the guy's shoulder, and yelled, "Fire in
the hole!"

The Papuan fired. *Click.* The missile *blooped* out and his upper
body jerked back, absorbing the initial recoil. The projectile lofted
twenty yards, then the booster ignited with a white flare and it powered upward.

Rocket-smoke shrouded them, but not for long. Hector grabbed
the guy and pulled him up into a trot away, headed for a yellow dumpster on the far side of the lot. As they ran, wheezing, staggering, he
glanced back over one shoulder, through the warped fogging lenses.
He tensed. The fucker was heading off downrange . . . no . . . it reoriented itself a hundred yards up, twisting in the air. At the same
moment a long burst from the bunker found the SUV. Projectiles
ripped through the passenger compartment, shredding it. Glass blew
out, and the car rocked on its springs before exploding into flame.

Above it the missile, still tailed by white fire, straightened,
plunged. Exploded in a modest distant *thud* on the roof of the bunker. Gray smoke and dust mushroomed up. The gun fell silent.

With a cheer, a line of soggy-uniformed, sand-frosted troops in
masks and suits surged up off the beach, yelling and firing. They
stormed the bunker, swarming to the firing slit and triggering magazine after magazine inside. Tossing in grenades. Hector panted, bent
over, elbows on his knees, drooling, wanting to yell at them to stop
wasting ammo, but couldn't force the words out. And he'd lost his
fucking terp back somewhere after the parking lot.

The colonel had shown him the division plan earlier. After taking the beach, they had about a klick to the firstphase line, "Bullet,"
on the far side of a north–south road and along the crest of a series
of defensible rises. Stop there and wait for air support to clear any
obstacles, then advance up the road to the reservoir. There they'd
link up with the Vietnamese, who were landing on the far side of
the main base. Meanwhile the follow-on waves were supposed to be
bringing in reinforcements, med teams, ammo.

But looking out to sea, which surged now a sullen and dreary black under a first light dulled by smoke the color of an unsheathed bayonet, he didn't see any armor. Other than the burning hulks. And without them, how could there be any follow-on waves?

Which meant they were on their own. Stranded. Still, they had to press ahead. He kept looking for officers, but if any had made it ashore they were keeping their heads down. Blending with their troops. Not exactly inspiring leadership. But to be fair, this was the first time these guys had been under fire. Things had been pretty fucking confused on Itbayat too. The first time the Corps had hit a defended beach since Inchon.

But nobody else seemed to be taking charge, so he waved together whoever would follow and led them down a depression with an open culvert at the bottom. They passed two light tanks, enemy 105s with cage armor. Something had burned through one hull, gutting it from the inside. It was still smoking so he snaked his guys around it, giving it a wide berth in case it felt like exploding. The other looked undamaged, but didn't move. One of the hatches was open. He considered manning it, trying to get it rolling, but he was no tanker. They grenaded it and moved on.

They seemed to sort-of get his hand signals, so he vee'd his fingers to show them: *Form wedges.* Where the fuck was the private . . . he sure could use a translator . . . finally he gave up and just trotted on at point, keeping a sharp eye out for cover and defilade.

The detector had stopped vibrating. He took a knee and tugged the mask off. Coughed, spat, wiped his eyes, and scrubbed dirt over the rubber. Noticing, as he stowed it back into its carrier, that a pack of the disk-drones had picked them up and were escorting them on both flanks. "Cool," he whispered. A large air support UAV howled over, heading inland, and he felt even better. If only the CHADs had made it ashore . . . or the armor . . . but they had Javelins and the Belgian MGs and air and drones. They could still make it.

Close with and destroy the enemy. The gut-level credo the Corps drummed into you from boot camp on.

But where was contact? Where *were* the fucking Chinese?

The king fucks the queen.

He was still thinking this when ahead of them something . . . *assembled* itself, as far as he could tell, from beneath the ground itself. It straightened, grew, lurching erect, like strung-together sticks picked up by a puppeteer, and began striding around their flank on long spiderlike legs. It vented a white plume that blew down toward them. Some of the Indos fumbled their masks back on again. Hector decided to wait. It smelled sulfury. Antitargeting smoke. He crouched in the ruins of a bungalow, peering at the thing. Nada. Just glimpses of something large lurching around out there. The Papuan said some urgent-sounding words, crouched beside him. He'd discarded the empty launcher and picked a rifle up somewhere.

Hector fought the desire to pull the world down on his head and cower. More and more Indos reached him, sprinting in short bursts down into the depression. "Shit," he muttered. He was gathering them into a perfect target. Whatever that thing was, or if enemy observation spotted them, one mortar shell would take everyone out. He kept trying to signal the Indos out onto the flanks, but they only huddled, as if in shock. Sure. The noise, for one thing. His own ears rang with ghost sirens. But he'd been on a battlefield before.

A taller guy he didn't recognize rolled over to face him. His dirty face was streaked with sweat. "I am Captain Andarwulan. You are the American." Hector nodded. "What is that thing like spider?"

"I don't know."

"We cannot stay here."

"Ya, pak," Hector said. "Do you have comms? Connectivity?"

"Nothing works. Jammed. We have to advance. Do you know where?"

Hector pointed where he figured the axis of advance lay. The watery smoke obliterated all sight, as if they floated in some milky netherworld that didn't really have sharp edges anywhere. "But if we get out of defilade, then what?"

"Then what?" The guy looked expectant.

"That's what I don't know," he shouted, suddenly impatient with this idiot, who seemed even denser than the usual officer.

Adarwulan hesitated, gripping a pistol. A fucking pistol? Hector thought. Seriously.

At that moment his hearing, sorting through the clamor, caught the unmistakable shriek of barrage rockets being launched.

The officer hurled himself to his feet and charged up the slope, yelling and brandishing the handgun. Hector grabbed for him, but hesitated an instant too long. If the meat robot wanted to self-destruct, let it.

Adarwulan stood atop the depression, shouting at his men, waving them forward.

The rockets screamed down, and he vanished in smoke and noise and fire.

This barrage bracketed them, then walked behind them, toward where some of the troops still lay prone, figuring probably they were sheltered. But just from the sound of the projectiles bursting Hector knew even before the detector began chirping. "Gas," he yelled again. His hands operated independently, jerking the mask out, spreading the thongs, snapping it on again. Around him the Indos were struggling with their protective gear, those who still had it. Those who didn't crouched as if struck dumb, or scrambled toward the rear. A crackle of fire meant they'd been quickly dealt with.

The lurching thing loomed through the smoke again, it or another like it, and he saw it clear just for a fraction of a second. A sleek, metallic insect-body, teardrop-shaped, with spiky antennas and a dozen bug-eyed oculars spaced around it. Not enough room in there for a man. Autonomous, like the CHADs. A bag or tank slung beneath, from which something was spraying. Needle-thin, only sporadically visible beams shot out from it through the smoke, searching its surroundings. One reached for him and he shrank back, ducking.

When he poked his helmet back up it was striding along on long black legs, many more than it seemed to need, insectile and obscene, the beams fingering the ground around it. Searching for victims. It moved with a dismaying fluid effortlessness even as it jerked from one microdecision to another. Something flashed overhead, spearing downward, but the silvery central body crouched with incredible quickness, hunkering down flat. The missile flashed past and buried itself in the soil before going off, throwing up clods of dirt. Only adding to the din of battle.

As the spider erected itself again Hector got his optic sight on it. He took the slack out of the trigger. But as if sensing the threat, it suddenly wheeled and stalked off, submerging, once more, into the smoke.

Hector stabbed at his cell again but got nowhere. It was all in Indonesian. He was going by guess and topo contours, trying to figure out where the phase line was. A road across their front. Hit that, dig in, wait for reinforcements. Maybe like what they'd done in Korea. Halt, sucker the enemy in, wait for the counterattack. Cut them to pieces with air and drones and arty. Maybe.

Desperately thirsty. Dizzy. Out of injectors now. But they had to keep moving. As soon as the shelling lifted he grabbed the Papuan and a couple others, pulled them to their feet, shoved them forward. Dismasked troops lay convulsing, unpupiled eyes staring up sightlessly as they died. Hector ignored them. He couldn't help. The others staggered out of the depression after him, their harsh agonized breathing snoring through the masks.

A brick building lay ahead. It was on fire. Smoke blew across a freshly mowed lawn. No . . . there was a soccer net. Not a lawn. A playing field.

The grass was soft under their boots, powdered with a light coating of gray dust. His breath rasped in his mask, buzzed in his ears. Perspiration fogged his lenses. The cicada chirruped, chirruped.

A body, torn and bleeding. Indo uniform. A pistol in the outstretched hand. The captain. Hector stepped over him and trudged on toward the building. Keeping the sun on his right. It shone ruddy and baleful through the drifting smoke. No one was firing at them. *Press on. To the road. Hold the road.* No entrenching tools, he hadn't seen one since the beach, so they'd have to make do with rifle butts and hands. He glanced back, alert for more of the spidery stalkers, but the smoke eddied past blank and ashen in opaque curtains. Tracers arched above it like blazing softballs. The stalkers were loose back there.

The Papuan buckled like a collapsing tower. He lay with chest heaving. Hector grabbed him by the web gear and pulled him to his feet again. Weepy brown eyes, terrified behind plastic. The other Indos stared at Hector. They were clumping up again. Making targets. He motioned *spread out* with an angry abrupt gesture.

They reached the red-brick building and took cover, crouching under the windows. Smoke blew across the field and blotted out the goals. Hector liked brick. Brick would stop a bullet. His mouth was stuffed with steel wool. Each time he tried to breathe powerful fists twisted his chest. The cicadas buzzed, panicked, dying. He didn't want to leave cover. But they had to press on. He let them rest for a couple minutes, then crept along the wall.

A bus was parked in front of the building. A bright orange bus with yellow and black piping. The engine was running but no one was around. No. A woman was slumped in the driver's seat. Motionless. Unmarked.

Hector followed his rifle's muzzle around the front fender. The grass between the bus and the school was . . . carpeted. For a moment he couldn't see anything but a patchwork quilt. A parti-colored rug unrolled on the gray grass.

Then he made out faces.

They were very small. He stared confused before his slowed brain assembled the colors into what they really were.

The children lay in windrows, ragged lines, as if they'd been in queues when they fell. Some were holding hands. All black-haired. Wearing colorful rain slickers. The boys were in blue. The girls in pink. By then he was walking in among them. The bodies crunched and yielded under his boots. He stepped on a pastic pencil box with a colorful cartoon. They all had the same pencil boxes. The Papuan was whimpering under his mask, making mewling sounds. The cicadas chirruped, chirruped.

Meat.

Robots.

No. Children.

What had killed them? Gas, or the violet shells?

He didn't know. Didn't care.

Do you hate the Chinese? The twisted, raving face of his boot camp DI. Brady. *Do you hate the Chinese, Private Ramos?*

I hate the fucking Chinese, sir.

I will stick my bayonet into them and blow their guts over my boots.

Some of the kids had been carrying plastic water bottles. Hector bent to scoop one up. The bottle sloshed half full. Other than raging thirst, he didn't feel anything now. Just an immense blankness. A void. The total absence of fear. Of terror. Even of rage. He pushed up the mask and sucked at the red plastic bottle.

He was a CHAD now. Autonomous. A mechanism. Hollow. Filled with swirling smoke. Assembled of muscle and bone and blood that very soon now would stop operating. The only meaning lay in the phase line. Bullet. Phase Line Bullet. Ahead. Reach it.

The cicadas chirruped, chirruped. He resealed his mask and threw the empty bottle away. The world darkened, tilting through dirty lenses. His lungs warped in his chest. He drooled and gagged and sweated. His bowels and bladder loosened and released.

He reeled forward over the carpeted dead, through the blowing smoke, gaze nailed to the axis of advance.

They passed the still idling bus and left the school behind. Trotting through streets now. Hector threw flankers out. Small houses. Tile roofs. All deserted. Corpses sprawled near the doors. One lay tangled in a toppled bicycle. Some of the houses were on fire. Others looked undamaged, pristine. Modest homes with little neatly kept gardens.

He led his improvised squad in slow staggering dashes from house to house, scanning behind and around them for the machines, for hidden snipers, machine guns. But aside from the spiders there was no resistance. Just smoke. And gas. As if the enemy had pulled back. Were refusing combat.

More bodies. These white-haired, spindly-legged, tumbled in a hedge, savagely torn, as if minced by huge blades while trying to run. Battle rumbled all around the horizon, hidden from the marines by a shifting curtain of smoke. Violet flashes deep in the murk.

Hector feels nothing. His chest is cast of solid pain. His eyes stream. He spits drool from a scorched mouth. Shapes shift within the smoke, striding about. They cast long mucus-yellow shadows from the bloody sun. A loose formation of silvery disks whirrs over a hundred feet up. He looks for cover, but they hum on inland, ignoring them. Far above, contrails scar the sky.

He stumbles across a lifeless land. Desolate, numb, hollow, still gripping his rifle, coughing and sobbing into his mask. And the cicadas chirrup, on and on, without pause.

20

The Pentagon

ER office was on the E Ring, considered the most prestigious. But she was on an upper floor, and the windows faced inward. All she could see was a wall, the offices of the next ring in, and the asphalted road between.

But since the war had started, Blair hadn't had much time to enjoy views anyway.

She was wrapping a meeting with her staff, and getting the ominous feeling Plans and Policy was being outrun by events. A television in her outer office was on 24/7. The screen on her desk linked direct to the "War Room"—formally, the Alert Center for Intelligence Fusion in the National Operations and Intelligence Watch Officer Network. Every half hour, the watch officer came on for an update. Even on a fast day, she was at most only fifteen minutes behind the White House Situation Room.

"Overall, it reminds me of the defeat of the Qing in the Opium Wars," one of her staffers was saying.

"The Opium Wars," she said flatly.

He nodded. "From 1839 on. Britain and France attacked in south China to protect their sales of opium. Which Peking was trying to stop. Ultimately, they invaded. China was forced to accede to unequal treaties, and cede land to the colonial powers."

"And this was a good idea?" she said. Humiliation often seemed like justice to the victors, but seemed rarely to lead to lasting peace. Reconstruction and Versailles, as examples. "All right, thanks for the update. Next issue—oculars?"

Another staffer unlimbered her tablet. "Ma'am. The enemy employed a vehicle-mounted pulsed ocular interruption system in Vietnam and Taiwan. The Army reports over four thousand troops blinded in Taiwan. We don't have Vietnamese figures. A 50-kilowatt-class unit was captured south of Hanoi and shipped to ARL. R&E contracted with General Atomics, Electromagnetic Systems Group, to reverse-engineer it into a squad-based system. It's completed tests and gone to contract award."

Four thousand blinded . . . she blinked, and forced her mind back to specifics. "The contract? And how soon can we field these systems?"

"Three hundred million with options up to nine hundred million, for fifty systems initial buy. First delivery in two months."

Two and a quarter million each, to blind enemy soldiers. She massaged her forehead. "Don't we issue some kind of goggles, something to protect the troops?"

The staffer said the Marines had fielded a cumbersome system adapted from a German welding mask, but the British had come up with a better one, polycarbonates coated with a dye that absorbed light in certain wavelengths. "They can be tuned for the precise frequencies the enemy system uses. It's effective, but at night it's like wearing sunglasses. And that's when the Chinese have been beaming our troops."

"We need something better, then. Ping DARPA, see if it's on their agenda. Anything else?"

They shook their heads. She nodded and thanked them. Her people flipped binders closed, slid tablets into briefcases. She waited until her door closed. Then shut her eyes and sank back into the padded chair with a sigh. Four thousand blinded . . . over fifty thousand Allied casualties taking back Taiwan, with no count at all yet on civilian deaths and woundings. Thirty thousand dead and wounded so far for the invasion of Hainan. A national debt so high it was a state secret.

The cost of war. And what had this one started over? Hardly anyone remembered now. A terror attack in Mumbai. Or had it been the shootdowns of satellites? Then Zhang's invasion of Taiwan. Like a greased slide downhill, rather than the single blazing jolt of Sumter or Pearl Harbor or 9/11. Some said it had been inevitable, the predestined conflict of a rising power with a legacy one. A clash as old as Athenians versus Spartans, as described by Thucydides.

But just now, there might be a lull. A hiatus as the scales vibrated, so delicately balanced a breath could disturb them.

"Dr. Titus? Call for you. From Europe."

Probably the Swedish defense ministry. They were worried about Russia again. Indications seemed to foreshadow some kind of military move. From time to time someone would call her, either from their Defense Commission or Parliament, and try to find out what the Americian reaction would be if the Russians came across the border. Or, more generally, asking about "coordinating defense plans," which amounted to the same thing. Each time she told them that if they wanted joint planning, they'd have to bite the bullet and join NATO. The EU Defense Community was great, but if they wanted security, NATO was where they wanted to be. Article Five would protect them. The EU might not.

What she left unsaid were her own doubts about how much the US could help in Europe, given that ninety percent of American forces were already engaged or on-call in theater in case the Hainan invasion turned into a disaster.

She picked up the phone. "Blair Titus."

"Blair. Liz McManus here."

She glanced at her door. Still closed, but she turned her chair away from it and the window anyway. "Um, Liz. Hello. What time is it in Dublin?"

"I'm actually in Tangier at the moment, but I wanted to let you know, your friends from Zurich want to talk again."

"Friends from Zurich" would be the Chinese. She glanced at the door again. "Um, I don't know how we could—"

"They're willing to undertake more substantive discussions. Would your Dr. Petrarka be available to talk?"

She hesitated, confused. There was no "Dr. Petrarka." Then she realized who they meant.

General Ricardo Petrarca Vincenzo.

"I think, um, Dr. Petrarka would be open to . . . a conversation," she said cautiously. "When would they like to call?"

"As soon as possible."

"It will take a little time to set up." She had Vincenzo on her cell, but maybe it wouldn't be smart to give it out over the phone. "Can I have a number?"

McManus supplied one, but said again that they wanted a swift response. Blair said she couldn't promise anything but would try. They chatted for fifteen more seconds, then McManus rang off.

Blair stared down at the phone, then hung up slowly. She looked at her cell again. Then thumbed up the contact for the chairman of the Joint Chiefs of Staff.

VINCENZO was in the J-3 spaces. Yes, he could make himself available to take an important call. She wondered, as she walked the corridors toward the NMCC, why the Chinese had decided to approach via the US military. But the question answered itself. The clique trying to negotiate were military themselves. This was a generals' revolt. Though the deputy minister for foreign affairs seemed to be involved too.

Reaching out must take brass balls, as Dan would have said. Zhang had ordered generals shot for much less.

Regardless, this was a huge development. She just had to make sure it didn't get derailed somehow.

Vincenzo was in short-sleeved greens. When he threw a beefy arm over Blair's shoulders his breath smelled of Tic-Tacs. "A huddle. Okay, what's going on?"

As she explained in terse sentences his eyes narrowed. "You've been doing this offstage? Who else knows? SecDef? CIA?"

"The national security advisor's in the picture. State knows a little. No one else."

"Not SecDef?"

"Not that I know of. It was important to—"

"I get it. The fewer ears, the fewer leaks." He drew back and regarded her quizzically. "But it could've been risky for you. Could still be, actually."

"I had to take the chance."

"Yeah. I guess so."

A colonel stuck his head in. "General? Call for you. From Zambia."

They exchanged glances. "Zambia?" Vincenzo muttered. "What the—"

"—Sorry, sir; correction; from the embassy of Zambia in Beijing."

A DIA officer spoke up. "China has significant investments in Zambia, General. A special trade and economic cooperation zone."

"They're using an embassy phone. From a friendly ambassador," Blair said. "To avoid the official networks."

The stocky general stood immobile for at least four seconds, frowning down at his hands. He glanced at the clock, then headed for the door. "In the annex," he snapped. "I'll take it in the MOLINK room. Get the translators. The J-2. The congressional liaison. Get the command historian in here too."

"We may not need translators," Blair told him. "If it's the contact I talked to, he speaks good English."

"I'd rather have the backup. Just in case. And yeah, get the JAG in on this too." He rounded on the astonished staffers. His shout "Let's go, people!" sent them into a flurry of activity.

The Moscow Link room was a walled-off cubicle with a table, one chair, and a dedicated computer for the old DC–Moscow hotline. One whole wall was stacked with bulging red-striped burn bags. Obviously, its main function these days was storage. A colonel said anxiously, "Shouldn't we call the White House, General? If they—"

Vincenzo hand-chopped him into silence. "I don't have anything to tell NCA yet. Let's see what they want first. But yeah, call the duty officer at the Sit Room and ask him—or her—to stand by." The colonel stood back after fussily centering a phone on the table. "This isn't a covered circuit, is it?" the general asked, grabbing the single chair.

"No sir. UNCLAS mode."

"Can we record this?"

"Already set up, General."

Vincenzo studied the phone, then the wall clock. He glanced around at the others crowding into the room. "Clear out," he snapped. "Ms. Titus, DIA, J-2, and JAG when she gets here. Everybody else, vamoose. And close that fucking door!"

When the chairman pressed a button for speakerphone the labored breathing of whoever was on the other end filled the little room.

"General Ricardo Petrarca Vincenzo here," Vincenzo said, enunciating clearly and speaking slowly.

A heavy deliberate voice came on the line. *"This is Deputy Minister Chen Jialuo."*

Vincenzo shot Blair a raised eyebrow. Shielding her mouth, she whispered, "The principal to the UN conference. We had a shouting match with him in Dublin. He ignored us in Zurich. Sent a junior guy to talk to me. But I think he's who we're dealing with. Or the channel to them, anyway."

Vincenzo nodded. A woman came in, looked around, and leaned against the wall. Air Force blues, with the silver-scales-and-laurel-wreath insignia of the Judge Advocate General Corps on her chest. "A reachout from China," the chairman told her, covering the mouthpiece. Then said into the phone, "Good morning, Deputy Minister. How can I help you?"

"Chairman Zhang has asked me to gain some idea of mutually acceptable terms."

Blair suppressed a gasp. Maybe she'd been wrong all along, about Yun fronting a resistance faction. Maybe he represented Zhang himself. But in the next moment she realized that couldn't be right. If so, why was he calling from a foreign embassy? Keeping this conversation from the rest of the governmental apparatus? Something wasn't kosher here.

Vincenzo glanced at the JAG rep, who shook her head, frowning.

He said slowly, "This is General Vincenzo. I certainly do not want to be negative, sir. We would welcome any chance to talk. But shouldn't such an approach be made through diplomatic channels? Rather than the Joint Chiefs. We try to keep military and political separate here."

5

Blair noticed the gleam of perspiration on Vincenzo's thick neck. The strain had to be terrific. One wrong word could derail the exchange. Extend the war. Cost hundreds of thousands more lives.

The lawyer was scribbling on a scratch pad. She shoved it in front of him. He frowned and nodded curtly. Pushed it away.

"Deputy Minister Chen here. Yes, I understand unorthodox way to contact. But necessary. China will never surrender. Invade, and you will lose millions of troops. Your country is riven by strife. Rioting. You cannot continue this war much longer. Again, what terms?"

Vincenzo took a slow deep breath; his shoulders rose and fell. But his voice remained steady. "Sir, your country is bleeding too. Allied terms were set out by the Jakarta Declaration. I have no authority to modify it. If I may, I would like to transfer this call to the White House."

The other's tone turned dire. *"We wish to stop suffering on both sides. Chairman is reaching out to you, General. I would not reject his overture."*

"This is not a rejection, sir."

"Then let us know what terms we can settle on."

"I would rather have you propose them, sir." Vincenzo shot Blair a look. Questioning, or uncertain?

She tried for an encouraging smile. "That's good. Keep him talking," she whispered as two more men stepped in. A junior officer followed, toting folding chairs which she snapped open across from where Vincenzo sat hunched over the phone.

"We have discussed acceptable terms with Dr. Titus. Is she there with you?"

Vincenzo glanced at her. "Yes, she is." His contracted frown asking: What the hell did you agree to, Blair? She shook her head furiously. Spread her hands and whispered, "I agreed to nothing. Just listened to what they had to say."

Chen spoke again. *"I have General Pei and Admiral Lianfeng here. We are entering fourth year of this war. We have given proof of our indestructible strength. So have you. But at enormous cost.*

"Therefore, we propose an armistice. All territory conquered

on either side, to be returned. All China's territories to which we have historical rights, you must cede back. A return to the status quo ante bellum."

Blair and Ricardo exchanged glances. Pei had commanded on Taiwan, but escaped before the island's fall. Lianfeng was China's naval chief of staff. If this feeler was being undertaken behind Zhang's back, it was from the highest level of the military establishment.

The J-2, the intel officer, leaned down to murmur in Vincenzo's ear. The general batted him away. "Please convey my greetings. However, those terms are not acceptable," he said into the phone, and a droplet of sweat rolled down his neck into his collar. "Your ally Korea has succumbed to our forces. We are firmly established on Hainan and preparing to take Hong Kong. It is time for you to capitulate."

Silence on the other end of the line. More heavy breathing. Then another voice, deeper, broke in, speaking in rapid Chinese.

"He says, the People's Empire will never surrender," the interpreter said. "You will regret not . . . uh, not accepting this extended hand of peace."

Vincenzo twiddled his fingers. The J-2 handed him a pen. He jotted on the scratch pad, signed it, and shoved it over. Blair caught a glimpse. It read *SACOM: DEFCON One Charlie*. The staffer cleared his throat, scanning it, then rushed out.

She shivered. Despite the bodies crowded into it, the temperature in the little room seemed to have fallen twenty degrees. Was this how the world ended? And what was *One Charlie*? The nuclear first strike Szernci had described? She put a hand on Vincenzo's shoulder. He clasped his free one over it, as if grateful for the reassurance. So she bent and murmured, "Keep him talking, Ricardo. At any cost, keep him on the line."

But the legal rep was muttering too, from Vincenzo's left. "You need to kick this upstairs, General. End the conversation! Tell them the White House will call back."

Vincenzo said levelly, ignoring her, "Sir, let me make clear that I welcome this initiative. We are open to the idea of an armistice. The United States, the Allies, would be glad to pause hostilities.

"But this decision is not a matter for generals. It's time to involve our president." He gestured to the interpreter. "Tell him we'll have the White House call back. Immediately. Will that be all right?"

The conversation shifted to Chinese. Blair hugged herself, afraid to breathe. The clock on the wall jerked steadily forward. More people kept crowding into the room, until Vincenzo angrily hissed, "Nonessential personnel, get the fuck out."

A subdued hubbub bled in from outside each time the door opened. She glanced through the crack into the command center. A throng hovered there, looking somber and frightened, though a few countenances seemed to glow with nervous hope. Sort of how she felt right now . . . if only they didn't drop the ball . . . but DEFCON One Charlie . . . and what about the Russians? They'd facilitated the contact, maybe pushed the Chinese toward making the call, but had their own irons in the fire.

She didn't know what to think, or how to feel. Only that the world seemed to have suspended its breath. And that she herself found it hard to keep on breathing.

The interpreter held up a hand. All their gazes shifted to her. "Sir, they are agreeing to talks with the White House," she said.

"And the armistice?" Vincenzo said.

"No armistice until an agreement is reached. Sorry, sir. I—"

"That's okay. I understand." He leaned toward the phone again. "Deputy Minister? Are you still on the line?"

"I am, General."

"I understand we have a path forward. The White House will call you back. At this number?"

"We will wait for the call. But cannot do so for long. Events move without us. The call must come soon."

Vincenzo nodded to the colonel who'd set up the room. "Sit Room on the line?"

"Yes, sir, and they're getting the chief of staff there. Mrs. Madhurika."

Vincenzo said, "Deputy Minister: You'll hear back within minutes. Thank you for reaching out. It's time we went forward together."

"I hope so as well. Goodbye, General."

"Goodbye, Deputy Minister. General. Admiral. Goodbye."

The chairman hung up, the handset rattling just a bit as he did. For a second no one spoke.

Then he glared around. *"No one discusses this outside these rooms. Is that clear? The White House makes the next move. This was just preliminary. Setting up the call. I said, is that understood?"*

Reluctantly, they all nodded. Blair did too.

Vincenzo got up and stretched. He patted her arm. Gave her a tired smile. "Let's hope this works out. No. Let's *pray* it does."

She nodded, unable to reply. And sank into a chair as soon as he left.

SHE was back in her office that night, unwilling to leave the building, when the Sit Room logo flashed on her official screen. She sat up straight, suddenly quickened with hope. This could be it. The armistice, put out to the government before the public announcement. Tonight crowds would celebrate in Times Square, in every city and hamlet in America. Would they call it V-C day?

Instead the logo dissolved to a map. *"From national reconnaissance assets. Troops and armored forces of the Russian Federation have crossed the northern Chinese border at three points. This is a major movement. It was possibly rehearsed in advance by the Vostok operational-strategic exercises Russia conducted last year.*

"Seven army brigades, along with airborne troops and tactical air forces, took part in that joint exercise, staged by the Far Eastern and Siberian Military Districts. This incursion is on an even larger scale. Chinese forces are falling back. DIA estimates they were denuded of advanced weapons and drawn down in numbers in response to the Allied offensives in the east and south, as well as internal unrest in Xianjiang and Tibet.

"Stand by . . ."

The map vanished, replaced by an Air Force officer's face. He looked harried. *"Moscow has just announced they are joining the Allies in bringing peace to Asia. Um, 'responding to Chinese aggression in the Blagoveshchensk region.' But we've seen so evidence yet of what they're referring to."*

Blair watched, disoriented at first, then suddenly comprehending.

The Russians wanted their money. But the White House had refused to guarantee their loans as part of the armistice deal. So their way of insuring they would be paid back had been to join the Allies. Demand a seat at the peace table, and insist on repayment there.

They'd stood aside as long as they could profit, waiting to see who would emerge as the victor. Now that the Opposed Powers were weakening, it was time to join the winning side.

Cold-blooded.

Machiavellian.

But perfectly rational, in the ruthless logic of great-power chess.

The Sit Room was still on the screen. The map came up again, updated. More Russian units were being identified. Their forces were advancing. Air strikes were taking out Chinese airfields.

This was a major attack. No, an invasion. Designed to gain land, eat territory, carve out China's northern heart. So it could be sold back later at a terrible price.

Events were sliding, tumbling. The whole planet shifting under their feet.

Her phone rang, startling her. Her secretary had gone home long ago. She looked at the ID. From Stanford, California. She picked up. "Kevin?"

"*Blair.*" Glancey sounded desperate. "*Are you watching this?*"

So the Sit Room was only thirty seconds behind cable news. "About Russia's entry into the war? I just heard. It's a stab in the back, considering they were sort-of allies with Zhang. But still, with us attacking from the south, the Russians from the north, that means the war's over." She debated telling him about the call to Vincenzo, but couldn't discuss it on an open line. "Maybe things will all turn out okay," she said cautiously.

"*That's what I'm calling about. The revolt.*"

She blinked, taken aback. "The . . . what revolt?"

"*You're not watching? Fox, BBC? There's been a coup in Beijing. Hard-line elements. It's confused. But no one knows what's going on. And that's not good.*"

"No, it isn't." She felt whiplashed, a sense of doom overtaking what had a moment before been hope.

"If Zhang's being overthrown, he's already told us what he'll do. He'll issue the orders. Some of the rocket forces will obey and launch. Even if he doesn't, I've studied their command and control structures. They're not as centralized as ours. They don't have PAL links on their warheads, and we cyber-degraded their automated command and control. Meaning, they'll have reverted to manual. Which means—"

"Which means individual theater commanders can launch," she murmured, and the fear grew until she bit her lip to stem rising panic. "What can we do, Kev? You're the expert on war termination. Help us."

"I don't know. I don't know! There's no template. No precedent. Maybe what Ed was saying is the only way left—"

She squeezed her eyes closed. A first strike, with the biggest thermonuclear warheads ever mounted. Earth Penetrators, to shake down mountains. That was the horror Szerenci had designed for the last act of this tragedy.

But no strike, massive as it might be, could take out everything.

She groped for words to reassure the frightened voice on the other end of the line. But nothing came to mind. Nothing she could say. Nothing she could do.

He was still talking when she hung up, and lowered her head into her shaking hands.

21

In the Golden Mountains

MASTER Chief Teddy Oberg was back in the Teams. Readying for a mission. But unable to assemble his dive gear. Missing the fins. Then his rebreather wouldn't give him air. He sucked and sucked, but his lungs stayed empty.

"Sumo" Kaulukukui was there. His old swim buddy. Teddy wondered at that. Vaguely recalling fast-roping into a night-shrouded city, being trapped in a kill room. Galleries above them. A machine gunner behind them. A grenade, bouncing between them . . . and Sumo . . .

War's a mothefucker, ain't it.

"You fatass Hawaiian shitbird," he told the other SEAL. "Thought you checked out on the way up to the roof. Waiting for the medevac."

"Look like I'm K?" the big SEAL said. He tapped his chest, where Teddy now saw a gaping but bloodless hole. "Stick your hand in, you retarded Laurel Canyon haole."

He woke to someone shaking him. He coughed, hacking out the fluid buildup that had dogged him since the chlorine attack, and reached for a green bottle. When the oxygen hit, icy life seared his lungs and his brain defogged like a cleared mask. "Yeah," he grunted.

"Lingxiù, it is time," the big bearded muj, Yusuf, said. Teddy's fingers tightened on the thin-blade inside his sleeping bag. But Yusuf backed away, visage unreadable.

It was still black dark. Oh-dark-thirty. But today was the day.

The day they'd find out if Jedburgh was a doable mission, or a massacre.

The supply drop had included the Stingers Vlad promised, plus ammunition, antibiotics, and the black, heavy teardrop-shape that might just give them a chance to cripple Zhang's remaining deterrent.

The Sandia TA-4 was an electromagnetic pulse generator driven by a nuclear microdevice. It had done the job on Teddy's last mission, but that installation hadn't been protected by solid rock.

Which meant they'd have to get in close before activating the initiation sequence.

He and most of their remaining rebels had trekked east through the mountains for weeks. A grueling, dangerous forced march conducted mainly by night, or when snow masked them from overhead observation. It had taken longer than he'd estimated. He'd had to cut their rations. Some had dropped out, deserters, losing the faith, but Teddy was ready for that. Three of his most trusted men had trailed the main body, to shoot anyone who turned back. Guldulla had stayed behind, to try to revive the rebellion. Spearheading a new recruiting drive, to rebuild their ranks after the cadre had been decimated by Chagatai's surprise attack.

Leaving Teddy and Qurban to honcho the raid to the east, with Teddy accompanied 24/7 by a guy he didn't trust and who outweighed him by at least fifty pounds.

He coughed again, spat, and rolled out. Dandan #3 knelt to make up his bedroll. A hefty girl, another captured Han, this time selected not for bed but her suitability as a pack animal. He couldn't carry his old loads, not with a bad leg and now crap lungs too. Fortunately Vlad had included several cylinders of oxygen in the drop. But sometimes, defiling up a cliff, Teddy had to stop and rest while the others waited.

Hotshot SEAL's getting old, dream-Sumo said in his mind.

Shut up, you dead motherfucker.

Gone south on us. Got religion and gone south.

I figured some things out, that's all. Mainly, that the fate of the fucking universe isn't up to me.

Gone over to the fucking ragheads. Bought into that "Allah rules" shit. Probably waste his old teammates, if they showed up there.

He pushed the dream out of his head and squatted in the ravine with his squad leaders, shielding a flashlight. The air was bitter cold this high. Vlad had downloaded him maps of the missile site. It looked impenetrable. Was designed to be, of course. Their last mission, against the computer facility, had been across open desert. This one was across terrain as rocky and precipitous as ITIM's old mountain hideout.

Of course, they weren't approaching by road.

In three weeks they'd traveled almost five hundred miles, first through mountains, then leaving the Taklimakan behind for rugged, treeless, blasted terrain that made the moon look friendly. The empty central heart of China. Mongolia lay to the north. Then south of the Jiuquan road the mountains began again.

Here, in the Altun-Shan, the Golden Mountains, China had dug in its most potent strategic deterrent. The massive missiles whose revelation had astonished the Allies, and overturned their comfortable assumptions of escalation superiority.

Or so Vlad had said. All Teddy could see was that after that trek, he was down to a hundred effectives. A paltry number to take on what was probably at least a regiment of security troops, barriering the area from intruders and ready to decimate any who tried.

"There is only one road in," he told them, showing it to them on the map. "Look at those tight turns. And cliffs. Must be hell in deep winter. These used to be lead mines. Silver too. They used the old mining roads to get their construction equipment up here."

"And where precisely are the missiles?" Qurban asked, in his exacting, slow Guantánamo English.

Teddy regarded him uneasily. The old al-Qaeda fighter marched up front, with the youngest rebels. His stocky form, shaggy with the sheepskins they wore against cold and infrared surveillance, seemed to take the steepest uphills in stride. Then he glanced at the younger man beside them. Yusuf was big, and smarter than he looked. He understood the squirt comms that connected them to their Agency handlers as well as Teddy did. The problem was, he was one of the ALQ veteran's guys. The squad leaders, too, seemed to defer to al-Nashiri as much as to their Lingxiù.

But for the moment at least, they seemed ready for a fight. "Uh, Higher says they're here. At the end of this side road." He called up the imagery. "See where it crosses what looks like an embankment? That's actually a dam. Coming down, we'll hit that road near this turn. But just now the stream will be dry. So we don't need to cross it during the approach phase.

"Should be two, three hours' march in from where we're sitting. In the dark. Total silence. Remember, the Han drones can detect electronics. So all radios must be off. The Stinger carriers will only turn their seekers on if we're attacked. Our shaheeds, martyrs, will not arm their loads until we are within sight of the enemy. They will go in last, after the scouts and the rocket grenade teams. And after that, the black idol."

That was what Qurban called the TA-4, with barely concealed scorn. In the faint light the guerrillas looked doubtful. Hey, he didn't feel that confident about this one himself. Their only advantage would be surprise. Lose that, and they'd be overwhelmed.

The only way he could see them actually accomplishing this mission, to disable or at least damage the missiles' guidance systems, was to detonate the electromagnetic weapon as close to the silos as they could get. Sandia put out a good product. After the previous mission, he was pretty sure the Package would work as advertised.

The question was whether they could fight it in close enough to penetrate the hundreds of feet of solid rock the Agency said protected their targets.

"All right, let's move," he told them, knees creaking as he cranked himself to his feet. "Follow the plan. Aim before you fire. Put the devils of fear behind you."

Qurban stood too. The old fighter said softly, "Say your du'a that I taught you. It will banish the djinn of fear that al-Amriki speaks of. Trust Allah and all will be well, whatever happens."

Their faces brightened. They pumped weapons in the air. The cheers were quiet, muted by the wind. But they seemed to be heartfelt.

HOURS later, exhausted from the climb down, breathless and hungry, Teddy lay full length in an overwatch position. The cold rock under his belly felt familiar. He'd lain like this before on so many missions, from Africa to the White Mountains: Serbia, Iraq, Ashaara, the high desert.

How many more did he have in him?

Vlad had offered a promotion. Warrant officer, which was a big deal in the Teams. Warrants were little gods. Even the Det COs avoided giving them direct orders. Back pay, which had to be a sizable chunk after war bonus, POW bonus, and hazard pay.

And California. Salena? Medical retirement?

Or a second career as a high-level operator, running special ops with the spooks?

All he had to do was offer up his guys on their fucking altar.

But lying here, freezing his fucking balls, he still didn't know what he wanted. Or what was right. Not since that night on the mountain, starving, lost, when everything he'd thought he knew had been turned upside down.

It wasn't up to him.

Somebody Else was in charge.

A scuffling behind him, and a heavy body thumped down alongside. Yusuf, by the sound of it. Teddy focused the binoculars on the installation's entrance. It was disguised by an overhang of natural rock. From overhead it would disappear into the mountainside. Only here, looking up from below, could he make it out.

Whoever had done the mission planning back at Langley had suggested two approaches. The first was this main entrance. If they couldn't get into the complex that way, they'd have to climb the mountain, hauling the Package all the way, to a fissure near the top. The guess was that this cleft might lessen the thickness of the rock shielding to an extent that could let the pulse penetrate.

As to what would happen then, when you blitzed four dozen

heavy multiple-reentry-vehicled nuclear warheads with an electro-magnetic storm, Vlad had gotten vague. Oh, no, they wouldn't go off, he'd said. The nukes would fry like poached eggs, but they wouldn't detonate.

Right, Teddy thought, tracking the creeping figures below with his optics as they neared what looked like observation posts.

Or they could tear this fucking mountain range apart with a flash you could see from Alpha Centauri.

Yeah. Maybe this should be your last mission, Obie. Hang it up. Take the offer. He could still go to worship in the States. Join a mosque. Keep his head down.

Leave Xinjiang? Leave ITIM? His guys, who'd followed him to battle?

Fuck no. At least, not yet.

They had to finish this fucking war first. Then leave the next one to the fucking new crop. He was done. Past time, to judge by the agony in his ruined foot, the desperate need for air when he took a strain.

Flashes below. Then the claps of distant explosions. The RPG teams were taking out the outposts. Breaching their perimeter. Teddy crept into the eyepieces. Smoke rose, obscuring the view. Machine guns ripped. Below, figures ran and then sprawled. As he'd trained them, fire and rush.

Only a few, pitifully few, rose again and dashed onward.

From somewhere he couldn't see, black specks darted skyward. They tilted and spread out like enraged hornets, seeking whatever had disturbed their nest.

Autonomous drones. But these seemed smaller, faster, more ma-neuverable than any he'd ever seen before. They dived more abruptly than the one he'd shot down during the attack on the computer cen-ter the year before. Yet unlike them, these didn't fire on the rebels. Instead they swooped around them in narrowing orbits, as if picking targets. The rebels took a knee, as he'd trained them. They aimed the long clumsy antidrone weapons, or fired out magazines at their tormentors.

Which suddenly ceased circling and dove in. When they hit their targets they exploded.

"Smoke," Teddy said into his cheap throwaway walkie-talkie. Line of sight, no scrambling, but a transmission now couldn't give anything away the enemy didn't already know.

Antitargeting grenades popped. A dense white smolder whirled up, blanketing the advance. Its upper layers braided into swirls as a second wave of larger, slower drones skittered back and forth above it, frustrated, unable to pick out targets in the haze. A pair collided, locked blades, and tumbled out of the sky into the murk.

Teddy sucked a hit of oxygen and glanced behind him. A four-man team crouched there, cradling the Package on an aluminum litter. As soon as the assault squad signaled they were in, he would order them forward. If this attack failed, he'd accompany them to the summit. Serve as sniper overwatch. They'd withdraw together, after emplacing the thing.

If anyone was left by then.

Heavier explosions thumped from within the murk below. The shaheeds were hurling themselves forward. With fifty pounds of C-4 strapped on back and chest, they were human torpedoes. Without artillery or mortars, he had to depend on them to reduce strong points. It was a wasteful way to fight. You lost your best, and kept the cowards. But the mission came first.

But it always did, didn't it?

A crackle on the radio. They saw a way through. Should he stay up here? Yeah, he should.

But he couldn't. Not watching them die, below.

Teddy hoisted himself, wincing as his leg nearly buckled despite the metal brace, but caught himself. He turned, and waved the litter team after him. They lurched down the slope, the swaying massive burden tugging them off balance. There. He was committed.

But who had committed him?

Had he done it himself?

There is no choice.

Everything that happened was inevitable as the sky.

They stumbled downhill two hundred meters and hit the smoke. It stank of sulfur, of burnt powder. It blotted out the entrance. Lost in it, Teddy led them toward where his compass told him it should be. Uphill now. Good.

But as the hill steepened bullets whined overhead. Someone was still laying down MG fire. Then a second gun joined in. Beneath the hammering, the pop of rifles, a faint chorus of high shouts.

A counterattack. He knelt, charged his carbine, and set the optic to his eye. A figure lurched toward him. He put a burst into it. Enemy, or one of his own who'd turned tail, didn't matter. As it fell he caught the black tactical gear of Han security. Good.

But at the same moment shells began screeching in. They exploded on the heights he'd just left. Two ranging rounds were followed by a continuous, earth-shaking barrage. The black blossoms of high explosive blanketed the rise. Air bursts sprayed steel down to slash white gashes into the rocks. If he'd stayed up there, he'd be dead now.

The voice had said it on the mountain, immense as space, more unyielding than granite . . . yet not without compassion.

There is no chance.

You have always done My will.

The assault squad leader, on the radio. *"Lingxiù. We are pinned down. In kill zone. All my men are wounded. We cannot break through."*

Without reflection, Teddy thrust a fist skyward. The men behind him braked too. A shell exploded mere steps ahead with a heave of earth and a shock wave that knocked him down. He lay full length as fragments whined and buzzed over.

When that salvo lifted he levered up again, only to have the damned leg fold under him. His searching hand came back bloody.

But he was still thinking even as his fingers scrabbled across the harrowed stony ground for his carbine. He couldn't find it. Then he did: a twisted hunk of plastic and steel. A hit, crunching the handguard and twisting the barrel. Smashed. Useless. Like him. He threw it aside and pulled his Makarov, trying to think amid the battering sound. He had one squad in reserve. Should he throw them in too?

Mortars screamed down, bursting one after the other across their line of retreat and spraying the ground with white phosphorous. Fiery flakes drifted down, cauterizing through sheepskin, clothing, flesh. Throwing their weapons away, the rebels ran, screaming and beating at themselves until they toppled and fell, unquenchable fire gnawing deep into their bodies. Mingled with that came the stinging reek of chlorine and the grinding bellow of some kind of armor, approaching from beyond the smoke.

As objectively as he could, he tried to decide. Push in the reserve? He should if there was a chance of fighting through.

But there really wasn't a decision here.

The enemy was too strong. Just as he'd feared. They hadn't even reached the entrance yet. Had been stopped at the second line of defenses. The Han had MGs, artillery, drones, mortars, white phosphorus, and gas.

They'd never break through.

Another nearby burst knocked him down again. He crawled to the litter. His men stared at him, those who were still alive, as he laid the pistol aside, fumbled open the cover, and went through the initiation sequence. Too far away to do the job, probably, but at least he wouldn't leave the Package to be captured and dissected.

When it was armed and the count started he hit Transmit. "Retire," he shouted. "This is the Lingxiù. Abandon the attack. Bring back those who can walk. Shoot those who cannot. Retire. *Retire!*"

But the only answers were fragmented bursts of static punctuated by screams.

THEY pulled back through a renewed barrage, clutching to their faces scarves soaked in the antigas liquid the Agency had supplied. Taking more losses as they stumbled through hell, the earth shaking, steel scything the air, an acrid haze stinging their eyes and stripping the linings from their throats.

Teddy sucked the last of his oxygen and tossed the bottle away. He emerged from the cloud, stumbling painfully on the reinjured leg. He oriented and headed for the rally point, a gap in the mountains not too far distant. The reserve squad would be waiting there. They'd serve as rear guard.

For a little while he wondered if he was the sole survivor. Then through the pre-morning dark a few other forms took shape, lurching along, many dragging wounded comrades.

But all too pitifully few. If drones or fresh troops pursued, they were lost. He felt naked without a rifle. But all he had left was the pistol.

Oh, fuck . . . where was it? He fumbled inside his coat, but the solid little Makarov was gone. He'd laid it aside to initiate the charge. Then *left it behind*. Fuck. *Fuck* . . . So all he had now was the thin-blade, until he could pick something else up. He pulled the knife from its sheath and carried it point up, but it seemed a paltry weapon after what the Chinese had just thrown at them.

And no doubt the black uniforms were putting together a pursuit force. Well, he'd mapped out the roughest, most precipitous route he could find for the retirement phase. With numerous opportunities to ambush anyone following them. Some of the wounded wouldn't make it. Maybe he wouldn't himself. But the toughest just might. All he could do now was give them a chance.

He was looking for a place to set up his rear guard when heavy, running footsteps thudded behind him.

He wheeled, alerted by Team-honed reflex just in time to block the descending knife. It slashed his palm, but he managed to grip his attacker's wrist and turn it outward, using the other's momentum to throw him rather clumsily over one hip. But the fucking bad leg gave way and they crashed to the rocky soil together.

Teddy rolled, recovered, and went to a combat crouch, facing the shadow that rose from the ground, steadied itself, and moved toward him again.

"Yusuf," he gasped. Then realized it wasn't.

It was Abu-Hamid al-Nashiri. Qurban. The hajji, who'd been undermining him ever since he'd come to these mountains.

Who'd probably poisoned the old sheykh, Akhmad, when the old man resisted his murderous interpretation of the Koran. And shot their young spymaster, without trial, without investigation.

So this was his next move. Teddy hawked fluid from deep in his lungs and spat. "Qurban. What are you doing? It's me."

"I see you, al-Amriki." Just the tone conveyed the smile. The thin, withholding, deadly stretch of the lips with which the al-Qaeda veteran had greeted him the first time Vlad had introduced them, and Teddy had tried, fruitlessly, to refuse the dangerous gift.

"Is this your true intent? To kill me?"

"Only if you survived."

The guy was up-front, anyway. Teddy felt a little better about the situation. This wasn't his first knife fight. They were about the same age. Qurban was a bit bigger, but that didn't mean a hell of a lot given the right circumstances.

Unfortunately, his own circumstances weren't that fantastic right now. Short of breath, half crippled, losing blood. So he'd better cut it short, so to speak. A knife fight? Bring it on.

The hajji gathered himself and rushed in again. Teddy feinted and tried to sidestep, but couldn't get out of his way. They crashed together and once more went to the ground. Qurban's knife grated into a rock beside Teddy's ear as he twisted his face away. A big fucking pigsticker too. Twice as long as the four-inch Boker ceramic-blade he held himself. But the Boker was double-edged and the Uighur blades generally weren't. He could use it stabbing or slicing, punching or thrusting.

Unfortunately al-Nashiri had an arm over his face and was trying for his throat. Looking for a spot to plant his blade that wasn't covered by the sheepskin, the thickly wrapped scarf, and the layers of shalwar kameez and thick insulated vest beneath those.

Teddy clapped his cupped hands on both sides of his attacker's head, and got the result he wanted. Screaming from a burst eardrum, holding his ear, the other rolled away again.

Qurban moved more warily now. Both on their feet again, they faced each other once more, panting, crouching. "You will die today," the Arab, if he was an Arab, snarled. Not even the CIA had seemed to know where he was originally from. Just that he'd been through the catch-and-release program in four different countries. No doubt, making converts all along the way.

Teddy glanced around. Where were the others? Were they getting to safety, before it was too late?

Then he saw them.

They made a circle in the dark, like a pack watching the old wolf fight a challenger. That big shadow in the front must be Yusuf. But the dark too was bleeding away. In a few minutes it would be light enough for whatever recon was circling overhead to make them out. And another artillery barrage, or another wing of killer drones, would be on its way. Though, what had happened to the armor? Their engines seemed to be dying away, not approaching. Taking a wrong turn, maybe.

Regardless, he had to wrap this up. *Don't wait for the attack*, he'd taught raw young SEALs in hand-to-hand training. *Be the attacker. I'm not training you to defend yourself. I'm going to show you how to take a human body apart, fast, quiet, and permanent.*

And maybe he was a little too caught up in remembering that, what he'd used to teach, instead of being here now, because he didn't see the kick coming. It was so swift and unexpected that somehow his hand, already slick with blood, lost the knife. It rattled down somewhere out in the dark.

No knife. Not good. Not facing the pigsticker his adversary was carving the air with. And grinning evilly, just like the bad guys in the video games.

Better get serious, Obie, someone said in his mind.

"Sumo?" he grunted.

He coughed up warm fluid and gagged. Flashes in front of his eyes. For the first time he wondered if this might be his last fight. On a mountainside deep in China, as the day hurtled toward them. With an aging but deceptive opponent, one who'd just surprised him with a kick that would have made a UFC champ proud. In what Brotherhood training camp had he picked that one up? Almost like savate. But the figure-eight business he was doing with the knife was straight tahtib.

He had to get this over with. He was losing blood and breath, while the other guy looked fresh. The circle was contracting around them, the watchers pressing in. Over Qurban's back Teddy glimpsed the big young disciple, holding now not the drone rifle but a pistol. Teddy's own Makarov. How had he gotten that? The answer was obvious. He'd picked it up where Teddy himself had laid it aside, left it . . . He pressed the back of his hand to his forehead. Getting confused. Feeling like heat stroke. But in this weather? Not a good sign.

Okay, identify his target . . . if the guy had actually trained tahtib, Egyptian traditional fighting, they watched the eyes, and their preferred target was the head. Which meant if he could sucker him in . . . Teddy went in just the barest bit slow, leaving his face unprotected. Concentrating on the knife hand. Grab, twist, groin strike.

But instead of engaging, al-Nashiri backed away, smiling deep in his gray beard, still spinning the knife, as if trying to hypnotize him with it.

The circle sighed.

The dawn light grew. The hum of engines swelled. One missile from a helo, or from one of those big drones . . . Teddy shook his arms out and circled with his partner. Allemande left. Do-si-do. The mortal dance that would end with one of them bleeding out. Qurban was sidestepping with him, the big blade weaving, just out of lunge-reach. The fucking guy was teasing him! Spinning it out, to entertain his fucking fanboys. So they could tell the story around their fires. Make one of their songs out of it. How the hajji killed the American. The CIA spy. The infidel.

Only Qurban was making a mistake. He was already thinking of that, of the song. Playing to his audience. Glancing past Teddy to grin at the men behind him.

Teddy hit the knife hand on the backswing, turned inside it, and back-elbowed him hard to the gut. The heavy sheepskin absorbed most of the strike, but he kept turning, jerked the knife arm up and close in, and gave it all he had to the groin with his knee.

But his bad leg gave way and the crotch strike barely connected. He toppled to the left. But he kept his death grip on the knife wrist, making sure the cutting edge was turned away. His weight pulled the other fighter off balance. Teddy kicked backward as he went down, sweeping away his legs, trying to break a knee.

Only Qurban went with it instead of resisting. The heavier man came down on him like a collapsing house as Teddy hit the deck, driving the breath from his lungs, caroming his head off the rocky dirt.

Teddy blinked away stars, concentrating on the knife, the *knife*. Finally he got the wrist twisted back enough that he could flat-hand the blade out of his opponent's grip. It spun away, clanging.

Another sigh traveled the in-pressing circle of intent faces.

But even weaponless, the other was stronger. His left knee locked Teddy's right hand. His left arm found his throat. A throat bar. He forced Teddy's head back, gradually crushing his windpipe as his free hand dug Teddy's face. The eyes . . . a thumb found his left eye, the sharpened long thumbnail digging in.

It was done in a second, with a dazzling flash and a shot of piercing pain. The man on top held up a fist, and at the sight of what dangled from it an excited hubbub broke out.

Teddy could still see out of the remaining eye, but blood was running into it. He couldn't breathe. The thin-blade . . . his left hand scrabbled for it . . . but the sheath was empty. Oh yeah. Lost it already.

No other weapon . . .

Going to black out . . .

So this was it. The last fight. The one you always knew was coming.

For a half second he almost welcomed it. The end of the struggle. Going down. Ringing the bell, at last.

Then he thought: Fuck that. And let this ass-jumping fanatic win?

Let him take over the resistance? And pattern it on what—Daesh? Boko Haram? Al-Shabab? Take a fighting, oppressed people back to the dark ages?

Not gonna happen.

If he only had a weapon . . .

His scrabbling fingers found hard metal. Hesitated. Then reached lower, for the buckle. He had to wriggle, shifting his hips beneath the weight pressing down. The man atop him shifted, trying to capture his left hand as well, but Teddy evaded it.

Red flooded his remaining vision. Fading fast. Time for one last blow. But it had to be done right. Delivered at the exact angle. With all the force he could muster.

It came free. Now turn the thing a little. Forget the lost eye. Forget the lack of breath. Get the sharp end, the end shaped for the toes of a drooping foot. But the red was turning black . . .

A bellow of sound.

A flash of light on the faces around him. They swung to ogle the mountain.

Where a pillar of flame was climbing skyward.

And at the same instant, a flash pulsed through his brain, as if every circuit in his mind had been shorted out, every thought stopped. Something fizzed and snapped in his pocket. His cell. Half a second later, the ground tremored uneasily. Not abruptly, as it had during the shelling, but a half-familiar shiver that disquieted his genitals. It was accompanied by a queer deep crackle, like focused lightning. A BOOOOM that went on and on.

Through the momentary daze he realized: The Package had detonated.

Interrupting every software program, and overloading and burning out every exposed circuit within a radius of at least a mile.

The pressure on his throat slackened. He blinked up through the scarlet curtains to see Qurban, also waggling his head, dazed, turned away, facing toward where the ascending missiles bellowed, louder now, shaking the very air.

Striking as hard as he could, Teddy drove the sharp end of the leg-brace into the side of al-Nashiri's neck. It was titanium, but that didn't mean it was light. And it wasn't all that sharp, either, but the toe end tapered enough that he could drive it in. He twisted it as the other screamed, pulled it back, and hammered it in again as the ground began shaking beneath him and the men around him shouted, pointing into the sky.

Teddy couldn't look. He was otherwise occupied, as the man on top of him stiffened. Went rigid. Teddy dragged in a deep breath and drove the end of the brace in again, jamming it into the vagus nerve as hard as he could. Just to the side of the windpipe. Where the heavy muscles of the neck didn't shield it. The thick, deeply entwined, crucial nerve that controlled breathing and heartbeat, and connected directly to the brainstem.

When Qurban went limp Teddy got his other arm free and backhanded him off. He rolled over him and with both hands forced the sharp end of the brace into his mouth. Straight down this time, digging deep. Until he felt the bony resistance of the spine.

Somewhere in there the man under him must have regained consciousness, because he shuddered, then started to struggle again. Something dripped onto his face from Teddy's. Blood, or jelly, from his empty socket, probably. Teddy leaned in even harder on the brace, probing for the gap between the vertebrae, hammering the spadelike point in with his free hand like a complexly curved chisel.

A grating snap deep in the neck, and the body beneath him went slack. Qurban's eyes were still focused. He was still conscious. But he couldn't move. Couldn't breathe.

The roaring went on, like some gigantic beast, unimaginably powerful, released at last from its shackles to rend and tear the earth and all who lived in it.

Teddy held the hajji down, pinning him to the rocky ground, until consciousness faded from those up-gazing, unblinking eyes. Then rolled off, wheezing, still gripping the brace like some primitive axe.

Only to stare up at pillars of smoke and flame. For a moment he thought the mountain had erupted. Then realized.

Something far worse had been unleashed.

He pressed himself upright, using the brace like a cane.

Facing the circle, which stirred uneasily. Murmuring. Teddy swayed on his feet, looking up at the climbing flames, registering the tremendous deep rumble of departing rocket engines.

One ascending torch faltered. It began to corkscrew, then detonated with a ripping sheet of flame from which smoking pieces tumbled slowly downward. But only one.

Operation Jedburgh had failed.

A long dying fart escaped the body that lay between him and Yusuf.

They faced each other. The big disciple looked uncertain now. Staring, appalled, at the ruin of Teddy's face, the empty socket weeping blood. But still pointing the Makarov as around them the muttering grew.

Fuck, Teddy thought, dismayed. Am I going to have to fight *this* asshole too? He took a step toward him, dragging the useless foot. "It is the will of Allah, Yusuf," he grated out, swaying.

He spread his arms, wheeling to face them all in turn. To let them see. "You have all witnessed it. Nothing in this world happens against His will. He has given me the leadership. And now, it is the end of the world. Imam Akhmad taught you of this. It is the Hour of Reckoning. The Great Massacre. Afterward, Allah will judge us all, the living and the dead."

He waited. There, a nod. A murmur of agreement.

"You will all obey me, and follow. In the final jihad." He held out his hand.

And after an endless moment, the big mujahideen reversed the Makarov. He handed the pistol over. He bowed.

As if that was a signal, the others crowded forward, patting Teddy's back, running their hands over his clothing, gazing with awe at his blood in their fingers, exclaiming and praising God. Praising his victory. Proclaiming their loyalty. Pressing bandages on him. An open palm offered back the ruined eye.

The Lingxiù pushed it away, snarling. He staggered under the hands, fighting with all his strength just to remain upright. Staring up at an apocalyptic sky. At the smoke that drifted now in enormous clouds, slowly, away into the scarlet-blazing east.

22

USS *Savo Island*

NIGHT came early this far north. Cheryl stood shivering on the starboard wing. Gray-black rollers glinted like phosphated steel in the waning light. The wind was fierce, chilling her even under the foul-weather jacket. The temperature had dropped precipitously as the task force beat north. Past Hokkaido, out to the Pacific. Past the Kuriles, then north again, into the Sea of Okhotsk.

She dogged the door behind her. The officer of the deck glanced her way, but said nothing. She scratched her neck, burying her face in the radar hood. Feeling boxed in. Claustrophobic.

As well as guilty.

She groped under her coveralls, nails mining furiously at an itch that never seemed to retreat, that seemed resolved to take over her entire body no matter what Doc Grissett prescribed. "Fuck," she muttered.

The surprise wake-homer attack off Korea. When she'd ordered *Sioux City* into *Savo*'s wake. The frigate had intercepted two of the incomers with her own CATs, but the last enemy weapon had evaded the antitorpedos and caught her on the port quarter, wrecking her so badly she had to be towed to Sasebo. With thirty-two dead, and dozens more injured or burned.

Cheryl shuddered. How was she going to face the families? Now she knew how Eddie's squadron commander had felt, when she'd upbraided him for the loss of her husband. And felt doubly culpable.

But maybe this war could be ended. Maybe it was even ending now. Drawing to a close, not with triumph, but in the hesitant, tacit acknowledgment of mutually exhausted combatants.

She hoped so. With a parting word to the OOD, she stepped into the elevator.

"GOT more company, Skipper," Matt Mills said as she slid into her seat at the command desk. Deep in the Citadel, in what was still called CIC by the old hands. The air was nearly as cold down here as up on the wing. The overhead was black as an Arctic night. The lighting was muted. No one else spoke. She nodded.

The combat systems team was doing an interoperability drill with the Japanese ships. Exchanging launch point estimates, surveillance tracks, IPPs, time of predicted impacts. The output would be a covariance error, or tracking error estimate, checking to what extent their systems returned consistent outputs if they had to carry out a coordinated engagement. She left them to it, studying the central display. The geo plot, first.

They were surrounded by Russia. Sakhalin and the mainland to the west and north. The Kamchatka Peninsula to the east. She leaned in, looking where Mills placed the laser trace.

"There," her exec muttered.

Twenty miles to the west. Three contacts. AALIS had labeled them friendly, but Cheryl didn't think that was entirely accurate.

Years before, the UN had declared this entire sea part of the Russian continental shelf, and thus part of the Exclusive Economic Zone of the Russian Federation. Oil and gas developments sprawled off Magadan, to the north. To her south, between her and the rest of the Allied forces, lay the main Russian naval base at Vladivostok. The Eastern Military District was led by Colonel-General Yevgeney Sharkov. PACOM had set her up with an HF radio link with his headquarters. A petty officer checked in once a day. A hotline, just in case.

The new contacts to the west, joining others to the east and an unknown number of submarines, were Russian.

The order of battle was sobering. The Russian Pacific Fleet had been beefed up throughout the war until the bulk of their navy was out here, including the latest ship types and a new carrier, *Admiral Istomin*, with fifth-generation T-50 fighters. Heavy-missile batteries, dense antiaircraft coverage, and a major airbase in Sakhalin lined the coasts. The EWs reported constant probing by radar.

An even more pointed threat, a stealthy Okhotnik drone, had shown up two days after they arrived on station. Relieved every twelve hours, a strike-and-recon UAV had stuck with them ever since, orbiting the task force at high altitude. She could see the hypersonic antiship missiles the drones carried through the telescopes on *Savo*'s lasers.

"China might be less of a threat, out here, than the Russians," Mills said.

She nodded grimly. "My thoughts exactly, XO. Finished the drill? How's it look?"

"*Chokai*'s still lagging us. The older software flight, probably. I'm not sure what we can do about it."

Terranova stopped on her way past. "Coffee, Captain? I'm getting some."

Cheryl shook her head and said no, thanks. Then almost immediately wished she hadn't, but the Terror was already gone.

She got up and stalked the aisles, checking screens over the shoulders of petty officers and junior officers. Parting the curtains into Sonar. The Keurig was lit. She dumped in a bottle of water, selected a Sumatran Dark, Ten Ounce, and hit the button.

The Sonar chief, Zotcher, cleared his throat. "Skipper, remember that guy Admiral Lenson brought aboard with his staff? Back on the old *Savo*? The submariner—Rit?"

Cheryl rolled her eyes as she stirred in two sugars. She could afford it; she'd lost weight every time she checked the scale. Besides, who was she supposed to look good for? The only man who'd shown any interest, after Eddie that is, was back with his family.

The resort had nestled in a green-forested canyon, facing a golden beach and a lapis sea. The floor-to-ceiling windows looked down a the nature trail on one side, and down onto a heated pool on the other. Two days of freedom, snatched from a hellish precom

*schedule. Forty-eight hours of sex, larded with guilt. His mother
Thai, father Nigerian. Cocoa skin she could close her eyes and still
feel. Black stubble in the morning . . .*

Zotcher cleared his throat and she flinched. "You mean Carpenter,"
she said. "The idiot who put that porn game on the ship's network?"

"It wasn't a—" Zotcher stopped himself in mid-sentence. "Uh,
right, Skipper. Anyway, he was telling me about how they used to
run subs up here. Against the Soviets. Tapped a comm cable that
ran along the bottom. Listened in on all the traffic from the base at
Kamchatka."

"Okay," she said, and waited. There was an awkward moment.

Zotcher broke it. "Anyway, another thing he said, you know, we
have to watch for ice up here."

"Too early in the season for that, Chief. And it's a lot warmer now
than it was back then."

"Sure, Skipper, but there's a lot of fresh water inflow. That means
low salinity in the upper levels of the water column. Ice from the
Amur River. And we're getting into autumn now."

"This'll be the fourth year of the war," she said, feeling her shoulders tense again. Not really sure she was following his meaning.

Zotcher blinked. "All I know is what the Armed Forces News puts
out. But it sounds like we're winning. Or at least, that the slants are
losing."

"I hope so. Okay, we'll stay alert for ice." She sighed, and carried
her mug back out into the main compartment. Looked at the elevator, wondering if she should be back on the bridge. Sometimes it
seemed strange, unseamanlike, sealed in by airlocks, running everything from screens, like a video game tournament.

At the moment the center display showed her formation. *Her* for-
mation. She was in tactical command of an augmented task group.
She stood before the display, absentmindedly scratching her flank.
Considering.

The centerpieces were *Savo Island*, two Japanese ABM-capable
Aegis destroyers, *Chokai* and *Ashigara*, and one Korean unit, ROKS
Jeonnam. *Jeonnam* was the northernmost, with *Savo* next, then the
Japanese, all spaced at thirty-mile intervals. With their coverage ar-

eas interlocked, they barriered the flight paths of any ballistic missiles launched from central China toward the US. Unless, of course, they were programmed for a nondirect suborbital trajectory. Unlikely, but in that case the orbiting ASM satellites would take the play.

Her force was submarine-heavy. That made sense, considering how little tasking was left for the undersea forces this late in the war. USS *Arkansas*, *Idaho*, *Guam*, and *John Warner*. Her surface escorts were two US missile frigates, *Goodrich* and *Montesano*. Spaced even farther out, in a defensive and early warning perimeter closer to the coast and extending down toward the Kuriles, were the unmanned hunters USV-34, 20, 7, and 16.

She had no carrier support up here. But four Aegis units should be able to fight off an air attack, considering the enemy's weakened state. In an emergency, JASDF F-3s were on call from Wakkanai, Hokkaido. That island was also her logistics support, via commercial tankers retrofitted for astern refueling. The US logistics fleet was occupied supporting operations in the South China Sea.

Hers was one of three Allied forces closing in on the enemy. One, based on Taipei, menaced the Chinese naval base at Ningbo and protected liberated Taiwan. The other, supported by three carriers, was supporting the invasion of Hainan.

A classified briefing via VTC had laid out her own mission. As the snare closed around China, the risk of all-out nuclear strikes rose. High-side chat said diplomatic feelers were under way, to try to end hostilities without the ultimate escalation. But no one could guarantee they'd succeed. Cheryl and her task force were the backstop. She was assigned to intercept any ICBMs targeted at US cities. The Armageddon Protocol, Admiral Yangerhans had called it, half jokingly. But also half in earnest, she figured.

She grimaced, turning toward the bulkhead to surreptitiously scratch her pits. If they could get through this . . . could the nightmare really end? It seemed surreal even to contemplate peace. The years before the war had been tense enough, with trade wars, friction over the islands, disgruntled allies, a bumbling administration fumbling everything it laid hands on. But looking back, they'd been good years. One long golden summer before the war . . .

A petty officer cleared his throat beside her. "Yeah," she grunted. "What you got?"

"Voice call for you, ma'am. Uncovered HF."

She frowned. Hardly anyone used conventional voice radio anymore. The first year of the war had shown how simple the older systems were to penetrate, even when they were scrambled. "Uncovered?"

"Affirmative, Captain. Simplex single sideband deconfliction frequency."

Cheryl glanced at her watch. "It's not time for the daily check."

"No, ma'am. It's Vladivostok calling. Want the task force commander. Personally."

"That's you," Mills said, but he looked puzzled too.

The petty officer set Cheryl up at his desk. She fitted on the earphones, feeling decidedly retro. "Remember, it's an uncovered net," the petty officer said.

She nodded. The working frequency was a mini-hotline, mainly to prevent collisions and other fatal misunderstandings. She looked at the printed test sentences and drew a breath. "Mishka, this is Albert. Mishka, this is Albert. Over."

The response was immediate. *"This is Mishka. Roger, over."*

"This is Albert. Understand you are calling. How copy. Over."

"I hear you loud, Albert. Stand by."

Stand by for what? This wasn't the protocol. She waited, and a new voice came on, male, rougher, older. *"This is Colonel-General Sharkov. Request to speak to your commanding officer."*

"This is Captain Staurulakis, General."

"Request to speak to commander, US Task Force in Okhotsk Sea."

Couldn't he hear her? "This is she, General," she said, louder.

"This is Admiral Lenson?" the voice sounded doubtful.

Well, thank God they didn't know *everything*. "Admiral Lenson is no longer aboard, General. I am in tactical command. Captain Cheryl Staurulakis."

The hiss of static. Faint wailing music, bleeding in from some nearby frequency. She waited, glancing past the consoles toward the displays. Finally she added, "I am standing by for your transmission, sir. Over."

"Sharkov here. I am passing urgent warning from Intelligence. Site Eleven is going to launch warning. I repeat, Site Eleven going to launch warning."

Cheryl glanced at the petty officer. "What is Site Eleven, General?"

"Site Eleven is Chinese intercontinental missile installation. I can give latitude and longitude."

She pulled a pad of paper over and unclipped her pen. "Tell Commander Mills, general quarters," she snapped to the petty officer. "SPY to max radiated power. Set Condition One ABM." They were already in Condition Three, but One would bring the rest of the crew on station. She leaned into the microphone. "We are acting on your heads-up, General. Over."

"Please record you are officially warned by commanding general, Eastern District."

"We are doing that, sir. All communications over this net are being taped. Over." She nodded to the enlisted woman, who reached for the circuit log. Almost signed off, then remembered something else and hit the transmit button again. "This is Captain Staurulakis. Over."

"Go ahead. Over."

"General, the flight path of these weapons may take them over Siberia. Over Russian territory. We may have to intrude on your airspace, to get a kill during boost phase."

The voice on the far end of the circuit turned steely. *"That is negative, Captain. Under no condition are you to intrude on Federation territory. That has been agreed at the highest levels. Moscow. Washington. Over."*

"Understand that, sir. We are not intruding. Only intercepting."

"You will not intercept nuclear weapons over Federation territory. You will not create a new Chernobyl on Russian land! You will not do this, Captain! Do you understand? Over."

Oh, God. No . . . she hesitated, torn between the inability to promise what he wanted—no way was she ruling out an intercept for political reasons—and the sure knowledge that the voice on the other end had the power to wipe out her whole task force. Finally she fell back on the good old military passive voice. "Your warning is acknowledged, General. This is Captain Staurulakis. Out."

WHEN she got back to the command desk Mills was taking manned-and-ready reports from the forward magazines, after magazines, laser and gun mounts. Around CIC, a muted bustle as the general quarters watch relieved the Condition Three watchstanders. Terranova was back. Cheryl handed her the lat and long Sharkov had given them.

Mills reported, "Captain: Circle William set. ABM Condition One set. Reducing speed to steerageway. Engines one through four on the line. Generators 1a, 2a, 2b on the line." The air-conditioning dropped to a low purr. Cheryl noticed the knot meter dropping as well. He added, "Freeing generator capacity for railgun and lasers."

"Very well. Pass that warning to *Ashigara* and *Chokai*. Inform Fleet."

"Sent it on nanochat, Skipper. Fleet should know from monitoring, but I'll shoot them a separate Flash. Who was that giving us the heads-up?"

"Did they—"

"Yes, ma'am. They all answered up, Captain." His handsome face impassive. "Was that PACOM?"

"No. A warning from the Russians, if you can believe it. HUMINT or COMINT, I guess." She wondered if she'd jumped the gun, setting Condition One. But the general hadn't sounded like a Chicken Little.

Mills looked doubtful, but kept taking reports. Cheryl settled her helmet over her head. The familiar near-agoraphobia as the sealed interior of the citadel gave way to the hovering-angel picture from high above. "Alice, this is the CO."

"Good afternoon, Skipper." AALIS's calm genderless tones.

"Scan and report."

"ABM Condition One set. Magazine report: twenty RIM-180 Block Ones forward, fifteen aft. Spinning up round four, six, and seven."

"Spin up *all* Alliance rounds," Cheryl ordered. It wouldn't pay to not be ready for anything. The AI acknowledged.

Her helmet video populated, downloading from the JTIDS via AALIS. The 3-D display reached out from formation center, out, out, up, up, until she gazed down on the entire sea, five hundred miles across. Circles, surface contacts—her own ships, her own Hunters, and the Russians. A green-for-neutral callout to the south identified a loitering Okhotnik. Blue semicircles indicated her subs. Yellow flashing trails tracked the nanosatellites she depended on for recon and comms. The Japanese had drones out to the south, extending their sensor range in case a missile was aimed at the home islands. There wasn't any X-band intel. This remote and bitter sea was far out of range of the Missile Defense Agency radars.

Mills hooked symbols and tapped. They began flashing. He touched his boom mike. "Alice, TAO: Fire control key inserted. Prepare for auto control."

"AALIS aye. Ready for auto control."

"Alice, CO: Initiate auto control mode, but remain batteries tight."

As the ship's computer acknowledged Cheryl concentrated on her formation. She couldn't see any realignments winning them anything. The intercept geometry looked good.

The Terror, Petty Officer First Class Terranova, on the command circuit. *"Ma'am, we don't show any PLP identified as Site Eleven."*

"Well, the Russkis probably got their own terminology. He gave you lat and long.—Alice, do you hold a possible launch point, terminology Site Eleven, in China?"

Terranova muttered, "Intel . . . wait a min . . . yeah. Okay, we got it."

The smooth genderless voice murmured, *"Identified from intel message traffic. Passed to Control."*

Cheryl ruminated, scratching at a sudden terrific itch just at her neckline. Okay, what else?

A raucous buzzer shocked the muffled voices, the click of keyboards. *"Launch cueing,"* AALIS said, one tenth of a second ahead of Terranova, so their voices overlapped in a disquieting duet. *"Launch cueing . . . cueing from JSDF. Consistent with DF-41 in boost phase."*

Her TF chat lit at the corner of her view.

Mount Ashigara: to Matador
FLASH FLASH FLASH
Launch cueing from national sources. Multiple ICBM launches,
    central China. Assign tracks please?

"XO: Tell him, *Savo* will take first three missiles," Cheryl said. "Three-round salvos each. Designate the next three to him. Assign *Chokai* two—she's only got uprated Standards. By then our screens will be clear and we can either refire on the first salvo or take additional rounds in the boost phase." She toggled to the comm net and snapped, "Inform Vladivostok we're firing on ICBMs from Site Eleven. Suggest all units stand clear."

She took a breath. Several seconds free now, not just to think, but to appreciate the full horror of what was happening. She put her hands to her head, but her fingertips met only the smooth rounded shell of the helmet.

This was it. The moment the experts had theorized about, the world had dreaded, for generations.

The decades of arming, years of conventional war, and the titanic struggle between two world-striding empires had reached its climax.

Armageddon had begun.

And she was expected to stop it.

Four tracks winked on simultaneously at the far southwest corner of her vision. Bright scarlet trails, the altitude callouts spinning upward.

No more clumsy reference point messages, laboriously transmitted from computer to computer via DAMA channels on Link 16. Now every node was networked. Every contact, instantly cross-referenced, identified, and displayed across the task force and simultaneously from Japan to Pearl. Not only that; each was evaluated as to degree of threat, and assigned to a ship, a weapons system, and a specific missile.

AALIS locked on automatically, brackets hooking the new contacts. Numbers flicked past at blurred speed at the upper left of her screens. As Cheryl toggled to the TF command net more contacts winked into existence to the southwest, over China itself. A second salvo, along slightly different paths. But all headed northeast.

Aimed, in the shortest-course Great Circle route, at North America.

Tangler: to all Tangler
Desig tracks 0032 through 0035 Meteor 1, 2, 3
Matador taking tracks Meteor 1, 2, 3 with Alliance. Mount Ashigara
    tracks 0036, 0037, 0038. Mount Shiomi tracks 0039, 0040

"Request batteries released," AALIS said in her earbuds.

Cheryl ignored it for the moment. "Terror, IPP for lead missiles yet?"

"No impact point yet, Cap'n. Trajectory so far consistent with west coast of US."

The command circuit: *"Lock on, tracks Meteor 1 through 3."*

"Warning bell forward deck. Warning bell aft. Visual confirm, forward deck clear. Aft deck clear. Bridge stations secured. Conn to after-Citadel. Topside clear for engagement."

"ECM reports: Okhotnik tracking outbound, headed south."

"Positive pressure throughout the ship."

"Capacitor banks armed and ready. Electrical control, manned and ready."

"CIWS manned and ready."

"Lasers, manned and ready."

"Nulka, chaff, decoys, railguns, CAT manned and ready."

She toggled back to the overhead view. The Russian surface units had turned, headed away from her task force. At flank speed, to judge from the readouts. Probably wise. No one knew the characteristics, safety interlocks, of the DF-41. If there were any. Each carried ten independently maneuverable warheads, of up to a megaton each.

Which meant an intercept, even if it took place sixty miles up, might wipe out every piece of unshielded electronics within hundreds of miles.

Which could leave a good portion of her task force helpless against any follow-on weapons.

She steered her mind away from might-bes to concentrate on *now*. Only seconds remained. The spew of new contacts from the southwest continued, like fireballs thrown out by a Fourth of July fountain. The last gasp of an expiring superpower. The dying spasm of an empire being overthrown, but still battling.

Or perhaps, of two empires dying.

She toggled to the exterior cameras, scanning the horizon. *Savo* steamed alone. The formation had accordioned out, expanding its footprint to reduce vulnerability. The gray sea rolled empty save for low clouds shadowing the dark horizon to the south. She toggled to the weather overlay. Rain, but headed away. So it would not interfere with either sensors or launch.

She toggled down one more level, to the cameras on her helmet. Curved by the short-focus lenses, the aisle between the consoles stretched to infinity. The large screen displays loomed up like drive-in movie screens.

AALIS said, *"Request batteries released, CO."* An added sharpness in his/her/its tone?

"SPY?" Cheryl prompted.

Terranova: *"We have firm lock-on. AOU still resolving. West coast 'a US."*

"XO: what about that covariance?"

"Within limits. Good to go."

Terranova said, *"Meteor One, pitchover."*

Once again, the familiar dilemma. The sooner one could fire, the better; ascending missiles were most vulnerable early in their flight regime. To catch one during its boost burn, or shortly after, while it was still ballistically ascending, the interceptor had to accelerate at about 8 g. Her own weapons had to first rise nearly vertically, to clear the thick lower atmosphere, then pitch over to meet the oncoming missile.

She scratched viciously at her neck under the helmet. Just now AALIS was feeding her an outer intercept range of about nine hundred miles and an inner range of four hundred miles. But intercept estimates got fudgy at the edges. Fire too soon, and the hit-to-kill homing body would run out of fuel for terminal maneuvering. Too late, and it would be impossible to reach the intercept point before the target passed overhead. ICBMs traveled so fast nothing could catch up in a stern chase. There were terminal phase interceptors farther downrange, fixed Ground Missile Defense sites in Alaska and THAAD batteries north of San Francisco and Los Angeles. But by then the bus would be dispensing its warheads, multiplying the targets and adding decoys and debris to the equation.

And added to that now, the warning just received from Sharkov. She manipulated the view, sliding southwest. Yeah. Here, Russia curved inward, along the coast, cupping Manchuria and cutting China off from the sea. Zhang had threatened that this too was historically Chinese, but hadn't yet moved to reclaim it. Doubtless due to the loans, technical assistance, natural gas, and arms Moscow had lavished him with. To keep Russia's two great enemies at each other's throats, and weaken them for whatever the postwar world held.

Now the orange pulsing trails were bending to the northward. They were leaving China. Crossing the Sikhote-Alin Mountains. Crossing Russia, on their way to America.

She looked on coldly, watching the flight path predictions and probabilities of kill that streamed up the sides of her screens, and knew she could not fulfill the Russian colonel-general's angry request. Or rather, threat. Delaying intercept until the targets were over Okhotsk would mean she'd launch too late. Her Alliances would have to climb vertically, pitch backward into a tail-chase geometry, and even then, couldn't match a final-stage ICBM warhead at suborbital velocity. They'd lag behind. Burn out, and fall uselessly into the sea.

No. *Savo*'s interceptors would have to violate Russian airspace.

She decided to leave it to the computers. Hoping that the latest patch had taken, the millions of lines of code properly written and flawlessly debugged. That all the engineers and designers and fabricators had done their jobs.

"Alice: batteries released," she said.

And instantly toggled back to the God view. To see the orange trails headed nearly straight overhead. They diverged only slightly, but with a considerable altitude differential. Different angles of climb. Meaning different targets. The West Coast? Spaced from north to south, perhaps. The highest-angled ones lofted to fly the farthest. San Diego? Los Angeles? Fresno, Long Beach?

She reminded herself to breathe, but it wasn't easy. The seconds ticked past.

The *seconds* ticked *past* . . .

"Is she gonna . . . ?" Mills muttered, low, as if the AI could overhear him. "Jesus . . . is it gonna fire?"

Cheryl pressed her thoat mike to transmit. "Alice, CO. What's the hold-up?"

"Parameters don't match. Ashigara *disagrees."*

The XO said angrily, "We checked covariance an hour ago. Tracking error was within tolerance. We—"

Cheryl clicked in, interrupting him. "This is the CO. Ignore the differences! Own-ship data only. JTIDS, network data only. Get those missiles out there. *Now.*"

"Manual launch?" Mills asked. She could hear him tapping away, setting it up on his keyboard.

"Too risky. Give her one more chance." She toggled to exterior cameras again.

The forward magazine hatches were cranking open. The new missiles didn't boost out of their launch cells vertically, the way the old Standards had. Their high-energy, exotically fueled engines burned too hot to confine inside the skin of a ship. Instead, like a submarine-launched missile, a gas generator impelled them out of the cells, blowing them out like a pea from a peashooter.

The first popped up as if spring-loaded. It seemed to hang there, sixty feet above the deck, for a shutter-flick, maybe a twentieth of a second, just long enough for her heart to catch and the fear to trigger: *Wasn't it—*

The booster ignited in a blinding glare. When the dazzle cleared the weapon was gone, ascending vertically, already out of the field of view. Succeeded by a second, and a third. Smoke swept aft and blanked the cameras, surrounding her in a woolly nothingness, a chemical whiteout. Cheryl could almost smell it, though she knew that was her imagination.

"Missile away," AALIS said. *"Alliances four, six, seven, away. One, three, eight preparing for launch."*

She toggled and the departing weapons reappeared, already miles distant, spearheads of violent flame trailing rapidly expanding cones of white smoke. "God, they go fast," she muttered.

No roar of engines reached them. Not this deep, this sound-isolated and shock-damped, armored by steel and Kevlar. Only the camera, and the flicker of numbers on the ordnance register above the displays, told her they were on their way. She breathed again and went back to overhead view. The blue inverted carets of outgoing interceptors leapt from the center of the screen and sped outward. Toward the advancing orange trails.

Now there was nothing to do but wait.

Except that suddenly Chief Zotcher spoke into the combat control circuit. *"CO, XO, this is Sonar. Suspected propulsor noises bearing one eight five. No range reading yet. Classification unknown."*

"Sonar, CO: need a classification, Chief."

"Classification unknown. Doesn't match any of our profiles."

Not again, she thought, closing her eyes. "Torpedo? Submarine?"

"Larger than a torpedo. Faster than a submarine. Not sure yet what it is, Captain. Freshwater layers . . . salinity clines . . . and a super-low radiated-noise signature. We're not getting consistent passive returns and it's too far to ping in mixed layers. Trying for cross-bearings with Chokai *on ASW chat."*

"Keep me advised." She double-clicked her mike and returned her attention to her rapidly climbing missiles.

But something about it nagged at her. From the *south?* There was nothing to the south. Only seven hundred miles of open sea, until the Kuriles. If it was a torpedo, or something like one, it would have to be incredibly long-ranged. She clicked to TF chat and warned her southernmost units, then back to the ASW circuit to activate Rimshot and stand by on bubble decoys and CATs.

Something changed on her screen. She blinked, unable to pinpoint exactly what it had been.

AALIS came up. *"USV-16 dropped data link. Fails to respond to query."*

Right, Cheryl thought. That contact, a blue half square a hundred and twenty miles to the south, had begun to blink. Its callout read NULL DATA.

The USVs were autonomous Hunters, originally built as antisubmarine platforms, now mainly deployed as radar pickets. They were controlled from the ASW supervisor's station. She clicked to that circuit. "ASW, CO. Why aren't we hearing from Sixteen?"

"Don't know, Skipper. No response to query."

"Sonar reported propulsor noise from the bearing."

A hesitation. Then, *"It's possible. Could just be a data glitch, though. Everything we get from the Hunters comes via nano."*

Meaning it went up to the circling microsatellites, then down again. "Any way we can confirm Sixteen's still on station?"

Mills, on the same circuit. *"We could ask* Chokai *to request Global Hawk out of Misawa."*

Terranova broke in. Unhurried. Calm. *"Stand by for intercept, Meteor One."*

Cheryl let it go for the moment and switched back to overhead. In the 3-D projection the trails described beautiful orange arches, like burning tracers. The Alliances had almost reached the lead projectile. It was in coast phase now, far above the troposphere. Trolleying along through space on a ballistic arc that would take it nearly halfway round the world.

"Stand by . . . intercept."

The radar picture showed vibrating brackets nailed around a speeding comet. Not its real shape, she knew. Its radar shape still tailed remnants of gas, atmosphere, and ablation from its fiery ascent. The Alliance wasn't on the screen.

Then, suddenly, a silent explosion ripped apart the comet, sending parts spreading and tumbling. Still traveling at that incredible velocity, they would coast on through near-vacuum until gravity pulled them down again into the blanket of air that would sear them into gas, charred metal, micrometeorites too small even to identify, drifting down at last as a metallic, poisonous, violently radioactive dust, somewhere over Siberia.

"Looks like a perfect intercept," Cheryl observed, feeling a slight weight lift from her chest. One down. Seven to go. On the other hand, that meant she'd expended three precious and irreplaceable weapons when only one would have sufficed. "Make it two-round salvos going forward," she ordered.

Mills and AALIS rogered up. At the radar systems coordination station, Terranova had already shifted the picture to the next warhead.

Then the surface warfare supervisor said, "*Montesano* reports explosion effects from bearing one five seven. Breaking-up noises."

"*USS* Guam, *lost data*," AALIS announced.

Terranova: "*Meteor two, stand by for intercept.*"

Cheryl froze. What was happening? The explosion and breaking-up effects, on that bearing from the escort, pointed straight to *Guam*.

Which meant . . . some as yet unclear but obviously dangerous threat was indeed approaching from the south. It had taken down the USV, one of her outermost sensors. And now, one of her escort submarines. The next unit in would be JNS *Chokai*, her southernmost ABM-capable unit.

But the older destroyer was already locked on the third wave of DF-41s. With an earlier version of Aegis, and less capable radars, *Chokai* would be keyholed on the missile threat, the way the old *Savo* had been. Leaving her nearly blind to an approaching attack from under the sea.

She was typing as fast as she could, putting the warning out on the command nanochat. "Matt, get Dagger in the air. Full ASW loadout. Vector them south. Find out what's going on. Tell Fleet we're under attack. Notify . . . *Idaho*. They're closest. Give them a course to intercept. Zotcher's best guess on the track. Tell them to close and take these things out. Whatever the fuck they are. But warn them to be careful."

But *what* was attacking them? Submarines, like the ones that had snuck in under cover of fishing boats, off Korea? No, they didn't seem to be. Zotcher would have identified them.

But then what?

AALIS's voice brought her back to her own mission. "*Meteor two, stand by . . .*" The brackets stayed steady. A flash, in the corner of the radar picture. But the cometlike cone did not disintegrate. It burned steadily, a cold candleflame of gas and ablating coatings fifty miles up, its trajectory gradually bending toward the horizontal.

"*Intercept round one failed. Second round arrives in three seconds . . . two . . . one.*"

Again, the silent burst, the spinning debris, the gradual emptying out of the field of view.

And once more, the switch to yet another target. Third of the first salvo of three DF-41s. The last of the weapons Cheryl had assigned to *Savo Island*. To the south, *Ashikara* would take the next three missiles under fire. And *Chokai*, the last two.

Unfortunately, each reentry body they failed to intercept would dispense up to ten other warheads. Even one would carry unimaginable destruction. And she couldn't help wondering what was coming the other way. Would StratCom retaliate, even if, as seemed likely, this was some kind of last-ditch launch by a rogue commander? Hundreds of American missiles could be in the air right now. From submarines, silos, alert bombers . . . the full weight of a strategic counterstrike.

She shuddered. Truly, the world might end today.

But all she could do was stand and fight.

AALIS said, "*Meteor three, stand by for intercept.*"

"*Sonar, CO: High-speed flow noises closing from the south. Two separate sources. Cross-bearings give speeds of sixty-plus knots. Advanced propulsion system. Not screws per se. Maybe propulsors.*"

Sixty-knots-plus propulsors? All she could come up with was some kind of high-speed autonomous weapon, half midget submarine, half torpedo. But Intel had warned of nothing like that in the enemy order of battle.

She hit her throat mike, but her eyes stayed riveted to the radar picture. The steady glow of the still ascending dispenser bus. "Copy, Chief. Is that what took out *Guam*?"

"*Sounded like it, CO. And . . . headed our way.*"

She chat-alerted *Chokai*, but wasn't sure what antitorpedo measures the older destroyer carried. And the Japanese unit couldn't be diverted from its ABM mission. It would have to fire when the incomers were close to the ship, since the Standards didn't have the range of the Alliances. The reason she'd assigned *Chokai* last . . . She toggled back to radar and searched the interior of Asia for additional cueing. Thank God, she didn't see any. Maybe the eight they'd already picked up would be all.

"Captain?" Dave Branscombe, her ops officer. "We're getting video from nano. *Guam*'s last reported position."

She clicked on it. A disturbed area of the sea. A spreading carpet of yellow and cream, flames guttering here and there on the gray waves. Smoke obscured it, then blew past. Already the seas were gentling, the slick drifting apart. She zoomed in, hoping for survivors. But couldn't see any. "Oh my God," she muttered.

In a horrifying déjà vu, she flashed back to the exercise off Hawaii again. This was all too much like it. She was bending all her attention to fending off an overt attack, while a dagger was being plunged into her back.

Only this was real, not an exercise. Not a game.

"Meteor three, stand by," AALIS said. Cheryl switched to the radar picture again. Waited, breathless once more, as the system counted down. *"Two . . One . . . intercept."*

The speeding contact, still trailing ionized gas, didn't waver. *"Failure to intercept,"* AALIS announced, as if they couldn't see that for themselves. Followed, almost in the same sentence, by, *"Round two, KKV failure to separate."*

"And then there was one," Mills breathed, beside her. Cheryl watched the wavering comet. The glowing cone was shrinking as it left the remnants of atmosphere behind. Cooling as it ascended too, presenting a smaller target to the secondary IR homing function of the Alliance's seeker head. The lock-on brackets quivered around it.

"TAO, Sonar: Incoming sonar contacts on constant bearing. Decreasing range. Estimate speed seventy knots . . . wait one . . . rocket effects. Rocket effects, in the water, bearing one seven six. Consistent with supercavitating projectile." A tension-filled voice in the background. *"Alerting* Montesano *on ASW net."*

A glance at the overhead view gave her the chills. Yeah. USS *Montesano* was on that bearing. One of her frigates. She clicked to

TF ASW and went out voice. "Thunderbolts, this is Tangler. Flash. Rimshot on! Confirm."

"Thunderbolts" was *Montesano*. If the incoming weapon was magnetically guided, the active magnetic-signature-management system could displace its apparent location, even trigger premature detonation. The answer came back at once, the voice sounding startled. *"Tangler, Thunderbolts: Confirm Rimshot activated."*

"Shkvals?" Mills said, beside her. She couldn't see him through the helmet. "But they were only at sixty knots before. And Shkvals don't have ranges that long."

"Agreed, it's something new. Maybe a conventional propulsor first stage, for long range. Then a hydro-reactive jet final stage to sprint in in to the target." That was why the Hunter hadn't transmitted any warning. Once the final stage was on its way, even the countermeasure torpedoes were useless, too slow, their warheads too small.

She clicked to the ASW circuit and quizzed Zotcher and the ASW officer. But the sonar analysis didn't match any Chinese weapon, and the Japanese arrays confirmed they hadn't detected any unidentified submarines to the southward.

"Tangler, this is Thunderbolts . . . heavy detonation close aboard. Intense shock. Engines offline. Damage report to follow."

She sighed, light-headed with relief. "Close aboard" . . . but not an actual hit. Okay, Shkvals . . . they traveled at almost two hundred knots, with a super-cavitating nose plate to tear a hole in the sea. And if the warheads were the same as the older models . . . shaped charges to burn through side armor. Then pyrophoric rods to tear through the hull, bursting into unquenchable flame on contact with air, water, or fuel. Even now, decades after the first models had been revealed, the Allies had nothing like it. Originally Russian technology, but proliferated now to all the Opposed Powers. Chinese? Iranian? Unlikely out here. But they could be North Korean, controlled by some bottom-hugging last-ditch survivor.

Or *were* they Russian? Approaching from the south, but Vladivostok lay in that general direction too. Timed to coincide with the onslaught of the Chinese ICBMs, to reduce her ability to respond?

Right now that didn't really matter. "Get all units around to the reciprocal. Open the range as much as we can." She searched her mind for something, anything, else to do. "Get the other units' helicopters out there. Sonobuoys. And run Mark 54s down the bearings. Maybe they can pick these things up. We've got to kill them before they fire the second stages."

"Worth a try," Mills muttered, typing rapidly.

"Meteor three, third intercept," AALIS said. *"Three. Two. One. Intercept."*

Her lips moved in a silent curse. She stared at the speeding comet, now shrunken almost to a pinpoint.

"Failure to intercept," AALIS said, with a note almost of regret. *"Round three, target too high for intercept maneuver. Initiate Alliance self-destruct."*

Mount Shiomi: to Tangler
Taking tracks 0039, 0040 with Standard

Tangler: to Mount Shiomi
Expend rounds ASAP and retire to north best speed. Deploy
    antitorpedo countermeasures immediately

She shoved herself back from the desk, panting as she snatched off the helmet. The black-ceilinged Citadel seemed impenetrably dark. Sweat ran down her neck. "We missed it. Fuck. Fuck!"

Mills laid comforting, or maybe restraining, fingers on her arm. "Fat lady hasn't sung yet, skipper. MDA has track. It's being passed to Fort Greely. They'll knock it down."

"God, I hope so," she muttered, but didn't like the odds. The ground-based interceptors didn't have a good test record, and had never engaged against a real threat.

Mount Shiomi: to Tangler
Missiles away. Increasing speed to flank. Countermeasures
    deployed

She felt slightly better. Maybe they could get out of the woods. Her task force, at least. Then she remembered *Guam*. No survivors. All dead. USV-16, gone, but at least it had been unmanned. *Montesano*, out of action, no casualty report yet.

They'd taken a hammering. But from whom? "Where's our helo? Is he there yet?"

"Vectoring to an intercept point. Full loadout, sonobuoys and fish."

She toggled to the ASW screen. They had a solid plot on the remaining intruder. The task force's northward turn, and increase in speed, were giving them more time to respond. Shkvals only had ranges of about six miles, so keeping the threat at arm's length would protect the rest of the task force.

Four minutes later, Dagger reported dropping on a sonobuoy contact. Then, seconds later, a massive, rumbling detonation.

Cheryl tried to think, but stringing coherent ideas together was like slogging through mud. Her neck felt sticky. Probably bleeding, where she'd clawed it. Her arms itched. She put her head in her hands, and concentrated on neither passing out nor throwing up.

Somewhere in there—it all got fuzzy, liquid, for a couple of minutes—*Chokai* reported one successful intercept and one miss.

So yet another bus of ten warheads was on its way to the US.

Terranova patted her back, voice gentle. "Skipper? Skipper? Your neck is bleedin'. Y'okay, ma'am? That was rough."

Cheryl uncovered her face. Tried to control the quiver in her larynx. "Yeah, Terror. Pretty . . . fucking . . . rough."

"What *were* those things? Where'd they come from?"

"We'll have to find out, Beth." Not exactly regulation, to call enlisted by their first names. But just now such formulas seemed too petty to care about. Yeah, where *had* they come from? The North Koreans? They seemed too advanced. Might have been the Chinese. Sure.

But who would benefit most from literally torpedoing the Allied defenses? Who would gain, at the end of the day, from triggering an all-out nuclear exchange between China and the United States?

She could think of only one player.

But then, why had Sharkov called to warn them?

It made no sense, but she could cogitate on it later. Right now . . . She shook off the dizziness like a boxer recovering from a hard blow. "Confirm MDA has track on our leakers. Keep a sharp eye on that launch site for more. I want more sonobuoy barriers to the south. Remain on station, Condition One. I need a damage report from Thunderbolts. And start a search for survivors, beginning with that last datum for *Guam*. We aren't out of the woods yet. Let's stay alert, God damn it."

She couldn't keep the anger from her tone. The disappointment. The shock. She scratched furiously between her fingers, then sucked at them. It might not be over. It might only be starting. She tasted salt blood, but didn't care. And at the same time she was frightened. So very frightened.

Eddie.

God.

God.

All the people.

I wish I'd done that better.

23

Seattle, Washington

NAN was walking across the campus when the sirens began. Short, staccato bursts, not the long-drawn-out wailing you heard in disaster movies. They'd drilled it over and over since the war had started. Archipelago had prepared, as much as anyone could.

Her phone chined. The text read MISSILE ATTACK. NOT A DRILL. TAKE IMMEDIATE SHELTER.

Nan glanced around, to see others in the quad dropping racquets, jumping up from benches, sprinting across the drought-stricken carpet of lawn. Dr. Jhingan hurried toward the concrete bunker that had been built beneath the carousel. Nan hesitated, torn between it and her assigned shelter beneath the biochemistry wing. Then pivoted midstep, and sprinted for the carousel. It was still playing that jaunty, incongruously merry tune, still revolving, though the painted horses bobbed and galloped with empty saddles.

Fifty feet down, a narrow, echoing concrete stairwell opened into long windowless rooms. She followed the crowd, and lost sight of Jhingan. The floors were raw unpolished concrete. The walls were painted brown up to chest level and pale green above that. The ceiling was reinforced with heavy cast-in beams. Yellow-tinted LEDs were spaced along the walls. They didn't really give enough light to see by, which added to the sense of claustrophobia as more and more scientists, technicians, administrators, and janitors crowded down the stairs. Save for one groundskeeper, who was calling on the

Mother of God loudly and eloquently in Spanish, they were unwontedly quiet. Many looked annoyed, as if irritated to be interrupted at
their desks and lab benches.

She checked her phone again, but got only NO SERVICE. Of
course, this deep underground . . . She spotted a gap on a bench between two very large women and wedged her butt into it. They gave
way grudgingly.

"So, where you from?" a dark-skinned woman with severely plucked
black eyebrows asked.

"Medical," Nan said.

"I'm from Neural Networks," the woman said, tapping her nametag. *Frederica*, it read.

"Attention please, everyone." A slender, white-coated black
woman who wore the pale pink badge of Administration turned a
control on the wall. The lights brightened somewhat, though it was
still dim. "I'm your shelter manager, people. Please listen up."

Her voice echoed as she began reading from a laminated summary.
"Welcome to Site 23, a FEMA and Washington State Civil Defense
Program Class II protective area. This is not a long-term shelter. It is
a blast-resistant safe room, to protect against active shooters, terrorist events, and other emergencies. The current emergency is"—she
faltered, looked around—"the current emergency is unclear. But the
alarm sirens have sounded, so you're in the right place.

"We have limited supplies of bottled water. Please restrict yourself to one one-liter bottle per person. Bathroom facilities are lo-
cated between the shelter areas. Do not dispose of feminine hygiene
products in the toilets. Plan to stay until the emergency is officially
declared over." She glanced toward the door and swallowed visibly.
"We will now, um, seal the shelter. Close that, please. Pull the red
handle all the way down."

Some people stirred as the door thunked closed. Others sat immobile, heads down, sunk within themselves. Nan checked her phone
again, then turned it off. No telling how long they'd be down here,
and she didn't see a recharge station.

Which left her with nothing to occupy her mind. She felt adrift,
atomized, suddenly cut off from the grid. There wasn't even a Patriot

News Service screen, though by law PNS had to be on 24/7 in every public space.

"So what were you working on?" said Frederica, who'd apparently appointed herself Nan's shelter buddy.

"Oh, medical stuff . . . immunizations." She wasn't supposed to discuss LJL. Jhingan had finalized the formulation, and Qwent Pharma had started preliminary bulk production. She'd gone out every other day to oversee it. Her initial misgivings about Qwent had pretty much been laid to rest. The drugs for medical use were produced in an entirely separate, completely new annex than those for pesticides, and the staff seemed dedicated to getting the new compound out quickly and in quantity. In fact, the first million doses were packaged and ready to ship, as soon as they got the official go-ahead.

As for her own personal disobedience . . . the release of the compound's existence and its formulation to scientists around the world . . . that had not gone as she'd envisioned. Old Dr. Lukajs had understood her veiled allusion instantly. "You are saying, this should be common possession of humanity," he'd said, stopping dead in the hallway and turning to stare at her.

"Uh . . . I guess so. Yes."

"So you have social conscience after all. I did not think your generation possessed."

"We're not all the same, Doctor," she snapped with a flash of anger.

"Maybe not. Your loyalty is not to corporation?"

"Only as long as they're doing the right thing."

And he'd grinned, showing stained crooked teeth, and patted her shoulder as a grandfather might. "You are too young to risk. But I have suffered at the hands of governments before. And they cannot punish me for long, whatever happens." He'd waved a hand airily. "Not when I am, how much, eighty-five years? Write up an email with test data and the formulary and dosage statistics. I will take it from there."

But now she wasn't so sure they'd done the right thing.

She'd been worried about enemy civilians. That they'd die without the drug.

But now, was that same enemy attacking her country, trying to kill them all?

If not, what was this alert for?

And more to the point . . . what was *she* doing down here? Maybe these others had nothing pressing to keep them above ground. But she did.

She took a deep breath. "Excuse me," she said, and got up. Her seatmate looked surprised. Nan forced herself into motion. Toward the shelter manager, who still stood looking uncertain beside the sealed door.

"I need to leave," Nan told the woman.

Who gaped at her, and recoiled. "What? B-but . . . that's not permitted. If you don't feel well, there's a bunk in the—"

"I'm not ill. I'm a medical researcher. And I have something important to see to. Let me out. Now."

"Against shelter regulations. Sorry." The woman shook her head and crossed her arms, tapping one foot like a stern schoolteacher.

"Oh, really? Show me where it says that. That no one can leave." Nan grabbed for the laminated sheet, but the woman jerked it away, lips set.

Instead of arguing, Nan reached around her for the red bar that sealed the door. They had hatches like that on the ships her Dad had taken her aboard. She jerked it up, pushed it open, and stepped through.

Back into the now deserted, dank-smelling, unlit stairwell. A child's pink sneaker lay forgotten in a dim corner. Strange, she hadn't seen any kids in the shelter. Maybe in one of the other rooms.

The steel door boomed shut again behind her, echoing like the door of a prison cell. Then, after a moment, grated as it was dogged again from inside.

She took a deep breath, looking back at it. Her heart started to race. Had she just made a *really* stupid choice? She poised knuckles above sheet steel, intending to knock. Then shook her head, angry at herself. No. She had work to do.

She was starting up the stairs when a bright light reached down it toward her. Like a sudden passing away of a dark cloud from the sun. But it brightened still more, very rapidly, until the glow was blinding, even attenuated by the concrete well.

She dropped to one side of the stairs, huddling, wrapping her head with both arms. Yet still the glare penetrated, a blazing throbbing scarlet red lighting up the insides of her eyeballs, of her very brain.

The brightness ebbed and instinct drove her sliding backward down the steps. Her coat rucked up; the concrete edges scraped her belly. She reached the corner where the stairwell made a right angle, crawled around it, and curled into a fetal position.

The shelter shuddered, then jolted. Concrete groaned and cracked. Dust filtered down like gray snow, seething the air. The noise arrived on its heels. A bellowing *crack*, then a tornado-howling that went on and on.

The stairwell banged and quivered and rocked. She lay with hands locked over her head, waiting for the roof to fall in, to collapse, to crush and bury her. A harsh scraping resounded from above, like a gigantic bulldozer blade passing over. Shards of blue glass and scraps of colored plastic bounced down the stairs. A chunk of fiberglass tumbled from step to step. It halted, spinning and rocking, beside her. Prying her eyes open, she made out the scarlet-white-and-gilt hoof and haunch of one of the carousel horses.

The roar lessened, the bulldozer blade roar waning. Rumbling away, into the distance.

She lay still for several seconds. Then cowered again as a second flash bounced down the stairwell. Not quite as bright as the first, and its shock and howl took longer to arrive. It too passed over, still deafening, but less loud than the first.

She crouched there for minute after minute, fists clenched, waiting for another detonation directly overhead. A final blast, to cave the world in on top of her.

But it didn't come.

Finally she stirred. Lifted her head, rose to hands and knees, coughing, and brushed the gray dust off. Broken glass prickled her fingers. She wiped the blood on her lab coat and backed down a few steps, glancing back at the shelter door. Still sealed.

She muttered, "I have something important to see to." And pushed herself forward again, up the steps, toward a diminished daylight.

THE whole lawn was on fire, the sod scorched, smoking, burning. Blue glass littered it, sparkling like early frost. The carousel and bandstand and bee arbor had been blasted across the quad, their silhouettes pressed into the grass like cutwork, their foundations ironed down into the soil. She crouched low, tensed for another flash, opposite the robotics wing. Its windows were empty of panes. Through their gaps she glimpsed wrecked interiors, desks flung through walls, a jumbled mass of wrecked and smashed equipment. Fire glowed in the windows. Smoke was streaming out of the roof, which was peeled back like the lid of a sardine can.

She turned in a circle, appalled. To the north, in the direction of the city, a tremendous black looming thunderhead flickered with internal lightning. Below it the familiar skyline was gone. Tall silhouettes of familiar buildings, vanished. The Columbia Center, erased. The Gateway Tower, obliterated. Lost in a growing pall of black smoke rising from a full quarter of the horizon as she gazed northeast, shaking, shocked to stillness again.

Seattle. The city she'd come to love. Barhopping in Belltown. The Republic of Fremont, where her artist friends lived. Her favorite bike trail, out to Alki Beach. And the tech and medical companies, the brilliant innovators that had pushed the envelope in so many ways. The places her friends worked. Josh, at Cray. Meredith, at Dendron. Ethan at Sporcle, which had converted to defense research with the coming of the war. No, wait—Ethan was at Microsoft now.

With a shock, she tried to grasp the fact they might all be dead.

Would anything be left of that splendor, that brilliant youth, that sense of standing on the cusp of the future?

And maybe Seattle wasn't the only city that had just been leveled. Two bombs, or missiles, or whatever those had been, must mean it had been a big attack. Maybe nationwide, with similar thunderheads over Los Angeles, Pittsburgh, New York, Washington, Atlanta.

The government had always warned it was possible. That was

why the Allies were fighting, they said. So nukes could be banned. So no country ever had to worry about annihilation again.

For a second Nan wondered, again, if she was screwing up. She was no expert on nuclear weapons, but every employee had had to sit through the emergency procedures and the state civil defense briefing. Many feet of concrete and earth had probably protected her from the initial neutron burst. The flash had nearly blinded her, but the blast had passed overhead. And the wind was from behind her, from the west.

She might be all right, if she could get to where she needed to be quickly.

But her destination lay toward the city center.

She couldn't really be sure, everything was so changed, but the ominous black cloud seemed to be towering over Mercer Island. Or somewhere to the north of it, maybe near Redmond. Qwent Pharma was south of that, between her and the cloud.

She checked her cell again, but the screen was blank. No, not just blank, but dead. She pressed the Home button again and again, to no avail.

Okay, she more or less knew her way . . . she jogged across the quad, avoiding the twisted remains of the bandstand. Skirting the grass fires, she came to the parking area.

One of the little self-driving company cars was plugged into a charge point. The others were wrecked, but this one had been partially protected from flash and blast in the shadow of a concrete pillar. Its blue paint was scorched and still smoking, but aside from that it looked undamaged. She unplugged it, pulled the door open, and slid in. "Start up," she ordered.

The car seemed to flinch. The dash screen lit. But when she gave it the address, and told it to go, it didn't. Just sat there, as if it didn't understand.

Okay, then, she'd have to drive manually. She was rusty, but remembered how. She touchscreened to Manual, moved the shift to reverse. The electrics whined as it backed out of the lot. She kept glancing at the sky. Maybe more missiles were coming. Because that had been a missile, hadn't it? Out here in the open, the flimsy plastic roof of the car wouldn't protect her for a second.

The only answer was to get to where she was going as quickly as possible, before another flash tore open the sky.

She bumped over a curb as she pulled up the ramp onto 509, then corrected and headed north. Past the airport. Since the war, rationed gas and scarce power had meant few cars on the road. So only a few trucks blocked the way, and most of them, whether human- or self-driven, had obviously pulled off to the side when they'd seen the flash. They lay knocked askew or toppled by the blast. The macadam of the road itself, though still smoking, seemed undamaged.

Peering ahead at the hovering cloud, she measured its edges with two fingers. Her dad had shown her how to judge the direction of a squall, when they were out sailing. If it widened over time, it was blowing toward them. So far this blackness seemed to be holding steady as she drove toward it, which should mean it was drifting to the north or northeast. She wasn't sure what the prevailing winds were. Maybe she should, but being a researcher at Archipelago during a war meant there wasn't much time for anything but work.

She pulled onto the breakdown lane to skirt a tangle of wrecked vehicles. A late-model Prius lay pinned beneath a truck. Both were burning fiercely, and one glance convinced her there was no point stopping to see if she could help.

Qwent was in Tukwila, near the golf course. Without thinking, she tried her phone again. But Google Maps didn't work . . . of course. She freaked for a moment. How was she going to get anywhere without directions? "You can do it," she whispered. She might make some wrong turns, but surely she could sort-of-remember the way.

A few minutes later she spotted the exit and pulled off. The streets were more congested here, and littered with smashed buildings, so she had to drive more carefully.

But now they weren't empty. Men—not many women among them— were edging out from basements, from the shelters FEMA had converted subways and lower floors into. She frowned. They were carrying things. Tools. Crowbars, mainly, but axes too, and baseball bats. A few halted, looking after her as she passed. Then up at the sky, fearfully.

Yeah. She guessed no American would look at the sky the same way ever again.

• • •

A FEW blocks farther on the smoke got heavier, to the point she couldn't make out the next intersection. This part of the city was on fire, but, by some freak of the explosions' effects was not totally destroyed yet. She steered gingerly around a fallen light pole. Glass littered the pavement like hail, crunching under her tires. All the windows had been blown out here. Now she saw what the crowbars were for.

For prying loose the bolts on security gratings. For jimmying open doors, and smashing them in.

More and more people filled the street. Some staggered, skin hanging in burned strips from their arms and faces. Those who hadn't reached shelter in time. Others looked unhurt, at least so far. Some of the men were carrying merchandise. Women were emerging too, skirting the blown-over cars and smashed buses. She braked hard to avoid one rushing out of a convenience store, arms filled with boxes of rationed infant formula and cereal. The woman didn't even glance her way.

Nan pressed harder on the accelerator, but the car felt sluggish. She glanced at the charge meter for the first time. Below the red line, and sinking fast. "Fuck," she muttered, peering up at the sky again. It was visible in slices of smoky black through the blasted-out upper stories of the buildings, where the interior walls had been blown out into the streets.

She steered around a woman lying in the street, curled like a roasted insect. Another block on, and her little vehicle was barely moving. A warning symbol pulsed on the dash. She wasn't just running out of charge. The debris littering the still steaming asphalt had done her tires in. The car whined to a halt, shuddered, and died.

"Just. Fucking. Great," she muttered. She checked the side- and rearviews to make sure no one was lurking back there. Then got out.

She stood in the middle of the street, looking around anxiously. Wondering if she should be helping the wounded, instead of her intended mission.

Shouting and thuds echoed down the block as the looters battered their way into another store. They hadn't noticed her yet, but they would soon. Unless she hid.

But then she couldn't get to Qwent.

She was pondering this dilemma, weighing her own safety against what she ought to do, when a shattering thunder rolled down between the shattered burning buildings. The rioters burst into furious activity, hastening their steps, casting apprehensive looks over their shoulders as the air vibrated.

From the street behind her, the roar grew. Of many engines. Of V-twins, unmuffled and full-throated.

She covered her ears as the Road Kings and Dyna Wides, Electra Glides, Ultra Classics, and Fat Boys swept past. The riders slid shotguns from scabbards as their tires crackled over the glass. Most of the looters scattered, though a few stood their ground, bats or crowbars at the ready. The wounded wandered among them, hands covering their faces. Blinded, burned, concussed . . . walking dead from the neutron burst. She shuddered, then ducked back into her car as bike after bike howled past. Their riders all wore the same sleeveless black leather vests. A colorful scarlet and black patch depicted an enraged Viking. Arched over it was the legend BERZERKERS, with a smaller Z on its side stamped over the larger one. Belatedly, she realized what ominous symbol it formed. They wore other insignias too: American flags, Confederate battle flags, POW/MIA stickers, and the back-to-back Bs of the Black Battalions.

One of the Harleys slowed as it approached her car. The engine blupped down to an idle. It coasted to a halt and its exhaust blew past her, heavy, laden with hydrocarbons, mixing with the rapidly thickening smoke.

"Need a hand there, little lady?" its rider said.

Huge legs straddled the black bike. The skin of his massive bare chest was reddened. A black tangled beard fell to his lap, braided with copper and silver beads, but his head was shaved except for a patch on the back where a braided queue dangled. BFFB was tattooed across his forehead, with other acronyms or slogans unscrolling from his cheeks down his neck. A medieval-looking axe dangled from a carpenter's belt, and he propped a black assault rifle on one gigantic thigh. He wore no helmet, just a red bandanna in a do-rag, and his eyes were concealed behind reflective wraparound sunglasses.

Nan glanced behind her. Screams and shouts echoed down the

street. The bikers were revving their machines after the looters, ignoring the wounded pointing shotguns and firing over their heads. The pedestrians faded, retreating into stairwells and alleys where the bikes couldn't go. A few Berzerkers dismounted and followed them in, but only for a few feet, as if establishing their dominance. After which, shouting threats, they swaggered back to their machines.

"I said, you need help here?"

He rolled the black machine closer. It was hard to hear him over the rumbling engine. As if realizing that, he gunned it, then shut it down. Extended a huge hand sheathed in black leather. Tattoos writhed up his arm. One she recognized: an eagle, globe, and anchor. "Hey," he said. "You a doctor?"

For a moment she was puzzled, then realized: she still wore her white lab coat. "Um, not exactly," she said. "Medical researcher."

"At the hospital? Harborview? VA?"

"No, no. Archipelago."

"That's government work, right? Defense work?"

"Um, that's right. I work on . . . new drugs." She coughed; the smoke was catching in her throat.

"For the troops. Got it. And what? Roller skate run out of gas?" He took off his glasses and bent to give her undercarriage a shaggy-browed inspection. "Right front's gone."

"It's electric. But yeah, it's out of charge."

Levi-blue eyes were fixed on her, so unblinking she had to drop her gaze. "What's your name, li'l honey?"

"Dr. . . . Dr. Lenson. What's yours?"

"Call me Ish. You hurt? Where you headed, so soon after the fucking slants clobbered us?"

She glanced back up the street, hoping to spot a cop car. But of course none appeared. Looters, or bikers? Some choice.

But when she turned back he was looking even more closely at her face. At her eyes . . . "Say, you ain't a fuckin' slant yourself?"

Her half-Asian heritage. "No," she lied. "Portuguese. Look, I'm on a—a mission. To rescue some, some vaccines. For the . . . for the Marines."

That seemed to be the magic word. He nodded and grinned, exposing stainless steel front teeth. "Oh, yeah? Where to?"

"Qwent Pharmaceuticals. Over by the golf course."

He patted the seat behind him, and blipped his horn in a long-short-long signal. She looked to where he'd turned his head. The other bikers were U-turning, heading back toward them. Re-scabbarding rifles and shotguns, tucking pistols back into leather vests. Pushing the wandering, shocked, zombie-like survivors out of their way.

She gnawed her lip and felt for her phone. Then remembered: It wasn't working.

"I get it," the big biker said. His grin was terrible to see. "Look, ain't no need to be afraid of us, honey. We're on the same side."

She frowned. "Side?"

"Yeah. Mobilized Militia." He rotated his offside shoulder to brandish a red, white, and blue armband. "Here to protect the good people and eliminate the bad ones. Which're you?"

She glanced at the nearest storefront. Make a dash? She considered that foolish idea for only a second.

Ish waved to the oncoming bikers and they braked, surrounding them. "Little lady needs help," he yelled. "She's a doctor, gettin' meds for the troops. Needs to go to Qwent. Anybody know where that is?"

She could feel them all examining her, but tried not to stare back. Tried to keep smiling, to not look terrified. "Cute," said one. "She can warm my back," muttered another. "Any day."

A smaller biker with an enormous red walrus mustache hoisted a fist. "It's over in Dunlap, I think."

"Okay, Rollvag, take point." Ish turned back to her. "Throw a leg over, Doc. Feet on the buddy pegs, but keep them pretty stems off the engine, it gets hot down there. Grab them two handles down by your sides. And hold on tight."

SHE wasn't sure of the route they took, and for a time wondered if they weren't just kidnaping her. Taking her somewhere they could do whatever they wanted. There wouldn't be much she could do in that case. The bikes tore along the highway at a frightening speed in a rolling blare of sound. They speeded past whole blocks on fire. A ball of ice settled into her belly. But finally they slowed, took an off-ramp, and she sort-of-recognized a street sign.

Quent was housed in a former shoe factory above a golf course, with Lake Washington beyond. The pharma building was set away from the rest of the facility. She rose in her pillion seat, clinging to Ish's broad shoulders, to look. The damage came in sight as they swept around the curve and motored up the rise.

The main building had taken the brunt of the blast, but it didn't seem to be on fire. Its roof was twisted wreckage and loose bricks littered the ground outside the fence. On the other hand, the metal roof lay canted across the chain link.

Meaning she could get in, whether or not anyone was around. She pointed. The motors roared, then slackened as the mass of machines and men rolled to a halt.

"This it?" Ish craned back at her.

"Yeah." She unslung her leg, fighting a cramp and wishing she was in jeans instead of a skirt under the lab coat. She kept looking for security, for the Qwent staff, workers. They should be here somewhere, but she didn't see anyone.

She turned, then, and looked out over the city.

Into the mouth of Hell.

To her left, the normally blue-gray waters of the Sound looked muddy and darker than before. The black thunderhead had drifted on north, though it still stained the horizon, but smoke streamed up from a hundred thousand fires, tinting the sunlight orange-red and making it impossible to see past the city center. Beacon Hill was on fire, its turn-of-the-previous-century mansions of brick and wood smashed and toppled, the rubble aflame. CenturyLink and Safeco Fields were gone, blasted from the earth, apparently; she couldn't make out any sign of them in the haze. The high-arching viaducts of the 90/5 Interchange lay collapsed in an avalanche-rubble of concrete, with here and there a sparkle of torn metal and broken glass. Whatever unfortunates had been on them when the warheads had fallen . . . she drew breath in a choked sob, fists to her mouth. It didn't seem real. Didn't seem possible.

Ish dismounted and came up beside her, laying a heavy arm over her shoulder. The assault rifle dangled in his other hand. He limped heavily as he walked, placing his boots carefully, as if he had spinal or hip damage. "There s'posed to be anybody here?"

"The drug . . . it was in production. Yeah. But I don't see any staff."

"Uh-huh. Still got to get inside, right? Know where you're going?"

She breathed deeply, trying to recover some calm. Pointed toward the pharma building, and stepped cautiously up onto the metal roofing. It creaked and shifted under her weight, and she grabbed for the big man as she started to fall. He stepped on too, counterbalancing the levering steel, and with arms linked they walked together across the crumpled chain link, then jumped down onto the scorched, smoking grass.

When she stepped through the empty floor-to-ceiling panels of the lobby of Building Four, employees were rushing to and fro inside, carrying extinguishers. She searched for a familiar face and finally found one. "Heremy. Heremy!" she yelled.

The manager, blue suit rumpled and neck smudged with soot, stared at her uncomprehendingly before recognition dawned. "Dr. Lenson? But . . . what are you doing here?" He switched his gaze to Ish, then dropped it to the black rifle. A frown crimped his eyebrows. "Uh—what's going on?"

"I'm here about our production run." Self-consciously, she took a step away from the huge man in gang colors. "He's my . . . security escort. Look, what's the status? Is our first shipment ready?"

"It's ready. Yeah. But we're evacuating." He cast a worried glance at the sky. "If that wind shifts, and sooner or later it will, it's going to drop fallout all across here. We've probably already have been exposed."

"That's pretty much what I thought about too. And another issue. What about refrigeration?"

The manager staggered as a worker carrying a desktop server caromed off him, and pushed him away. "Out on the lawn," he snapped. Then, to Nan, "Still working. Until the freezer warms up. But we don't have more than an hour's power on the battery banks. Once those go down, we lose power, we lose the cold."

Unfortunately, LJL 4789, named after Lujaks, Jhingan, and Lenson, was a heat-sensitive molecule. They had only rough tests of stability at elevated temperatures and no idea yet of duration of storage. But based on related compounds, every hour at ten degrees above the freezing point meant a measurable loss of potency. And with the reports of outbreaks to the south . . .

But was she just rearranging deck chairs? The whole city was on fire. If this was a nationwide attack, maybe it didn't matter if they could forestall an epidemic. Like putting a Band-Aid on a chest, when the heart within was staggering from a massive infarction.

She shook the doubt off. The drug was their best hope against the virus, which would remain a threat to survivors no matter what else was happening. In fact, if this was a nationwide attack, weakening the population might mean it would strike even more virulently. "Um, have you heard any news? Is it just Seattle, or—?"

The manager shook his head, shrugged. "No idea."

"Well, look, dude," Ish said, stepping up. "Got a reefer?"

"A reefer." The manager stared at him, from his shaved head to the massive black boots studded with steel spikes.

"A reefer truck.—I've driven 'em," the biker asided to her.

She rubbed her face. Her hands came away black. How much of this soot, this smoke, was radioactive already? The wind had blown the thunderhead north, but it couldn't have dissipated all the fission products. "Um. So, you're a trucker?"

"Until the fucking layoffs, when they automated."

"Can we get a refrigerated truck?" she asked the manager.

"We had one . . . hey, Jerry, that white fridge truck still run?"

It seemed that it might, but hadn't been used for a while. "If we can get it cranked up, where would you take this important shipment of yours?" the big biker asked her.

She thought hard. The FEMA Region Ten Support Facility was in Lynnwood, about fifteen miles north . . . no. the plume would have passed directly over it. Even if the facility was still intact, no point going there. A hospital, then. Overlake? Issaquah? A hospital would have a blood bank or plasma center, with low-temp storage and emergency generators.

Or a military base? No, they wouldn't let her in without a long explanation. Endless complications. They'd see the looting as their biggest problem. Restoring order. Deploying the National Guard. Setting up to handle mass casualties.

"You know the roads pretty well, right?" she asked the biker.

"Oh yeah. We run the pipelines, the power lines. Protectin' 'em. Got in a shootout with some copper thieves last week."

"Could you get me to Issaquah?"

He tapped steel teeth with the rifle muzzle, reflecting. "Have to go east, then north. Stick to back roads. What, you want a hospital? I'd go south on Five. Tacoma. Be faster. Tacoma General? We took brothers there once when we had a run-in with the Pagans."

When she nodded he beckoned to the small biker. "Get 'em out of the saddle, Roller. We got some work to do."

IT took an hour to pull the ampules, already boxed, wrapped, and palleted for shipment, out of the freezers. A million doses. They were still cold, but wouldn't stay that way long. Ish got the truck started and backed it up to the loading dock. He left it running, air blasting out of the back with the refrigeration unit turned to high, then stood watching as the Qwent people forklifted the pallets in. "There any mercury in this stuff?" he asked her.

"What? Oh—this isn't a vaccine. It's a drug. No, there's no thimerosol."

"I heard it was bad shit. Toxic."

"No mercury. No." Great, an antivaxer. She almost rolled her eyes, but stopped herself. So far the bikers seemed to be on her side. The last thing she wanted to do now was to show disrespect.

The manager came out holding a clipboard. "My tablet's dead, so I drew up a paper receipt."

She pushed it away. "Come on, Heremy. It's just gonna go bad if it stays here."

"We're on FEMA contract. No way can I release it without at least a signature. And what about our truck?"

Beside her Ish stirred. The manager cut his eyes at him apprehensively. "This asshole hassling you, Doc?" the biker growled, hefting the rifle. Behind him the other Berzerkers wheeled as one to face the manager, each man putting a hand on a gun or knife.

The manager held his ground for a moment, then buckled in the face of dozens of tattooed, scowling gang members obviously eager to unleash carnal violence. "Uh, uh, sure . . . I guess it's all right," he said hastily. "Sure, whatever, take it. It's just gonna degrade, once the batteries run out. Right?" He scrawled something on the clipboard.

He started away, looking relieved, then wheeled back. "Oh. I forgot. One of the guys just pulled CBC in on his scanner. Public radio, from Canada. They said Seattle, Montana, and North Dakota got hit. The White House launched on Shanghai and another city in retaliation. I forget which."

The bikers cheered. Nan stood silent, turning it over in her mind. Imagining it. And what might come next. "And if they hit us again?" she said at last.

"Then fuck 'em," Ish grated. "We'll wipe every yellow monkey off the face of the earth."

Rollvag sauntered up. The diminutive biker looked at the truck, then at Ish's Harley. "You drivin'?"

"Oh, yeah." The big man clambered awkwardly back on his hog and revved it. He gunned it, let out the clutch, and piloted it skillfully up the ramp to the loading dock, then into the back of the truck as the others climbed onto their hogs and started up.

Nan closed her eyes. Apparently they were all coming with her.

Ish climbed out of the back of the truck, lowered himself clumsily and obviously painfully to the ground, and slammed the doors. He jerked a thumb at her and limped around to the cab. Beckoned her to climb up.

When she was belting in he peered over at her again. "Hey. Sure you're not a chink?"

"Told you. I'm Portuguese."

"I guess that's okay . . . but maybe you better wear this."

He fished in an inside pocket of the vest, and held out a patch. It read PROPERTY OF BERZERKERS. "Put it on. There's a pin stuck in the back."

What the . . . "Put it on . . . ?"

"On that pretty white coat. Yeah. Right there." He poked a big index with a blackened nail into her upper breast, and leered again, just as he had when he'd pulled up beside her stalled car as she sat wondering what to do.

She wanted to ask what this meant, exactly what she was signing up for, then realized she didn't have a choice. Reluctantly, she pinned it on.

The roar of Harley engines resounded like a wing of bombers readying for takeoff. The bikers maneuvered complexly, to some silent drill they all knew, wheeling into what looked like rehearsed positions. Their touring formation, probably. There had to be two dozen of them in front of her and just as many behind the truck. All armed. They faced forward, ignoring the Qwent employees who'd come out of the annex to watch.

Ish leaned out of the window, spun a finger in the air, and jabbed it ahead. The lead bikes, Roller up front, leapt forward, front wheels popping off the road, then thumping down as they gunned the engines. When the wave of motion reached the truck Ish jammed the gear in and they started rolling. Surrounded by sound so thick it was nearly a solid wall, the vibrating throbbing roar of heavy, large-displacement pistons, the column inchwormed into motion. A right turn out the gate. Another right, through the streaming, stinking black smoke of a burning gas station.

The convoy, two hundred yards long, two bikers abreast, charged up the exit ramp onto the highway. The reverberating clamor of their approach alone cleared the street. As they accelerated the noise rose in pitch and volume until it rolled out over the crushed, burning city.

Crouched tensely in the passenger seat, Nan glanced out the side window, up at the sky. It was empty. Shrouded by smoke. The sun barely peered through, an obscured, lusterless, ruddy disk. Ish drove with utter concentration, eyes narrowed, face intent. His rifle was propped against the console between them.

The caravan hit fifty, then sixty, then eighty. The engines bellowed all around her. She clutched a hand grip on the headliner and squeezed her eyes shut.

Motors roaring like a pride of lions, swerving violently between stalled cars and trucks, the glittering column of silver and black thundered southward, out of the dying city.

24

USS *Franklin D. Roosevelt,* the South China Sea

DAN lay with one arm over his face, trying to fight through anxiety and nausea toward something resembling sleep. After days of half-hour naps in his command chair, every cell yearned for unconsciousness. For a few seconds after he'd kicked off his shoes, turned off the light, and rolled into the narrow bunk in his flag cabin, they'd sighed in relief.

But sleep was still far away.

It wasn't his body.

It was his mind that was in the way.

After years at sea, the sound of rotating machinery was a lullaby. One arm anchored him to the bunk frame. After years in destroyers and frigates, he could only sleep clutching some solid handhold. Even before the war, in the rare times he'd spent at home, he needed a fist wrapped around the headboard. Which had made it complicated years before, when he'd slept cuddling a little girl. His daughter. So small. So vulnerable.

He lay with eyes closed, listening to the whoosh of ventilation, and gave way at last to the burning tears he'd held back since getting the news.

FDR was still under way. Escorted by two destroyers, south of Dongsha Island, also known as Pratas Reef. The circular atoll had been neglected during the war, until a Japanese landing force occupied it for the Allies. Now Lee Custer was there setting up the shore facilities, barges, tugs, and floating piers of the Mobile Logistic Force and coordinating ground-based antiair and missile defense coverage.

Dongsha was only a hundred and fifty miles from the coast. With a landing strip suitable for F-35s and C-17s, the island and lagoon were being converted into a base for the next campaign, into southern China.

Hainan had fallen. The Indonesians and Vietnamese had joined hands in mid-island at Phase Line Bullet. But instead of surrendering, the People's Liberation Army had withdrawn across the strait. Dan had done his best to pound them as they crossed. Troops were most vulnerable during retreats. But overcoming the island's defenses had degraded his airpower, depleting already low missile and bomb stocks to the point he'd had to accept a reduced sortie rate. So there weren't as many POWs as they'd hoped for. Not nearly as many as had been taken on Taiwan.

Still, General Isnanta said deserters and the captured reported low morale, scarce rations, sickness, and general disintegration. The shattered remnants on the mainland would take many weeks to resupply, reinforce, and rebuild into combat-worthy forces again. JCS estimated the Allies had wrecked at least four first-class enemy divisions in the fighting.

But the victory on Hainan had been overshadowed by the nuclear laydown on the American homeland, and the violent retaliation for it. Dan had gotten the news via high-side chat. The exchange had been triggered by an ICBM launch from northern China. Some of the missiles had been taken down by the combined US-Japanese task force in the Sea of Okhotsk as they arched overhead. Others were shot down by Army ground-based missile defense, in Alaska. Still more, blasted out of existence by microsatellites steered to impact at orbital velocities.

But a few had gotten through. The terminal vehicles spun off warheads and decoys as they burned down toward the continental United States. These in turn were taken under fire by Patriots and THAAD interceptors that had been pulled out of Europe and the Mideast early in the war. Cued, tracked, and attacked nearly continuously through the boost, midcourse, and terminal phases, only a remnant had succeeded in penetrating the layers of defense. And not all of those had survived reentry with their fuzing mechanisms still functioning.

But still, the damage was incalculable. Millions were missing, presumed dead.

Nan was one of them. No one knew who had survived and who had not.

Zhang had disavowed having provided release authority, blaming "renegade elements" in the military, "adventurers" and "traitors" who'd despaired of ultimate victory for the People's Empire. But the Joint Chiefs had rejected his apology, and acted in savage revenge.

SLEEP took another step away. He breathed hard, remembering, denying, wet face buried in the pillow. He turned over angrily. Shouldn't have let her stay in Seattle. Should have insisted she evacuate. But even as he reproached himself, he knew she wouldn't have obeyed. She'd told him it was her duty to stay, to keep working on the drug that would bear her name. Or at least her initial.

Not much to hang on to, to remember her by. A single initial.

He punched the pillow away and rolled out, coughing. Doubled, hacking so hard he almost vomited, clutching his stomach. When air finally returned he lurched up and staggered into the little attached head.

He rubbed his face, staring into the mirror. Facing the fact he'd tried to push away. Trying to accept the unacceptable.

His daughter was dead. She had to be.

Seattle, where she'd worked, had been one of the worst-hit population centers. Neither Dan, Blair, nor Nan's mother had heard from her, despite calls and emails.

The Patriot Network said central and north Seattle were obliterated, hit by two megaton-range airbursts. A dud had impacted south of Port Orchard, apparently aimed at the submarine base at Kitsap. San Francisco had been hit by one leaker, detonating over Pacifica.

Montana and North Dakota, where the ground-based deterrent was sited, had been hammered hardest of all. Sixteen ground-penetrating warheads had detonated near and around Karlsruhe, Velva, Max, Ryder, Mohall, Bowbells, Makoti, and other small towns, the obvious intent being to blast out and degrade the US retaliatory capability dug into silos there. Omaha had absorbed three ground penetrators, two of which hadn't detonated and were being investigated. Dan wondered who was doing the investigations. Whoever it was, they had brass balls. Montana had been struck hard too, Augusta, Cascade, and Judith Gap, so heavily no one really knew how many missiles had fallen. Duds and decoys were still being discovered and evaluated, some buried many feet below the soil's surface.

It would take time even to guess at how costly the attack had been. The casualties were still being counted. Both from the blast and from radiation; the ground bursts had smeared thick plumes of radioactive dust across the Midwest as far as Ohio and Ontario.

American retaliation had been swift and violent. But with only a part of the strategic arsenal, and none of the surviving ICBMs. Instead Trident submarines in the Pacific had launched against strategic assets, command sites, and bases.

In exchange for North Dakota and Montana, every large military base in south China had been wiped clean. In revenge for Seattle and San Francisco, Shanghai, Shenzhen, Hangzhou, and Changsha had also been destroyed. Going forward, the president had announced, the price exacted would be double whatever America suffered. Dan suspected Szerenci had designed this: a wintry, blood-curdling strategy that sequentially degraded the enemy's ability to defend himself, while daring the leadership to strike back. At which time, no one doubted the rest of China would be obliterated, while StratCom still retained enough warheads to take on Russia and Iran—if they cared to join the game.

So far, though, both Moscow and Tehran were lying low. Neither had issued so much as a press release about the exchange.

Dan washed his face, trying to think past emotions to what he had to do next.

Notified thirty minutes in advance of launch of the counterstrike, he'd disaggregated the task force, spreading across the sea to minimize the effects if the next exchange targeted them. But in the days since the attack, not a missile, not a single plane had triggered the sensor net reticulated across South China and the western Pacific.

But if Nan was gone . . .

He sighed. Went out into his stateroom, switched on the desk light, and reached for a red-and-white-sriped binder. OPERATION OVERTHROW, its cover read.

The next step.

The invasion of south China.

No one expected to actually conquer China. It was too vast. Too populous. But a foothold, stubbornly maintained, would exert ever more pressure. Forcing Zhang to the conference table at last. If the destruction of four cities and most of his remaining conventional forces was not enough.

He sat with head down, trying to lose himself in the tables and graphs and maps. Based on the lack of reinforcements for Hainan, and intel about the enemy's growing weakness, his staff was modifying the plan to provide for a hasty landing of Vietnamese and Indonesians, along with American air support, in Hong Kong. That city was already in open revolt, and the unrest was spreading to other regions of the south, as well as Xinjiang and Tibet.

The world was coming apart. And as much as he grieved, he couldn't shake the knowledge that many more were grieving, terrified, mourning, bereft. Millions. He wasn't alone.

War did that.

He muttered "Fuck this," and snapped the desk light off. He blinked in the sudden absolute darkness. Fear for his daughter was an icy stone in his chest. A paralysis of the heart, draining the world of light.

He had only one resort. The power that had never failed him, when he asked it for help.

If he asked for strength, he'd get it. If he begged for courage, it would come. It always had.

But it couldn't take away grief. And even if it could, he wouldn't accept that.

Grief was the memory of love. Its opposite wasn't happiness, but oblivion.

No matter how he felt, he had to go forward. Into a cave of everlasting darkness, out of which he could see no way out. No light, no warmth, no solace.

Only the razor edges of memory, slicing his flesh again and again whenever he moved.

HE must have fallen asleep there at his desk, because when the chime sounded he was facedown on the op plan. He coughed and unstuck his cheek from the pages, grabbing for the red phone. "Lenson," he grunted.

"*Sir, comm-oh. Stand by for quantum voice with Fleet.*"

Christ, the fucking conference call. He logged into the LAN and scrolled though the TF chat, trying to refresh a groggy brain while he chinned the handset, waiting for Higher to come on.

"*Barbarian, this is Replay. Barbarian, this is Replay. Over.*"

Dan recognized Dick Enders, his classmate, now J-3 of Ninth Fleet. "Hello, Dick."

"*Dan. Wish we had time to talk. Maybe after. Stand by for Replay actual.*"

"Standing by. Over."

A tap on his door. It cracked, and the red night-lighting from the passageway leaned in past Enzweiler's silhouette. Dan waved his deputy to come in and sit, and hit the button for speaker so he could hear.

A hiss of unmodulated air. Quantum comms were new to the Fleet, limited to the most secure command links so far. They used regular STANAG 4591 scrambler technology, but assured security by using quantum information protocols to distribute the keys. Then a new voice came on. The Fleet commander, Bren Verstegen. "*Dan. Very sorry to hear about your daughter. I lost people too. Most everyone here has. Over.*"

Dan let a breath out slowly. "Roger, sir. Let's press ahead. Get this over with."

"*Could not agree more. Dick recommends we speed up the timetable for Overthrow. We're drawing up a frag order to bring it forward. How soon can you go? Over.*"

A frag order modified a previous op plan. Dan said carefully, "This is Barbarian. Sir, I can move forces, but my limiter is support. We're below forty percent fuel. Heavy losses to strike aircraft. Low on ordnance, parts, tech support. Over."

"Understand your concerns, but this is the time to be aggressive. Even if we're not totally ready. Speed over preparation."

Dan said, "The enemy could have reserves we don't know about."

"They probably do, but overall, he's softening. If at all possible, we want to advance the landing to seventy-two hours from now. What's the issue here, Dan? You stood tall when it looked like we might not get ashore, in Hainan."

Yeah, he wanted to say, but this isn't a night in Las Vegas. They couldn't keep gambling and not expect to lose big at some point. He coughed into a fist. Enzweiler was keying numbers into his notebook, head bent. Dan pulled the op order over, unfolded a chart, and swung dividers. He and his chief of staff exchanged glances. Enzweiler shook his head and tilted the screen. Dan grimaced.

Finally he pressed Transmit. "This is Barbarian actual. I can't commit to that, sir. Too much damage to my air wings. Not enough time to clear the lanes in."

Impatience edged the distant voice. *"Then when? The governor's left. The last Interior Ministry troops went with him. The people are flying the Dragon and Lion, the old Crown Colony flag. The city administration's proposed they join Taiwan in what they call the Commonwealth of Chinese States. We need to move ASAP, Dan."*

Dan took another deep breath, and committed. "I understand, sir. Assuming we can refuel passing Dongsha, I can move advance elements into Hong Kong harbor five days from now. That's flat out the best we can do. Over."

A new voice broke in. *"All stations, this is Coronet. Who do I have on the line? I need actuals. Over."*

Dan was confused for a moment. Coronet was Indo-PaCom, the overall theater commander. But movement orders, operational, and frag orders came down through the operational commander. The theater commander wasn't scheduled to be on this call. WTF? "Uh— roger. This is Barbarian actual, over."

"This is Replay actual."

"Very well. This is Coronet. Stand by for actual."

A familiar voice: Admiral Justin "Jim" Yangerhans. Dan recognized it as clearly as if the lanky, homely four-star who'd steered the Allied war across half the globe stood in front of him.

"This is Coronet. Flash message on the way. But I wanted to give each of the forward commanders this personally." A pause; excited voices clamored in the background. *"We're getting reports of a coup in Beijing. Military commanders are asking for an armistice. They say Zhang's dead, but our diplomatic sources say no, he's left the country. If so, no indication where yet. One source guessed Russia. Storming and looting of Party headquarters is reported from Tibet and south China."* A pause, more muffled shouting. *"Over."*

Dan's heart was pumping harder than it ought to. He felt unreal, as if brushing webs aside as he descended into a dark basement. So many deaths. So much danger. For so many years. Could this finally be the end? "Roger, copy all," he managed, glancing at Enzweiler. Who was typing busily, head down so far the bald patch was visible.

"This is Replay. What's your intent, Admiral? Our last orders were to expedite Overthrow."

Yangerhans said, *"Continue that effort. Regardless of what just happened in Beijing, we need an early presence in the south. But be aware, hard-line elements may continue to resist. We're still on a war footing. Until I tell you otherwise. Over."*

Dan and Verstegen acknowledged. Yangerhans promised more details as they became available, and signed off.

DAN put the task force in an east–west racetrack south of Dongsha, while warning Custer to press on with the buildup in case the invasion went ahead. He reminded his screen, ASW, and air commanders to keep their guard up. He tasked Captain Pickles to revisit the plan to see if a permissive landing could take place early. He had Enzweiler start detaching ships, two by two, to refuel.

Then he tried to get his head down again. After lying awake for a long time, he managed to get in a solid hour.

Before Blair called. Also on a covered circuit, direct from the

Tank. *"I'm here with General Vincenzo. Wanted to make sure you got the word about the armistice."*

"Jim Yangerhans passed it. But I'm still glad you called. Over." Of course they both already knew he had; Blair was using it as an excuse for a personal call. "How are you doing?" he asked. "Have you heard anything yet?"

"You mean about Nan. Not yet. FEMA's overwhelmed. Millions are unaccounted for. Presumed . . . anyway, unaccounted for." She sighed audibly. *"We won't know even rough casualty totals for weeks. I'm really sorry. I hate to tell you this."*

"I . . . understand. Thanks for trying. And don't stop. Please."

"I won't. But, another issue's come up. The ICC."

"ICC?" He didn't recognize the acronym

"The International Criminal Court's issued a summons for you. Stemming, but maybe not limited to, that German tanker episode, back when the war started."

Unexpected, but it seemed trivial, compared to what he'd lost. "You're kidding me. A summons . . . am I supposed to respond?"

"No. State's working on a formal response. The Hague's talking about a series of trials once the war's over. Zhang, if he's still alive. Chagatai. Lianfeng. Pei. For aggressive war and crimes against humanity. But they're planning to indict from both sides, to show impartiality. Uh . . . over."

Dan rubbed his face, torn between apathy and outrage. "Uh-huh. Like Nuremberg?"

"Sort of. I guess."

"Great. So who'll they indict on our side? Szerenci? Yangerhans? The president? You?"

"We'll have to wait and see. Maybe we can derail the issue. Or simply refuse to participate. The US never signed the Rome Treaty. But then, the Chinese could do the same. So that might not be the best reaction. Anyway, we're still studying options. No need for you worry. I probably shouldn't even have mentioned it. But I didn't want you to be blindsided."

They chatted a little longer, but finally she said she had to go. Dan blinked blurrily at his watch, considered, but finally got up, shaved, and dressed.

Getting ready for another day. Even though he still felt done in.

Even though, without his daughter in the world, he didn't really see the point.

THE confirmation came just before dawn. Captain Skinner read the announcement to the crew over the IMC. *"An armistice has been brokered by Switzerland. A cease-fire has been declared. All Allied and Opposed forces are to withdraw from contact and halt in place. Discussions are under way for a peace conference. The location will be announced.*

"All hands are cautioned that this doesn't mean we can't still be attacked. Some elements may refuse to surrender. We will stay at Condition Three until further notice."

Dan had gone up to the bridge to catch the sunrise. He stood on the wing, leaning on the splinter shield, staring out as the horizon gradually sharpened, into a far-off, jagged line. The brightness grew behind it, bleaching the sky.

A intensely bright golden dollop popped up, quivering. It shimmered for a second, hovering, indescribably bright, then ran down again into the sea and vanished. And darkness rushed back across the face of the sea.

The central fire slowly reappeared as its upper limb pushed up into view, orange-reddish at first, then gradually brightening to a glare that reached across the waves to them, picking out the crests while leaving the troughs in shadow.

Dan stared down at the passing waves. Decades before, back when he'd first gone to sea, he'd thought of their endless rolling as some kind of metaphor for existence. So many years before . . .

"Think this is really it, sir?" Donnie Wenck, cowlick ruffling in the sea-wind, stood beside him for a moment. Then leaned forward, placing his elbows alongside Dan's.

"I sure hope so, Master Chief." Dan glanced back. The rest of the staff stood inside the wing. Looking expectant. So he beckoned them out to join him.

They let themselves out the door, dogged it, and ranged in a ragged rank, going to a loose parade rest. Enzweiler. Pickles. Singh. Tomlin. And the others. Captain Skinner peered up at them from the next deck down, eyebrows raised; Dan gave him a nodded acknowledgment.

He surveyed their faces. Expectant. Exhausted. Etched with the sleeplessness and stress of years of war. The strain of battle and loss. Some hadn't heard from their folks back in the States, either. And from what little news was being released, the final casualty numbers were going to be horrifying. Even if this was truly over, it would take the world many years to recover. If ever.

No one had gained from this war, in the end. The two greatest countries on earth had striven to the very limits of their strength; and nearly destroyed each other. One coalition, one empire had fallen. The other still stood, but shaken to its foundations and nearly toppled.

What could he say to those who'd fought through it?

Only that this must never happen again.

But didn't the leaders say the same thing after every war?

And hadn't they been wrong, time after time? As the sacrifices and danger were forgotten, and the old habits of fear and aggression returned?

"It looks like this cease-fire might stick," he told them.

Heads lifted. A muted cheer, and a few clapped. He waved them to silence. "Too soon to celebrate, okay? We still have to stay on our toes. I can't emphasize that enough.

"But even if active hostilities terminate, we've still got a job to do. We need to start planning for a permissive landing and some kind of occupation. At least, a maintenance-of-order mission, until civilian authority can be reconstituted."

He cleared his throat, looking down at the flight deck as a fighter catapulted off, engines howling at full power. When the noise lessened, the plane canting off over the sea, he resumed. "Look at the governing factors, evaluation criteria, and task elements for the post-combat stabilization phase. Hit Joint Pubs 3-07, 3-29. And 3-57 too, since we'll probably have to transition to humanitarian operations. Both for the surrendering forces, as they disband, and the ci-vilian population.

"In a lot of ways, this is going to be more complicated than war. But it'll still have to be done. And since we're here, it'll probably be our job."

He nodded curtly, looking past them to the rising sun. The symbol of new life. The symbol of regeneration.

At least now, maybe, the killing could stop.

"I think I'm going to bow my head," he said. "And give thanks. Those who'd like to can join me."

They still had their heads lowered, standing quietly in the sun and wind, when a lieutenant commander tapped on the bridge window, holding up a clipboard. Dan recognized *Roosevelt*'s comm officer. He gave it another moment, then beckoned her out.

The message fluttered on the board. He ran his eyes down it once, then again, more slowly.

CONFIDENTIAL
FM: CNO WASH DC
TO: CTF 91

INFO: NINTH FLEET
INDOPACOM
NAVPERS DC

1. (C) EFFECTIVE IMMEDIATELY ADMIRAL DANIEL V
LENSON RELIEVED OF COMMAND TASK FORCE 91 BY
ADMIRAL LEE C CUSTER.

2. (C) UPON RELIEF ADM LENSON RETURN WASH DC FIRST
AVAIL REG SCHEDULED FLIGHT.

3. (C) SNM AUTHORIZED ONE WEEK COMPASSIONATE
LEAVE. THEN PROCEED AND REPORT CNO STAFF WASH DC
FOR TEMPORARY DUTY AS ASSIGNED.

CONFIDENTIAL/OADR
BT

"Need an initial on that, Admiral," the commander said, offering a pen.

The staff began filing off the bridge. Dan stood aside, letting them pass. The comm officer handed Dan his copy, then turned to leave. Enzweiler lagged the others, glancing askance at his senior.

Dan didn't respond, just settled his elbows back on the varnished teak rail atop the gray steel bulwark.

The rays of the rising sun struck deep into the passing sea, turning gold into emerald and emerald into a deep endless turquoise that fell away to a deeper violet blue. The rocking surface was furrowed, laced with foam. A brisk wind cooled his cheeks. A lone swallow skimmed the crests, dipping and weaving with unutterable grace.

So this was probably the last time he'd command. Or even go to sea, unless his sailboat was still in shape. He'd left it in Norfolk at the start of the war, moored at the Little Creek marina. He'd hoped to sail it again once peace came. Maybe the big circuit, through the Canal to the West Coast, and take Nan out with her friends . . . no.

It didn't sound like the America he'd left would be the one he'd return to.

And he wouldn't go sailing with his daughter. Ever again.

His eyes burned again, but he pushed the grief and anger back savagely. She was gone. But he'd never forget her. Never let a day pass without regret.

And now . . . he had to defend his actions? So be it. That had always come with command, in the service to which he'd given his life.

Whatever happened, he felt certain he'd done his duty. As he saw it, to the best of his ability.

The lean, gray-eyed, middle-aged man stood unmoving in the sea wind until it chilled his bones and blurred his sight. Then he turned away from the brightness of the dawn, and went below.

The story of the turbulent aftermath of the war with China will continue in David Poyer's Violent Peace.

ACKNOWLEDGMENTS

*E*X *nihilo nihil fit.* I began this novel with the advantage of notes accumulated for previous books as well as my own experiences in Asia and the Pacific. In addition to those cited earlier in the series, the following sources were helpful for this volume:

Hector's chapters were reviewed and commented on by Peter Gibbons-Neff, for which many thanks, as well as to Katie and Drew Davis. Other useful references included David E. Jones et al., "Placement of Combat Stress Teams in Afghanistan: Reducing Barriers to Care," *Military Medicine*, 178, 2:121, 2013. "Combat and Operational Stress Control," U.S. Department of the Army: Field Manual 4-02.51. TACT 3022, "Offensive Combat 1 and Combat Signs," USMC Officer Candidates School, April 2011.

Blair's Zurich, White House, and Pentagon scenes were based on personal experience. Other references that proved useful for her chapters included Keren Yarhi-Milo and George Yin, "Can You Keep a Secret? Reputation and Secret Diplomacy in World Politics," *Princeton Scholar.* David Szondy, "Ministry of Defence Developing New Anti-Laser Eyewear," *New Atlas*, October 14, 2012. Simon Saradzhyan, "The Role of China in Russia's Military Thinking," Harvard Kennedy School Belfer Center for Science and International Affairs, May 4, 2010. Thanks also to the real Liz McManus for her cameo in this and the previous book.

For Nan's passages: Jon Cohen, "Why Flu Vaccines So Often Fail,"

American Association for the Advancement of Science, September 20, 2017. Han Altae-Tran, Bharath Ramsundar, Aneesh S. Pappu, and Vijay Pande, "Low Data Drug Discovery with One-Shot Learning," *ACS Central Science*, 2017, 3 (4), pp. 283–93. "Transition State Analog," Wikipedia, accessed March 1, 2018. Food and Drug Administration, "Impact of Severe Weather Conditions on Biological Products," accessed August 30, 2018. Also Karl Haugh for Harley details.

For Navy passages: Previous research aboard USS *San Jacinto*, USS *George Washington*, USS *Wasp*, Strike Group One, and USS *Rafael Peralta*. A deep bow and "fair winds" to all! The following additional sources were valuable as background for tactics, mind-sets, and strategic decisions, with Phil Wisecup and Matthew Stroup being especially generous with their advice. Forrest E. Morgan et al., *Dangerous Thresholds: Managing Escalation in the 21st Century*, RAND Corporation, 2008. "Aegis Ballistic Missile Defense," Missile Defense Agency, accessed January 22, 2018. John Harper, "Pentagon Examining Options for Space-Based Missile Interceptors," *National Defense Magazine*, June 30, 2017. David Hambling, "What Is an EMP, and Could North Korea Really Use One Against the U.S.?" *Popular Mechanics*, September 28, 2017. Rebecca Perring, "Kim's Fortress," *Daily Mail*, November 11, 2017. Japanese Ministry of Defense, "Ballistic Missile Defense," accessed July 20, 2018. Ronald O'Rourke, "Navy Virginia (SSN-774) Class Attack Submarine Procurement: Background and Issues," Congressional Research Service, June 29, 2018. "Satellite Study Proves Global Quantum Communication Will Be Possible," *Scienmag*, December 20, 2018.

For Teddy Oberg's strand of the story, the references listed in the previous volume, plus "China Uses Facial Recognition to Fence In Villagers in Far West," Bloomberg News, January 17, 2018. "Apartheid with Chinese Characteristics," *The Economist*, June 2, 2018.

For overall help and encouragement along this lengthy pilgrimage, I owe recognition to the Surface Navy Association, Hampton Roads Chapter; to Charle Ricci and Stacia Childers of the Eastern Shore Public Library; the ESO Writers' Workshop; with bows to Bill Doughty, James W. Neuman, Alan Smith, John T. Fusselman, Dick Enderly, and others (they know who they are), both retired and still on active duty, who put in many hours patiently leading me down the path of righteousness. If I left anyone out, apologies!

Let me reemphasize that these sources were consulted for the purposes of *fiction*. The specifics of tactics, units, and locales are employed as the materials of story, not reportage. Some details have been altered to protect classified capabilities and procedures.

My deepest gratitude goes to George Witte, editor and friend of over three decades, without whom this series would not exist. And Sally Richardson, Sara Thwaite, Young Jin Lim, Steve Gardner, Ken Silver, Naia Poyer, Sally Lotz, Fred Chase, and Sarah Schoof at St. Martin's/Macmillan.

And finally to Lenore Hart, trenchant critic, anchor on lee shores, and my North Star when skies are clear.

As always, all errors and deficiencies are my own.

"MARKS"

record that you have

may use the spaces

system code. Please do